MALENA

a novel

edgardo david
holzman

NORTIA
PRESS

Orange County, California

www.nortiapress.com

2321 E 4th Street, C-219
Santa Ana, CA 92705
contact @ nortiapress.com

This book is a work of fiction. Names, characters, places and incidents are products of the author's imagination or are used fictitiously. Any resemblance to actual events or locales or persons, living or dead, is entirely coincidental.

ISBN: 978-0984225279
Library of Congress Control Number: 2012932103

Manufactured in the United States of America

"Many of the events described in this report defy belief. The people of this country have only heard of such horrors from distant lands. The enormity of what happened, the offenses against the very foundations of our species, may still prompt the 'Can it be true?' by which some have tried to ward off the pain and the horror, but also the responsibility of being aware, of knowing. For knowing leads inevitably to the question of how to prevent its ever happening again, and to the anguish of realizing that the victims and their tormentors were our contemporaries, that the tragedy took place in our midst..."

—Introduction to *Never Again: The Report of the Argentine National Commission on the Disappeared*
(Buenos Aires: EUDEBA, 1984)

"Any life, however long and complicated, is actually made up of a single moment: the moment when a man forever learns who he is."

—Jorge Luis Borges, *The Life of Tadeo Isidoro Cruz*

AUTHOR'S NOTE

The author is indebted to CONADEP, the Argentine National Commission on the Disappeared, and its 1984 report, *Never Again*. He also wishes to express his gratitude to the peerless set of professionals he had the privilege to work with in bringing Malena to print: his editor David Groff, his agent Jill Marsal, and his publisher Nathan Gonzalez.

Translations of quotations from *Never Again*, Jorge Luis Borges, and the tango "Malena," are the author's.

For Daphne

PART I

September 1979

1

Malena sings the tango...

Diego smiled. His forearm reached out to encircle Inés and he looked past the dance floor to the orchestra. The grainy voice delivering the familiar lyrics belonged to a young woman in a sequined blue gown. She saw him looking and smiled back.

"You asked them to play it..." Diego said to Inés. His thumb glided across her back and wriggled into her armpit.

"Stop it!" she gasped and laughed, jerking her arm down. "I said nothing, I swear. Everybody loves 'Malena.'"

"Malena" was their tango, the first they ever danced together that rainy afternoon in the seedy splendor of the Ideal cafe. Ever since, Diego felt as though "Malena" had been written for their private delectation. It had no business being played here in front of all these people in the Club Español in the heart of Buenos Aires. Except that these people—this tango crowd of diners and dancers—were the reason he had brought Inés here tonight: to show her off. It was juvenile. And dangerous. He should know better than to let Inés be seen with him in this classy tango ballroom. Someone might recognize him and carry the word back to Colonel Indart. The colonel would be very interested to learn that Captain Diego Fioravanti, his protégé, had a girlfriend he had never cared to mention. Colonel Indart would want to know who she was.

The thought sent a dagger's edge down Diego's spine. He had promised himself not to do this, not to press his luck with Inés and risk connecting her to him in any way. Tonight he had broken that pledge, foolishly succumbing to a craving to feel normal, if only for a few hours, to lay aside his vigilance and pretend that they were a regular couple on a night out: free to go anywhere, run into anybody, without fear of being recognized.

> *Malena pours her heart out*
> *In every verse...*

The lyrics echoed in his head. He sighed and pulled Inés closer, heads together, her breath on his cheek, her scent in his nostrils—and Malena's broken voice, her oblivion-dark eyes, swept them into her world of back alleys, into the chill of a last encounter, into the trance of the tango.

Their legs interlaced and parted intuitively, divining each other's intent. Long gone was the hesitation of her first dances with him. The music alone now dictated their coupling and uncoupling, the flicks and walks and pencil turns she read from the language of his torso and executed with the style and abandon of a true tanguera. He had felt that gift in her from the first, though she herself seemed unaware of it: the sensibility to dance the heartache that was a tango. He knew it from the intimacy in her eyes, from the grievously sensual energy in that long-stemmed body. He just hadn't realized how quickly she would blossom.

Their sweep and leg wrap brought the first bravos, as other couples receded to give them more room or stopped dancing to watch. Diego felt the pulse of the music rise, as it always did when the orchestra became aware of exceptional dancers on the floor, the piano, bass, and violins following the lead of the bandoneon, driving the rhythm sharply on the counterbeat.

A carousel and a chain. A coil and a windmill. He stepped forward, and the pressure of his hand on her back cut short her backward eight. As he pivoted in the center of the figure, Inés grapevined around him, her peep-toe pumps gently stroking the parquet, tracing circular caressing motions with tense, exquisite grace.

The singer's voice faded and they ended on the dramatic flourish of a *sentada*, as the illusion of Inés sitting on his leg died out in two vibrant notes. They were alone on the dance floor, harvesting the applause. Inés was blushing.

On their way back to their table, Diego checked his watch. Almost time. Colonel Indart wanted him to call in at eleven sharp, Sergeant Maidana had said. The colonel had never before asked him to check in at this hour. And Maidana had delivered the message at the last minute, just as Diego was leaving headquarters on his way to meet Inés. Diego didn't know what it meant. He did know that no one kept Colonel Indart waiting.

After pouring them each a glass of Torrontés from the bottle in the ice bucket, he looked at his watch again. The hands of his father's Tissot were a reprimand; he had been waiting far too long to do what he had to do and didn't want to. The orchestra was taking a break. Under the painted ceilings framed by elaborate moldings, the crackle of conversation and scraping of silverware had resumed. He swirled the wine in his glass and drank a long draft, but the gnawing in his stomach did not ease.

He said, "I have to make a phone call."

"A phone call," Inés said, giving him a keener look.

He turned up his palms. "Routine. I'll be right back." He forced his voice to keep casual.

She had opened her mouth to question him further, but the waiter in a black vest, apron, and bow tie arrived with menus. Diego got up and left the ballroom, descending the winding art nouveau staircase to the public telephone by the Club Español's famed ground-floor restaurant. He picked up the receiver. The line was dead. Of course. What did he expect? Not even a military government could make the phones in this country work. He swore at the phone and slapped the heavy metal casing twice, which got him a dial tone. With his second token he got through to headquarters. He gave the operator Maidana's extension.

He could picture Maidana in his small office, the windowless room assigned to the basic-training instructor in a corner of the gym, surrounded by his martial arts trophies.

"Sergeant Maidana," answered the gruff voice with the lilt of Córdoba. Diego gripped the phone hard. Before meeting Maidana, he had always found that singsong pleasing.

"It's Captain Fioravanti, Sergeant," Diego said.

"Yes, Captain. You are late."

"Time got away from me," Diego said.

"You mean a woman got hold of you," Maidana gave a throaty chuckle. "Where are you?"

"Downtown, in a bar," Diego lied.

"Captain, Colonel Indart wants you back here."

Diego's hand tightened on the phone. "What—now?"

"Now. A car is coming for you. It'll be waiting at the Club."

Diego felt his stomach knot. How did Maidana know he was at the Club Español? Was he being followed?

"The Club..." he said.

"The Athletic Club," Maidana said, drawing out the words. Diego knew that the sergeant's pockmarked face must be wearing a sneer. Only the uninitiated needed to be told which Club. Officially the so-called Athletic Club was the basement of the supplies and maintenance building of the federal police. Unofficially... Dread jagged through Diego. Indart wanted him to meet the car at the Athletic Club. The colonel's message was getting louder and clearer.

"Corner of Paseo Colón and—" Maidana started to say.

"I know where it is."

No use asking questions. Maidana was a messenger.

"I knew it," Inés raised her eyes to the ceiling when he told her. "Can you at least do me the courtesy of explaining why you have to go, what the big emergency is?"

Diego made a move to take her hand but she removed it and put it on the table. The orchestra's pianist was back on his bench, warming up with a come-hither riff on "Malena."

He said sheepishly, "I'm sorry. Obviously, I wouldn't have taken you dancing if I'd known."

"But you never know—do you. Or if you do, you can't talk about it. Everything is a big secret, even your address and your phone number. And you expect me to just click my heels and play follow the Führer. Well, I didn't go to obedience school—or whatever the military call your training."

Her mouth wore an angry lipsticked frown, but he could tell by her strained tone that she was torn between resentment and worry. She hated that he was in the military. His unexplained duties were a wedge between them, the threat of an unexpected summons an irritant that corrupted their time together. And for him, there was no escaping the guilt.

"Look," he said, "this will change soon, I promise. I'm going to quit."

Inés wrinkled a corner of her mouth. "You say that once a month. It's Pavlovian."

He scowled. "I've told you—it takes time. I need an ironclad case. And I think I have one now. I'm going to ask for a medical discharge."

She stared at him. "You're all right, aren't you?"

He drew his chair closer to her and leaned over, calling up his best smile. "I'm fine. But—" he lowered his voice even as the music rose, "I can arrange something, make them not want me." She squinted at him, dubious. "I was going to tell you as soon as I put in the papers."

He knew he shouldn't even hint at the plan that could rescue him and erase the risk to both of them. But Lucas said he had it all worked out, and Lucas could be counted on. He was a respected doctor. He had been researching the condition for months, studying patients at his hospital, figuring out how to fake the symptoms and line up the lab work that would free Diego from Colonel Indart, from the constant fear that the colonel would order him to do more than he could bear to do. He had scars enough as it was, thanks to Indart.

"I can't tell you any more than that," Diego whispered against the music. "Trust me. And not a word to anyone. It could ruin everything."

He could see that she wanted to believe him, but doubted him too. He stood up. "I have to go. I'll get us a taxi."

"For yourself," Inés said, her voice suddenly hard. She fixed her eyes on the orchestra. "I'm staying right here, enjoying the wine and the music. Then I'll have dinner and maybe dance with some of these gentlemen."

Diego waited for a cab outside the Club Español, eyeing the dressy diners who wafted into the entrance to its popular restaurant intent on a good time, as if nothing was wrong with Argentina. It was what he too had hoped to do earlier this evening. His gaze traveled up the inset tiles, elaborate friezes and ironwork of the illuminated façade to the bronze winged figure of the cupola. He had often seen this Moorish-modernist building featured in design books, magazines, and film, and he could never help thinking how different Argentina must have been in 1911, when Henry Folkers, a Dutchman, designed it for a thriving Spanish community, many of whose grandchildren now wished their ancestors had stayed in Europe.

He took off his suit jacket and slung it over a shoulder, savoring the dregs of his shortened civilian night. The cold spell gripping Buenos Aires the past two days had broken, and the night's balminess surprised him with its premonition of spring. A breeze off the River Plate cradled the jacarandas along the wide span of 9 de Julio Avenue. He looked half a dozen blocks to the north where, like a giant fertility symbol dominating the teeming city, the lit-up obelisk stood stark against a starry sky. How fitting it seemed these days for the "monument to the phallus" to preside over Buenos Aires. In the three years since Perón had died and his feckless wife had been muscled out of the presidency, the country's military, with their cult of machismo, ruled with an iron rod.

Inés worried him. She had been genuinely upset, and despite his misgivings about sharing his plan, he had caved in and revealed he would be applying for a discharge. The disclosure had mollified her, he knew, sucking the sting out of their ruined evening. But now he wished he hadn't told her. The less she knew the better.

A black-and-yellow was cruising his way, its red *Libre* sign lighted, the radio on loud. He waved to it and got in.

"Good evening," he said over the blaring radio.

"Good evening, sir."

"Paseo Colón and Garay, please."

Diego could have sworn that the driver shot him a quick look in the mirror before flipping down the meter flag. A sticker pasted on the glove compartment read *I love my Argentina. Do you?*

The newscaster droned on about a high-level delegation headed by Admiral Rinaldi, the Argentine Foreign Minister, arriving in Washington to smooth out relations with the Carter Administration. The driver snorted and switched off the radio.

"Sucking up to the Americans again," he said.

Diego shrugged. "I guess Rinaldi wants to stay on their good side."

"Sure," the man sneered. "But there's a big difference between bending over backward—and forward. This Carter has no idea what's going on here."

And you do, Diego thought. His thumb slid back and forth over the face of the ring on his left hand, the engraved laurel wreaths and

sunburst of the Argentine Army. If only rubbing it could summon the
spirit of its original owner, his grandfather, Sergeant Major Arambillet. His grandfather had earned the framed letters and commendations
that Aunt Finia still kept on her wall, under his saber, next to a faded
early photograph of him wearing a shaggy beard and a worn, dusty
uniform. But grandfather Arambillet was long dead; Diego was on his
own. Whatever it was that Colonel Indart wanted with him tonight, he
would have to keep his wits about him. It might be just routine. The
colonel might want nothing more from him than another urgent forg-
ery, a false passport or death certificate. Diego nibbled on his lower lip.
Deliverance was so close. Just a few more days, Lucas had said.

Half a block before reaching the Club, Diego told the driver, "Just
drop me here."

The green Ford Falcon was waiting at the curb in front of the dark
façade of the Athletic Club. No other vehicles were parked on either
side of the street. Diego made out the dark police uniforms leaning
against the wall, Uzis slung across their chests. He felt a prickling of
goose flesh on his neck as he climbed into the back seat of the car.

"God is Argentine, Father," Colonel Indart said, gazing out the open
window of his office at the moon-laced park surrounding the headquarters of the First Infantry Regiment, First Army Corps. Diego
could hear the choruses of cicadas rising from the pink-blossomed
lapacho trees through which goldfinches darted in the daytime. Colonel Indart breathed in the sweet night air and smiled at Father Bauer.

"Amen, Colonel." The priest smiled back from his wing chair, in
its usual place next to the colonel's desk. "A splendid night to serve
God and country."

Diego stood in the center of the room, waiting. The smell of freshly mown grass outside could not overpower Father Bauer's expensive
cologne. As always when he came into the colonel's office, Diego's
eyes strayed to the oil portrait by the window, with its small black

velvet ribbon hanging from the frame. That bright, intelligent gaze, the golden hair and sunny smile of Mrs. Indart as a young girl. The colonel had brought the painting here after her funeral and hung it on that wall as a constant reminder of her murder. That any of his subordinates, but especially Diego, might not share his zeal for retribution was a possibility that never seemed to enter the colonel's mind.

"Will that be all, sir?" Diego asked. Hands crossed behind his back, he kept his face impassive.

"Yes, Captain," Colonel Indart turned his watery blue eyes back to him. Time was nosing its way into the colonel's hairline, enlarging his pouchy face. "Let me repeat: This is a simple operation. The prisoners are three broken subversives who have cooperated with the government and are being allowed to leave the country. You are driving them to Ezeiza Airport and putting them on a commercial flight to Brazil. Understood?"

"Yes, sir."

"Very well. You will drive the first car, Captain. You are leaving in five minutes. Father Bauer has already talked to the prisoners."

The chaplain hitched up the sharp crease of his trousers on his crossed leg and nodded. "I had a talk with them after our little farewell party. Now I will just bless them before we go. I'm coming along," he added with a smile to Diego.

"And Captain," Colonel Indart went on with a penetrating look, "remember: no guns. That goes for all of you."

"I understand, sir."

"Good. You often hear me say that our war on subversion is fought on many fronts. Your work in our documentation section has been very valuable, Captain. But this will be your first field operation—your chance to join the rest of your comrades in the trenches, so to speak. I have every confidence in you. You come from a proud army tradition. Your grandfather served the country with distinction. I know you will acquit yourself well. Carry on."

Diego saluted and left the office.

The three cars were waiting outside. He hurried past the room where the elaborate farewell get-together had been held, catching a glimpse of bottles, paper cups, balloons, and the flowers some family members of the prisoners had sent from Brazil, where they would be meeting the flight. He frowned. Maybe the three prisoners were being released.

Nobody in the locker room. He dialed the combination on his locker, took off his coat, and exchanged it for the leather jacket inside. With quick motions he took out the semi-automatic, checked the magazine, and slipped the gun into the large inside pocket of his jacket. No guns, Colonel Indart said, but what if the stage was being set for a phony clash with guerrillas, in which not only the prisoners but guards would be gunned down to make it look real for the media? It would not be the first time.

Outside, in the amber light of the driveway, Sergeant Maidana and his flunky, Corporal Elizalde, waited by the open rear door of the first car. Maidana's face, dry and pitted as an almond shell, inclined in a nod. Diego nodded back. They too were packing, he was sure. He got in behind the wheel.

Father Bauer came out of the building with two men and a woman. No handcuffs, no hoods, just as the colonel said. The prisoners were in their early twenties, Diego guessed, though even in this light he could see that the woman's shoulder-length hair was gray. She gave Diego a wary, flickering glance as she gingerly entered the rear of the third car, a guard on either side. One of the male prisoners was ushered into the second car while the priest came towards the front vehicle with the second man. Diego felt a sheen of perspiration on his forehead.

"I'll ride up front," Father Bauer said. The prisoner was placed in the back between Sergeant Maidana and Corporal Elizalde. Diego adjusted the rear-view mirror to take in Maidana and the prisoner, a sunken-eyed youth of scraggy features and bloodless lips drawn tight in stony silence. His body sagged into the seat, eyes on the car floor.

A hand-held receiver on Maidana's lap crackled as they eased out.

The sergeant answered, "On our way. Over."

They exited the regimental compound through the gate on Bull-rich Avenue, a tree-fringed boulevard now guarded, as were all streets bordering military installations, by small bunkers and armed soldiers. Signs posted at regular intervals warned motorists not to stop or stand anywhere along the boundary, as the sentries had orders to shoot.

The car left the Palermo district behind. As instructed, Diego took the route to Ezeiza Airport. Just a drive to the airport, the colonel said. Maybe. He wanted to believe the colonel, and there was nothing so far to indicate he should not. The prisoners were unhooded and uncuffed and had been given a send-off. But why was he driving instead of Maidana or Elizalde? And why drag him in and tell him about it at the last minute? His arm pressed against the bulk of the gun in his pocket.

The city rolled by. They were in Mataderos now, approaching the General Paz beltway. Traffic dwindled and street lamps grew sparse in this poor neighborhood of meatpacking plants scattered among small houses with tiny front lawns. Diego flicked on his brights, highlighting a parade of whitewashed tree trunks along narrow sidewalks. Garbage bags awaited collection on shoulder-high wire baskets mounted on metal poles, out of reach of dogs and rodents. The fetid smell of the slaughterhouses seeped into the car. Father Bauer produced a scented handkerchief and held it to his nose. "How can people live here..." he muttered.

The receiver rang again. This time, instead of Sergeant Maidana's voice answering, Diego heard a thud and a cry of pain from the back seat. He looked in the mirror. By the fitful light of oncoming head-lights, he saw the prisoner, bleeding, struggling for the pistol the sergeant had drawn. Corporal Elizalde was pistol-whipping the prisoner's head. Diego jerked as he felt warm blood spatter his neck and shoulders, and his foot sank for a split second into the accelerator. Seconds later he heard the scuffle cease.

"He's out," Maidana said. One of the cars behind them suddenly overtook them with a honk and shot ahead. The other two cars had taken care of their prisoners and signaled Maidana, Diego realized.

"Follow them," Father Bauer said. Diego saw him use his handkerchief to wipe the prisoner's blood from his cheek and jacket.

"The airport...?" Diego knew that his question was pointless.

"New orders from the colonel," Maidana called from the back seat. Father Bauer nodded.

Diego felt sweat bead down his rib cage. They had all known the real orders from the start. All except him. He was the odd man out. And he was not supposed to be carrying a gun.

He kept his grip tight on the wheel, his foot steady on the gas, following the lead car southwest into the La Matanza district, edging out of the city limits into industrial suburbs that were soon replaced by sparsely populated areas he didn't recognize. Twenty minutes later the three vehicles arrived at a large open field surrounded by woods. Dr. Bergman, the unit's medical officer, was waiting for them, his silhouette a dark cutout against the high beams of his covered pick-up truck.

"Bring them out," the doctor called.

Diego shut off the lights and the engine and got out of the car with the others.

"It's warm," Father Bauer said. "You won't need that jacket, Captain."

The priest was standing by the open door of the car, his face in shadow above the slant of the interior overhead light.

Diego hesitated. Then, without a word, he removed his jacket with the gun in the inside pocket and dropped it on the driver's seat.

The guards carried from the cars the unconscious bodies of the three prisoners and laid them out on the grass in the twin ovals of light from the truck. The chirring of crickets ceased. Diego tried to keep his eyes off the three forms curled in the grass. He saw Dr. Bergman reach into a black leather bag, take out a syringe, and fill it with a red liquid.

A deep stillness crept over the group. Each man, Diego sensed, felt the presence of death. He stood a step behind the ring encircling the doctor, saw him insert the needle into the chest of one of the male prisoners and press the plunger, then refill the syringe and repeat the operation with the second man.

Diego remained stone-still, his eyes now locked on the bodies inside the beams of light. As the doctor readied the syringe for the woman, he felt a cry rise from his viscera and die in his throat.

Suddenly, the woman moaned and came to life. Diego could not see her eyes, but he imagined them wide with panic as she shook her gray hair and yelled, "Help me! Please! I'm Beatriz Suárez..."

The doctor clamped a hand over her mouth and drove the needle into the flesh above her left breast. She squirmed for a second in his grasp, but almost at once stopped moving. He waited a moment longer before plucking out the hypodermic and getting to his feet. His eyes swept the bodies, then Diego and the other men.

"Three fewer," he said. "Throw them in the truck."

2

At last, Solo would see Inés again. Once he finished a day of interpreting for Admiral Rinaldi, the Argentine Foreign Minister visiting Washington, he would be off on assignment to Buenos Aires for two whole weeks. And maybe he would reconnect with the woman he once thought he would marry.

Ever since last week, when somebody named Doris had called from the Organization of American States to offer him the job, he had been so wired with expectation that he had hardly slept. The timing could not be worse, of course; a custody fight over his children had ignited, and he had to contend with his ex-wife Phyllis's lawsuit. But the thought of seeing Inés again had trumped his qualms. The interpreter normally employed by the OAS human rights commission had fallen ill, Solo was told, and he was asked to keep the matter to himself until his visa was approved and issued by the Argentine embassy. That would be today. It would be his first visit to Argentina in sixteen years, since he had left it after his father's drowning and returned home to the United States. He couldn't wait to tell Alberto, even though his friend seldom mentioned his native country these days. Solo suspected that Alberto was none too happy with the demise of Argentina's Peronist democracy, however dubious it had been, ended by the military three years ago.

He was in Alberto's car now, getting a ride to work. His friend jerked into third gear and Solo's head snapped back. His hand found the seat belt buckle and tightened the strap. His own junk heap was in the shop, and bus service from Alexandria to the District was abysmal, and yet maybe he should have splurged on a taxi instead of letting Alberto drive him. Alberto was hunched over the steering wheel, peering into the road ahead like a lookout on Magellan's ship.

In the distance the District of Columbia lay shrouded in the milky pollution that had been settling on it since daybreak. Government employees heading to work early sped through the tallowy air towards the northwest quadrant of the city, a vanguard of the armies of civil servants massing for their daily assault on the nation's capital. He and Alberto were now part of the flood of suburbanites pouring onto every highway, plunging into the tide that would empty itself in the city.

"You know Serge, the French translator in my office?" Alberto asked. "He's back from a meeting in Buenos Aires. I asked him to look up our common friend."

"Our common friend..." Solo repeated, trying to sound casual. He knew Alberto meant Inés and he felt a rush, the secret thrill of anticipation. Tomorrow he would be off to see her. As they said in Argentina, he had one foot on the stirrup.

"Yeah," Alberto said. "Come on, guys. It's green. Wake up."

Solo waited for Alberto to elaborate. Finally, he said, "All right, Serge looked up Inés. And...?"

"Oh, nothing. Just thought you might be interested."

Solo tapped his foot on the floor mat.

Alberto smiled. "She sends her regards. She's living with her parents, working part-time and studying to be a literary translator. She asked about you. She knew you and Phyllis had divorced."

Solo looked at his friend. "Actually, it's not over. I just found out Phyllis is suing me for joint custody."

"I thought that was settled with the divorce."

"So did I. I'm still paying my lawyer on top of my mother's last medical bills."

"*Lontano da questa casa stia il medico e l'avvocato*," Alberto quoted. "May the doctor and the lawyer stay far away from this house."

Pick a lane, Solo wanted to tell him. They were cruising along the George Washington Parkway. Patches of fog hung over sections of the Potomac, clinging to the dense greenery of its banks before drifting upward to dissolve in the humid light above the spires of Georgetown. A pair of single scullers scored the surface of the river, white needles stitching a brown body. With a soft shudder, Alberto's large sedan picked up speed and the boats become distant water striders tracing threads over the caramel.

"How about Lisa and John? Do they know their mother wants joint custody?" Alberto ran a hand through his thinning white hair.

Keep hands on wheel, please, Solo thought as the car briefly straddled the solid line dividing the highway. Age was catching up with Alberto. His hands were dappled with liver spots, there seemed to be new lines on his face daily, and he looked anxious. The steady progress of macular degeneration was pushing him into early retirement from his senior linguist job at the Organization of American States. He had already quit teaching at Georgetown. Driving was what he needed to quit next.

Solo shrugged. "I haven't told them. Six and four is too young to be worrying about these things. I can see Lisa sometimes trying to play mother and protect her little brother. They've been through enough." Phyllis had walked out on the family eight months before, to Solo's shock, saying only that she just couldn't be with him, that she needed to be alone to figure out her life. When he demanded to know if there was someone else, she refused to answer. Then Solo's mother died after a long struggle with cancer. Her old housekeeper, Saturnina, had been the one godsend in a wretched year, moving in with Solo and the children and helping Solo adjust to being a parent on his own.

Jefferson, Washington, Lincoln—highway signs for the memorials flashed past. Busloads of American pilgrims, in shorts and baseball caps and jackets bearing names of high schools and fire departments and bowling teams, were already unloading at the nation's shrines. Alberto's car crossed the Potomac and skirted the dreary box of the Kennedy Center, squatting on its hillock like a sumo wrestler on a footstool. On Pennsylvania Avenue, along the barricades of cranes and pile drivers of subway construction, they had to slow to a crawl.

"Looks like the Iranian students again," Alberto pointed to groups of protesters headed for the White House, carrying signs with pictures of the Shah above the legend "Reza Pahlavi, Criminal," and "American Puppet." They no longer wore the masks Solo remembered as their trademark before the Shah fled Iran and his secret police was disbanded. Alberto shook his head. "They've been demonstrating for twenty-five years. I first saw them in New York when I came from Argentina to work at the U.N. soon after the coup that overthrew Mossadegh. Those students must be the parents of these."

They waited for more protesters to cross in front of them. "Who called you for today's little tête-à-tête with the leaders of the Free World?" Alberto asked.

"Malena did. The Argentine embassy is running the show. She's become the ambassador's personal aide, so she's in charge."

"Malena?" Alberto's eyebrows went up. "I haven't seen much of her since you and Phyllis broke up."

"Nor have I," Solo said. He seldom heard anymore from most of the friends he and Phyllis had in common. People have their allegiances; or they feel uncomfortable dealing separately with two fragments of a former couple. That was how his shrink explained it. Whatever the reasons, his social circle, which the parenting of young children had inevitably constricted to mostly parents of other young children, had spun away from him.

Alberto cut left towards Dupont Circle across oncoming cars. Relax, Solo told himself as they left the horn blasts behind. One more day and he would be off to Argentina. He was dying to tell Alberto.

"So," Alberto said, "one more day and you'll be off to Argentina."

Solo stared, slack-jawed, then grinned. "You recommended me."

"Oh, I wouldn't go that far. They need an interpreter with top security clearance and their regulations bar them from hiring anyone in the country they're inspecting. I just gave them your name and your ridiculum vitae."

"Thanks," Solo said simply. Alberto had given him too many referrals to dwell on it, though they both knew how special this one was.

"But I had ulterior motives," Alberto's tone grew serious. He groped up from his coat pocket a bulky envelope. "Laura and Héctor Mahler. Have I told you about them?"

"For years." Solo smiled. The Mahlers were Alberto's aunt and uncle in Buenos Aires. Alberto shot him a look. "Good. I need you to take this money to them. I've told them you're coming and they'll pick it up at your hotel, but just in case, their address and phone number are written there. Tell them I hope to send the same amount again soon."

"Will do," Solo said, taking the envelope.

Alberto paused. He grimaced into the windshield's sunlight. "Débora and David are missing."

Solo cocked his head. Débora and David were the Mahlers' children and, despite the age difference, Alberto's favorite cousins. Débora was a university student and David worked at a Ford factory. "Missing? What do you mean?"

The car stopped at the light. Alberto turned and looked at him levelly. "Solo, you know that I think of you as family. There's no one in whom I would sooner confide. But I can't."

"Okay..." Solo said, not sure what to make of this and surprised at Alberto's grave tone. "I didn't mean to pry. I was just wondering what the circumstances were—you know, how long they've been missing."

"Months."

"*Months?*"

"Yes. My aunt and uncle haven't been able to find out what happened to them. That's all I can tell you."

"Sure—anything I can do..." Solo let the rest of the sentence drop.

"Taking the money to them is a big help." Alberto regarded him solemnly. Then his face shifted into a half-smile. "And here's your reward," Alberto offered him a small piece of paper. "Inés's number. Say hello to her for me."

Alberto narrowly missed a hydrant as he turned into the driveway of the Argentine embassy on New Hampshire Avenue.

"You haven't complimented me on my driving," he said as Solo stepped out.

Solo watched him go. Alberto was right: they were more like family than friends, and he felt a little hurt that Alberto wouldn't tell him what was going on with his cousins. Now that he thought about it, Alberto hadn't mentioned them in quite a while. Solo had worked as an interpreter at enough missing persons proceedings in this country to know that most adults dropped out by choice; or, if they were mentally ill, they returned home on their own or were ultimately found. People didn't simply vanish.

Except for his father. No, that wasn't really true. His father's body had never been recovered, but there was no question that he had drowned. For Alberto's cousins, too, there had to be an explanation. His relatives probably didn't know the right people to get answers, and in a country like Argentina it was always *who* you knew.

He was ten minutes early for the interview with Henry. Entering the embassy, he checked in with the doorman and went straight to the ballroom where Malena had said she would be spending the day supervising arrangements for tonight's reception in honor of the visiting foreign minister. Malena had once told him, to his surprise, that this handsome mansion was the 1907 creation of a black architect, a man by the name of Julian Abele, who remained virtually unknown despite having designed wonderful buildings all over the country. Solo had never heard of Abele, but the simple grandeur of the oval grand ballroom he now stepped into was a testament to the man's talent. Arched transoms graced the beautiful French doors through which waiters scampered in and out, setting up buffet tables. A man on a ladder was testing above the crown molding the concealed lights that accented a wide frieze of lovely gilded plaster girdling the ovoid ceiling.

"*O Solo mio…!*" trilled a woman's voice behind him, and Solo turned to see Malena, a fist over her heart, an impish grin on her face. He loved that smile, made the more captivating by the chignon that set off her hazel eyes and high forehead. She always reminded him of a Renaissance Madonna.

"Magdalena!" he answered teasingly. She often joked that to be possessed of her highfalutin last name, Uriburu-Basavilbaso, was an unspeakable misfortune in an English-speaking country. Back home she had long ago offset its stuffiness by shortening her first name to the trampy Malena, a moniker considered more suitable for a lady of the night. "Malena" was the title of a well-known tango about a singer with a sultry voice and a checkered past.

She came over beaming and kissed his cheek, then quickly brought out a tissue and began wiping away the imprint.

"Now I've done it. A public display of affection by two people not married to each other. What will my government say? A sign of degeneracy, no doubt."

"Maybe we can hush it up," he said. Her cheongsam dress of red brocade with embroidered dragons and phoenixes, high-necked and closefitting, accentuated her tall, pale figure and her delicate hands and features, revealing a long stretch of lovely leg along the side slits. "You look stunning. It's so good to see you."

He meant it. Of the friends who had drifted away in the aftermath of his divorce, he missed her the most. She was at once irreverent and elegant, footloose and serious, full of adventure yet engagé to a degree he would have thought unlikely from her moneyed background. He had liked her the instant they met—on the very night in Manhattan that things had gone so wrong with Inés. And that first favorable impression was never later belied. Their friendship had survived his breakup and departure for D.C. and her return to Argentina after working in New York for her uncle, the polo breeder, and had flourished again when she became a diplomat and was posted to the embassy here.

"I'm sorry we've been out of touch," Malena said. "How are your darling children? I miss them. We need to get together. I need the escape—the visit of this delegation is driving me crazy."

"Why is that?"

"The wives. Tax-free shopping on diplomatic passports. They all know three English words: *give me two*. They have military planeloads flying from Andrews Air Force Base directly to Argentina. Appliances, electronics, furniture, you name it. Free shipping and no customs when it gets there. Disgusting."

Same old Malena, Solo thought. It was a wonder she survived in the foreign service. But then again, quick-witted sexy polyglots at ease in every drawing room, and bred to the silly proprieties revered by diplomatic life, would not be easy to come by.

"I saw your name on the visa list from the OAS commission," she went on. "It happened awfully quick, didn't it?"

"Yes," he said. "I'm subbing because their interpreter is sick."

She nodded. "I've been summoned home for consultations myself. I'm flying tonight and there's something I need to talk to you..."

She stopped. Her eyes had left his and flicked over his shoulder. Somebody was coming towards them, and he saw her underlip push forward almost imperceptibly in annoyance.

A man attired in an elegant navy-blue suit came up to them and said, "Is this the young man who will make sense of what I say?"

Malena smiled. "Admiral, this is my friend Kevin Solórzano. Solo, meet Admiral Rinaldi, our foreign minister and a friend of my father's."

"Ah, yes, our interpreter," the admiral gave Solo a crushing handshake. Tall, dark, with lustrous black hair and dusky eyes set under an outcrop of heavy eyebrows, Admiral Rinaldi bore a strong resemblance to a well known Italian film actor whose name now escaped

Solo. "And you're on the OAS visa list as well. You run with the hare and hunt with the hounds, do you?" he added good-humoredly.

Solo gave a little grin. "My job, Admiral."

An embassy staffer appeared in the hallway and called Malena's name.

"If you gentlemen will excuse me," she said, heading off. "I'll talk to you later, Solo. Fernanda, in my office, has your passport with our official visa stamped on the last page. You need a new passport."

"Marvelous woman," the admiral said, following her retreating figure with appreciation. "I take it you've known her for some time?"

"We met in New York, Admiral, when she was working there years ago, and have been friends ever since."

The admiral nodded. "A most distinguished family, you know, prominent in politics, business, the arts."

Solo knew. Malena's uncle had been president of Argentina, albeit with another military government—"and so it doesn't really count," Malena had once wryly told him. Her father was one of the country's leading politicians, in semi-retirement now that the military had taken over the government yet again.

"Malena tells me," the admiral went on, "that you've lived in a number of countries. I could have taken you for an Argentine: you have no accent."

"Thank you, Admiral. I learned Spanish when I was young. My father was stationed for five years in Buenos Aires."

"Government?"

Solo nodded. "He was a harbor facilities expert with the Agency for International Development. He died in Argentina, actually, in a shipwreck on the River Plate."

The admiral gave him a look. "I'm sorry to hear that. When did it happen?"

"Nineteen sixty-three."

Now the admiral seemed startled. "In nineteen sixty-three—the *Ciudad de Asunción*?"

Solo nodded, not surprised that the admiral knew the ship's name. It *had* been a major shipwreck.

"I remember," the admiral said, and Solo was struck by the note of sympathy in his voice. "It was July, midwinter, an impenetrable fog. The radar malfunctioned on the way from Montevideo to Buenos Aires and the ship strayed from the navigation channel and hit a sunken wreck. It split in two and fire and panic broke out. Thirty missing, over fifty confirmed dead, mostly from hypothermia."

Solo was impressed. Sixteen years had passed. The particulars of his father's death, which his mother had always found too painful to talk about, were packed away in the mental warehouse of his youth. And this man was familiar with the details.

"I took part in the search for survivors," the admiral said, as though reading Solo's thoughts. "Your father's body..."

Solo felt the vague ache that stole up on him when he thought about his father's death. "It was never found."

The admiral nodded to the floor before looking up. "I hope you have other, better memories of Argentina. If there's anything I can do for you during your stay—let me know. Any friend of Malena's is a friend of mine."

"Thank you, Admiral..." Solo began. Then, on an impulse, he said, "Maybe there is something."

"Yes?"

"I have this friend—I just found out that his cousins are missing in Argentina."

"Missing?" The admiral's face clouded.

"Yes, their names are Débora and David Mahler."

"Mahler." The admiral grew thoughtful. "The name is not familiar to me. How long have they been missing?"

"Months, I'm told."

"Months..." Now Admiral Rinaldi frowned. "An accident? Have the hospitals been checked? Is it a police matter?"

Solo felt foolish. He couldn't answer these questions, reasonable as they were. He realized how little he knew, how vague it all sounded, and he chided himself for not trying to obtain a fuller account from Alberto, however reluctant his friend had seemed.

"I'm not sure, Admiral," Solo finally said in a half-apologetic tone. "All I know is that she is a student and he works in a car factory."

Admiral Rinaldi kneaded his chin between thumb and forefinger. "Many business executives have been kidnapped for ransom by the guerrillas that plague us, but this sounds nothing like that."

He teased out a pair of eyeglasses from his breast pocket and put them on, then produced a small notebook and a fountain pen.

"Let me look into this," he said, writing down the names. "I appreciate your bringing the matter to my attention. It's often these third-party requests and tips that prompt investigations and help us shed light on cases. I don't know how much I can help, but I'll make some inquiries right away." He smiled at Solo. "Come and see me in Buenos Aires."

In the embassy library, after the handshakes and greetings, Solo sat between the admiral and Henry, opposite Ambassador Capdevila, who cut his usual superb figure in a double breasted suit, finely tuned cravat, and exquisitely trimmed moustache. The ambassador, Malena said, was one of several respected politicians recruited by the military to present a more civilian face abroad.

As for Henry, he looked portlier and older than Solo remembered, but the curly hair, now graying, and the gravelly voice made him as distinctive as ever. Though the media no longer sat at his feet, Henry still held much of the foreign affairs establishment beneath his sway, traveling the lecture circuit, accepting the occasional honorary degree, and running his international lobbying firm. Allegations were lately coming to light about the many coups engineered during Henry's long foreign policy reign, but Solo knew that in American politics these were peccadilloes readily brushed aside with the magic words "national security."

Solo turned to Henry to convey the admiral's first words: "How long has it been?"

"Since last year's World Cup, when I was a guest of your government," Henry replied. He was known to be an avid soccer fan, Solo remembered.

"Yes," the admiral concurred. "You've been a true friend. Your praise for our war on terrorism has been very helpful."

Henry smiled on hearing Solo's rendering. "I have an old-fashioned view that friends ought to be supported. As I told your government when you took over: we want you to succeed, the quicker the better."

The admiral smiled back and sighed. "Do what you have to do before the U.S. Congress meets again, I remember you advised. How right you were. Mr. Carter won the election and aid was cut off. We've had three difficult years without someone to speak for us in the Oval Office."

Conversation turned to the recent toppling of Nicaragua's Somoza by the Sandinistas, and the possibility of a domino effect in the region. Admiral Rinaldi noted that Argentina had dispatched military advisers to Honduras and other neighbors of Nicaragua, discreetly of course, to reorganize the remains of Somoza's National Guard and give governments the benefit of Argentina's experience in fighting subversion.

Henry sipped his coffee and nodded. "Unfortunately, our present administration has been actively working to overthrow Somoza without having any idea of what to replace him with. The outcome in the region is crucial to maintaining our credibility in other parts of the world. If we cannot manage Central America..."

The admiral and the ambassador smiled and nodded their agreement.

"Three hundred seven, sir." The cashier at the garage returned Solo's credit card while the mechanic drove up his brown Volkswagen—"a lovely caca color with beige pentimenti," as Phyllis had once described it.

"It's got one wheel in the junkyard," the mechanic warned him again as he drove out. Yes, Solo thought, but with gas skyrocketing to eighty cents a gallon and lines at the pump, the beetle's camel-like thirst was its one saving grace.

Next event: Congress, a private, informal meeting with select members of the Senate foreign relations committee and its counterpart in the House. Thank God the admiral was first delivering a lecture at the Georgetown University Center for Strategic and International Studies, which provided its own interpreter. That left Solo enough time to pick up both the car and Tracy Spencer, his partner today, and make it to Congress before the admiral and the ambassador arrived.

Asking the admiral about Alberto's cousins had made Solo feel better. Odd how the idea had suddenly suggested itself, prompted perhaps by the admiral's cordiality and his unexpected connection to the shipwreck that had taken Solo's father. Personal access to a top official who also happened to be a friend of Malena's family presented a rare opportunity. He had seized it, and the admiral seemed to take a genuine interest in the matter. If nothing came of it, at least he had tried.

He spotted Tracy waiting at the entrance to the World Bank.

"I'm so excited!" she said, getting in. "My first job in Congress. Is my skirt too short?"

"Way too long," he said, eyeing her shapely legs.

She laughed. "Don't get any ideas. It's not payback for getting me the gig."

He turned east on Pennsylvania Avenue. A block before the White House, traffic stalled. The demonstrators. He'd forgotten the damned demonstrators. In Lafayette Park, across from the White House, a handful of marchers cordoned off by police were orbiting a woman with a bullhorn. But they were not the Iranian students Solo had expected; they waved a U.S. and a blue-and-white-flag unfamiliar to Solo. The sight took him back to his own demonstrations in college, protesting Nixon and Vietnam. He had done things like that, in his age of innocence, before coming to this town and getting his top security clearance, before reality bared its teeth. Vietnam would still be going on for all the good demonstrations did.

"Can you make out what they're chanting?" he asked Tracy.

She rolled down her window an inch, then looked at him. "It's stuck."

"Yeah, sorry. Mine doesn't open at all."

She listened through the crack, "They want Somoza extradited to Nicaragua."

Dream on, Solo thought, as a cop with a whistle waved them past. Somoza had fled to Miami with the entire contents of the Nicaraguan treasury, but radio and television in America were still dominated by the fallout of Three Mile Island. Besides, as FDR would have put it, Somoza was *our* SOB.

"We in the military looked on as our country drifted into anarchy..."

Through the tinted glass of the portable interpreters' booth that had been set up for this meeting, Solo watched Admiral Rinaldi recite the remarks prepared for him by the American public relations firm hired by his government to manage its image abroad. Most faces around the racetrack table in the conference room—"the aquarium" to the interpreters—were familiar: Jesse Helms, favorite son of the Old South, and his antithesis Claiborne Pell, scion of New England nobility and paladin of every liberal cause. The astronaut John Glenn was here, and Bill Bradley the basketball star, and others whose long survival in office had scored their names and faces into the public mind. Tall men, strong jaws, telegenic faces. Only one woman among them, Susan Segal, the New York representative. Solo saw the ambassador's eyes registering her presence.

"Schools were in ferment, policemen shot at, businessmen kidnapped. Even military installations were attacked. Voices rose on every side urging us to intervene..."

At the far end of the table, while seemingly absorbed in mental consideration of the issues at hand, the congressman from Utah was running a private eye over his leggy neighbor, a striking brunette aide to his Massachusetts colleague. Tracy had noticed how deftly Utah operated his swivel chair, casually tilting and reclining it into coigns of vantage. The Massachusetts legs shifted position once more, setting off fresh contortions in Utah, and Solo caught Tracy's smile and shake of the head as she talked into the mic.

Her amusement at the shenanigans in the aquarium made him feel—what? Old? Thirty-four wasn't old. But he had long ago learned the odd voyeurism of life as an interpreter. Alberto—Professor Dellacroce in those days—had warned him and his fellow trainees: You are invisible. It was true. People entered the aquarium fully aware of the interpreters' booths. They sat down, put on headphones, turned knobs to the desired language and volume, and settled back. Soon they had lost all consciousness of the eyes focused on them through the tinted glass. And once that happened, every privately intended move they made was forced on the hidden audience. Solo too had once been amused by it. Now *he* was the veteran, Tracy the rookie.

She was good, too, with the quick mental reflexes and extensive vocabularies of a first-rate interpreter. No college-trained linguist liable to trip over slang or become tongue-tied at the first barbarism, Tracy was bilingual from the nursery. He had known it the minute he heard her; he hadn't needed to ask in what language she dreamt or counted her numbers. Her prepositions said it all. The spontaneously correct use of prepositions, as Alberto lectured when Solo attended his classes at Georgetown, gives the native speaker away.

"You play *with* her," Alberto would say, leaning against the blackboard and smudging chalk across the shoulders of the same brown suit he had worn for thirty years, "but if she's not around, you play *by* yourself, not *with* yourself—I trust."

Solo too had grown up with the prepositions. And the nursery rhymes and school songs, the tongue twisters, the swear words and the idioms. The idioms above all. In this country you ran around like a chicken with its head cut off, but in Brazil you ran around like a dazed cockroach. He recognized in Tracy his own feel for idiom and usage that could not be taught—or even learned, he thought, but only absorbed while the brain was still a sponge.

"The IMF and the World Bank hold up my country as a model for developing nations..."

Solo glanced at the wall clock and Tracy followed his gaze. Her half hour was nearly up. Two more minutes and she would hand him the baton. And everybody in the aquarium would give a start as a new voice in their ears broke the spell and brought back awareness of the invisible interpreters.

"Well put, Admiral," said a senatorial voice. "Cutting off military aid was exceedingly ill-advised when our own vital interests are at stake in Argentina."

Solo saw Ambassador Capdevila steady a drooping frond of his breast-pocket handkerchief and make a show of looking at his wrist-watch.

"Thank you for being so candid with us, Admiral," Susan Segal, the New York congresswoman, said. "Allow me to reciprocate."

Solo smirked. Across the glass, he could feel the ambassador tense. On this turf doublespeak was the lingua franca. Nothing was ever a problem but always a challenge or an opportunity. Aging dictators became senior leaders, and taking full responsibility meant there was no way in hell you were going to resign. Freedom of information meant miles of files protected by layers of lawyers. Tracy's current favorite was "appearance of impropriety," which could be used after the standard denials to play down anything from soliciting a bribe—always a campaign contribution—to extorting sex from your underlings. Unless you were caught red-handed and had to settle for "error in judgment."

The New York congresswoman had uttered the word candid. She was about to step on the admiral's toes.

"After three years of rejecting inspections, Argentina is letting in a group from the OAS, our regional organization headquartered here in D.C. Let me be clear, Admiral: under our current law, there can be no resumption of aid without a favorable OAS report."

Ambassador Capdevila had stopped fidgeting with his handkerchief and was on pink alert. Tracy signaled. Solo turned on his mic, waited for her to finish the sentence, and began.

"If I may put in a word..." Ambassador Capdevila interposed in his heavily accented English. "With your permission and the indulgence of our interpreters Ms. Spencer and Mr. Solórzano"—the ambassador could never bring himself to pronounce Solo's surname without the vestigial Spanish accent never used in America—"I will take advantage of my diplomatic immunity in order to murder the English language."

His unexpected drollery raised a laugh, draining some of the tension from the room.

"We have no doubt that the OAS report will vindicate us, and that you will consequently rejoin our battle against the common enemy." The ambassador turned to Admiral Rinaldi. "Admiral..."

It was time for the final humorous line from the PR team, Solo guessed.

"Yes," Admiral Rinaldi said, picking up his cue. "As we well know in Argentina, it takes two to tango."

Monique Nguyen, Esquire, looked at Solo sternly across her file-strewn desk and said, "Why didn't you tell me your housekeeper is an illegal?"

He was too surprised to answer.

"I'm your attorney, Solo. I don't appreciate learning these things from Phyllis's lawyer. Did you speak to him, or to Phyllis?"

"I didn't talk to anybody," he said defensively. "You said not to."

Monique scowled. "I wonder how he found out. Well, two can play the same game. We need something on Phyllis's boyfriend, if she has one. Any dirt we can dig up."

Solo shrugged. "I don't know any. I never wanted to find out dirt. Couldn't we hire a private detective or something?"

Monique crossed her arms and didn't answer. Her look said: Can you afford one?

Money. Always money. His mother's long, final illness in her little apartment in Chevy Chase had taken the last of his savings, such as they were after Phyllis left and he had to support his family on a single paycheck—and a sporadic one at that, since he had decided against finding a full-time job in order to spend more time with the kids. When he and Phyllis were still together, the money she made as a freelance editor had made a big difference. Later, he had considered declaring personal bankruptcy, but with the divorce and custody pending, Monique had advised against it. And then, there was the issue of affording Monique herself. They had remained good friends after attending Rutgers together, and she never mentioned her fees, which made him feel even guiltier. He had yet to pay her for the divorce, and now Phyllis was after the kids.

"Forget detectives," Monique said. "See what you can remember over the next few days."

"Thanks. I really want to think about it. Anyway, I won't be here. I'm going on a job to Argentina for two weeks."

She stared. "You don't say. How about a few months in Tahiti? Are you out of your mind? What on earth will you be doing in Argentina?"

"The usual: meetings, interviews. It's a commission."

"Solo, we have a crucial hearing coming up!"

"I'll be back before that. I need the money, Monique, you know that. The kids will be fine with Saturnina."

She gave him a very serious, teacherly look. "Solo, your divorce was a breeze because Phyllis took off and contested nothing. But now there'll be a parade of expert witnesses to claim she had mental or emotional or whatever problems at the time and to swear she's all better and needs her kids back. Read the papers: politicians are getting hammered on their illegal nannies; the INS is under pressure to crack down. Yes, we've got to show you're earning real income, but we also need to prove the children are being properly cared for at home when you're not there."

"I know that. A couple of neighbors and friends will drop by to keep an eye on them."

"Sure, and with a little nudge from Phyllis's lawyer the INS could drop by, too. You've got to get rid of her."

"I can't."

"Solo, it's your kids we're talking about."

He shook his head. "They've already lost one mother figure. I don't want them to lose another."

"Would you rather lose custody?"

He sighed. "Look, my mother was bedridden for months before she died. Saturnina took care of her. We are the only family she has. I'm not letting her go."

Monique grunted in exasperation. She picked up a pen. "Who's the friend you're leaving in charge?"

From the cardholder on her desk, Solo took one of her business cards and handed it to her.

When he got back home to the saltbox that Phyllis and he had rented on the edge of Alexandria soon after their marriage, the first thing he did was to go to his bedroom and call Inés's phone number in Buenos Aires, his fingers hurried and shaky as he dialed. Inés and her parents were out, their cleaning lady said. He left word of his arrival and the name of his hotel.

Inés sends her regards. Alberto's phrase kept running through his head. Was that Serge the French translator talking or could she really have uttered something so impersonal, so inane? Well, why wouldn't she? She probably wanted to keep her distance—or distance came naturally to her whenever she thought of him. A dozen years, after all, had passed since their painful parting in Manhattan. He kept tunneling into the past, to their younger days in Argentina—Inés silently hugging him after he learned of his father's drowning—and to their reunion in New York years later, wandering the streets of the city hand in hand with her, feeling life could have no greater gifts to offer. Raking over, his analyst called it. But Inés had probably erased him from her memory long ago. To her, he might be nothing but a youthful mistake.

An impulse seized him and, climbing on a chair, he rummaged in the rearmost reaches of the bedroom closet until he found the large box with his old photo albums and family papers. He sat down on the bed with it. His father's papers, which his mother had bagged and buried away in this box when he died, lay on top. He took out his father's State Department picture ID and looked at it, lingering over the dark wavy hair and trenchant gray eyes he had inherited. He still missed his father, he realized as he put back the card. In so many ways, Argentina seemed no longer ago than yesterday. He sighed and picked up a photo album.

There they were in Buenos Aires sixteen years ago, he and Inés standing with his father in front of the *Ciudad de Asunción* that winter afternoon when they drove him to the pier for his regular, and that time fateful, trip to Montevideo. His father, hands inside the pockets of his fur-lined coat, looked happy, a broad smile crinkling his face. Solo and Inés, one arm around each other's waist, looked absurdly young. In another photo of them, taken at Jones Beach four years later when they were living together in Manhattan, her girlishness had ripened into womanhood, and his own teenage shaggy hair and rangy look had given way to a beard and pony tail. They looked at ease, their arms again wrapped around each other, grinning into the sunlight, lovestruck. After twelve more years, what would they think of each other now?

That evening Solo and his children sat around the kitchen table as Saturnina made them empanadas. Knowing he was leaving, Lisa and John were clingier than usual and Saturnina even quieter than her normally imperturbable self. With Tita, their tabby, purring on his lap, Solo watched Saturnina's calloused hands roll the dough and wondered, not for the first time, how old she was. She herself didn't know. In her soft Quechua-inflected Spanish she had told Solo she was born in a small village in the Cochabamba region of Bolivia, not far from a mining town, many years ago—that was all she knew. Around her thin lips and sad, dark eyes the burning winds of the altiplano had etched a tight web of lines. Chicken tracks, she once told the kids, in her fragments of English, when they asked; when she was little and slept on the floor on a thin straw mattress, the chickens would walk all over her. It was the only humor Solo had ever heard from her. Her long black hair was still parted into twin braids, but she no longer dressed in the colorful skirt and petticoats, the alpaca poncho, or the flat brown bowler of the framed photograph visible through the open door of her room facing the kitchen. She stood in that shot with a grim, wide-cheeked man whose name she had never mentioned.

On a shelf above that photograph stood the large figurine of Ekeko, god of prosperity and good fortune. The kids loved that terracotta doll, the squat mustachioed hunchback in a poncho and wide sandals, woven cap with earflaps, and a cigarette in his mouth. Ekeko was laden front and back with representations of every object desirable in the puna: little llamas, chickens and goats, reed flutes and panflutes, fabrics, fruit and pots, baskets and banknotes. Except that tonight, Solo had noticed that Ekeko was covered down to his sandals with a paper bag. Solo knew what that meant. Saturnina did not like it when he traveled.

"Are you worried?" he asked her, pointing to Ekeko.

"Ay, señor," she said, "I told Ekeko I wouldn't let him out until you returned safely."

After dinner they sat in the living room, all except Tita, who was hiding under Solo's bed after being declared gata non grata for chewing up the stereo wires. While Saturnina knitted, Solo began to tell Lisa and John a story about a princess with long blonde hair...

"Make it black hair," Lisa interrupted, knitting her little brows. "Like my mom."

This caught Solo off guard.

"Okay, like your mom. The princess had long black hair and her name was..."

"Phyllis," Lisa said.

"Phyllis?"

"Yes, like my mom."

"Okay. Her name was Phyllis..."

After telling him the story, in which Phyllis rescued the king and queen from a mean wizard who had imprisoned them in his castle, Lisa began to deploy her bedtime filibuster, ably abetted by her brother. John had been fighting off sleep in a superhuman battle of heavy yawning and eye rubbing that did credit to his Superman pajamas, but when his sister said she wouldn't be able to sleep because she had a headache, he announced that he had two headaches. Eventually he toddled off to bed clutching his stuffed beaver. Solo swept up Lisa and carried her to bed, where she squeezed out permission for two straight-face contests that became five—because twice she messed up and once he flared his nostrils and that was no fair. Finally, she kissed him good night and went to sleep.

He didn't. Lisa's insistent mention of Phyllis was something new. Had she overheard him during one of his many phone conversations with Monique? His analyst had said the children would miss Phyllis and grieve as if she had died. An exaggeration, Solo had thought. Mommy and he, he told them, had not gotten along and had divorced. She had gone away for a time, but she loved them very much. He wondered if they were going to start asking about Phyllis again, if they still missed her as much. Saturnina was terrific, but all kids needed a real mother, didn't they? And Phyllis had been a good mother—he had to give her that. Which had made her abrupt departure all the more painful.

He stared at Phyllis's three beautiful Iznik tiles, still hanging on the bedroom wall: a profusion of pomegranates, artichokes and hyacinths, a floral scrollwork in lapis lazuli, coral and emerald, and a very un-Turkish looking ship, more like a Chinese junk, in the vivid turquoise she loved. She hadn't bothered to take the tiles or anything else. Just her clothes in a suitcase, and her car.

Get on with your life, the shrink had told him. Phyllis was her own person, and women all over America were struggling to find themselves in the uncertainties of these times. Go out, meet other women. Solo had. Except for sex, he hadn't gotten much out of it. It was hard enough making friends, let alone finding your soul mate, in Washington and its suburbs—a world of transient, work-obsessed bureaucrats, as Malena had correctly diagnosed soon after being sent here. How she detested the restaurant kitchens that closed at ten, the giant malls with their satellite suburbs of dead streets, the nightlong wailing of sirens over the empty boulevards of D.C. In those early months following Malena's arrival from Buenos Aires, Solo and Phyllis and their kids had been Malena's refuge, her foster family, as she tried to adjust to the loneliness of Washington.

But in his case, he knew, Washington wasn't the problem; Solo was the problem. Maybe Monique was right. Why *was* he going to Argentina? Not simply for the unexpected extra income, vital as that was. He had a soft spot for the country. Except for the tragic death of his father, the five years he had spent there had been happy. Sixteen years later, he still looked back on those days as his personal belle époque. First sex, first love: Inés had been his induction into adulthood. And his parents had been alive then, his life slower, carefree. Maybe he was kidding himself. Maybe it had all been about adolescence, a time of life you are desperate to outgrow, only to miss it later.

It did not diminish the value or intensity of his memories that Argentina had changed since his time there, or that the country was troubled. Argentina was always troubled. It was a country of loonies. Didn't Buenos Aires have more shrinks per capita than any city in the world? Crises were something Argentina never tired of falling into and bouncing back from. Whatever the trouble, a couple of good harvests and all would be well again. The locals had a saying for it: God is Argentine.

The doorbell rang.

When he answered it, Malena stood in the lighted doorway, a taxi waiting at the curb. She had changed out of her formal attire into a more comfortable Jacquard cropped jacket and skirt and low-heels. But she did not look comfortable. There was an air of disquietude about her, an odd nervous unease.

"Hi," he said, surprised. "I got my passport from Fernanda in your office, but you were out."

She nodded and gave him a peck on the cheek as he let her in. "I'm on my way to the airport, but I had to see you first. Are the kids asleep? Can I see them?"

"Yes to both," he said. "Is everything okay?"

She smiled, saying nothing, and he led her down the hallway to the kids' room. By the faint glow of the night light he watched her re-enact his own late homecomings, tiptoeing in, sitting down first on one bed, then the other, to admire Lisa and John.

"They are so beautiful, thank you," she said softly, just minutes later, when she followed him into the hallway to the front door. He heard in her voice a twinge of sympathy, sadness perhaps, nostalgia for the days when the family was whole, when Lisa and John had their mother with them. And he was grateful for her delicacy in leaving it unsaid.

Malena took the purse she had hung on the doorknob. She looped the strap over her shoulder and said, "I need a favor, Solo. And I couldn't ask you at the embassy. This must be strictly between us."

Her tone was intense, her eyes troubled.

He took her hand, that slender wrist with long fingers, and said reassuringly. "Consider it done, whatever it is. Would you like to sit down?"

She smiled. "No. I have only a minute. Listen, the chairman of your OAS group is a lawyer named Hardoy..."

"Yes, he's from Uruguay." The name was in the file the OAS had given him.

Malena nodded. "The note from the OAS said he's arriving in Buenos Aires tomorrow. I need a private interview with him, and it can't be at the Hotel Metropole where you're all staying. I need you to arrange it."

"Sure, but—"

"Don't, please," she said. "I'll tell you everything in Buenos Aires. Except for Hardoy, you, and me—nobody else must know about this. It's very important. Will you do this for me?"

He looked at her quizzically. She was mortally serious. He nodded.

She took from her purse a sealed envelope addressed to Dr. Bruno Hardoy and handed it to Solo with her business card. "The letter has the time and place for the meeting. The phone numbers of my father and a friend of mine are on the card. Call me as soon as you get in."

He took the letter and the card. "What makes you so sure Hardoy will do it?"

A smile crossed her lips, and for an instant he saw in her eyes the teasing playfulness he always loved in her.

"You," she said, squeezing his hand. "You are irresistible."

She opened the door and hurried to her taxi.

Diego woke up on the cot he kept in the printing shop and saw through the undrawn window blinds that it was already nighttime. Lights were blazing across the regimental compound. How long had he slept?

It had been early afternoon when they arrived back at headquarters after the operation. Sergeant Maidana was at the wheel of the car and Corporal Elizalde at his side, Diego sitting in the back. Father Bauer had been driven to his apartment before the bodies of the prisoners were taken to a different location and burned along with old tires to hide the smell of incinerating flesh. Thank God Dr. Bergman had picked the four guards in the other cars to help him with that task. During the ride back to headquarters Diego had kept silent, unable to think past the vision in his head: Beatriz Suárez's gray hair, aflame.

"Well, well," Maidana had exclaimed as they came through the gates and were met by the smell of barbecue. They could see in the rear of the compound large hunks of skewered beef cooking in open-air pits. "A real *asado* for a change."

Elizalde laughed. "Smells like big money, doesn't it? Our guests have loving families. You have to hand it to the priest: he's done it again."

Another large ransom negotiated by Father Bauer, Diego had surmised as he went directly to his locker to return the jacket and gun and retrieve the spare set of clothes he kept there. The families of the dead would soon realize that their ransom had not won them their loved ones' freedom, and there was nothing they could do about it. He met no one in the locker room or on the way to the small printing shop behind the quartermaster building, and was more than ever thankful that his duties here allowed him to work alone, bringing in help only when the job was too much for one man.

Now he rubbed his eyes, got up from the cot, and walked past the copperplate press into the shop's bathroom. His shirt lay on the floor, where he had tossed it when he scrubbed the dried blood from his neck and hair. The face staring back at him from the washbasin mirror was chalky and his eyes looked raw.

It had been a test. The farewell party was Colonel Indart's elaborate charade to keep the prisoners docile, and Diego had been left in the dark to see how he would react. Father Bauer had caught a glimpse of the gun and made him take off the jacket to show he knew it was there. It all made sense now. The priest had been watching him as Diego stared at the three bodies sprawled on the grass, the doctor straddling them with his poison syringe. Colonel Indart was signaling that Captain Diego Fioravanti would no longer be allowed to spend his days in the printing shop, that he had more serious business to attend to in the future.

A knock on the door of the shop made him jump.

"Come in!" he shouted through the bathroom's open door.

Father Bauer walked in, dressed in blue gabardine trousers and a gray herringbone sport coat over a black polo shirt, his thin gray hair neatly combed. Diego could not recall ever seeing him in clerical dress, a robe, or even a collar. His clothes were expensive, as was the imported Toyota he drove, a red coupe equipped with the police siren authorized by Colonel Indart. They were old friends, the colonel and the priest.

"I didn't mean to disturb you, Captain," Father Bauer said, coming forward and standing in the doorway of the bathroom. "The colonel will be congratulating everybody who took part in the operation, but I wanted a word with you first. I saw that last night's events made a deep impression on you."

"Father, I was not prepared—"

"For what happened. I know, I know," Father Bauer raised his hand. He looked as if he might lean against the tile wall, then thought better of it. "Once you've been on as many operations as I have, you'll be used to it. For security reasons, not everybody can be in on the actual plan. But it was your first operation. I could see it in your face: you were shocked, weren't you?"

"Yes," Diego said. No point in denying it. The priest's searching eyes, set wide apart under the shaggy eyebrows, did not miss much.

"It's understandable, Diego. May I call you Diego?"

"Yes, Father."

"What we did today, Diego, was for the good of the country. God knows that. And God is grateful. It was a patriotic duty, Diego. You, more than most, should realize that."

Diego followed the priest's gaze. He was looking into the mirror behind Diego, at the scars on his back.

"Come see me in my office. I'd like you to join me in a visit to one of our guests." He left.

It was a patriotic duty, Diego. You, more than most, should realize that.

He should. He had the scars to remind him of that night four years ago in the Indarts' apartment on Zabala Street, sitting in the living room, waiting for their daughter Graciela and her friend Ana María to finish their homework so he could take Ana María home.

"Lieutenant..." Ana María had called to him from the dining room door. "We're finished. Give me a minute to use the bathroom and we can go."

He had smiled and nodded from his chair, putting away the graphic design magazine he brought along to his usual day of guard duty. Ana María disappeared down the hallway while Graciela gathered the books scattered over the dining room table.

Same routine, he remembered thinking. Ride shotgun in the police cruiser. Pick up the girls at the Foreign Language Institute, bring them back to Colonel Indart's apartment for their evening homework session, wait until they finish, take the friend home. But he understood the reason for all the security. The head of the federal police and his wife had been blown up while boarding a river cruise. The next chief had barely escaped an ambush. The colonel was taking no chances.

Diego liked the girls and they liked him. It wasn't hard to impress eighteen-year-olds. Graciela was not very outgoing, but Ana María was lively—she made a point of flirting with him.

Above the fireplace in the Indarts' living room, a young Mrs. Indart always smiled at him from a romantic portrait. The subdued light in the painting brought out the chartreuse of the single orchid held in her hand and the soft green of her eyes, kindled by the hint of a smile. Diego studied the face on the canvas. The eyes of the present Mrs. Indart still held a gleam of the girlish innocence depicted in this painting.

"Graciela, dear," Mrs. Indart said, coming out of the kitchen with her younger children, a boy and a girl, both in pajamas, ready for bed. "Have you girls offered Diego even a cup of coffee?"

"No, please, Mrs. Indart," Diego said. "Thank you. I'm about to take Ana María home. I was admiring your portrait."

She laughed, her eyes lighting up. "Oh, that. Highly utopian, I'm afraid. If only I looked like that even then."

Ana María returned and picked up her purse and books. "Ready," she said with a smile.

After a round of goodbye kisses between Ana María and the Indarts, he and Ana María were out the door. In the street, the driver of the patrol car was chatting with the two guards posted at the entrance to the building.

"Ride with me in the back." Ana María laced her arm through his when he opened the rear door for her. "Please."

He climbed in beside her. The driver didn't need to be told where to go. They had been taking Ana María home for a week now.

"Graciela's family is so nice to me," she said as the car picked up speed. She paused. "I was called in for questioning, you know."

He did know. Word was that they let her go because the colonel intervened.

"They let me go because of the colonel. Because I am a friend of his daughter."

"Why did they want to question you?" Her thigh was pressed against his.

"My parents. They're leftists." She revealed this information in a bored tone, as though saying they were vegetarians. "My father was fired from the hospital because of his leftist ideas. He is a surgeon. My mother is a psychologist. They're separated now, but I went through hell with them this past year. I told Graciela that I don't know what I would do without her and her family."

She rested her hand on his thigh, and he felt his body reacting to the contact. She smiled, then said offhandedly, "Do you think it's true what they say about the colonel—that he executed all those guerrillas out west in Catamarca after they surrendered?"

"I don't know," Diego said. What kind of game was this girl playing?

"That's what they say in school. That he's the head of that secret Argentine Anticommunist Alliance, the AAA, that's been killing subversives."

"Is that what you think?"

"Oh no. I don't believe that. He's such a nice man."

"Lieutenant," the driver said. "I'm going to hit the siren or we'll never get out of here."

Only now did Diego notice the traffic jam they were in. The siren made further conversation futile as Ana María's hand glided back and forth along his pants leg.

"See you," she said, grinning, when they dropped her off.

He stayed in the back seat to collect himself while they drove back. Minutes later he was back at the Indarts' building. The colonel wasn't home yet, the street guards said. Graciela opened the door of the apartment.

"Hello," she said, a shiny smile on her face. He felt she had been waiting for this moment, when she could be alone with him without Ana María.

"Is that Diego?" Mrs. Indart's voice came from her bedroom.

"Yes, Mrs. Indart. "If you won't be needing me any more tonight..."

"You go home, young man. Thank you. The children are asleep and I'm going to bed right—"

She never finished that sentence. Or maybe she did but he and Graciela didn't hear. The explosion dashed them both against the front wall of the apartment.

From his bed in the military hospital, only blocks from the Indarts' building, he watched for weeks the same television footage of the wrecked apartment, which, as the investigation unfolded, was constantly featured—reporters and commentators declaring it a cautionary tale of the horrors subversives were capable of, and a call to arms to fight them by any means possible. The force of the blast had ripped through the interior walls of the apartment, demolishing large sections of masonry, smashing doors and windows and blowing out glass panes throughout the building and the neighborhood. In the television shots splintered furniture lay all about. Mrs. Indart had died instantly. Graciela and her siblings had been hospitalized with serious injuries but were expected to recover. Ana María and her family were still at large. Montoneros, one of the largest guerrilla groups, had taken credit for the bomb—brought into the apartment in a small bottle of perfume in Ana Maria's purse. The guards checking bags at the building entrance had thought nothing of the container. Seven hundred grams of trotyl had been placed under the Indarts' mattress. Ana María had snuck into their bedroom on her way to or from the bathroom, before Diego escorted her home. That was the only time she had left the dining room while he sat there reading his magazine.

He retained a dim recollection of a visit by Colonel Indart in the early days of his hospital stay, when his senses were dulled by medication and he drifted in and out of consciousness. In his uncertain vision, the colonel looked spectral, withered. His shoulders sagged and his features had grayed, coarsened somehow. He had stood over the bed, gazing at him for a long time, then turned and left the room without uttering a word.

Gradually Diego's body healed. He would later tell Inés that the scars on his back were from a chemical explosion in a printing establishment where he once worked. The truth was they had earned him a promotion to captain instead of the disability retirement he had hoped for. Colonel Indart, he was sure, had pulled strings to get him promoted and keep him in the army. By the time he returned to active duty, with Perón dead from cancer, a rising tide of violence was engulfing the country under Peron's second wife, Isabel. She was ousted in a coup and Captain Diego Fioravanti had been transferred to this special counterinsurgency unit run by Colonel Indart himself.

Ever since his arrival here, Diego's one aim had been to be as unobtrusive as furniture. He had managed to avoid fieldwork, the death squads that went under the name of task forces, because his skills inside the printing shop outweighed his usefulness outside. But no more.

He left the shop and walked to the main building to knock on the open door of the office marked by a small wooden crucifix.

"Well, you do look much better, Diego," Father Bauer said, closing one of two tall filing cabinets that took up most of the space left over by a desk, a table, and two chairs. In a wall niche, a kneeling statuette of the Virgin Mary clasped her hands in prayer. "It seems you needed a good long nap and tidying up. Very good. Let's go."

The guardhouse was a squat structure two buildings away in the direction of Dorrego Avenue. A soldier flipped on a light switch by the door of a small cell and let them in. In the rank odor that filled the air Diego saw a lanky blindfolded man in tattered pants and a buttonless shirt sitting on a canvas cot.

"It's Father Bauer," the priest told the man. "You may take off the blindfold."

The man didn't respond. Father Bauer went up to him and removed the blindfold, revealing under the crusty eyebrows a pair of red, swollen eyes—badly infected, Diego thought. It took him a long moment to recognize the prisoner. Nobody who laid eyes on those sunken cheeks, the emaciated body, would easily recognize in this wretch the newspaper publisher whose picture had been splashed across the media when he was kidnapped, supposedly by subversives. Over time, Diego had seen the man's face recede from the headlines as more publishers, reporters, cartoonists, writers, psychiatrists and lawyers disappeared. The man's family had publicly admitted paying the large ransom demanded by the kidnappers. Yet here he was.

"Oh," The priest was looking in apparent amusement at the prisoner's chest. "They burned off your chest hairs. You have no chest hair left."

The man stared dully at the priest, as if trying to decide whether to speak. Crimson rings under his eyes contrasted with the ash of his skin. At last, he seemed to muster his strength.

"Father," he said in a thread of a voice, "I don't want to die."

The priest assented gravely. "Nobody does. Your life depends on God and your cooperation. Have you thought about what I said yesterday?"

The man shut his eyes and seemed to shrink further. "How can I name people I don't know?"

Father Bauer shook his head. "Do you expect the colonel to believe that? Why do you think you are here? Why are these terrible things happening to you?"

This drew no reply.

"When your newspaper published that letter from the Marxist terrorist, did you think there would be no consequences? Confession is good for the soul, my son." He glanced up instructively at Diego, then regarded the prisoner again. "I am ready to hear yours at any time. Just tell the guard and I'll come."

The publisher closed his eyes again and made no answer.

"Here," Father Bauer took a small bottle out of his pocket and placed it on the cot. "This will help your eyes."

"He's a stubborn one," Father Bauer said when they were seated in his office. "But he'll come around. They all deny everything at first. Nobody knows anything about the guerrillas, the People's Revolutionary Army, the Montoneros. The bombs, kidnappings, executions—nobody is responsible; they're all acts of God—may God forgive me for saying that."

Diego said nothing, but he listened carefully. This was Colonel Indart speaking.

"You know, Diego, that the colonel has a special regard for you because of his beloved wife." Father Bauer crossed himself. "You too were a victim of terrorism. It left you scarred. But you must learn to trust your comrades and your colonel's orders."

The gun. Diego had known that Maidana and Elizalde and the rest of the party would be armed, orders or no orders. Nobody trusted anybody. But he hadn't counted on the priest spotting the gun.

The priest looked at him through slitted eyes, as if trying to read his thoughts. "We all have to do our part, Diego. I wanted you to see me doing mine, which is to extract information from the prisoners because that information may save lives. This is a dirty war, and we all have to get our hands dirty. Otherwise, it's not fair to your comrades. Do you understand?"

"Yes, Father."

"Good." Father Bauer seemed to relax. "An OAS inspection group is coming, and there is much work to be done. We'll need every available man. Then, if you do a good job—well, you know that the colonel has high hopes for you. Your file says you speak fluent French. Is that right?"

Diego was unprepared for the question. Warily, he said, "Yes."

"How would you like to go to Paris?"

Diego's uncomprehending expression brought a smile to the chaplain's lips. "We're opening an office there as part of Operation Condor, to counter the exiles' anti-Argentine campaign."

Diego nodded. He had heard about the network to track down and neutralize exiles. Father Bauer himself, it was rumored, had been involved in one such mission last year in New York, where he had been sent as a visiting parish priest to a church in the Bronx.

The priest stood up. "Colonel Indart thinks you might be very helpful in Paris. But we'll talk about it when the time comes. You know, as a man of the cloth I suppose I shouldn't say this, but perhaps what you need to take your mind off this gloomy work is a girlfriend. Or do you already have a girlfriend?"

Outside the regimental gates, Diego walked along Santa Fe Avenue until he found a working pay phone inside the Pacífico train station. He dialed Lucas.

Or do you already have a girlfriend? He hoped to God that his face had not changed expression or color in response to Father Bauer's question. Did he know about Inés? No, how could he? But what if he did?

He finished dialing and got another dial tone. Muttering an oath, he pummeled the phone and began dialing again. In American movies they called the operator when this happened. Here, you'd have a coronary if an operator even answered.

This time it rang. And rang.

"Hello..." Lucas's sleepy voice.

"Lucas, it's me, Diego. Wake up."

"Diego?" A loud crash, then, "Sorry. I dropped the phone. I was in surgery all night. What's the matter?"

Diego heard his own voice, raspy, terse, strangely subdued, "I've run out of time."

4

"So, you are our interpreter," Justiniano Fonseca, the vice chairman of the OAS commission, said in Portuguese after carefully placing his briefcase and hat in the overhead luggage compartment and taking the aisle seat next to Solo. He was a pale-complexioned man with affable eyes and shiny black hair parted in the center and fringed by a glossy sliver of gray above each ear. "Allow me to apologize in advance. I'm afraid my Portuñol will test you to the utmost."

Solo smiled and replied in the same language, "I doubt that, sir. Doris says your Spanish is better than hers."

Doris Pereira, the plump, fortyish Brazilian office manager of the OAS human rights commission, was sitting three rows behind them. At Solo's hiring interview in Washington she had indicated that her compatriot Fonseca and Professor Summerhay, the American delegate, would be the main beneficiaries of Solo's services on this trip. Summerhay had already left for Argentina, but Fonseca was in New York on business and would be boarding their connecting flight to Buenos Aires at JFK. Doris had also let slip that Fonseca was a dresser of the old school, perpetually decked out in a three-piece suit, cuff links, tie pin, and felt hat, a feat of remarkable endurance in the torrid summers of Washington, let alone his native Rio.

Fonseca returned the smile and undid the bottom button on his vest in preparation for the long flight. "Is this your first trip to Argentina?" he asked.

"No, sir, my first was twenty-one years ago," Solo said. He had gone to Buenos Aires with his parents when he was just thirteen, no stranger even then to travel and its dislocations. Twice before his family had relocated abroad as his father was posted first to Haiti, then to Brazil. With what he now recognized as rare foresight in an era when Americans were still caught up in the mentality of the melting pot, his parents had shunned the American schools in Port-au-Prince, Rio, and Buenos Aires, enrolling him instead in regular local schools where he had been forced to sink or swim in French, Portuguese, and Spanish. That parental decision, more than any other factor, he credited as his springboard to his present profession, even if each new destination meant a painful uprooting from friends, schoolmates, environment and language. He still vividly remembered his curiosity and excitement during the voyage from Manhattan to Buenos Aires. He had been fascinated with the albatrosses and dolphins, thrilled at the exotic ports of call—La Guaira, Port of Spain, Recife, Santos, Montevideo. There had been in that crossing a magical sense of passage. Scenery and climate unfolded like a Chinese scroll, heightening his sense of exhilaration, adventure, and discovery.

A string of announcements over the plane's speakers, followed by a revving up of engines, cut off conversation. Solo settled into his seat and thought of Malena and her mysterious request. It was a reasonable surmise that she did not want to approach Hardoy herself because she was a government official. Maybe she had been given a hush-hush assignment to contact Hardoy off the record about something embarrassing that the government preferred to discuss in private. Or maybe it had to do with her father the politician; his party, Malena said, had been banned by the military along with all other political parties. Or it might be a personal matter he had no business speculating about.

As the plane gained altitude, he lifted the plastic eyelid of the window and gazed down at Manhattan. From here the city looked muscular, monumental. Skyscrapers thrust themselves into the sky, head and shoulders above the ranks of lesser buildings. But on the ground, he knew, so much of it was devastation, an urban battleground of fortified ground-floor windows, treeless streets and childless parks surrendered to winos, beggars, and pushers. Half the buildings in the South Bronx were gone, either torched or abandoned. Ed Koch, the new mayor, acknowledged that New York was again on the brink of bankruptcy. The 1970s had not been kind to a city that seemed less the capital of the world than a half-ruined metropolis.

The U.N. rose rectangular against the East River: Alberto's old office, where Solo's own interpreting career had begun. To the west lay the rent-controlled loft behind Penn Station where Inés and he had lived together in 1967, until the night of Venus Adonis.

It hadn't worried them that the neighborhood was iffy. In the daytime, it teemed with pedestrians and cyclists, skaters and hawkers, monte sharks and their shills. At rush hour, a parade of commuters streamed in and out of the station's maze of tunnels, sidestepping the bodies sprawled on stairways, hunched in corners, slumped against walls. At night, a woman huddled in the doorway of their building, talking to the wall, while a fellow homeless man shadowboxed as he ate from a garbage receptacle. From their window they could see a bearded wino in grimy pajamas lying on a traffic island, his head inches away from death.

They had been lucky to sublet the rent-controlled loft through Alberto, Inés's friend, then a translator with the U.N. A former flame of Alberto's, Kimberley, was off to photograph the Australian outback and let them have the apartment for what she herself paid. For Inés and Solo—neither of them much interested in working beyond the minimum needed to keep themselves in groceries, wine, and smoke— it was a real break, the only way they could have afforded a ninth floor with thirteen-foot ceilings, wraparound windows, and a skylight over the shower. Not to mention the little terrace with the southern exposure: a view of the Empire State Building standing mountainous on the brink of the skyline's plunge into the valley of lower midtown before it rose again along the distant palisades of downtown towers. Winter nights when it snowed, he and Inés would wrap themselves in blankets and stretch out on recliners, Swiss sanitarium-style, on that little terrace. There, under the overhang of the floor above, they would sip hot toddies in the white stillness of the city, watching the flakes dissolve into rainbows across the blue, green and gold lights trained on the skyscraper—a giant filament steepling the night.

He and Inés had shut out the outside world in that loft. News of the usual calamities filtered in to them but barely registered: an Arab-Israeli war, a summer of urban race riots and protests against Johnson's Vietnam draft. Solo remembered worrying about the draft: he was out of school and able-bodied. But he was too happy to dwell on it.

They lived together in the splendid isolation of a new love affair, with their books, their music and their drugs, losing themselves in the anonymity of the big city, breaking off sex when the Chinese food came, going to concerts in the Village, kung-fu movies in Chinatown, cinema-noir festivals at sleazy revival houses on the Lower East Side. Remembering it now, he could almost recapture that sweet feeling of abandonment, that luxuriant slide into seediness, the seduction of a life lived in an intimate world meant for two.

It didn't last. Venus Adonis had seen to that. But even before Venus appeared at their door that cold November night, reality reasserted itself: Inés became pregnant and, awed by the abrupt idea of motherhood, insisted on having the baby. And he wasn't sure he was ready to be a parent. They had not broached the subject of marriage, but at twenty-three, fresh out of college, the idea of heading a family daunted him.

The prospect of the baby had unsettled him as much as it had elated her. Out of a sense of duty, it now seemed clear to him in the light of afterknowledge, he began to look for ways to supplement the modest language-tutoring income he earned from Park Avenue parents of underperforming students. It was then that the idea of interpreting had

first come up—Inés's idea, inspired by the dubbing he would sometimes do when they sat up late at night, stoned, watching the strangest
movies they could find on TV. Inés found his dubbing hysterical, especially the foreign movies he rendered in their native accents. He had
never thought it that funny, but he loved to hear her laugh. Inés laughed
with her whole body, her whole being, often in spasms that left her
helpless and flan-like and set off sympathetic chuckles in everybody
around her. He would often do the dubbing just to hear her laugh.

One night he turned off the sound on an early Bollywood film
and started, as always, straight-faced, to put words into the characters'
mouths, weaving some ridiculous plot and cracking her up almost immediately. Then, at the height of his performance, she let out something like a shriek and rolled off the bed.

"Stop! Stop!" she cried through her laughter, dragging herself to
the bathroom.

She returned moments later, still teary-eyed and vulnerable, to find
him on bended knee in the center of the bed, declaring the loincloth-
clad hero's love for the beautiful young girl in the elephant's canopied
seat. That sent her back to the john, and this time he followed her, to
calm her down. Instead, her laughter infected him and they lay on the
bathroom rug, laughing, tears streaming, shaken by fresh fits every
time they tried to speak—until they fell asleep.

"You know," she told him later when, both of them sober now, they
showered together, "your timing for dialogue is remarkable. And you
speak several languages. Have you ever considered interpreting?"

She knew a good deal about interpreting and translating from Alberto, who often gave her tapes to transcribe. The money was good,
and she had taken to doing her transcriptions at home, investing in a
secondhand electric typewriter and a transcriber machine. Earphones
on, one foot on the pedal, she would pound away at the keyboard a few
hours a day, sometimes breaking into her musical laughter over the
side comments Alberto had slyly inserted on the tape for her benefit.

"Why don't I ask Alberto to arrange a test for you?" she proposed.

At first he was lukewarm to the idea. Dubbing movies for her amusement—he viewed it as hardly more than mimicry—was one thing, but real interpreting was a profession, something that serious people did, in serious places, and he had entertained no thought of being serious about anything but Inés. Still, whether for his sake or that of the coming baby, or both, she insisted. And he humored her. Alberto arranged a test for him at the Dag Hammarskjöld Library of the U.N. headquarters building, and to Solo's surprise, the instant he put on the headset and started talking into the mic, he knew Inés was right. He had a talent for it. He felt an unforeseen competence in the quick give and take of it, the adaptation to the myriad accents, regionalisms and speech patterns of Spanish, French, and Portuguese—his three companion languages—the unthinking adjustment to tone, speed of delivery, and mannerisms, and the instantaneous choices required to render not just meaning but mood and nuance.

Ahead lay years of study and training, but the day he passed that first interpretation test he came home flushed with excitement, feeling as if he had stumbled onto a vocation and the final element of his adult life was primed to fall into place.

That evening, he, Inés, and Malena, Alberto's new friend, converged at the loft with the makings of a celebratory dinner while Alberto went off to the liquor store for wine. As Inés stuck her key in their apartment door, they saw their neighbor Venus Adonis, a large blonde woman in a yellow muumuu, open the door of her own apartment, filling the doorway, smiling her bright lipstick and heavily rouged cheeks at them.

"Hello..." Solo and Malena smiled back from the opposite end of the short hallway while Inés fumbled with the locks.

Inés looked up. "Hi, Venus..."

The woman just kept grinning at them as they let themselves in.

"Who is *that*?" Malena asked after they shut the door.

"Odd woman, isn't she?" Solo said, placing the bag of groceries on the dining room table. "That's our neighbor, Venus."

"That's what she calls herself," Inés said, opening a cupboard. "Venus Adonis, mother of divinity, daughter of Zeus and the stars and I forget what else. She runs these tiny ads in newspapers—total nonsense. Kimberly said she's strange but harmless. Yesterday was actually the first time I talked to her. We took the elevator together and she asked me if I was pregnant. It's not that noticeable. Is it?"

"Just a bit, and very becoming," Malena said. "Can I fix you anything?"

"No, no. I've stopped smoking, too. I'll get busy in the kitchen." She picked up the groceries and carried them into the kitchen.

"What a charming apartment—I wish I could find something like this," Malena said, standing in front of the color blow-up on the living room wall, a photo portrait of Kimberly, her bright red hair fluttering in the wind, with Alberto, the two of them holding hands in Central Park. Alberto's t-shirt read: *I'm not the Answer.*

Solo came into the kitchen for ice. He was glad Alberto had brought Malena along to introduce her to "my young friends," as he put it. Alberto had met her at a recent anti-war march from Central Park to the U.N. They had watched the speeches by Martin Luther King, Stokely Carmichael and Benjamin Spock from the front-row comfort of his office and had later gone out together a few times as friends, Alberto said. Solo wondered if there was more to it than that, though Malena was half Alberto's age. She was new to New York, having recently arrived to set up an office to sell polo ponies for an Argentine breeders association her uncle headed. She was his own age, Solo guessed, and very attractive, with a finespun beauty highlighted by a haircut *a la garçon*, soft gleaming eyes, and a simple strand of pearls gracing the gentle curve of her neck. Even though the three of them had just met, he felt that Inés liked her as much as he did. There was something disarming about her, a frankness and forwardness of mind that put them at ease.

Solo cracked an ice tray as Malena leaned in the kitchen doorway and said to Inés, "Alberto tells me you're here temporarily, in an exchange program."

"Was. My family in Argentina doesn't even know I'm living with Solo, let alone that I'm pregnant. They think I'm still in the program, perfecting my English. I'm not supposed to go back to Buenos Aires for two months."

She finished washing the lettuce and transferred some from colander to salad drier.

"So, you're not telling them? Why not? Excuse me for prying, but I can't resist."

Solo saw Inés jut out her jaw. "Because my love life is my own business," she said, and Solo wondered if she was aware of the contradiction, aware that she was explaining her love life to a stranger. Maybe it was easier to talk to a stranger—this stranger, anyway, another woman who shared her nationality and, perhaps, her sensibility.

In the breath of silence among them, they all distinctly heard a rustle by the front door. Malena peered out from the kitchen. "There's a paper under your door. Shall I get it?"

"Thank you," Solo said as he refilled the ice tray. "It's probably a notice of a tenants' rent strike or something."

Malena came back holding an index card and handed it to him.

"What is it?" Inés said.

He stared at the card as he read aloud: "*You've changed but I know you. You can't hide from me.*"

"What...?" Inés screwed up her face and reached for a dishtowel. "Let me see that."

Solo handed her the card and went to open the front door. The hallway was empty. Both the door of Venus's apartment and the elevator door were shut. He closed the door and went back to the kitchen.

"Nobody."

Inés was still looking at the card. "Creepy," she said.

"Could it be your neighbor?" Malena asked.

"That's what I was thinking," Solo said. "Did you hear her door?"

"No."

The doorbell rang.

"I'll get it," Malena said. "Must be Alberto."

Solo saw her look first through the peephole, then bend down to pick up another index card.

"It's your neighbor, all right," Malena said, coming back. "I saw her yellow muumuu disappearing into her apartment. This one says, *"You dyed your red hair but I know you. I'll be back for you."*

Solo felt a surge of anger. "That does it," he said, starting for the door.

Inés put her arm on his. "No. Wait. Let's wait and ask Alberto if..."

The doorbell rang again, followed by a loud bang on the door.

Solo went back to the door and was about to put his eye to the peephole when he heard Inés yell "Solo, no!" and felt Malena's arm around his neck, yanking him back, the two of them tumbling to the floor, colliding hard with Inés and hurling her to the floor. As they fell he heard Inés scream again, but this time it was more like a howl.

He looked up. The plastic lens of the peephole had exploded into splinters, and the pointed end of a heavy tool protruded from the empty socket.

"You devil!" Venus yelled from the hallway.

Solo scrambled to his feet and stood stunned as the sharp metal point disappeared from the peephole—and then stabbed through again, and again. It looked like the head of a pickaxe. "Don't think you can escape me! I knew it was you!"

"My God!" Solo turned from the door. "Are you all right?" he asked the women. "How did you...?" He saw Inés, doubled over, one hand holding her belly, the other gripping the edge of the knee-high metal bookcase she had crashed down on as the three of them fell.

Frantically, he and Malena grabbed her arms, hurried her into the bedroom, and laid her down on the bed. Her face was drained of blood. Her breath came in gasps.

"Don't try to move," Malena told her. "I'll be right back." She disappeared from the room. Solo watched Inés's face crumple into fresh pain.

He could still hear Venus at the door, shrieking, swinging the pick furiously at the frame, the hinges, the locks, kicking and throwing her weight against the panels. Please don't let her have a gun, Solo prayed, rushing out of the bedroom. Malena had grabbed the phone and was moving with it as far from the door as the cord allowed. A thin line of blood trickled down her forehead.

"And an ambulance, yes. Nine B. She's attacking the door with a pickaxe! Hurry! She's going to break through!"

Solo glanced at the door and saw the empty peephole darken with what he realized in horror were the deranged woman's lips. "The police can't help you!" she bellowed. Her voice was with them, inside the apartment. "That woman, she thought she was so clever dyeing her red hair! But she can't fool me. Open this door!" The door shuddered as she pounded and kicked it.

With a loud snap from one of the locks, the door listed to one side—and Solo threw his body against it, trying with both hands to turn the dead bolt. The door was askew in the jamb—he couldn't get the bolt to budge. He felt Venus's body give way, saw through the butchered peephole that she had stepped back. His hand darted to the door chain and hooked it an instant before he felt her bulk smash into the door, sending him sprawling against the couch.

He raised himself on all fours, shook his head clear, and saw the door narrowly ajar. Through the crack, the pickaxe struck wildly at the chain's mounting plate, gouging out chunks of wood with every blow.

He dragged himself to the cupboard, grabbed a vodka bottle, and crawled back to the door. When the pick fell again, he brought the bottle down on it with all his strength, knocking it out of her hand.

Venus screamed. "You bastard! Now I'll get you too!"

The intercom sounded. Solo lifted it and pressed the buzzer. "Hurry!" he yelled into the mouthpiece, his voice shaky. "Inés! The police are here!"

Through the mutilated door frame he saw Venus retreat into her apartment and shut the door behind her. His body let out a long breath, then tensed again. Moments later the elevator door opened and a sergeant and two patrolmen stepped out. Solo unhooked the chain and the door tottered and thudded against his shoulder, dangling from a single hinge.

"She's in there." He pointed to Venus' door. "The...the psycho who did this. She took off as soon as she heard you. Where's the fucking ambulance?"

"Coming, sir." The sergeant strode over and rang Venus' doorbell.

One of the patrolmen studied the mangled door. "Christ! You say a woman did this?" He was staring at the vodka bottle still clutched in Solo's hand.

"Hello, boys." Venus opened the door and flashed a smile at the uniforms. Solo blinked hard: she had changed into a pink chiffon dress and applied even more lipstick and makeup. He could tell her hand was swollen, but there was no trace of anger in her voice or manner. "I've been waiting for you," she said

"I'm afraid you'll have to come with us, ma'am," the sergeant said.

"Of course." Venus grinned, her eyes fixed on the policeman. Never once did her gaze stray to Solo. "I was just getting ready."

She shut the door of her apartment behind her and the two patrolmen escorted her into the elevator.

"Is this the weapon?" The sergeant turned to Solo and pointed to the pickaxe on the floor.

Solo started forward, then heard a loud, prolonged moan from the bedroom and rushed back inside, followed by the sergeant.

"Inés, what is it?" Malena was at her side, holding her hand. Inés's eyes were tightly shut, her face contorted.

The sergeant went to the phone. Solo stood looking at Inés's agonized grimace, his mind floundering. He didn't know how to help her.

"The ambulance is on its way, sir," the sergeant said when he came back. "Don't worry. She'll be all right."

She wasn't. That evening at Bellevue Hospital she had a miscarriage. Then, in the days and weeks that followed, came her deep depression, the panic attacks, the relentless nightmares. She seemed to withdraw into her trauma; he could not follow her there. They lasted three more months in the loft, its door now steel, Venus Adonis in temporary custody in a psych ward on Rikers Island, he and Inés separate planets, each spinning out from the other's gravitational pull. At one of their nearly wordless dinners together, Inés told him she was going back to Argentina. He did not try to talk her out of it.

It was Alberto, himself moving to D.C. to his new job at the OAS, who helped him get a trainee interpreter position at the World Bank and enroll in the interpretation program at Georgetown University. And it was Malena, when Solo was packing, who tried to help him make sense of Inés's departure. Malena had spoken to him kindly, as a friend, to help him understand what she thought she had gleaned from her conversations with Inés.

"She took your ambivalence about the baby as a rejection," Malena said, her hazel eyes gentle, full of the affection that had grown up between them. "She felt you were secretly glad, or at least relieved, that she lost the baby. And she just couldn't deal with it."

That hurt, not least because he knew there was a measure of truth in it. "Why didn't she tell me that?" he said.

Malena sighed. "Maybe she thought it would make matters worse. Maybe what you both need is distance and time."

Distance and time. Over the next years, he and Inés would stay in touch, but the phone calls recounting the day's or week's events would give way to letters, regular at first, then sent at lengthening intervals, until Solo wrote to tell her he had married Phyllis, then sent announcements that his children had been born. All through their conversations and correspondence he had never found the words to start discussing what Inés felt or the two of them had endured.

Even in the years when he and Phyllis were happy, he thought about that November night constantly. What if they had never rented Kimberly's apartment? What if Venus hadn't chosen them when she snapped? What if he had called the police sooner, or had charged into the hall to confront Venus, instead of simply defending the door? If he hadn't fallen into Inés when the pickaxe struck the peephole, would the two of them be raising a child, now twelve years old?

Moot questions. But now, years and years after the violent insanity of Venus Adonis had destroyed their life together, now that he was free and—he hoped—wiser than he had been at twenty-three, maybe time and distance had salved their wounds. Maybe Malena was right, and the mantle of silence that had fallen between them had been balm.

During the one-hour stopover in Santiago, Chile, passengers in transit disembarked to stretch their legs at Pudahuel Airport. The first veins of dawn ruddled the eastern sky. The terminal was deserted, save for uniformed guards with short Tommy guns stationed at the exits.

"We were here five years ago, a year after Pinochet's coup," Doris told Solo as they sat with Fonseca in the empty cafeteria. She glanced around at the guards. "Nothing much seems to have changed."

Fonseca smiled philosophically. "These things take time. I think our report did some good. But this worries me." He pointed to a headline in a Chilean newspaper abandoned on their table: *Supreme Court bars extradition of Chileans in Letelier and Prats cases*. "A bad business. It may land on our lap."

Doris nodded. Solo knew that the Carter administration had demanded the extradition of Chilean military officers implicated in killings of dissidents abroad. He wasn't sure who Prats was but he remembered Letelier, a former foreign minister of Salvador Allende's government killed with his American associate three years ago in D.C. That day Solo and Phyllis had gone with their kids to visit Malena and had seen Letelier's blown-up car in Sheridan Circle, not far from Malena's apartment.

He picked up the discarded newspaper as the speakers announced the reboarding of their flight.

On takeoff, with the day breaking clear, they winged their way above the coastal belt of lowland valleys, over tartans of green and brown fields along the foothills of the Andes. Solo watched the snowy eminences rise to meet the plane and escort it across the icy barrier sown with black craters, great canyons, and blue glacial lakes. The captain came on to point out the better-known peaks: Mercedario, Tupungato, Aconcagua.

Soon they were leaving the Andes behind and soaring above the tableland pinched by the cordillera, on their way to the pampas. The sea of grass sparked in him memories of the summer vacation his family and Inés's, the Maldonados, had spent at an estancia, the ranch where she and he had discovered each other. His father had met hers at the port authority of Buenos Aires, where Mr. Maldonado worked at the time. The friendship they struck up had cemented and brought the two families closer after Inés and Solo developed a crush on each other that summer. He could almost smell again that pervasive scent of earth and cattle, rawhide and alfalfa, see himself sipping bitter maté with the *peones* as they strummed guitars and sang old *milongas* about the plight of the landless gaucho. Those long horseback rides to nowhere: watching the sun drop past an infinite scarlet horizon; making love under a lone chinaberry tree in the measureless green plain. Could he and Inés start by remembering their teenage Eden at the bottom of the world?

An hour later, against the backdrop of an endless estuary, he watched Buenos Aires emerge into distinctiveness, opening out on the shores of the River Plate and stretching away beyond where he could see, suburbs burgeoning in every direction. He could barely discern the scatterings of lower structures and older gabled roofs among the masses of high-rises and new construction. My, my, Buenos Aires, he thought, how you've grown.

Something stirred inside him at the sight of the vast river basin, his father's boundless grave. The Freshwater Sea, the first Spanish explorers had dubbed it. Sixteen years ago, those umber waters, forever journeying to the ocean, had closed over his father, closing as well a chapter in Solo's own life. Now they stared up at him like an immense memento mori, indifferent to his return.

A jolt of landing gear contacting the tarmac. A roar of thrust reversers. As the plane lost speed and began taxiing to the terminal at Ezeiza Airport, the Argentine passengers burst into applause. Solo found himself applauding too.

"Miss Pereira, Dr. Fonseca, Mr. Solórzano," the protocol officer smiled and read off the names on the stamped passports he had taken from them in the V.I.P. lounge, returning each to its owner as their van pulled away from the Ezeiza terminal. "Welcome to Argentina. You're the last of the OAS group to arrive. We hope you have a pleasant stay."

Well, he *was* back, Solo thought—he was Mr. Solórzano again, accent on the second "o." He better remember that. People here would find it strange if he didn't know how to pronounce his own name.

The police motorcycle raced ahead of the van, the two vehicles' flashing lights streaking yellow and red glitter over the wet pavement. On the bike's rear mudguard Solo could make out the bright yellow bumper sticker *I LOVE MY ARGENTINA. DO YOU?*

He could already see that some things had changed. They were not driving over the same ungentle roads he remembered. A stretch of superhighway, de rigueur in even the poorest of countries, had been built to fast-forward visitors past the beltway of shantytowns ringing the capital. Sitting by himself behind Doris and Fonseca, Solo longed to take in the scenery, but their escort's chatter about the new construction sprouting all over a rejuvenated Buenos Aires kept sabotaging him.

"Very impressive," Fonseca replied propitiatingly. "I understand that major public works programs are under way."

"Oh, yes," the protocol officer said, launching into a description of various projects.

At times like these the tools of Solo's trade came in handy. Trained to listen with divided attention while the buffer in his brain stored incoming speech, he could retain enough meaning for coherent replies even as the greater part of his mind disengaged and wandered off. He selected an appropriate expression to wear, a thoughtful stare relieved by sporadic nods and smiles, and slipped away to watch the city glide by.

Traffic, at any rate, hadn't changed. Brightly painted minibuses fumigated black clouds of diesel smoke. Vehicles still enjoyed the right of way over pedestrians. Black-and-yellow kamikaze taxis wove in and out of forgotten traffic lanes, gearing down at intersections just long enough to duel for the right of way. The unwritten rules, he recalled, were simple. Pedestrians yielded to cars, cars to buses, buses to big trucks. Vehicles of equal size played a game of chicken. With regrettable exceptions, the system seemed to work. Like Argentina itself.

A recalcitrant car swerved swiftly from their path when their lead motorized Cossack, with practiced aim and perfect balance, delivered en passant a vicious kick to its rear door. They were now downtown, in the old section of the city. Buildings Solo vaguely remembered came into view and passed out of sight in quick succession.

He looked down at his passport and saw, tucked into it, a small envelope addressed to him. He tore it open and found a note from the admiral:

Dear Mr. Solórzano,

I have been working on your request concerning the Mahlers. I'll be in my office this afternoon and could see you, if you're not too tired from your trip.

Solo was pleased, if a trifle uneasy at the prospect. He wanted nothing better than to be the bearer of news when he met Alberto's aunt and uncle. Provided the news was good.

The car made a sharp turn and stopped before the mansard silhouette of the Hotel Metropole. One of two doormen, brass-buttoned in uniforms made comical by their thick epaulets, sprang to attention and dashed forward to open the door of the van.

Fonseca turned to Solo with mock solemnity and said, "Presidential—aren't they?"

5

Inés was one of no more than a dozen students outside the law school, carrying signs and handing out leaflets along the enormous portico. She tried to stifle her disappointment. A dozen students in the country's largest law school, with an enrollment of thousands. When she offered them the handbill, many of the students coming in and out refused it. *It's your student union too that the government has just banned*, she felt like shouting in their faces. But she knew her fury wouldn't do any good. Don't get involved: that was the Argentine national motto.

A young man in a double-breasted suit brushed past the flyer in her outstretched hand without so much as a look at it. She fervently wished that her literary translation program were not being taught here. She detested this ridiculous, pretentious, neo-classical enormity of a building with its fluted columns and carved capitals, filled with magisterial peddlers of Latin maxims and dead laws, and a student body more concerned with snazzy dressing and grooming than the state of their own country. What was wrong with these people? As if Argentina needed more lawyers. As if laws mattered in this country.

Stop it, she ordered herself—you're just anxious and you're taking it out on others. True. And she knew why she was so testy. Solo was coming.

She had been in a state of nervous agitation ever since getting his message after returning from the Club Español last night. Two weeks ago, when she had seen Serge, Alberto's visiting friend, she had done nothing more than send Solo her regards. Regards. They might as well be distant acquaintances.

Well, weren't they by now? Their history in New York was just that—history, buried though unforgotten. Yet as hard as she had worked to exile her memories of their New York life, images of that year with Solo flashed unbidden into her thoughts and rose up rashly in her dreams. Months ago, when Malena came briefly to Buenos Aires for her sister's wedding and called to say hello, the news of Solo's divorce had left her stunned and shaken. She tried to imagine what his life was like now, the faces of his children, his own face after all these years. Why did he keep shouldering his way into her mind? The two of them had broken up and drifted apart the way failed couples do.

Another fashion plate on cork platform shoes waved off her pamphlet.

That terrible night in New York still haunted her. She ran it over and over in her mind like police evidence, its pain as fresh as if the last wound had closed just yesterday—the aftermath of silence with Solo as resonant as ever. The urge to get away from New York had been overwhelming, irrational, but off and on for the past twelve years she had wondered what would have happened if she had somehow shaken off her trauma and sorrow before it was too late.

She sighed. Things without remedy should be without regard, said Lady Macbeth. Or, as Inés's father put it, if grandma hadn't died she'd be alive.

And now there was Diego. Handsome, kindhearted, smart, sexy Diego. Mysterious Diego. She had yet to meet any of his family or friends, and she was wary of his renewed assurances that he was leaving the army. But he was no longer the passing crush she had once judged him to be. The affair of the body had become an affair of the heart. Could she be in love with two men? That wasn't allowed.

"Inés!"

She turned. Diego was coming up the steps in long strides, his lips grim, a frown creasing his forehead.

"What's wrong?" she asked as soon as he reached her.

"Come with me," he said, grabbing her by the arm.

"Wait." She pulled back hard. "I can't leave now."

"It's urgent! Please!" He unwrapped her fingers from the sign and wrested the fliers from under her arm, laying them against the wall.

"I'll be right back," she shouted to her fellow leafleteers as she let herself be propelled down the steps to the curb on Libertador Avenue, growing more annoyed and worried with each step. When the light turned, they dashed across the broad boulevard to the Café de las Artes. The café was a popular hangout for the better-heeled students who scorned the law school's basement cafeteria, a smoke-filled room wallpapered in ancient political posters that nobody ever bothered to remove. Diego led her to a table by a picture window facing the school.

"Well?" she said when they were seated. The place was empty, no one in sight to take their order.

"When you said we should meet up there by the entrance"—he took a deep breath—"you didn't mention you'd be in a demonstration."

"A demonstration? If only." She didn't want to sound bitter, but couldn't help it. "They've outlawed the student union, fired tenured professors and brought in their own. They're burning books, banning songs, plays, movies. We have policemen posing as students in class." She glared at him. "The whole student body should be out there protesting. How many do you see?"

He looked pained and seemed to decide to say nothing.

"Don't you understand, Diego? If we're going to have rights we have to stand up for them. If anyone should know that, it's future lawyers. You're not defending what the government is doing, are you?"

"I'm not defending anything," he said, his face hardening. "You know me better than that."

"Do I?" she shot back.

He glanced warily out the window. "I don't want to argue with you. Just promise me you won't do this again."

She looked at him with disbelief. "You dragged me in here to tell me that? Is this another emergency like the other night at the Club Español?"

He ignored the barb. "No. I need to ask you something and I don't have much time. I have to get back." He paused, as if groping for the right words. "Have you noticed anybody—anybody you don't know... a stranger, somebody you've never seen before, following you around or watching you?"

She sat back in her chair. A siren sounded a few blocks away. "What are you talking about?"

"Look, it's probably nothing. It has to do with my work."

"It always has to do with your work. You are not in any trouble, are you?"

"No. It's just that somebody may be—making inquiries about me and I want to make sure they don't involve you."

She shook her head. "What's gotten into you? How should I know if somebody is watching or following me? What am I, a trained spy? Anyway, no, I haven't noticed anybody."

"No one trying to strike up a conversation, asking about you, or me?"

"No," she said, her irritation growing. She hated it when he got into this cloak-and-dagger routine. It always ended the same way— with him never saying what it was about. Always the secrecy. Except this time he was talking about her. Because of him, he was saying, someone might be following her. She felt the tug of an inner tripwire. Suddenly the long shadow cast by a woman in a yellow muumuu seemed to step out of the past and loom over her. "I need to get back." She shoved back her chair.

"Wait!" He seized her wrist and looked out the window.

The sirens they had been hearing suddenly materialized into a patrol car and two trucks halting in front of the law school. They disgorged police in full riot gear.

Inés looked at them in shock. As a swarm of helmets rushed up the steps, she saw some protesters drop their signs and flee through the revolving doors into the building. The rest, cornered or too slow, huddled like petrified sheep. She shot up from the chair.

"Let me go!" She tried to free herself from Diego's grasp. But he held her fast.

The truncheon-wielding uniforms closed in on the small group of students and started to hustle them down the steps, while another detachment pushed through the revolving doors in pursuit of the fugitives.

"Bastards," Inés said. Her body went slack as she sat down again. It was too late to do anything and there was nothing she could have done anyway, except get herself arrested as well. She glowered at Diego. "You knew they were coming."

A wounded look sprang into his eyes. "I knew—and didn't warn you? Is that what you think?"

Now she regretted her words. No, she could not believe that of him. "Then how—" She let the words hang.

"How?" he snapped back. "For Christ's sake, Inés, this is a military government! They can do anything they want. There's nothing to stop them. No, I didn't know they were coming here. But I knew they could."

Diego leaned back in his chair, as if the outburst had depleted his anger, and she was struck by how worn out he looked. She shifted her gaze past his bleak eyes, and saw across the street that it was all over. The handcuffed protesters were being herded into the trucks. The portico was empty.

The engines of the police car and trucks came back to life, and rubbernecking vehicles veered aside as the convoy, sirens blaring, disappeared down the avenue.

Diego released her arm.

"I'm sorry," was all he said as he got up to leave. His voice was full of grief.

A waiter finally appeared and she ordered a cortado, an espresso cut with steamed milk.

She tried to sort out the play of emotions within her. Shame. Shame at not being arrested with the others. What would they think of her leaving the protest just before the police showed up—pulled away by a man who had appeared as if to rescue her just in time? How convenient. It looked as if she had been tipped off to the raid—or worse, had a hand in it. But they knew her better than that. Or did they?

She should have been at their side. It was her moral duty to be arrested with them and suffer the same petty indignities and harassment that could be expected from the police before they were released. And Diego had prevented it. Even if she took him at his word that he hadn't known about the raid, she still didn't know whether to be grateful or offended that he had taken it upon himself to decide for her. He had kept her here, in the safety of the cafe, stalling for time with some story about suspicious characters following her—until the police had come and gone. She didn't know whether he was being paranoid or had reason to be suspicious. It spooked her to think that he could be right, that someone in fact was following her.

Once again, Diego had left her with more questions than answers.

A tango filtered out of the café's kitchen. "Malena," again. It was enjoying a revival. The melody wafted over the empty tables, enveloping her in its seductive melancholy.

> *Perhaps in childhood her lark song*
> *Took on that back-street dark tone*
> *Or else that romance she'll only name*
> *When alcohol dulls the pain.*
> *Malena sings the tango in a voice of shadow*
> *Malena feels the bandoneon's sorrow.*

This tango always made Inés think of Malena Uriburu, of Solo and New York—but also of Diego. The night they met. The first tango they danced together.

"That's it," Diego had murmured in her ear after the first few bars, "head up, shoulders back, weight forward."

They were on the dance floor of the Ideal, on Suipacha Street, one of a few surviving grand dames of old cafes. The place, declassé since the heyday of tango, had not been proof against the depredations of time. The intricate stained glass panels in the dome above the dance floor cried out for cleaning, and the leather chairs were cracked and crumbling. Among the old photographs on one wall was a snapshot of the *orquesta de señoritas*, the orchestra of young women for which the Ideal was renowned in the 1920s, when, as an elegant tearoom, it catered to an after-office clientele of working women in the downtown area.

It was the regular barman's day off and Fermín, the solitary old waiter, manned the enormous mahogany bar at the far end of the ballroom. She and Diego and one other couple were on the dance floor. Glassed back by the wall mirrors, their entwined bodies glided past the marble columns encircling the floor. Inés remembered now how rain thrummed the windows, making her feel enclosed in a safe and magical space.

For once she hadn't felt vaguely silly in her high heels, fishnet stockings and short, side-slit skirt. Their legs crossed and recrossed, hooked and spun into double eights, half-moons, grapevine turns. His hold on her was light, yet so close that she forgot her feet. His torso guided her in and out of each figure, challenging, retreating, capturing and releasing her. The other couple disappeared for her; she and Diego were alone. She had never danced like that with any other instructor— or with anybody; she had never known such intimate fluency. And she had not felt so attracted to a man since Solo. She wished "Malena" would never end.

But it did. They dropped into chairs at a table and Diego signaled the waiter as another familiar tango purled out of the speakers. She searched her mind for the title.

"'Armenonville'?"

The way she said it made him cock his head and look at her with curiosity. Nice green eyes, she thought, deep-set under thick eyebrows matching a head of auburn hair.

"Yes. 'Armenonville.' Do you speak French?"

"Not very well. I'm learning."

Karina, the female half of the other couple, came up to their table. "We better be going, Diego," she announced. She and Max, her partner, were both good-looking and smartly dressed. Karina adjusted her beaded black outfit. "With the rest of the class not showing up, it's been a private lesson,"

"And quite a workout," added Max, unfolding a handkerchief to wipe his forehead. He was older than Karina; in his forties, Inés thought. Polished, urbane, tanned. A winegrower, she guessed, or a yachtsman. Tango was definitely coming back. It was no longer something the upper class looked down on; everybody was taking lessons.

"What a nice couple," she said when Karina and Max had gone and the waiter brought them two Negronis.

Diego agreed. "Good people. They started learning because it was good for business, but now they keep coming because they enjoy it."

"What kind of business?"

He smiled. "They're a team. In the—how shall I put it... the hospitality industry."

She looked at him.

Diego raised his shoulders. "My mother was French Basque— Northern Basque, excuse me. I'd never hear the end of it if I said French Basque. She would have said that Karina is a *dame de compagnie* and Max her chargé d'affaires."

Inés stared at him. Was he teasing?

"Tango is popular again," he went on matter-of-factly. "Lots of foreign tourists come to learn. Karina and Max provide... additional amenities."

He was serious.

"What about you?" he asked.

"Me? I'm not in the hospitality industry." They both smiled. "In fact, I'm still trying to figure out what I want to be when I grow up." She knew she was being evasive, holding back, feeling an inexplicable need for caution. "I work afternoons in a bookstore, take French and tango lessons. I'm getting ready to go back to school but haven't decided what to study. Languages, maybe. And you? Do you do this for a living?"

He shook his head. "I have a regular job with the government."

"But you dance like a pro," she said, and meant it.

"I learned with the pros. My father played flute and violin in second-rate tango orchestras way back when. No fancy cabarets like the Armenonville—nothing that classy. He used to take me with him. I never really liked it back then. I was more into stamp collecting."

She laughed. "You could have fooled me."

"You know," he said, "with most students it might as well be Gregorian chants coming out of the speakers. It's like pushing a refrigerator around the floor." He leaned over, his eyes on hers. "Then, one day, you find someone who can dance as if she knows her body." She felt the color surge into her face.

And now Solo was coming.

Still shaken, Inés hung up her coat in the office she shared with her boss on the second floor of the bookstore and went down to join her in the storeroom.

Rita sat hunched over on the first rung of one of the stepladders, surrounded by piles of books and cardboard boxes.

"Sorry," Inés said as she came in. "The police raided our feeble little protest."

"Are you all right?" Rita said, her eyes darkening.

"Yes. I was across the street when it happened." She did not mention how Diego had rushed her away.

Rita nodded as she tore off a cover and dropped the remainder of the book into a box. She brushed back a strand of black hair, revealing white roots, and squinted through her thick eyeglasses at the next title on her lap.

They had undertaken a job that was mammoth for just two people. The books had to be identified and their covers removed for the pulping mill. And in this small business there weren't many people Rita could trust. Nor was there much time. Inspectors and volunteers were checking publishing houses, distributors, and bookstores for titles the government had banned. Inés knew that publishers and booksellers and even ordinary people were burying their books, hiding them in cellars, switching their covers or, like Rita, destroying them. People in this country were inured to military coups and the predictably ensuing censorship, but this time there was a definite truculence that filled Inés with helpless unease.

"What time is the truck coming?" she asked.

"After dark. The pulping mill is doing us a favor. They won't take the load during regular hours. Too dangerous."

Inés took books from a pile.

"*The Industrial Revolution*?" She grimaced.

Rita nodded. "You saw the list. Anything with 'revolution' in it. Or 'sex,'" she added, holding up *Sex, Death and the Collective Unconscious: A Freudian Perspective*. "Highly erotic, no doubt."

Inés tore off the cover of her book and threw it in the box. She picked up a paperback. "*Mother*, by Maxim Gorki?"

"Russian," Rita said without looking up. "And this one"—she used scissors to dismember a hardbound tome—"has a red cover. That's enough to get you arrested."

Inés looked at her next book: Stendhal's *The Red and the Black*. Suddenly she felt worn out. She sat on the floor, drew up her knees, and clasped her arms around them.

Rita went on. "They've just raided the biggest children's library up north, in Rosario. They took the typewriters, movie projectors—everything. The whole PTA board was arrested."

"I heard about it," Inés said in a limp voice. "Another book burning."

"Twenty tons," Rita said. "Four more than Hitler in nineteen-thirty-three. We are lucky. If we were a publishing house we might be firebombed. As it is, we haven't even been raided—yet."

Inés pillowed her forehead on her knees and spoke to the floor. "Rita, do you think societies can go collectively insane—like individuals?"

"I just threw out the Freud book. Want me to look?"

Inés said, "Valeria says she'll leave."

"Your friend?"

"She's fed up. Her sister's in Canada. She could help Valeria get papers and a job."

Rita was quiet, then said, "And you are considering it? Is that why you're telling me?"

Inés raised her head. "It has crossed my mind."

"What about Diego?"

"I could send for him when I'm settled. You know, the sweetheart from the Old Country."

"Tell me about it when you're serious," Rita replied.

Inés sat up and tore the binding off *The Red and the Black*, tossing the pages into a box, then reached for another volume: Antoine de Saint-Exupéry.

"*The Little Prince*..." she said in a tiny voice.

Rita looked up from the book she was ripping apart, and only now did Inés see her tears.

"I know. It's like killing friends."

6

Solo gave the hotel operator his home number and unpacked while he waited for her to call him back. When she put him through, he told Saturnina he had arrived safely and spoke briefly to Lisa and John. "Will you be home tomorrow?" Lisa asked.

Next, he called the Maldonados. Busy. He tried the Mahlers' phone and got no answer, so he dialed the Maldonados again. Still busy. He looked at the alarm clock on the bedside table. Hardoy and the OAS group were about to start the welcome meeting in the conference room on the third floor.

He took from his wallet Malena's card with the two telephone numbers she had written down: that of her father, Dr. Victorino Uriburu-Basavilbaso, and a friend named Néstor Reidlonger. He dialed Malena's father and asked for her. The *señorita* was not home, he was told. Would her father be available? He was.

"Hello?"

"Dr. Uriburu? I'm a friend of your daughter's from Washington. I don't know whether she ever mentioned me to you: Solo. I've just arrived in Buenos Aires. Malena gave me your number to get in touch with her."

"No, I can't say that I recall your name. But Malena isn't here." The voice was rich, cultivated, accustomed to public speaking. And yet—was there a certain wary frostiness in it as well?

"You mean she's not in Buenos Aires?"

"No, no. She called from the airport to say she would be staying with a friend for a few days."

"Oh, I see. I assumed she would be with you."

"So did I," Dr. Uriburu retorted. "Well, you know my daughter. She's very independent. She's done this before, staying with friends and coming to see me later. But I trust she'll show up soon."

"In that case, may I leave you my room number at the Hotel Metropole?"

Malena's father took down the information and Solo rang off.

Strange conversation. He knew he was hypersensitive to voices and tone, but there was a certain defensiveness, he thought, a distance in Malena's father, who hadn't even offered to take his number until he was asked. Solo realized he hadn't given the man his full name. But Malena knew he was at the Metropole.

One more try. He dialed her friend.

"Hello." A man's voice.

"May I speak to Néstor Reidlonger, please?"

"Who is this?"

"A friend of Malena's."

"Your name?"

"Solo."

"Solo?" A pause.

"Yes, Kevin Solórzano, a friend of Malena's from Washington. Is Mr. Reidlonger there?"

"Kevin? You are American? From Washington?"

"Yes."

Another pause. Was this Reidlonger? Why didn't he say so?

"Néstor isn't in right now. I'll have him call you back. What's your number?"

"I'm at..." The dial on the alarm clock warned him that he was five minutes late. "Never mind, I'll call again. Thank you."

"Two reminders: carry your passport with you at all times, and never discuss business in the government cars or taxis we'll be using," said a well-knit though portly Bruno Hardoy sitting in the conference room. He looked to be in his mid-sixties, judging by the slightly bowed shoulders where gravity was beginning to leave its imprint. Thick eyeglasses over wide brown eyes, with the large jaw, nose, and ears set in a broad fleshy face so common in the Basque. Not handsome, but purposeful. There was in those eyes sagacity but also a deep guardedness. They struck Solo as solitary, the eyes of a man who kept a lonely vigil.

"We have much to do in very little time. Given our mix of nationalities, I propose that we conduct our meetings in Spanish. We all speak it to some extent. Mr. Solórzano, our interpreter, will be our linguistic fire extinguisher amongst ourselves and with local officials and any foreigners we encounter in detention facilities." Hardoy smiled gravely at Solo. "He is a professional interpreter bound by an oath, sworn to silence about anything learned in the course of his work, so we may speak freely in his presence."

All eyes turned to him. Solo kept his face solemn.

After a murmur of assent, Professor Summerhay, the American delegate, raised a finger. His pea-green plaid jacket and bow tie stood out among his more charily dressed colleagues.

"Dr. Hardoy, I have question," the professor began in his Tarzanesque Spanish. "Are offices secure?"

"I shouldn't think so, Professor. These are regular hotel rooms assigned to us by the Metropole, refurnished to serve as office space and equipped with extra phone lines. We will periodically remove all important papers to the safe in the local office of the OAS."

"What about transportation?" Fonseca asked.

"I was coming to that, Dr. Fonseca..."

Dr. Hardoy, Dr. Fonseca—it felt funny to Solo to hear lawyers being referred to as *doctors*. But Latin etiquette made doctors of lawyers and he better get into the habit himself.

"We have two government cars with drivers," Hardoy went on. "We'll hire other vehicles as needed and fly longer distances. I am more concerned about manpower. Our regulations bar local hiring and our budget is, as usual, minimal. So we'll be short-staffed. Our Washington office manager, Doris, and two secretaries will work in the hotel. That leaves nine of us, counting Mr. Solórzano. I suggest we split up evenly into three groups. Each group will take turns dealing with the public at the hotel while the other two visit detention centers and make other outside calls. I've drawn up a tentative chart."

He passed out copies and waited until heads began to nod, then crossed his arms and rested his elbows on the table. "I've been getting the courtesy calls to government officials out of the way. They've promised us official passes to visit detention facilities unannounced, including military installations. Any questions?"

Professor Summerhay said: "One thing, Dr. Hardoy. Has everyone seen that?" He gestured at a stack of papers by a telephone on a side table.

"Yes, yes, Professor, we know." Hardoy allowed himself another smile. "The pile of anonymous letters and telephone messages urging us to leave the country on pain of bodily harm. It will probably grow. I wouldn't pay too much attention beyond exercising the usual caution. Now, if there are no other questions, let us adjourn and get some rest. Mr. Solórzano, you wanted to see me?"

"She wants me to meet her on Tuesday at the Palermo polo fields," Hardoy said thoughtfully after opening and reading Malena's letter. From across the table, Solo saw what looked like a page of writing and a drawing.

Hardoy took off his glasses, closed his eyes, and rubbed the bridge of his nose. "We have to be very careful with outside meetings. We've had some bad experiences."

"I will vouch for her, sir," Solo said.

Hardoy looked at him and Solo was glad the chairman didn't ask the obvious: And who will vouch for you? Instead, Hardoy said, "You say she's an Argentine diplomat posted to the embassy in Washington."

"Yes, sir, and a good friend of mine. I've known her for years."

Hardoy jutted out his jaw; he seemed to be arguing with himself. Finally he said, "All right. I will go see your friend. You can tell her that for me."

"Thank you," Solo said, getting up.

"One more thing, Mr. Solórzano. Have you seen the contents of her letter?"

"No, sir."

"Did she tell you what it says?"

"No, she didn't."

"So, you have no idea what it is that she wants to see me about."

"She said she would tell me here, in Buenos Aires."

For a moment Solo had the impression that the chairman was going to say more, but he simply nodded, folded Malena's letter back into its envelope, and put the envelope in his briefcase.

"Taxi, *señor*?"

"*No, gracias.*" Solo waved aside the doorman's offer and strode past the line of parked cabs. After the flight, the long walk to the admiral's office would stretch his legs. In his pocket was the message the desk clerk handed him on his way out of the hotel: an invitation to dine with the Maldonados tomorrow night. He would have preferred a chance to see her alone, free from family and the need to swap pleasantries. But perhaps it was just as well. Perhaps he was getting ahead of himself. Twelve years was a long time.

He buttoned his jacket against the cold and set off. He was in the historic district of the city, the cradle of the republic, as his schoolbooks here had called it. In 1810, porteños, the inhabitants of Buenos Aires, had thronged through these streets to Plaza de Mayo, the main square, assembling in the rain outside the town hall known as the cabildo, where the country's founders were planting the seed of independence from Spain. This district had grown and prospered with the floodtide of immigration, investment, and commerce that followed those turbulent early days. As in North America, the natives had been slaughtered or driven out and the land occupied. Farm machinery, barbed wire, roads, and railways had transformed the pampas. Now, no more than a handful of mansions with carved balconies, wrought-iron work, and Sevillean patios remained here among the banking houses, trading concerns, and insurance companies.

He passed a boarded-up fleapit of a movie theater. *AS ALWAYS, EXPLICIT SEX AT THE HIGHEST LEVEL*, screamed the hand-painted marquee. Farther down the block, a man and a woman were coming out of a nondescript three-story building. A small sign next to the door read, "Trocadero Lodging."

So. Something else hadn't changed. The *hotel d'amour* was still here, still required by law to identify itself by the word "lodging." When he lived here there was another option: the officially winked-at lover's lane in the Palermo woods, the local Bois de Boulogne. He and Inés frequented it when he could wangle the car keys from his dad. You could park there all night, undisturbed by the police as long as you kept your parking lights on. Nearby bars did a thriving business sending out discreet waiters to keep the cars in food and drink. Very civilized, if cramped.

He passed a stationery store and went back to it—he needed to buy postcards for the kids. They always got a thrill from his postcards, even if the cards arrived after he did. He chose two trick shots of King Kong: one diving into Iguazú Falls, the other wrapping himself around the giant obelisk in downtown Buenos Aires—the monument to the phallus, as some locals called it. In all his years in D.C., Solo reflected, he had never heard anybody refer to the Washington Monument in a similar vein. Americans, he guessed, took their monuments much more seriously.

At a post office on the same block he scribbled notes on the cards, bought stamps, and went over to the mailboxes respectively labeled *Domestic, Foreign*, and *Airmail*. The head and shoulders of a postal worker emerged from behind the boxes and held out a hand.

"Just give them to me." He dropped the cards into a canvas satchel into which he was dumping together the contents of all three boxes.

"Amazing!" exclaimed a man in a brown suit "Only in this country." Then, turning to Solo, "If your mail ever gets there, you'll know it's true: God is Argentine."

The street he continued on debouched into the Plaza de Mayo, next to a building whose façade appeared to be pitted by the impact of heavy-caliber bullets. He stopped to take in the square. At one end lay the white arcade of the colonial city hall; at the other, the government palace known as the Pink House. From its balconies in the late forties and early fifties Perón and his first wife, Evita, would address the banner-choked square packed with cheering multitudes. The cathedral rose to one side, as did the Renaissance beefiness of the Bank of the Argentine Nation. In the days of the world wars, when the country's coffers brimmed with revenue from its exports to a warring world, the Bank's corridors had been lined with excess bullion that could not fit in its gold-glutted vaults. Those were the days when the expression "rich as an Argentine" was coined, when the country's upper classes wintered in Europe and imported New Orleans jazz bands to play at their children's birthday parties. Malena's family, the Uriburu-Basavilbasos, had probably done that. He should ask her.

In the center of the square stood a monument known as the May Pyramid, a sixty-foot obelisk surmounted by a statue representing the republic. Scattering pigeons drew his eye to a group of figures walking around it. Women. All women. Two dozen, maybe, wearing white scarves over their heads, some holding hands as they circled the pyramid. A few carried signs that he couldn't read from here. People walking across the square seemed to be keeping their distance.

Intrigued, he walked the length of the block and stopped at the corner facing the center of the square. Though he was still too far to read the signs, he now saw that a framed photograph dangled from the neck of each woman.

"*Caballero...*"

He turned and faced a helmeted policeman in blue uniform. Twenty feet behind him, near the corner of the side street, stood a whole row of officers, with German shepherds at their side. A dark blue truck filled with more policemen was parked down the street.

"What is your business here?" the officer asked curtly. His hands were crossed behind his back.

Solo was taken aback. "My business? I'm taking a walk."

"Move on," the policeman ordered. "The crazy women don't need people staring at them."

"The crazy women...?"

The policeman shifted his weight from one foot to the other and eyed Solo closely. "*¡Documento!*" he snapped.

Subduing his irritation, Solo brought out his passport. The policeman looked at it and immediately relaxed.

"Ah, a North American friend," he said smiling, and turned to the men behind him. "It's all right. He's a tourist."

"What's the trouble?" Solo said.

"No trouble, *señor*. You have no accent, so I didn't realize you were a foreign tourist." He was amiable now. "Sorry to inconvenience you, but it's better if you come back some other time, when the crazy women are not here."

He handed back the passport and strode back to his comrades.

Goons will be goons, Solo thought as he walked away. But as he continued on his way to the admiral, he kept one eye on the women circling the pyramid.

The Ministry of Foreign Affairs, an imposing palazzo once inhabited by the Anchorenas, one of the country's leading families, overlooked Plaza San Martín, where gracefully curving benches reposed by a fountain that gurgled in the shade of basswoods, ceibos, and araucarias.

Solo approached the ornate wrought-iron and bronze gate guarded by two uniformed sailors bearing submachine guns. A policeman in a booth by the gate took his passport, made a phone call, and led him into the courtyard, where a young protocol officer in pinstripes waited under the porte-cochere. He escorted Solo through massive French doors into an ancient elevator that lifted off with a spasm, inched its way up to the third floor, and clanked to a halt. At the end of a carpeted hall his guide opened a door.

"The admiral will be with you shortly. Please make yourself comfortable," he said before leaving.

Solo sat down in an armchair facing the admiral's marble-top desk, behind which hung a large canvas depicting hand-to-hand combat at Lepanto, lions of St. Mark and Ottoman standards flying from Venetian and Turkish galleys. Two iron crucifixes held down stacks of papers on the desk. On the wall nearest Solo was a large photograph of a vintage warplane with a young Admiral Rinaldi standing next to it in pilot uniform. Painted on the plane's tail was an Argentine flag, and on the nose and engine cowlings a crucifix inside a large V. The caption read *Meteor, Argentine Naval Aviation, 1955.*

The door flew open and the admiral came in, dressed in sweat pants and a cable-knit tennis sweater.

"Mr. Solórzano," he said, smiling. They shook hands. "Please excuse my informal attire. Today is my regular tennis date with the Papal Nuncio. I didn't really expect to see you after your long flight. Have you been in touch with Malena yet?"

"No, Admiral. I expect to see her soon. I wanted to thank you for your quick response to..."

Admiral Rinaldi waved away his thanks. "Any friend of the Uriburus is a friend of mine. Besides, I have a special fondness for Americans. I did all my advanced training in your country, you know. You've been our staunch ally— our present differences with Mr. Carter notwithstanding." He opened a desk drawer and took out a folder. "But let's get down to business. I know you're anxious to have news of your friend's relatives."

Donning eyeglasses, he scanned the folder, then leaned back against the desk. "My people are still checking, but so far there is no record of admittance to hospitals or any police reports involving the Mahlers. That may not be good news."

"Why is that?"

The admiral sat down in the armchair opposite Solo and took off his spectacles. "I'm going to be frank with you, my friend, and say things that I would not say to your OAS group. How much do you know about this country's recent history?"

"I know there's been constant turmoil ever since Perón died," Solo said cautiously.

The admiral nodded. "We, the military, have made many mistakes. We've been ousting elected governments since nineteen-thirty. We ousted Perón in fifty-five." He motioned towards the photograph of the warplane on the wall. "As I'm sure you know, Mr. Solórzano, by the time we allowed him back from exile two decades later, we had a leftist insurgency on our hands, complete with guerrilla groups and Marxist priests."

Admiral Rinaldi drew a weary sigh. "This is a Western Christian country. We were not about to surrender it to the left. Violence was answered with violence. If you go by Plaza de Mayo, you'll see a group of women with signs..."

"I just did," Solo said.

"The crazy women." The admiral circled his index finger by his temple and frowned. "It's sad, but that's what the media call them. Their children are missing. We know that some are guerrillas who fled abroad or are in hiding. Others may have died in clashes with rival groups or government forces. But many may be innocent people caught in the middle, perhaps like your friend's cousins—although I hope that's not the case."

So do I, Solo thought. He did not relish the role of bearer of bad tidings to the Mahlers, whom he had yet to meet. "What do you think may have happened to them?"

"It's hard to say. The military in this country are like a dog whose tail has been stepped on time and again, until it bites back. There have been excesses—why not be frank about it?" The admiral opened his palms. "Coordination among security forces is not all it should be, and there are rogue elements in both the military and the police."

He slipped his glasses back on and glanced at the open folder on his lap. "Then, again, we have little to go on here. It might help if we knew more. If the family doesn't know what happened to Débora and David, maybe their friends or acquaintances might offer a lead we could follow."

It made sense. He could ask the Mahlers when he met them. "I'll see if I can find out more, admiral. Thanks so much for your help."

The admiral took a business card from his desk and wrote on the back. "My private numbers. Call me anytime."

7

A *No Funciona* sign dangled from the public telephone in the cafe closest to the regimental headquarters. Two blocks away, five people stood in line for the phone outside a movie theater.

It must be some sort of hereditary curse, Diego thought, an excommunication placed on one of the ancestral Fioravantis in Tuscany. Unless the hex came from the Basque side of his family. What would it feel like, he wondered, to live in a country where the phone system worked, where people didn't request telephone service only to die thirty years later without ever getting it, where a phone number wasn't handed down from generation to generation like a family heirloom? Not that having a phone in your home did you much good if you couldn't trust the line. And he didn't. Especially now that Colonel Indart considered him a regular member of the squad. There was no way he would let Inés have his number. Or his address. Not until he could break loose from Indart.

After cheating him out of two tokens, the phone at a tiny Japanese dry cleaner's finally put him through to Valeria's. Inés should be there now, Saturday afternoon, on her visit to her friend's after their class at the Alliance Française. He hoped she wasn't still angry with him for spiriting her away from the law school protest.

"Valeria? This is Diego. Is Inés there?"

Two soldiers in fatigues came into the dry cleaner's and stood behind him.

"Hello." Inés's voice.

"I want to see you," he said. "Can you meet me tonight?"

"I can't."

"You're not still mad, are you?"

"I'm sorry. I can't. An old friend is coming to dinner."

"Who?"

She hesitated.

"Solo."

He was stunned. He finally broke the heavy silence. "I see."

"You see what?"

"Your *yanqui* boyfriend."

"Ex," she replied dryly.

Don't make matters worse, he cautioned himself. He's just a friend from the past. "What's he doing here?" he said.

"He came with the OAS human rights group. He's the interpreter."

Diego exhaled into the phone. One of the soldiers was shuffling his feet, letting his impatience show.

"Can we meet tomorrow?" he said.

"All right."

"Our usual time and place, then. And..."

"Yes?"

"Nothing. I love you."

"Gentlemen," Colonel Indart paced his office as he addressed the men before him. "I have already thanked those of you who took part in our last operation, including Father Bauer and our good doctor. A job well done."

Diego stood with the rest of the men next to Major Ferrer, the other officer called in by the colonel. His eyes found and settled on the portrait of Mrs. Indart. Tonight, more than ever, she beckoned to him. Suddenly he wondered if it was the other way around—if it was he who sought her out, who desperately needed her to remind him why he was here. But his mute appeal was fruitless. Her young eyes knew nothing of retribution; they met his with a guileless gaze. Did the Mrs. Indart he had known, middle-aged and married to the colonel, harbor any suspicion about her husband's activities? The colonel would have kept her in the dark, Diego was certain. He himself lived such a life of withholding and dissembling with Inés. He and the colonel had more in common than a uniform and a bomb blast.

"As you know, an international inspection group is here. This has made it necessary for us to take certain steps in close coordination with other branches of the services. Some operations have been moved forward. Major Ferrer..."

"Yes, sir!" The major squared his shoulders.

"You will command the operation tonight."

"Yes, sir."

Colonel Indart stopped in front of the men. "You've heard me say this before: to serve his country, a soldier must have two kinds of courage—the courage to die and the courage to kill. The second is often harder than the first."

Diego's eyes met the priest's and Father Bauer smiled thinly. Colonel Indart scanned the faces before him and came to rest on Diego's.

"Captain Fioravanti, you will second Major Ferrer."

"Yes, sir."

The colonel returned to his desk and sat down. He looked up. "You will confine yourselves to headquarters until it's time to go. And you will all carry your regulation firearms. Dismissed."

Diego let himself into the regiment's dark printing shop and turned on the light. At least he could sit here alone.

Too late. All the careful planning, the research Lucas had done on a disorder of the nervous system that could be faked with drugs, the medical exams and lab tests that were already scheduled—there would be no time to put any of it into effect. The colonel was sending him out again this very night. Another operation, another load of prisoners, another deserted location. And this time it would be his turn to kill. And if he did his job well he might be rewarded, might be sent to Paris as part of Operation Condor to kill again.

There was no more time. He got up and went over to the flat files. His hand groped the rear of the bottom drawer until he found the plates he had made. He pulled them out, turned on a floor lamp, and examined them critically: a national identity card, a passport, and an international driver's license, all issued to one Francisco Aguirre—a recently deceased real person from the supply of assumable identities he kept for Colonel Indart. The hair color was different, but the age, height and weight were close enough. With more time he could have cut better plates, made nearly perfect papers. But these items had been part of his backup plan, if his scheme with Lucas failed. He had not counted on actually needing the documents, least of all in a hurry. And now they were no use to him. He had printed and aged them and put them with all his money in a safe deposit at the bank. Today was Saturday. He had no access until Monday.

Inés had been on his mind all day—the narrow escape from the police at the law school, what might have happened had he not shown up when he did. How could she be so naive? She was just asking to be arrested. And then, her reaction. *Don't you understand, Diego?* Inés, Father Bauer—everybody seemed to think he didn't understand. He understood only too well.

She had hidden nothing from him. When he had finally broken through her reserve and she had told him the story of her relationship with Solo and what happened to them in New York, he had seen how she was still troubled by that part of her past—and he could not reciprocate with his own story. Don't involve her, he had told himself; wait it out. But every falsehood he uttered, every pretext, every false impression he left undisturbed in her mind, filled him with disgust.

Was he even fooling her?

It was almost a relief to think that he had reached the knife point of decision. The army wanted everybody to get their hands dirty, so no one would later be able to say "I didn't know, I had nothing to do with it"—so there would be a pact of silence. His father would have had a name for it: omertà.

You will all carry your regulation firearms.

He had never killed anybody in his life. He had thought about it before enrolling in the Colegio Militar, when the country was going through one of its recurrent bouts with recession and hyperinflation and there were few jobs to be had. His parents were dead; he could not afford to study graphic design as he had wanted. Grandfather Arambillet's name had eased his entry into the military. He believed he had been ready to kill, or be killed, in combat, to defend his country. And that was what Colonel Indart said they were doing now: defending the country, defending Western Christian civilization. We are the country's moral guardian, the colonel always said, its last moral reserve.

Diego shook his head. Was he a coward? Did he have the two kinds of courage Colonel Indart talked about? To find out, all he needed to do was wait. Or he could run. Right now. Run and hide until Monday, when the bank opened. Or forget the bank and just run, take his chances without the money and documents.

No. Without papers and money, he wouldn't get far. He had to survive this night.

He picked up the plates, dropped them in the acid tray, and watched Francisco Aguirre dissolve.

8

"I could tell something was wrong the minute I switched on the radio and a military march came on," Mrs. Maldonado said. She smiled at Solo happily. She and her husband had always been partial to him. "How many lumps, Solo?"

"Two, please."

"One, two. There. I'll stir it for you. So I tried another station, and another. I went through the whole dial and every station had the same march. You know what that means."

"No, mother, he doesn't," Inés said. "They don't have military coups in his country."

As Solo had expected, Inés had changed, though he couldn't decipher exactly how. She looked the same, hardly older except for the emerging parentheses around her mouth and the commas at the corners of her eyes. She was quieter than the exuberant Inés he knew. In front of her parents, wishing he could still the beating of his heart, they had hugged and kissed on the cheek, demurely, even bashfully.

Mrs. Maldonado tittered, sending a light tremor over matronly cheeks that had been less fleshy sixteen years ago when Solo had last seen her. "Of course; Solo knows nothing about coups. Here"—she passed the tray of bonbons—"try one of these, Solo. No, that's the smallest. This one, the fat one. And please help yourself. You look so thin, much thinner than when you lived here."

"Are you joking?" Mr. Maldonado objected. "He's put on weight since we last saw him. Remember how skinny he was? And he ate like a piranha. His father used to say a teenager's best friend is the refrigerator."

Solo smiled at him. With his sparse hair, gray temples, and features rounded out with age, Inés's father had grown blunter in every way.

"Nonsense," Mrs. Maldonado chided. "Don't pay any attention to him, Solo. You need to stay here for a while. I'll make sure you eat properly. Where was I?"

"Telling me about the coup," Solo said.

"Ah yes. I'm sure you were too young to notice any of this when you lived here, but the first thing you do in a coup is run into the bathroom. It may sound strange, but that comes first. You run into the bathroom and fill the tub, in case the water is cut off. Which it never is—at least not in the many coups we've been through. In fact, you may expect the water to be cut off at any and all other times, but never during a coup. I don't know why. Nobody does. But I fill the tub, even as my mother did."

"Tradition is important," Mr. Maldonado said.

"Next"—Mrs. Maldonado plunged her fork into a morsel of chocolate cake on her spouse's plate—"you race to the grocery store. Notice all the running you're doing—speed is vital in a coup to keep up with everybody else who is doing the same things. Otherwise, you get to the store and the shelves are bare. You fight the crowds and stock up on food essentials. You get cans, in case the electricity goes. Which, again, it doesn't. And you get candles, which will prove equally useless. These are largely symbolic actions, left over from the days of the first coups, when they were primitive affairs and there were no refrigerators." She swallowed the forkful of cake.

Mr. Maldonado nodded. "Then, you can relax and watch the tanks roll past. This happens after they take over the telephone exchanges, radio and television stations, labor unions, and so on. It's quite a sight and people come out to watch. The weight of the tanks cracks the pavement and later they have to tear everything up and we have crews idling around the ditches yakking and smoking and barbecuing for the next three years. But that's another story."

"Or," Mrs. Maldonado added, "if you choose to stay indoors, you can tune in Uruguay on your short-wave radio. Except Uruguay too has a military government now."

Solo chuckled. He had felt self-conscious at first, but the Maldonados' easy intimacy made him feel at home right away. They had expressed their condolences over the death of his mother and had shown him the familiar photograph of his parents still hanging in the study, next to baby pictures of Inés and other family shots.

"Speaking of coups," Solo said, "I saw a photograph of an old warplane with this sign painted on it. Let me show you." He brought out a pen and a small notepad and drew a letter "v" with a crucifix in it. "What is it?"

Mr. Maldonado smiled, obviously pleased to know the answer. "That's from nineteen fifty-five, before you and your family arrived. It means Christ Victorious. It was painted on the tanks and planes that toppled Perón."

"They bombed and strafed a rally in Plaza de Mayo," Inés added. "They didn't get Perón, but they killed hundreds of men, women, and children. You can still see the bullet holes on buildings."

"Perón dug his own grave when he took on the Church," Mr. Maldonado said, bringing out a case of cigars from the breakfront behind him. "He and the Vatican got along famously for years, running the Nazi relocation program here. I worked for the immigration service at the time, so I saw it up close. They brought in Mengele, Eichmann, Priebke, Barbie—thousands of war criminals hiding all over Europe— and their loot. They gave them Argentine citizenship and jobs. Then, Perón fell out with the Church..."

Inés interrupted, scoffing. "What he means is that Perón tried to separate church and state: he gave the vote to women and equal rights to illegitimate children; he legalized divorce and repealed religious subsidies. So, the Pope excommunicated him and the generals deposed him."

Her father waved his hand at her. "That's all ancient history." He reached for a long cheroot and offered one to Solo, who declined. "I want to ask Solo about the present. Tell me, Solo, what do Americans really think of the Argentine situation?"

Solo dreaded this sort of question. The answer was, of course, that the Argentine situation never entered their minds. America simply ended at the Rio Grande. South of the border was a sort of Steinberg poster, a dim patchwork of countries receding from Mexico into the distance, each owned by a handful of families and ruled by a dictator—preferably our SOB. Solo groped for the right diplospeak, but Mr. Maldonado barreled right through his start of an answer.

"I mean, you're here with the OAS and there's all this fuss about human rights, the bad publicity from those crazy women in Plaza de Mayo..."

Inés gave her father a soft Bronx cheer.

"I know my daughter doesn't agree with me." Smoke, thickly curling from Mr. Maldonado's cigar, undulated over the table. "But let me tell you, three years ago: kidnappings, people's jails, bombs—we were all praying for a coup. That's what we always do: go knock on the barracks doors to ask the boots to step in."

Inés leaned toward Solo. "Those poor women are not crazy, Solo. Their family members are missing and they want the government to tell them where they are."

"That's what I heard," Solo said, though the admiral had not put it quite that way.

Mr. Maldonado grunted. "Those poor women, as you call them, are the mothers of terrorists. If their children were arrested, they must have done something."

"Now, don't you two start again," Mrs. Maldonado cut in, all maternal cheer. "I'm sorry Solo—this must be very boring for you. Inés, dear, would you help me with the dishes?" She plucked away Solo's plate and her husband's and hurried into the kitchen. Inés stayed where she was.

"Why do women find so much to criticize about the military?" Mr. Maldonado went on. "When the military stage a coup, we know the drill: they shut down the gay bars, raid the hourly hotels, and set up a censor's office with a priest in it." He released a particularly dense whorl of smoke. "But they restore order and fix the economy. No more strikes, walkouts, or slowdowns. I applaud the government and keep my money in Miami. They've promised to end rent control and priva- tize our ridiculous phone system. The streets are clean, and the stu- dents, instead of demonstrating all day long, have to go to school to learn something."

"Learn something!" Inés exploded. "They've shut down entire schools. They burn books. They closed down Lovers' Lane. Bravo!"

Her father shook his head. "What would Diego say if he heard you?"

Inés lifted her chin and leaned her head back. "He knows how I feel. We talk about it."

"Who's Diego?" Solo asked.

"Diego Fioravanti, Inés's boyfriend," Mrs. Maldonado said, re- turning from the kitchen. "He's an army captain. And we haven't seen him in a while. Where is he?"

Solo deflated instantly. Inés's boyfriend. Mrs. Maldonado had det- onated the news with utter casualness, blowing away his idiot hopes. He tried to rearrange his features, hide the stricken look he knew had flashed across his face.

"Who knows where he is or what he's up to," Inés was saying. "They are so secretive I can never get a straight answer. I guess I'll see him tomorrow. He called me at Valeria's."

Mr. Maldonado groaned. "Not Valeria again."

Inés turned to Solo. "Valeria is a friend of mine. She used to study psychology and sociology, but the military shut down both schools because they 'breed subversives.' Father doesn't like Valeria."

"It's not that I don't like her. She's harmless, I suppose, although her sister had to leave the country. And Valeria and her boyfriend were detained by the police—"

"Because he wears a beard and she was wearing pants." Inés broke in. "Pants, not a skirt, which apparently threatens your generals' masculinity."

"Yes, I'm sure that's what she would say, little Miss Psychosexuality. Her boyfriend could use a shave and a haircut, if you ask me. And her parents had to bribe half the police department to get her out. You'd have to meet this girl, Solo. A real radical."

"She is not! You are just saying that to annoy me."

Mr. Maldonado's cheroot had stopped burning but he took no notice. "This Valeria, she says things like, 'If this or that happens, people will take to the streets.' Our people take to the streets? Don't make me laugh. Don't get involved, that's the Argentine motto."

"Now, now, calm down," Mrs. Maldonado intervened. "Remember what the doctor said."

Mr. Maldonado struck a match and put it to his cigar. "We are a nation of nitpickers, Solo. To err is human, to criticize divine. People here will put up with anything."

"Including his cigars," Mrs. Maldonado sighed.

"Sorry about my father," Inés said as they started down in the elevator. "His wisdom falls like the rain: heavy at times."

In the brief intimacy of the tight enclosure, her scent enveloped him. He took hold of her hand.

"How are you?" he said.

"All right... And you?"

"All right."

Silence.

"Your children are beautiful."

"Thanks," he said. "My wallet pictures are old. Lisa is a foot taller now."

On the ground floor they held the door open for an elderly couple, then walked to the front of the lobby to stand by the plate glass wall facing the street.

"You know," he said, "Malena's in town, too."

Inés brightened. "Is she? I haven't talked to her since she came for her sister's wedding months ago. I'd love to see her."

"We'll get together. I'll let you know. And Alberto says hello."

"Oh, how is he? I've been so bad at keeping in touch."

"He's okay. Still doing his yoga, eating health food, gardening in the nude—you know... But his eyesight is deteriorating. He stopped teaching and he's taking early retirement. He gave me something to deliver to relatives of his here." For a moment he thought of telling her about the Mahlers, then changed his mind. Best to wait until he spoke to them himself and the admiral finished looking into the matter. He hesitated. "Look—is this it? I mean, your boyfriend, Diego..."

It took her a moment to answer.

"I don't know," she said, looking away. "We're so different. I never would have imagined going out with somebody like him. It just—happened."

"What do you mean?"

"We met by chance, dancing. I guess I'm trying to make a fresh start. I've been drifting, waiting for something, I don't know what. I need to get my feet on the ground. Diego, going back to school—it's all part of that. I'm not getting any younger, you know." She laughed softly, with a tinge of what he thought was melancholy. It was the first time he had heard her laugh tonight.

"We were both so young, back then," Solo said. "I didn't handle it well—especially after that night."

She looked at him. "I was young too. And in love with my independence."

"I..." he began. But she went on.

"Later, after the miscarriage, it felt, well, almost like a punishment. I blamed myself. I realized I had no right to be so selfish. Oh, it's all so complicated. And what does it matter now..."

The taxi pulled up to the curb and honked.

"What are you doing tomorrow?" she asked.

She wanted to see him again. The thought buoyed him. "I'm going to visit my father's plaque in the morning, then go back to the hotel to get in touch with Malena and Alberto's relatives. We're supposed to get very busy on Monday."

She nodded. "May I come with you to see the plaque?" She must have heard the traces of sadness and anxiety in his voice.

"I'd like that very much."

She drew closer and kissed him gently. "I'll borrow my father's car and pick you up at the Metropole at nine."

Solo walked out to the cab. He had barely shut the door when the car blasted off along the broad arteries.

She has a boyfriend, he said to himself as he sagged into the seat. But at the dinner table she seemed rather annoyed with this Diego. Which did not mean that the American visitor was any more to her than an old boyfriend in town for a few days, a reminder of pain.

He was thankful he was holding on to the door grip when the cab turned into a narrow street and the driver jammed on the brakes, then crawled forward. A disabled van was parked under a street lamp, a man's legs and lower torso protruding from its raised hood into the street. Drawing alongside, the taxi driver reached out with his left arm and gently goosed the vulnerable backside.

As they sped away, Solo glanced back and saw the man shaking a fist at them.

"Couldn't resist. He was asking for it," the driver said with a waggish look into the rear-view mirror. Dangling from the mirror was a pennant with the likeness of the famous tango singer Carlos Gardel, his trilby at a rakish angle, over the caption "Sings Better Every Day."

"I know, I know," the cabbie went on, "don't say it: how can this country ever get ahead with grown men like me pulling such childish pranks? You're right. This one's going to cost me several sessions with my analyst."

Crazy country, Solo thought. No wonder it had so many shrinks.

Seconds later they were at the Metropole. The cab discharged him and zoomed off into the night.

Solo got his key from the desk and went up to his room. His bed-side phone was ringing when he entered.

"Hello."

"Hi, Solo. It's Monique. Sorry to call this late, but I thought I'd better."

He didn't like the sound of that. "Anything wrong?"

"First the good news: As a certain attorney tried to warn you, the INS is after your housekeeper, compliments of Phyllis and her lawyer."

He sat down on the bed and let himself collapse onto his back, one hand holding the handset to his ear. He let out a long breath. "That's the good news?"

"Yes. By a singular stroke of good fortune your friend Alberto happened to be visiting your house when the INS showed up. He called me and I arrived just in time to prevent them from taking Saturnina away. I am now her attorney of record in her forthcoming deportation hearing." She paused, waiting. "Solo, are you there?"

"Yes," he finally said. "I'm sorry. I—how could Phyllis do this?"

"Fortunately as well, your kids were playing next door and missed seeing it."

Thank God, he thought. They would have been terrified for Saturnina.

"Now for the bad news," Monique went on. "Phyllis's lawyer told the court that you knew all along that Saturnina is an illegal. He says they have evidence to prove it."

Evidence? How could Phyllis or her lawyer know anything about that? He had made a promise to his mother on her sickbed. How could anybody know?

"You're looking at big bucks in unpaid taxes, fines, and so on," Monique said. "Plus deportation for Saturnina. But that's not the worst of it. It could put a big hole in our custody case."

"What do you mean they have evidence? What evidence?"

He could hear the reproach in Monique's voice thousands of miles away. "You tell me, Solo."

9

It was four-thirty in the morning when they picked up the four hand-cuffed, hooded prisoners at the Athletic Club. The sky had been pre-saging rain all day, and Diego heard the first swishes of water across the windshield as the truck cut the engine in the dead stretch of street in front of the Club. Policemen posted at either end of the block di-verted the few vehicles coming their way at this hour.

Major Ferrer and Father Bauer had arrived ahead of them. The priest had blessed the prisoners, two men and two women, and gone home before they were loaded into the truck. In the cone of light from the doorway as they were brought out, Diego saw that one of the wom-en was badly hurt, her face and neck bruised, skinned raw, and her pain apparent in every wincing step. The second woman was pregnant. At her appearance the soldiers went silent; Diego could feel their un-ease.

In the quiet before dawn, they traversed the city and its suburbs. High-rises gave way to handsome lawny houses hedged about with shrubbery in the outlying residential districts of Acassuso, San Isidro, Beccar. Then, the truck turned west. When they reached the poor-er outskirts of the metropolis, the asphalt faltered and stubble grass took over along the unpaved side streets. Houses became sparse; tilled fields began to pock the landscape. Soon they were jouncing over back roads. Diego wondered where they were going. The truck driver next to him knew, as did Major Ferrer in the car behind them.

On either side of this dirt road, the quickening light spread a ruddy glow over fenced-in pastureland that rolled away into the distance. All signs of human habitation—the double rows of eucalypti leading to farmhouses, the occasional windmill and rusted-out tractor—had now vanished. A ranch hand on horseback, his poncho soaked, his broad-brimmed hat pulled down over his eyes against the driving rain, was the last human being they had passed. Diego fingered the ring on his left hand and glanced again into the rain-spattered side mirror of the truck. Major Ferrer's Ford Falcon was still close behind. Closer. It would not be long now.

Suddenly he knew that he should have run, should have tried to slip out of the gates of the regimental compound as soon as the colonel dismissed them from his office. He could have made a break for it and taken his chances in the maze of the big city, in the back streets he knew so well. Now it was too late.

The rain stopped. A rainbow was rising over the sodden fields. He rolled down the window to let in fresh air just as they bounced heavily over a pothole, prompting curses from the soldiers guarding the four prisoners in the rear of the truck.

"Sorry," the driver muttered. It was the only word spoken since they had picked up their captives.

Major Ferrer honked. Acknowledging him with a hand signal, the driver turned the truck into a narrow lane and came to a stop by a clump of trees. Diego took a deep breath. He jumped off the cab as the major pulled up behind them.

"Out!" Major Ferrer shouted through the open window of his car even before he stepped onto the dirt.

One by one, the two men and two women were helped down the back of the truck. The pregnant woman was last, leaning on the arm of a soldier to steady herself.

"Captain." The major tossed him a key chain and pointed to the two male prisoners. "Uncuff those two and take off their hoods."

Diego moved behind the prisoners. His own hands, shielded from the view of the others, trembled as he fumbled free the prisoners' wrists. The major walked back to his car, opened the trunk, and returned with two shovels, which he threw at the men's feet.

"Dig!"

Diego removed their hoods. Both men were in their thirties, he saw, frail-looking, one with a thick beard, the other balding. They seemed startled, dazzled by the light of day that threw into relief their wasted faces, their swollen red eyes, their waxy skin.

"Dig!" the major repeated, menace now in his tone.

The prisoners looked at each other, picked up the shovels, and began scooping away moist earth. Diego and the soldiers guarded the two handcuffed, hooded women. Major Ferrer smoked and paced.

"All right, climb out!" the major rapped out when the muddy prisoners had produced a shallow pit. To the soldiers he shouted, "Line them up! Hoods off!"

They placed the prisoners in front of the pit and removed the women's hoods, leaving the handcuffs in place, before retreating some ten paces to form a firing line.

Mouths moving in silent prayer, the two men and the pregnant woman wept. Diego could now see that she was middle-aged, wild-eyed, with sunken cheeks and matted yellowish hair. The other woman was much younger; she hunched her shoulders as if the pain of breathing raked her. Her nose was bent, broken. Blood empurpled her swollen cheeks and caked her left arm above a deep gash at the elbow, where a blood-soaked bandage curled down to her cuffed wrists. Diego felt a shiver. There was something familiar in that battered face, something that tugged at his memory.

Nobody spoke. Diego saw the rainbow behind the prisoners fade into banks of iridescent clouds. A light wind brought from the neighboring fields a fragrance of wet earth and honeysuckle and a chirping of birds.

The bearded man and the pregnant woman sank to their knees. She crossed herself and said, in a broken voice loud enough for all to hear: "*Por piedad...*"

"Captain," the major said, and Diego realized he was being spoken to. He had been staring at the younger woman. "Take your place."

Diego didn't move.

"Captain!" The major's eyes narrowed, his tone was sharp. "I gave you an order!"

Diego saw himself reaching for the holster on his hip. He drew the gun as he moved forward to join the near end of the firing line. He found himself standing directly across from the younger woman, her eyes pinioning his.

"Ready...!"

"No, no, don't..." The balding man moaned, lifting a thin forearm against the guns.

Diego raised his gun with the others. In that instant, he saw the flash of recognition in the woman's eyes. And he too remembered.

"Fire!"

Diego squeezed off his shot into the deafening burst of gunfire.

His hand shook from the recoil. Through the acrid haze, he saw three figures lying motionless on the ground, their limbs twisted grotesquely under them. But the pregnant woman remained on her knees. Her eyes had been closed and now she opened them. Awkwardly, with her hands cuffed behind her, she moved—starting to get up and step away from the pit.

Major Ferrer walked up to her, put his pistol to her head, and fired. Her knees buckled instantly and her body collapsed.

The men stood by in sullen silence as the major inspected the bodies. The high-pitched *teru-teru* squawks of teros, disturbed by the gunfire, rose nearby. Dry lightning tore through the sky to the west and a thunderclap drowned out the cries of the birds. Very slowly, as if coming out of sleep, Diego returned the gun to its holster.

"Into the pit!" Major Ferrer ordered. "Get the gasoline."

Two soldiers went to the truck and came back with gasoline containers. They poured the pink liquid over the bodies. A match, framed by a hand, flared and flew into the pit. Flames erupted, leaped out. The men stood back from the stench while the fire consumed the bodies. Diego was suddenly aware of his own shallow breathing. A chill had crept over him, numbing him from his limbs to his core.

When the fire finally died out, the bodies had shrunk to half their size. The soldiers shoveled soil back into the grave and spread twigs and dead leaves over it. It still looked unnatural, like a bruise on the earth.

"Captain!" the major called as the men were getting back into the vehicles. Diego walked over to him.

"Do you understand that we're at war?"

Diego opened his mouth to speak but Major Ferrer waved him to silence. "In wartime, the penalty for disobeying an order is death."

The major strode off to his car.

PART II

10

In the dilapidated harbor district of Puerto Madero, east of Plaza de Mayo, the small riverside monument was just as Inés remembered it: a shoulder-high monolith aproned by evergreen ground cover. Its bronze plaque read, *In memory of those who died in the shipwreck of the* Ciudad de Asunción *on the River Plate on July 11, 1963.* Charles Benjamin Solórzano was among the names in the long list below the inscription.

She watched from a distance as Solo gazed at the pillar. After a time, she knelt and arranged in one of the built-in side vases the flowers they had stopped to buy at a corner stand. Years ago in New York, when she told Solo that a memorial had been erected, he seemed only mildly curious. Now he looked fascinated. She was realizing that not just the circumstances of his life had changed in the years they had been apart, but some barometer had altered in him as well, just as it had in her, There were few signs of this change in his outward appearance. Although the pony tail and beard were gone, exposing the willful chin that suited his delving gray eyes and energetic movements, his body remained lean and his voice retained its dark, rich timbre. And yet his forehead was visibly seamed. He seemed tougher, hardened, sadder.

A sullen sky brooded over the grayness of the River Plate, where distant silhouettes of ships crisscrossed the navigation channels. It was so quiet here, even for a Sunday. The city fell away and its tumult died down in this ghostly harbor area. She glanced around at the abandoned structure of the old cargo terminal that loomed between the river and the city, its dikes and jetties bordered by empty brick warehouses, the rusting silos, tanks, grain elevators, and cranes that had once handled trainloads of grain, beef, and wine before losing out to the new facilities of Puerto Nuevo farther north.

"I've read that there are plans to redevelop this area," she said at last.

Solo looked at her. "You mean they might move this memorial?"

"Yes."

His shoulders lifted and dropped. "He's not here, anyway."

She knew he was not affecting indifference. His father's sudden death, the ordeal of waiting weeks and months for the body to turn up until it became clear that it probably never would, and then his mother's painful decision to leave Argentina and go back home—those had been cataclysms in Solo's life. She felt sure that he was not trivializing them. Rather, it seemed to her that he had come here seeking from this slab of stone some answer, only to find that his heart remained unawakened, that he could not rouse it to feel whatever it was he had hoped for.

"Is it important?" Inés asked. "To locate him?"

He smiled. "My therapist thinks so. Something to do with closure and being able to properly grieve."

"And you're just humoring your therapist."

"I'm hoping he's right. I loved my father, though I never knew him very well. His family were Sephardic Jews, from Santander in northern Spain, but he called himself an atheist. When my mother died I found papers, photographs, navy medals from his war service in the Pacific that he never talked about—but I can't say I knew him."

Inés wondered what it would be like to lose her father, and immediately felt guilty for even entertaining the notion. She too loved her father, though lately she found herself so irritated by their political wrangling that she had considered moving out. But his heart condition, which had prompted her to move back in with her parents, worried her, and she knew that her mother appreciated having her home.

"He would be gone for days on end," Solo went on, "inspecting port facilities most of the time—or so I thought."

She looked at him. "What do you mean?"

He hung back, his words hesitant, almost trickling out. "His papers from when we lived here—my mother saved them. I went through them to decide what to keep. There was almost nothing on ports and harbors—which was his expertise. But I found maps of residential sections of Buenos Aires and Montevideo, organizational charts with initials and acronyms that made no sense to me, lists of names and bank accounts... It made me wonder—"

She waited. His eyes took in the vastness of the river.

"It made me wonder if—well, if maybe he was not what we thought he was. Maybe he was some sort of spy..."

Inés gave her head a disbelieving shake. "Are you serious? Wouldn't your mother have told you after he died?"

"Maybe she didn't know. Or she promised not to tell. Or maybe she didn't think I needed to know."

Inés took him by the arm. "And maybe she was right. What difference does it make now? Come on."

On the broad riverfront promenade of the Costanera Sur, they encountered only the odd jogger and weekend fisherman. The boulevard, bordered by turn-of-the-century lampposts, wound its way along a wave-lapped balustrade flanked in places by alamos, acacias, the prickly trunks of flask-shaped *palo borracho* trees, and jacarandas that would burst into thick clusters of purple flowers in November. Gulls wheeled overhead.

"A few years ago," Inés said, "I think it was on the tenth anniversary, there was a newspaper article about the *Ciudad de Asunción*. It focused on the captain, who died in jail, but the reporter also interviewed survivors and there was a photograph of a woman who survived, her husband, your father and the captain. I thought of sending you the article, but..."

"I know," he said. "You didn't even have my address."

"No, it wasn't that. I could have located you. I just didn't know whether—you wanted to go back there."

It was clear he knew what she meant—that the past included not just the loss of his father but their life together. The idea of not sending him the article had been part of a conscious decision to stay out of his new life.

A timid sun peered out from behind the cloud cover. They arrived at the Fountain of the Nereids and sat down on a bench by the elaborate marble sculpture. Seagulls and pigeons perched on the nude Venus emerging from a seashell among sea nymphs, Tritons, horses, and waves, in a depiction that in the early 1900s had been considered too risqué for its intended location in Plaza de Mayo, so close to the cathedral. Inés was glad that this lovely work of art had been exiled here, by the river, where it seemed to belong. The military and the priests, she thought, would have covered Venus' breasts.

She tucked her crossed ankles under the bench and looked at her watch. Solo had to get back to the hotel. "If I can track down that survivor," she said, "would you be interested in talking to her?"

"Yes," he said without hesitation. And suddenly she saw his face darken. She turned around to see what he was looking at. On the wall of the building across the way from the fountain, large graffiti in block letters read *SERVE YOUR COUNTRY, KILL A JEW*. Under it, by way of signature, was scrawled *Long Live Christ the King*.

She felt herself reddening. "I'm sorry," she said, falteringly, as if she were to blame.

11

"In the end they all ask to be killed." Doctor Bergman took one final pull on the metal straw and handed back the maté gourd to Sergeant Maidana, wiping a hand across his salt-and-pepper mustache that looked more grizzled every day. "But a premature death means you've failed. That's why the first thing I determine is the physical condition of the subject."

Diego was sitting by himself at a table to one side of the room. He saw out of the corner of his eye that the doctor was looking at him, as though expecting him to be pointedly attentive to any discussion of the work of the unit now that he was a full-fledged member. He pretended to be absorbed in examining the property deed in front of him; one more residence of a prisoner about to change hands thanks to Captain Fioravanti's skills in the printing shop. He had become an expert at forging titles and deeds.

"I don't expect you knuckleheads to understand it," the doctor said, looking from Sergeant Maidana to Corporal Elizalde, "but interrogation is a science."

Maidana laughed. "You mean you took a course in medical school, doc?"

"No, in Uruguay, with the American advisor. The man was a real expert. An artist."

I'll bet, Diego thought. And he was also willing to bet that Colonel Indart and Father Bauer had put the doctor up to today's lesson: Captain Fioravanti may need some breaking in; he's still wet behind the ears, a little squeamish.

"He had done a lot of work in Latin America," the doctor went on. "Some of the other students knew him from the International Police Academy in Washington."

"And all you got was a trip to Uruguay? How come you didn't go to Washington?"

"They were shutting down the Academy." Doctor Berman shrugged. "American politics. And now they're going to move the School of the Americas out of Panama because Carter is giving back the Canal. You can still go to Los Fresnos, a place in Texas, to learn bomb making. But this was strictly interrogation and the course was in Uruguay. You want to hear this or not?"

Maidana smiled. "If I have to."

The doctor glanced unsubtly in Diego's direction. "He had this house in the Malvín area of Montevideo, with a soundproof cellar and a separate entrance from the garage. First thing he taught us was this: the whole purpose of softening them up is to humiliate them. That's why you assign them a number. No names, no questions. Just blows and insults, and then just blows in silence. But you have to be careful to leave them some hope."

"Want a maté, Captain?" Maidana refilled the gourd with hot water from a kettle kept warm on a small electric burner.

Diego dropped the magnifying glass onto the deed and looked up. "No, thanks. I have an upset stomach. I think I'll skip lunch, too."

The doctor said, "I'm going to need one of those deeds soon, Captain, if I can get these bums here to do what I ask."

Corporal Elizalde, cleaning a gun on a table by the window, piped up. "We're waiting for the right time, doc. We can't just shoot up the house in broad daylight."

"Why not?" the doctor countered. "They need one final push to sell."

Sergeant Maidana smirked. "You mean you're actually going to pay them something?"

"Good morning, gentlemen."

Father Bauer was at the door. Diego tensed. He had not expected the priest to be here today.

"Morning, Father," Doctor Bergman said. "Didn't think we'd see you here on a Sunday."

Father Bauer smiled. "Why do you think I became a priest? Work Sunday and relax the rest of the week."

The men laughed. Diego produced a smile.

"Actually, I had some filing to do and I wanted to see the captain. Do you have a minute for me, Captain?"

Diego got up and followed the chaplain down the hall to his office.

"I just wanted to find out how the operation went," Father Bauer said when they were seated. "The colonel got a report from Major Ferrer, who seemed—not entirely satisfied with your performance."

The phone rang and the priest picked it up. "Yes, good morning, Colonel. Yes, I'm doing that right now. We are discussing it."

Diego fixed his eyes on the kneeling Virgin Mary in the niche behind the priest's desk. Only she could divine if this was a pre-arranged call, if it was even Colonel Indart on the other end of the line.

"I certainly will, Colonel. Goodbye, sir." The priest replaced the receiver. "Diego, Major Ferrer said that, after some hesitation, you obeyed his order, took your place in the firing line, and fired your weapon. Is that right?"

Diego assented with a nod.

"Of course, he had no way of knowing whether you fired into the air..." Father Bauer raised a hand to forestall any answer. "I'm not saying you did that. But if you did, you were not the only one. A woman was pregnant, so it's perfectly understandable—it's a shame that the sins of the parents are visited on the unborn." He lowered his voice as if to share a secret. "Some of the other men told me they fired to miss her. Maybe you did too. But you don't have to tell me if you don't want to."

Diego swallowed hard. He sensed another trap. It was clear that Major Ferrer had been watching him closely. "I fired over their heads," he said.

Father Bauer smiled. "The major thought so too. As I tell our guests, it's always best to get things off your chest. Now"—the priest left his chair and came around to stand behind Diego, placing a hand on his shoulder—"You come from good military stock, Diego. Your service record is excellent and your work in the printing shop has been very useful. In my opinion, what you need is a couple of days off. To think things over, to reflect on what we've talked about before. How does that sound? I'll speak to the colonel."

Diego picked up the deed and his magnifying glass in the squad room and went to the printing shop. He couldn't shun the squad room altogether; it would draw attention to him. Only here, in the shop, could he be alone with his thoughts.

He sat at the drafting table and began tapping a pencil against the palm of his hand. Disobeying a direct order and then firing to miss—it had all been juggled away by Father Bauer as misguided but understandable qualms over killing a pregnant woman. With this short furlough, he was expected to think matters over, to come to his senses. Was the colonel giving him one last chance?

Diego sat up and wheeled away from the table, then began walking the room. The younger woman had remembered him, he was sure. In that fleeting moment before death, he had seen recognition flicker in those haunted eyes. They had burned into his; a memory had sparked. A memory of her, smiling, undisfigured.

The night he met her, some five or six months ago, he had been sitting at his table by the bar in the second-floor ballroom of the Ideal. She and a man had stepped out of the wrought-iron cage elevator and seated themselves at a remote table. Mondays were slow nights, when the old cafe recovered from a hectic weekend of big-name orchestras and singers that attracted sizable crowds: the exhibitionists, the acrobats of tango showing off their high-kick steps, the old men with dyed brillantined hair and 1940s suits redolent of mothballs; the elegant women in hat and veil waving cigarette holders. Tango was fashionable again, and the Ideal's magnificent ballroom, with its seven-meter plaster-relief ceilings, French art deco chandeliers, and Italian stained-glass cupola, was enjoying a revival. There was even talk of re-buffing the polished marble floors, stairs, and columns, burnishing the mahogany *boisserie*, and rewiring the ancient ceiling fans. But on Monday nights the Ideal's entrepreneurial spirit sagged and the cafe sank back into the comfortable shabbiness Diego liked. Small groups of foreign visitors watched the regulars, a mix of sure-footed older men and their dangerously corseted partners, younger couples and singles out for fun or romance, and the shady-looking characters that titillated the tourists. Three lovely Ingrids—the name that Fermín, the old headwaiter, gave to all Scandinavian blondes—languished at a nearby table for lack of available males. Soon Diego would ask them to dance. Part of his job. And not the most disagreeable part.

He watched the new couple with curiosity. They were good, if rusty. There was something old-fashioned about the way they danced. No intricate footwork, nothing showy. Very salon-like, but poised, old-school. She was a looker. And much younger than her partner. It was hard to tell how old he was, but he was definitely on the debit side of life, as a tango would put it. Her sugar daddy? She looked expensive. Maybe they were another Karina-and-Max team, out to hook tourists. Or just a boss and secretary. Cut it out, he told himself; there were plenty of younger women married to older men.

"Diego." Fermín, a crisp napkin dangling from one arm, came over. "Forget the Ingrids. The young lady over there is asking for the instructor."

Fermín nodded towards the couple Diego had been watching. The music was over and they were reseating themselves at their table. Diego walked over.

"Good evening, I'm Diego Fioravanti, the tango instructor here." They were drinking vermouth; the small marbletop table was covered with little plates of cheese, olives, peanuts and sausage.

"Violeta, Violeta Argerich," she said. "And this is Inspector Argerich."

Inspector. Diego saw no wedding rings when they all shook hands. Inspector Argerich was wearing lightly tinted eyeglasses. Not quite dark but shaded enough to obscure his eyes in this dim light and make him look a little sinister.

"I'm afraid we're out of practice," Violeta said. Whatever perfume she was wearing was delicious. "We were wondering if you could give us a quick refresher."

"Glad to. But from what I've seen, you don't need much help. How long have you been dancing tango?"

Violeta smiled and shrugged. "I learned years ago."

"And I," the inspector said, "many more years ago. Why don't you two get started while I take a breather."

Diego escorted her to the dance floor. They embraced and swayed briefly in place, establishing in silent conversation the terms of their physical proximity, the distance each wanted. She was not defensive, he found, but pliant, unafraid of closeness.

"Your husband," he said as they flowed into the music—and thought, let her correct me if he's not— "what kind of inspector is he? Police?"

"Intelligence."

"Oh." It was a conversation killer, a signal to let it go. But he said, "Did I pass?"

At least she smiled. He was just kidding around, not chatting her up to make a pass. But she made sure.

"Look," she said, still smiling. "You're cute. But you're not my type."

Argerich. Violeta Argerich. The name had stuck in his mind because his friend Lucas the doctor had been on the staff of the Argerich Hospital for years before transferring to the Hospital Italiano. And Violeta was such an unusual name, so old-fashioned.

He had forgotten all about Violeta Argerich. Until yesterday. Beatriz Suárez and Violeta Argerich. Two names that a week ago had meant nothing to him. Two faces he now carried with him, each wearing the ghastly mask of its last breath: the agonies of poison, the plunging darkness of a hail of bullets. He wondered how long each woman had been held before being killed. And why. He knew nothing about the poison victims, but Violeta Argerich, if he could believe what she said when he met her, had been in the company of an intelligence official. Was he dead too?

Diego understood that there was nothing he could have done to change the fate of either woman. But he had been there. He knew what happened to them. And the families of Beatriz Suárez and Violeta Argerich never would. They would go on looking for them, endlessly wandering through government offices, telling their story over and over, imploring help, feeding on empty hopes. Unless he told them.

Lunchtime. The men would have left the squad room for the canteen. Father Bauer was probably with them. There was nothing he liked better than to be considered one of the boys.

The priest's presence here on a Sunday made his plan riskier, but there was nothing to be done about it now. Tomorrow the place would be crawling with people again. Diego felt in his pocket for the set of lock picks he had brought along and was surprised, when he tried the knob, that the door was unlocked. One good thing about Father Bauer's being here today.

He shut the door behind him and moved quickly to the files. His luck was holding, he saw at a glance. The priest had been examining the files. A folder lay open on the desk, and the locks in the filing cabinets were not pushed in.

He opened the first cabinet and was met with dozens of hanging folders neatly labeled with plastic tabs over handwritten names in alphabetical order. He thumbed through them. No Argerich. No Suárez.

He heard footsteps out in the hallway. They were coming this way. He stood still, one hand frozen on the files. If it was Father Bauer he was finished. He could try shutting the cabinet, sitting in one of the chairs and pretending to be waiting. But the priest wouldn't be fooled. I hope you're praying for me, his eyes told the Madonna in the wall niche.

The steps went past the door and faded down the corridor.

No Argerich in the second cabinet. But two Suárez folders. There: Beatriz. He took it out and rested it on the open drawer. How long did he have?

Moments later he was out the door, walking down the empty hallway towards the canteen. He reached the end of the corridor, turned, and felt his breathing ease.

"Captain Fioravanti!"

Father Bauer's shout came from behind him, from the hallway he had just left.

Diego shut his eyes and clenched his teeth. Where had the priest been lurking? And for how long? Had he seen him come out of his office?

"Ah, there you are, father," he said loudly as he turned on his heel and headed back.

Father Bauer was coming toward him, his face unreadable.

"I was going to look for you in the canteen," he said, trying not to sound too urgent or hearty. "I stopped by your office to see if you had any word for me from the colonel."

Father Bauer's eyes remained on his. Finally he said, "Yes, Diego. Your two-day leave has been approved."

It took him twenty minutes to find a working phone in a pharmacy four blocks away. In his pocket address book, he looked up the office number of Aunt Finia and dialed. It was Sunday but he knew she would be there. Sunday was her catch-up day, she often said, when she was alone in the office and could get something done for a change.

"Euskal Herria, Basque Nation. Good afternoon."

"Good afternoon, Aunt Finia. It's your nephew."

"That's redundant," she said.

"What?"

"What you just said is redundant. If I'm your aunt, then you, a male and the only offspring of my only sibling, are my nephew—aren't you?"

He rolled his eyes, then forced a chuckle. "I was just following your lead, Aunt. Doesn't Euskal Herria mean Basque Nation? "

Now he heard a smile in her voice. "What kind of trouble are you in now? Women, as usual?"

If only. "A friend of mine will be coming to see you, Aunt. His name is Francisco Aguirre. He's in need of your expertise. He'll explain."

"Francisco Aguirre. All right. Is that all you want to tell me?"

"Yes."

"Fine," she said, and hung up.

He was used to it, but it still amazed him that Aunt Finia ended all her phone conversations by simply disconnecting. No goodbye, no nothing.

Nobody hovered behind him, waiting for the phone. Unbelievable. He dropped in another token and dialed Lucas's apartment. The machine answered.

"I'm going home, Lucas; I'll call you," was all he said.

12

Nothing in this trip was turning out the way Solo had envisioned. Over the past twenty-four hours his buoyancy at the prospect of coming to Argentina had been subsumed by a presentiment, a dark feeling he was hard put to explain. In a book he had read to Lisa and John last week, dogs howled, leaped, and ran in circles just before an earthquake. The image had stayed with him. So had the specter of the hundreds of civilians killed in Plaza de Mayo that he had never heard about until yesterday.

Last night's conversation with Monique had added to his foreboding. There would be a deportation hearing for Saturnina. Millions of illegals worked openly for major employers all over the country, but the INS had to come after Saturnina, and they had to do it when he was halfway round the world. Not that staying home would have made much difference if Phyllis had proof that he had knowingly hired an illegal. But how could there be any proof? It had been a private conversation between him and his mother. How could Phyllis possibly know?

He pictured Phyllis again that night eight months ago, loading her suitcase into the trunk of her car, tearfully asking him to look after himself and Lisa and John. All his questioning and argument had been unavailing—she was determined to leave. But they had not parted as enemies. Deeply wounding as her departure was, he had been lost in a welter of confusion more than anger. And she too seemed torn, uncertain rather than resentful. Why this vindictiveness now?

This morning, walking along the river with Inés, he had come close to telling her his troubles with Phyllis and the custody fight, but decided against it. Talking about your ex is a turnoff—how often had he heard that? Then, the graffiti had fouled their remaining time together. Inés had apologized as though the inscriptions were her fault. He had played them down, but on the way back to the hotel he had swiftly examined the wall scrawlings they passed. Most dealt with local politicians whose names meant nothing to him, but he had spotted several *Long Live Christ the King* accompanied by swastikas, and an older, faded *Bring Eichmann Back*.

Alberto always said antisemitism was endemic here, in the Catholic Church, in the monolithically Catholic military, in the labor unions and the landed gentry. Before and during World War II, Alberto knew from his relatives in the foreign service, Argentine consulates had been secretly ordered to deny entry visas to Jews trapped in Hitler's Europe. This directive had enriched many consuls who sold the visas anyway to desperate Jews posing as Catholics.

In Alberto's own family, his Aunt Laura's marriage to Héctor Mahler had been a scandal: Dellacroces, the people of the cross, did not marry Jews. Though the money was gone, Alberto said, the Dellacroces still revered hyphenated last names and fancied themselves upper class, which in Argentina meant sending your children to private schools with English or French names, spending part of the year in Europe, and, above all, owning many cows—all things the Dellacroce family could no longer afford. But it could still afford to look down on Héctor Mahler, a lathe operator and a Jew.

Mr. Maldonado's account of the Nazi ratline squared with what Solo was seeing. He had been too young to notice certain things when he lived here, as Mrs. Maldonado had casually remarked last night. He knew it now: something was rotten here.

There was a knock on the door and he answered. A waiter in a tux wheeled in a gurney and with great ceremony set up a table for one, uncovering plates and tureens. Solo signed the check, tipped the man, and sat down to eat. He had overslept and then skipped breakfast this morning to meet Inés, and now he was famished. He made short work of the leek soup, a terrific steak with fries à la provençale and a salad of greens, accompanied by a half-liter of Argentine Malbec. By the time he finished the charlotte with hazelnut praline, he felt better.

As he folded the gurney and rolled it out into the hallway, he noticed the small sheet of paper tucked under the door. He picked it up.

MUST SEE YOU. IT'S URGENT. WILL BE BACK.

There was no signature. He stepped out into the hallway. Nobody. A hollowness thrummed in his chest, and a vision arose of a grinning woman in a yellow muumuu hacking away at the apartment door, her grotesquely made-up face drawing closer with every blow.

He dialed Malena's father's home. An answering machine took the call. It was Sunday, so the maid must have the day off. He left no message and again tried Malena's friend, Néstor Reidlonger. This time there was no answer. He dialed the Mahlers once more. Busy.

Things would get hectic tomorrow, Hardoy had said. Solo could take a chance and go see the Mahlers now, since they appeared to be home. The address on Alberto's envelope was not far from the hotel.

The taxi took him to Parque Lezama, an area of tarnished old apartment buildings and houses radiating from a park with an Italianate-style museum in it. They passed an ancient Bar Británico, a Russian Orthodox church with star-spangled blue domes, and skirted the park where old men played chess on stone tables under tall palm trees.

In the tangle of streets south of the park, the cab stopped at a small one-story house of modest appearance. Solo paid the driver and got out. On the front door, flanked by two shuttered windows with ornamental ironwork grilles, he found no bell to ring, only a heavy door knocker in the shape of a fist. He rapped twice while his eyes registered the traces of graffiti on the whitewashed wall, and the large plywood patch and shiny new hinges on the aged wooden door.

The door opened and an older couple stood in the doorway, looking at him.

"Mr. and Mrs. Mahler?" he said. "I'm Kevin Solórzano, Alberto's friend..."

They were still looking at him.

"Perhaps this is not a good time..." he added. Something was wrong. They seemed befuddled, as if the knock on the door had woken them, their shoulders drooping, their air forlorn.

"Alberto's friend," Mr. Mahler repeated absently. He was tall and slim, bleary-eyed under iron-brown eyebrows and hoary hair. "Yes, come in."

Solo stepped into a room with no furniture save a small table, several mismatched chairs, and a cupboard standing meagerly in one corner. The walls, too, were bare, except for a cracked floor-to-ceiling mirror and a photograph he had often seen a copy of on the wall of Alberto's apartment back home: a much younger Alberto with his little cousins Débora and David blowing soap bubbles across a fence.

"I'm sorry," Mrs. Mahler said, encompassing the emptiness of the room in a wave of her hand and gesturing to the table. She was petite, with a shock of blond hair over dark sunglasses.

"I didn't want to delay giving you this," Solo said when they were seated around the table. He produced the envelope from the inside pocket of his jacket and handed it to Mrs. Mahler. "Alberto says he expects to follow it up soon with the same amount."

Mrs. Mahler took the envelope almost distractedly. "Thank you. Alberto is such a good man."

Solo said: "He told me about your children, that they're missing. I wanted to talk to you about that."

Mrs. Mahler's head trembled. "Yes, our children, Débora and David and our daughter-in-law. And their friends. And our grandchildren." Mrs. Mahler seemed to waver, looked at Solo again as though finally placing him, then reached under the tabletop and pulled from a shallow drawer a handful of papers, removing her sunglasses at the same time. Framed by reddened lids, her pale brown eyes seemed pillaged of life.

"Yes, you're American. You came with the OAS people, and Alberto says you're like family. He doesn't know... about this. If something happens to us—you could tell him. Here..." She pushed the papers toward him.

He took them. A newspaper clipping on top was a day old. *Four Subversives Killed*, read the headline. In the picture under it, police kept passers-by away from a car sprawled on the curb. Four subversives in a speeding car were killed late last night in a shootout with police, the article said. A shotgun and two handguns were found on the bodies of two unidentified men in the back seat. In the front passenger seat was the bullet-riddled body of Carmen Fiorelli, twenty-seven; behind the steering wheel, that of twenty-three-year-old Débora Mahler.

Solo lifted his eyes to Mrs. Mahler's. "Débora..."

She nodded.

"I'm so sorry."

"She was taken from this house eight months ago," Mrs. Mahler said. "Carmen was a friend of hers, visiting with her six-year-old daughter, Ana. It was late and they were about to leave, when our front door was kicked down and two dozen men with guns came in. There was a helicopter overhead and an army truck shone searchlights on the house."

Her voice was flat. Solo heard in it no emotion, as if the story had nothing to do with her. "Most of the men were in combat uniform. They were from the First Army Corps, they said, looking for our son David. They had his photo ID from when he was hired at the Ford factory, before he married and moved to his own apartment. He had just been elected shop steward, you see, and the military were arresting people at the factory. David argued with the manager about the arrests. We told him not to get mixed up in the problems there, but he wouldn't listen."

Her voice caught but she went on. "They tied us up and looted the house, taking everything of value, even the small frames on family photographs. When we told them that the deed of this house was in a safe deposit box in the bank, they cut the wire from our bedroom fan, plugged it in and gave us electric shocks. They poured water on our heads to intensify the jolts while..." She faltered, and looked to her husband, whose face was a scored stone.

"W—what?" Solo blurted.

"... one of them beat us with a belt. I still have the scars. But we still couldn't tell them where David was, so they threatened to do the same to Carmen's little girl, Ana."

Ana. A six-year-old. Solo wanted to say more, but no words came. Like the reflex action of a camera shutter, an image of Lisa had clicked in his brain.

"They finally loaded all our belongings on the truck and took Débora, Carmen, and Ana with them. We tried to comfort Ana before the soldiers put hoods over their heads and threw them into the trunks of three Ford Falcons waiting outside." Mrs. Mahler swallowed. "The cars had no license plates, the neighbors told us. Before they left, they spray-painted *Long live Christ the King* all over the outside of our house and said that if David didn't turn himself in to the police we would never see Débora, Carmen, or Ana again."

Her words trailed off. Her husband put his hand over hers and said, "David and his wife—she was pregnant—were arrested later that day when they went back to their apartment."

Solo's voice finally stirred. "What about the police?"

"The police?" Mrs. Mahler said. "Our neighbors called them. The police said they could do nothing because the operation had 'green light.' We went to the police ourselves to report the kidnapping. They laughed when we said 'kidnapping.'"

Héctor Mahler's eyes found Solo's. "Débora was studying biology, sir. She was such a good girl: clever, pretty, hard-working. We were so proud of her. Last night I bribed an orderly at the morgue and saw her body. She was covered with cuts, bruises, burns. All her teeth were missing. Her lips and gums were burned. She had no eyes—no eyes, sir, just empty sockets. There were scabs on her wrists, from ropes or chains or God knows what. I—I'm sorry..."

Tears coursed down his face. He wiped them with a handkerchief and continued haltingly. "There was no money, identification, or underwear on the bodies. And, you see, Débora couldn't drive. She had no license and didn't know how. How could she be behind the wheel?"

Solo drew a long breath and let it out slowly, trying to keep down his rising nausea, the disgust and anger churning in him. He glanced at the photograph on the wall, remembering the sparkle in Alberto's eyes when he talked about visiting the Mahlers in their first home in Wilde, a semi-rural suburb of Buenos Aires. Little Débora and David would be waiting for him on the station platform, holding on to their father's hand but letting go to hug each other and jump up and down in their excitement as the train pulled in. The day the photograph was taken Alberto had brought them wire loops and soap to blow bubbles in their backyard, and a group of curious cows had congregated across the fence to watch the drifting ovals. We're entertaining the cows, Débora and David told him. Alberto had never forgotten that.

"We went to see everybody we could, to try to find out where they were being held," Héctor Mahler went on. "The Monsignor at the Military Vicariate looked up the names in a file he keeps in his office and told us that these are difficult times but everything that is happening is for the good of the country." His voice grew coarse with the irony of it. "Our children were in a rehabilitation program for wayward young people, he said, in houses set up by the government to reclaim them, with doctors, psychiatrists, and sociologists. He said the church has only a pastoral mission and can't interfere in temporal matters, and he advised us to keep quiet."

A priest? Solo wanted to ask, a priest had a file on your children? Instead, he said, "And that was the last you heard?"

"No," Mrs. Mahler said. "A police inspector called us to say our children would be secretly released from the Intelligence Brigade. He warned us to tell nobody and asked us for money. A chaplain, Father Bauer, was our go-between in the arrangements. We gave him all the money we had. He said our grandsons were baptized when our daughter-in-law gave birth. They are twins, you see."

Mr. Mahler said, "We took turns waiting at the door of the Brigade for two days and two nights. Then they told us to go away, that our children had come out the back door. That was the last we heard about them."

He stopped speaking. There was a long silence that Solo finally broke. "Did you go to the courts?"

Mrs. Mahler's lips tightened and she shook her head dismissively. "We filed habeas corpus petitions. We must have been mad. But we didn't know what else to do. Months without word, without being able to find out anything. After we filed, they called us to say we would never see our children again. Our lawyer was kidnapped. Then the courts refused to hear our case because there was no record of any arrest."

Solo looked at the Mahlers. There was nothing he could say.

He understood now why Alberto had been tight-lipped in Washington. His aunt and uncle were at the mercy of predators who could return at any time to claim them too, or do to the remaining captives what they had done to Débora and Carmen. He knew what the answer to his question would be, but he still asked, "Will you come with me to talk to the OAS people?"

Mrs. Mahler shook her head heavily, almost somnolently, in a gesture of infinite defeat.

"Then—will you let me tell them...?"

"You mustn't breathe a word," she said gently. "Débora and Carmen are dead, but David and his wife and the babies, and Ana—they may be still alive."

She said it without conviction. Hope, her eyes said, was blighted to the root.

13

Diego stepped off the bus into a chilly wind at the intersection of Boedo and San Juan avenues. He lingered on the corner in the failing evening light, scrutinizing the familiar face of his neighborhood.

Sitting in the back of the bus, he had spotted no cars keeping suspicious pace with it. And here, in the subdued Sunday streets of his barrio, nothing caught his attention. The corner flower stand and most storefronts were shuttered. Halfway down the block he could see the magazine-choked profile of Amilcar's newsstand; the old man was working late on Sunday as usual. He watched the four subway staircases, but only three teenage girls and an old woman with shopping bags climbed to the surface.

Two days. Two days to find a way out. The plan with Lucas to fake the neuropathy with the unpronounceable name was useless now. He was under suspicion, his chance for a discharge gone. But no matter what happened, he would keep the vow he had made to himself: he would never again take part in an operation.

He looked at the luminous dial on the clock above the Canadian Cafe. In less than two hours he would be meeting Inés. He felt a pang of hunger. There would be little to eat at home, and he needed food to think. Eyeing the brand new traffic light on the corner, he crossed the street to the Canadian.

A good-looking young woman in a chic tight dress, menus under one arm, intercepted him as he went in.

"Table for one, sir?" she said, smiling.

He smiled back, startled. A greeter at this ancient neighborhood cafe?

"Unless you care to join me," he replied, off the cuff.

Her smile widened and she led him to a table near the bar, leaving a menu before going back to a lectern by the front door.

Had he walked into the wrong cafe? The place looked far too clean, almost bourgeois. Some tables were decked out in red table-cloths with napkins fanned artistically upright on plates. There was a new leather cover on the menu, showing a telephone number for reservations, and each offering inside was now followed by an English translation. He looked around. The regulars were still here, reading the paper in front of their empty espresso cups. This was the same cafe his dead father never stopped calling the Aeroplano, after the airplane painted on an inside wall that had been removed by a new set of own-ers who were Japanese and had rechristened the place the Nipón. The present name, Canadian, would have been equally sacrilegious to his old man. This cafe was hallowed ground, a second home to genera-tions of *tangueros*—composers, conductors, singers, writers and poets. Homero Manzi, his father's idol, was said to have written some of his best tangos here, including the lyrics of "Malena," which his friend Lucio Demare, another regular here, then set to music. And now the place had a greeter?

"*Hola, Dieguito.*" Turco, one of the waiters, came over, escorting his stomach. Turco was legally Sergio Driss, his last name Moroccan. In this country that made him a *turco*, just as Eastern Europeans were *rusos* and Asians *chinos* or *japoneses*, depending on the sound of their last name. Turco had been a decent tango singer in his day, Diego's father always said.

"*Hola*, Turco. What's with the beautiful gatekeeper?"

Turco shrugged and leaned forward. He was very shortsighted and drew uncomfortably close to people when talking to them. "We're try-ing it out. You know—like the fancy restaurants in the movies. She's Amilcar's youngest."

Excuse me while I burst into flames, Diego thought. Amilcar's daughter. Before leaving, he would apologize to her for his flip remark. "Pretty quiet today," he said to change the subject.

"Everybody's at the game," Turco said, pointing to his San Lo-renzo apron, which sported the soccer club's shield on a background of blue and red vertical stripes.

Diego looked at the menu he knew by heart, then arched his eye-brows. "The Swiss chard ravioli?"

Turco frowned and tilted an open hand from side to side.

"The ossobuco?"

Turco shook his head, agitating his gray hair and moustache.

"Why not?" Diego pointed to the menu. "It's the Sunday special."

Another shake of the head.

Diego gave up. "Give me a blood sausage, a portion of sweet-breads, mixed salad with watercress, and a glass of red."

"I knew you'd see it my way." Turco took back the menu.

A few minutes later he was back with a crispy slice of grilled pro-volone "On the house. You look hungry. Oh, your neighbor came by looking for you."

Diego tensed. "My neighbor?"

"Yeah, the old lady who's always dressed like a funeral."

"Doña Asunta. What did she want?"

"Something to do with the gas guys. She'll tell you." Turco re-treated towards the kitchen.

Diego ate hurriedly, left money on the table, and waved to Turco on his way out, uneasiness dogging him. Amilcar's daughter was no-where in sight.

It was just as well his father was dead, he thought as he strode toward the newsstand. Not much left of the old man's beloved bar-rio. Long gone from Boedo were the union organizers, anarchists,

and working-class intellectuals whose literary groups, amateur theaters, and immigrant presses challenged the cultural supremacy of the
Frenchified northern part of Buenos Aires, which gloried in its mansions, parks and boulevards, and statues of generals. The lecherías that
served fresh yogurt were gone, as were the kids playing soccer on
the street and building bonfires on June 29th—St. Peter and St. Paul's
night. Even the streetcars and trolley cars had disappeared, though the
rails and traffic islands remained embedded in the cobblestone, and
the wires still hung overhead. And he himself was still here, in the
decrepit rent-controlled apartment his parents had occupied. He was
still here living alone, instead of with Inés. He had given up the idea
of asking her to move in with him or finding an apartment together. It
was too dangerous.

Amilcar was in his wheelchair inside the kiosk, under the glare of
two bare bulbs, listening to the soccer match and refreshing his maté
gourd with more ground tea leaves.

"Don't even ask me how the game's going," he growled when he
saw Diego. He turned down the radio and inserted the metal straw
into the gourd, pouring in hot water from a thermos. "There are no
real players anymore. Overpaid prima donnas is what they are. What
do you need?"

"How about the *Buenos Aires Herald*?"

Amilcar sucked on the straw until it made a long slurpy sound.
"Not your usual French magazines? You taking up English?"

"It's never too late." Diego said, paying for the newspaper.

Amilcar said, "Doña Asunta was looking for you."

"I know. Turco told me."

"She came by to ask me to tell you if I saw you coming home.
Wants to talk to you."

A second alert. Doña Asunta would not have come out to the newsstand and the Canadian unless she thought it was important to head
him off. But if she didn't want him to go home, she could have said
so to Amilcar or Turco. That could mean she wasn't sure. He thought

of retreating, not going home at all but taking refuge with Lucas and figuring out some other escape. No. The key to the bank security box with the IDs and the money was in the duffel bag at home. He had to go there.

He thanked Amilcar and, with one eye looking over his shoulder, began walking home.

As he approached the tall wrought-iron-and-glass door of his building, a light came on in the vestibule of the house next door and Doña Asunta stepped out, dressed as always in black, the black tortoiseshell backcomb gleaming in her white hair. How long had it been since her husband died? Ten years? Fifteen?

"The gas people came by today," she said immediately, standing in the pool of light cast by the lantern behind her.

The building's heavy antique key was in his hand, but he did not slip it into the keyhole. She hadn't just happened to come out. The indoor light leaking through the adjustable louvers on her balcony told him that the slats angled in the direction he had come. She had been watching for him.

"Good evening, Doña Asunta. The gas people?"

She shoved her hands into the pockets of her black smock and began rocking back and forth on her heels. "I saw him looking into your doorway when I came out to sweep the sidewalk this afternoon. He asked me who lives in the apartment in the back. I told him. He said there is a leak and they need access and will be back tomorrow."

"Thank you, Doña Asunta."

"The gas inspectors that come here—I think I know them all. This one was wearing the uniform, but I never saw him before." She jutted out her chin. "And I've never seen one on Sunday, leaks or no leaks. You asked me to keep an eye out..." she added almost apologetically.

He moved closer to her and before she could step back he grasped her by the shoulders and kissed her cheek.

"Thank you," he said again. Her face was steeped in shadow, but he sensed she was blushing.

He had to keep his movements calm, as if he had exchanged words of no importance with her. If they were already inside his apartment, all was lost. But he couldn't turn back now. He unlocked the door and stepped into the inner hallway lighted by a naked bulb. Without hurrying or trying to scan the street through the glass pane, he shut the heavy door behind him, slid the key back into the lock, and gave it a full turn before removing it.

The inner hall led into an open-air corridor lined with Doña Asunta's potted plants that ran in a straight line past her side door to his rear, ground-floor apartment. He could not hurry; his figure was visible through the street door. One more patch of plaster, he noted to quiet his racing mind, had crumbled high up in the wall, sprinkling fine dust over the tiled floor and plants. With the same deliberate movements, he unlocked the door to his apartment and let himself in.

Nobody.

He moved fast. He didn't think they were going to wait until the neighbors were asleep. They hadn't wanted to take him in the street— put on a show for the whole neighborhood. And they knew he had a gun. But they had to be watching. They must have seen him talking to Doña Asunta and figured she had been waiting just inside her doorway, to warn him.

He kept the lights off. In the kitchen, he groped through the refrigerator for the paper bag with the two steaks in it, and carried it to the patio, placing it on the rim of the stone sink built into the high wall that separated his patio from the backyard of his neighbor, the jeweler. The rope ladder he had secured to the top of the wall hung next to the sink.

Going back for the duffel bag, he heard glass shatter in the street. That won't help them, he thought. The street door was ancient, couldn't be opened without the key. Even with its glass pane gone, there wasn't room enough for a man to wiggle through the door's iron grille. But it wouldn't take them long to force the lock.

He swung the strap of the duffel bag over his head and darted to the front door. Through the grille of the peephole, he looked in the angled mirror he had anchored in the opposite wall.

Men were rushing single-file into the corridor.

He ran back out to the patio, snatched the paper bag from the sink, and clamped it between his teeth as he hoisted himself up on the first wobbly rung of the rope ladder. Scrambling up the wall in the dark, his hands and feet groping for the crosspieces, he heard the clumping boots in the corridor come to a halt outside his front door. Keep calm, he reminded himself, his nose twitching from the pungent smell of the garlic he had smeared on the raw beefsteaks in the bag—they'll have to slow down now; they know you're armed.

From his perch atop the wall, he reeled in the ladder and dropped it down his neighbor's side, then climbed down to the man's yard. He yanked the ladder loose from the wall and rolled it into a bundle, stashing it under a bush. It might buy him precious minutes if they didn't spot it right away.

The two Argentine *dogos* were tethered to a post not far from the small gate to the back street. He had tried to befriend the white mastiffs in casual encounters on the street, when they were being walked. They obviously needed reminding: both were up on all fours, hackles raised. He had to get to them before their low growling turned to barks. Taking the first piece of beef from the paper bag, he threw it between them. The growling intensified as they pounced on it.

He heard a loud crash from the other side of the wall—his front door being kicked in, he guessed. Lights came on in his apartment and he heard men fanning out inside. He threw the other piece of meat and waited to hear chomping before advancing to the gate. The dogs were tearing into the meat. One of them looked up and barked ferociously at something behind him.

He turned. Backlit from the patio, the head and arm of a man, a gun in his hand, was outlined above the wall.

Diego was conscious of a muzzle flash, a report, and a searing pain in his left arm as his right hand brought out the pistol and fired. A chunk of plaster from the top of the wall flew into the man's face.

With a volley of curses, the figure toppled backward off the shoulders holding him up.

The dogs were barking furiously now. Floodlights suddenly came on, their broad beams bathing the yard with a burst of radiance. Diego ran for the gate, unbolted it, and sprinted out.

He crossed the street, ran to the corner, and turned away from his building, forcing himself to walk as casually as he could, ignoring the insistent siren of his wounded arm, hugging the wall and its shadows. If they had thought of posting cars and men on the side streets, he had no chance. But maybe they had been overconfident. On paper, there was only one way in and out of his apartment. His pounding heart outstripped his steps.

When he turned the second corner, he put away the gun he had been gripping inside his jacket and switched the duffel to his right shoulder to ease the pain in his left arm.

He walked three more blocks to the construction site. The street was empty except for a couple kissing in a doorway. He strode past them, wondering why his footfall was so loud; the whole street seemed to resound with his steps. Fifty meters down the block, at the far end of the construction fence of an unfinished nine-story building, the loose boards he had noticed three days ago looked undisturbed. He pried them open with his right hand, slipped in and replaced them. Moving cautiously in the darkness, one hand on the bare brick wall and one foot scouting the bare cement under his feet, he skirted the stairwell pit and found the rear wall of the ground floor. A cat leapt away into the night as he spread the *Buenos Aires Herald* and settled into a corner.

When his heart stopped pounding he felt the pain in his forearm more acutely and knew that the wetness was blood. He probed with his right hand. It hurt too much to be a flesh wound, he thought, but he was too shaken to examine it calmly. Out of the back pocket of his pants he fished a handkerchief, ripped it with the help of his teeth, and tied it around the wound. He had to keep the blood off his clothes.

Thoughts milled about in his head. It would be a long night. Inés would wait for him at the cafe until she figured out he wasn't coming and left, probably more angry than worried. And Lucas would have left the hospital at this hour. It suddenly occurred to Diego that it would be too risky to contact either one at home from now on. Everything had changed.

The bank opened mid-morning, but he would leave at dawn, before the neighborhood stirred and the construction crew arrived. He would be more vulnerable in daylight, but there was no help for it.

Sleeping was out of the question, even if he attempted it; it was colder under this concrete skeleton than out in the street. His teeth started chattering. Come on, he told himself, it's nothing more than the adrenaline spike and a little cold. He opened the duffel bag, took out a thin poncho, and wrapped himself in it. Better cold than dead.

He was finally out, though not in the way he had expected. At this hour he should have been sitting in a cafe with Inés, worrying about her gringo and about Colonel Indart and Father Bauer and how to leave the military behind safely and for good. Instead, the choices had been made for him. The colonel and his chaplain had figured it would be bad for morale to arrest him at headquarters. Better to let him go home and make his death look like the work of terrorists.

He had slipped through their fingers. Now he was a fugitive. But he was alive.

14

"And what is your interest in my article?" the reporter asked Inés, suspicion rife in his voice. He sounded like a crusty old man, Inés decided, but she wasn't about to complain. It was a minor miracle that the man still worked for the same newspaper and she had been able to locate him after only three phone calls. She switched the receiver to her left hand and picked up the foxed newspaper clipping with its grainy shot of four people: a young couple, Solo's father, and the captain of the *Ciudad de Asunción*, all raising their glasses in a toast. The caption read: *Haydée and Leandro Madariaga, and Charles Solórzano, dining at the captain's table on the night of the shipwreck.*

"Your article says that Mrs. Madariaga survived the shipwreck," Inés said. "I'm a friend of the family of Charles Solórzano, the American passenger in the picture. His son is in town after sixteen years and would like to speak with Mrs. Madariaga if she can be located." Looking at this photograph, Inés wondered how the reporter had come by it, and whether the photographer too had survived. She conjured up a vision of a camera inside a castaway suitcase, bobbing in the immensity of the great river.

There was a silence. She could tell the reporter was trying to decide if he could be bothered.

"Please," she said. "it would mean a lot to Mr. Solórzano's son."

The man uttered something between a sigh and a grunt. "Look, that article is six years old. I'll have to get the file from our morgue—our old records. Call me back in a half hour."

She thanked him extravagantly and hung up. Half an hour. She did not want to keep tying up the line in case Diego should call. He hadn't shown up last night. She had lingered in the cafe for over an hour, but he never came. That in itself was unusual. He might be called away when they were together, as he was last Tuesday at the Club Español, but he had never stood her up. Worse, he hadn't phoned to explain. Well, it was still early. She would probably hear from him in the course of the day. But she could not put off dealing with the issue that gnawed at her: her fellow students arrested by the police. She dialed the number for Judge Rodolfo Molinari, Fito to her, a criminal court judge and one of her father's oldest friends. Maybe she could nudge the wheels of justice.

"He's in a meeting," his secretary replied when Inés identified herself and asked if the judge could see her for five minutes this morning. "Hold on while I ask him."

Inés waited impatiently.

The secretary came back. "Can you be here in an hour?"

Inés said yes and wrote down the directions to the judge's court, located deep within the inner maze of the Tribunales building.

When she called the reporter back, he had the file with him. "There's not too much more in it," he said. "The survivors I contacted were right here in the city. I never tried to interview Mrs. Madariaga because the address I had for her was up north in Posadas, in the province of Misiones. That's a thousand kilometers away. Later I learned that she died not long after the shipwreck."

Inés felt her elation drain. Her quest was over just as it was beginning. Haydée Madariaga was also dead.

"There's a name in the file: Gladys Iturralde," the reporter went on, "and a contact number for the Madariagas here in the city. I don't know if the number is still good. Do you want it?"

It seemed hardly worth pursuing now. But she said, "Yes. Thank you."

She got off the subway at the Tribunales station and took the escalator to the surface. Her meeting with Fito should not take long, but she had called Rita just in case to say she might be a few minutes late for work this afternoon.

Lion-faced masks topped the neo-Greek columns of the arcaded entrance to the Palace of Justice. She hurried up the flight of steps and wended her way through crowded hallways to an inner courtyard lined with pilasters, then took the set of stairs that led to the criminal courts.

As she had been warned, the door to Judge Rodolfo Molinari's court was shut. In front of it, a press of people was listening to a voice that seemed to come from a sliding peephole in the door. She didn't stop but walked past the crowd, turning into the next hallway and knocking on the second door down, where she gave her name and was let in by an orderly.

A nattily dressed young woman, unnecessarily blonde, identified herself as the judge's secretary and motioned Inés to a chair. She sat down. Across the room, a middle-aged man smoked and read a news-paper at a desk equipped with a telephone and an antique typewriter, while a young man in coat and tie, probably a law student, bent over a small table wielding an oversized needle. Inés watched him labori-ously stitch together the pages of a thick case file. Stacks of similar files covered the ceiling-high shelves on three sides of the room.

A few minutes later Judge Molinari's secretary returned and led Inés through a hallway to the judge's chambers, opened the door for her and left.

"Ah, Inesita..." The short figure of Judge Molinari rose from his desk to greet her with his tobacco-roughened voice and an avuncular kiss on the cheek. Despite the custom-tailored suit and silk tie, her fa-ther's friend did not look well. Under the carefully groomed gray hair, his face seemed sallow, his good-humored eyes harried, his forehead a fretwork of wrinkles.

"I'm sorry for the back-door welcome," he said, waving a hand toward the front office in exasperation, "but you see how it is... How are your parents, my dear?" He led her across the wood-paneled room to a set of armchairs and coffee table by one of the heavily curtained windows.

"Fito," she began, using the familiar diminutive that had always seemed made to his measure, "my father doesn't know I'm here. I think it would upset him." She took a deep breath. "I'm trying to find out what happened to schoolmates of mine who were detained by the police last Friday. I called the police precinct for the law school, but they wouldn't tell me anything. So, I thought if I could impose on you to..." She saw the consternation on his face.

"You phoned the police precinct?" he asked. "Did you give your name?"

"No, I—"

"Tell me what happened. From the beginning."

"We were handing out leaflets at the entrance, protesting the firing of professors and asking for the reinstatement of the student council. I was across the street, at the cafe, when the police came..." She didn't mention Diego in her account of the police raid.

When she finished, he massaged his chin, then went to his desk and picked up the phone. "Get me the comisario in the seventeenth precinct. I think it's Llorens." He capped the mouthpiece and turned to Inés with a scowl. "I hope I'm wrong."

Unnerved, she watched him rock thoughtfully in his chair against the rows of bound legal volumes in the bookcase behind him. "Comisario Llorens? Yes, yes, Molinari, that's right. Two years ago, indeed. I remember. Well, Llorens, I'm actually looking for a little advice. You see, we're planning a legal seminar at the law school with some prominent foreign officials and scholars, and it's just come to my attention that last Friday there was a major disturbance there involving arrests—

so, naturally..."

Inés listened as the judge spun a tale of concern over potential embarrassment in the presence of foreign dignitaries.

"Just a few troublemakers—I see. So, you don't think there is any risk of..."

Fito listened, thanked the comisario, and hung up. He looked at her, troubled. "Your schoolmates are very lucky. This Llorens—well, never mind. Luckily, he says he's been ordered to let the students go."

Inés felt her burden finally lifting. "Oh, I'm so relieved. I can't thank you enough."

"Llorens doesn't know why they're being released—a bad idea, if you ask him. He thinks it's because the OAS people are in town. Inés..." Fito rose wearily from his desk and came over to sit by her again. "I'm going to tell you something for your ears alone, do you understand?"

There was a warning in his tone and his eyebrows were set in a frown. She nodded.

"When you came in, you saw the people in the hallway outside."

"Yes."

"It's like that every day. They are the families. We have orders not to interfere, not to involve ourselves in any way with the families of subversives. Their briefs are refused, their petitions denied. But they keep coming anyway."

She stared at him. "Orders? But—you're a judge..."

"Yes, and judges don't make the law, do they. ... Do you understand what I'm telling you?"

"I—I think so," she said, though she wasn't at all sure.

"Good. From now on, please make sure you are nowhere near demonstrations or protests." He stood up.

She got to her feet and they said goodbye. As he walked her to the door, he said, "And remember, dear, I never told you what I told you."

15

Long before the business district awoke from its Sunday torpor the line of people in front of the Hotel Metropole had turned the far corner of the street and crept halfway down the block, its lengthening tail fed by new arrivals issuing from the silent streets.

Solo stood by the window regarding them, wondering how many came bearing stories like the Mahlers'. As he awaited the arrival of Fonseca and Hardoy, he watched the two secretaries take turns rattling away at their typewriters, answering phones, and handing out forms up and down the staircase packed with the earliest arrivals waiting to be heard.

The Mahlers' harrowing story had played havoc with his sleep. Only near dawn did exhaustion get the better of insomnia, and even then he parried nightmares. He wondered if Alberto now knew, if the Mahlers had called him to say Débora was dead. They would have spared him the ghastly details, Solo was sure. He had heard those details because he had intruded on the Mahlers' private grief when they were at their most vulnerable. They had poured out their hearts to him, an accidental witness to their anguish, because he was Alberto's friend, someone they could trust to tell Alberto what happened—if it turned out they could not.

Trust. The word made him writhe with guilt and recrimination.

Beware the fool with initiative, his father used to say. The Mahlers had been warned to tell nobody, yet last Wednesday, in Washington, Solo himself had brought to the admiral's attention the disappearance of Débora and David. Friday night, Débora and her friend had turned up dead in Buenos Aires.

It made him cringe even to form the words of the question: had he, by his meddling, by setting in motion the admiral's inquiries, somehow triggered the deaths of the two women? He could not bring himself to voice this possibility to the Mahlers, shattered as they were. He had kept silent partly out of guilt, and partly because he couldn't be sure what role, if any, the admiral had played. Had he been helping or simply stringing Solo along, unlocking his confidence, fishing for information on the OAS inspectors or the Mahlers?

But the man was an admiral, the country's Foreign Minister. He met with the U.S. Congress, lectured at Georgetown University, played tennis with the Vatican ambassador. More than any of that, he was Malena's boss, a friend of her family. Solo had to talk to her. She was meeting Hardoy at the polo field tomorrow. If he couldn't get hold of her before that, he had to make sure he went with Hardoy to see her.

"Mr. Solórzano," Hardoy called to him as he and Fonseca emerged from the conference room. The chairman carried his fedora and a pocket-size recorder, which he handed to Solo. "Can you work it?"

Solo studied it. "I think so," he said, putting the small device and spare cassettes in a pocket of his jacket as they made for the elevators.

"Dr. Hardoy!" someone shouted from among the throng on the stairway. Doris was racing up the steps. She gasped for breath as she reached the top. "Please come, quickly! They're taking pictures of the people in line!"

The chairman bolted, shouting ahead for people to move out of the way. His stocky figure surged down the stairs, grappling his way among the bodies on steps and landings. Doris and Solo followed. They reached the ground floor and ran through the hotel lobby into the street.

Solo saw Hardoy confronting a tall man whose neck and shoulders were strung with cameras and flashes. Across the street, a second man holding a large camera scampered away toward the corner.

"But I tell you he wasn't with me," the first man was saying. "I never saw him in my life. I am a legitimate photojournalist. My newspaper sent me. Look, here's my ID." He reached for his wallet but the chairman stopped him.

"I don't care who you are. No pictures are allowed here, do you hear? If you are a journalist you ought to be ashamed of yourself. Will you have the decency to go away?"

A hush had fallen over the line. Solo cast his eyes along the first stretch from the hotel door to the street corner and saw that dark sunglasses, hats and scarves had materialized as if by magic. Small children had been picked up in arms, their heads turned away and shielded from the photographer.

"Look, sir," the photographer said, seemingly abashed. "I don't know who you are but I assure you that I didn't mean any harm. I'm just doing my job."

Behind Hardoy and the photographer, Solo saw an old woman in a black dress detach herself from the line and move unsteadily towards the two men.

"Maybe it was thoughtless of me to try to shoot the line going into the hotel," the photographer went on, "but would you object to my taking pictures from a distance and from the back, so that no faces can be made out?"

Hardoy had no chance to reply.

"Please, sir!" the old woman called out to the photographer. He and the line turned to look at her. Her face gaunt and white, she moved with visible difficulty. Her tone was plaintive, but something in her voice belied her appearance. Amplified by the silence, her words carried along the line. "Please take my picture, will you? Please."

The reporter looked at her, bewildered.

"I would like it very much if you took my picture and put it on your front page—on the front page of every newspaper."

The man seemed to shrink back. "*Señora...*"

"I mean it. Didn't you say you want to take pictures of us? Well, here I am. Take mine. You can take as many pictures of me as you like. And I will tell your newspaper what they did to my family."

The woman's words chilled Solo. He looked at the queue. Behind magazines and newspapers, raised lapels and half-turned shoulders, the line watched in stony anticipation.

The photographer stood still, all will to argue broken. He looked from the woman to Hardoy and back again, then turned around and walked silently away.

The old woman hobbled back to her place in the line.

"Dr. Hardoy," Doris said while they waited for Fonseca at the entrance to the hotel, "I called the Ministry of Foreign Affairs and spoke to the Chief of Protocol. I told him what you said: we've been waiting for two days for the passes to visit jails at our own discretion. He said the passes are on their way. They should be here any minute."

Hardoy sighed. "Thank you, Doris. Please carry on here." He looked at his watch. "In case of an emergency, we will be at the Villa Devoto jail."

"Villa Devoto? But—what about the passes?"

"If they arrive, hold on to them."

Their car pulled up to the curb just as Fonseca came out the door. "I missed all the street theater, didn't I?" he said. He must have waited for the elevator, Solo thought as Doris, in rapid-fire Portuguese, related to Fonseca the incident with the photographer.

"Where to, sir?" the driver asked as they climbed into the car.

"The Villa Devoto jail."

"Villa Devoto?"

"Yes, the jail," Hardoy said testily. "You *do* know the way, don't you?"

"Yes, sir." The driver eased out into traffic. The line of people, now punctuated with umbrellas held up against a fine drizzle, inched into the hotel. Solo looked for the old woman in black and did not see her.

They rode in silence. Questions swirled in Solo's mind, but he remembered Hardoy's injunction against discussing business in government cars. Villa Devoto was the first of a number of detention facilities they were supposed to visit. They didn't have the passes, so they might not be let in. What then? There might be a confrontation. Unless Hardoy was bluffing. Or calling the government's bluff.

The business district dissolved into avenues lined with apartment buildings, followed by barrios of cobblestone streets and low-rise dwellings. After a while, a sign over a shop told Solo that they were in Villa Devoto: broad, quiet streets, heavily treed, with occasional gardens. Mixed in with working-class homes were older mansions and mini-palazzi of Italianate style. Solo did not remember ever being in this part of Buenos Aires.

The car turned into a side street and drove a few hundred feet along a high wall bristling with glass shards and barbed wire, halting in front of a solid iron gate. The armed soldier standing guard in front of the gate followed the car with his eyes but made no move to come near it.

"Please wait here," Hardoy told the driver. The three men got out of the car.

The drizzle had stopped. Near the gate, one of two scrawny dogs sleeping in an abandoned section of sewer pipe rose on wobbly legs and switched its tail. Hardoy went up to the soldier and said something Solo couldn't hear. The guard motioned with his rifle in the direction of a small door next to the gate.

"This way," the chairman called out.

They walked up to the wicket and rang the bell. After a long pause, a peephole opened in the center of the door, exposing an eyeball that looked them over. Hardoy spoke to the eyeball.

"Good morning. We are the delegates from the human rights commission. We've come to visit the jail."

The peephole clicked shut, setting off a commotion inside. Solo heard indistinct orders shouted, followed by complete silence. Hardoy was on the point of ringing again when heavy footsteps tramped towards the gate and the door clanged open and exposed an olive uniform.

"Good morning. I am the sergeant on duty. Please follow me to the office of my commandant."

They stepped through the low-browed entrance into a cement courtyard bounded on three sides by large five-story buildings, the fourth side being shut in by a smaller structure for which they were headed.

Barking over his shoulder some comment or injunction—Solo caught only the words "my commandant"—the sergeant showed them into an office. The officer behind the desk stood up. He was short and burly, with muscular arms and a tendoned neck showing above the necktie of his khaki shirt.

"Please have a seat, gentlemen," he said after Hardoy introduced himself, Fonseca and Solo. "I am Major Alvarado, the commanding officer here. Forgive our surprise. We didn't know you were coming."

"That's just the idea, major," Hardoy said. "I'm sure you are accustomed to both routine and surprise inspections."

"Of course. No doubt everything is in order. But our security is very strict and we cannot admit visitors without prior authorization. I have telephoned my superior. He is on his way. In the meantime, may I offer you coffee?"

He said something to the sergeant, who uttered the same yelp as before, wheeled about, and left. Solo ran his eyes around the room: desk, chairs, filing cabinets. On the wall behind the major hung a crucifix, a large map of Buenos Aires sprinkled with red dots and circles, and four black-framed photographs of men in uniform under the caption "Victims of Subversion."

Hardoy folded his hands in his lap. "While we wait, Major, would you mind telling us about the prison? We understand that it holds both men and women. Any minors?"

"No minors. Women are housed separately and closely monitored to prevent abuse. We have medical facilities, a chapel, and a school for prisoners who have not completed elementary school."

"What is the diet?" Fonseca asked, preparing to write on a notepad.

"The usual: beef, eggs, fish, fresh fruits and vegetables. Our inmates also receive food from their families, and their nutrition is supervised by doctors."

"Is there hot water in the bathrooms?"

"Yes. And we have televisions, and sewing machines for the women to make items for their personal use or to sell outside the jail."

"Visitors?"

"Mondays and Thursdays for the men; Wednesdays and Fridays for the women."

"And your disciplinary system?"

"Isolation is our only punishment. Fortunately we don't need to use it much."

"What about mail?" Fonseca asked, still writing.

Instead of answering, Major Alvarado suddenly got to his feet. Solo turned to see a heavy-set man in green fatigues, his receding black hair flecked with gray and slicked back, standing in the doorway behind them. He was in his early fifties, Solo judged, with pale blue eyes set in a deeply seamed face. There was a smile on the face, but not in the eyes.

"Pardon the delay, gentlemen. I'm Colonel Indart."

16

Diego waited until the crowd of government pensioners laying siege to the small branch of the River Plate Bank piled through the bank's doors to collect their monthly checks. He crossed the street and walked in behind them.

As he hoped, the multitude of old people outside had discouraged most other customers. He made his way past the swarming teller windows to the rear of the bank, where a lone clerk stood behind a counter by the open vault. There were two posters on the wall by the counter. One proclaimed, *To shrink the State is to enlarge the Nation*, the new maxim for the economy. The other featured the city's noise-abatement slogan that had become the object of dark jokes since the coup: *Silence is Health*.

"Good morning." Diego handed over his ID and signature card and signed the register. The clerk looked at him and retreated with the cards to a filing cabinet.

Diego gingerly rested his forearms on the counter, shifting his weight to his right arm and leg. The pain was dull and constant, but the makeshift bandage fashioned out of a sock was holding. There was a dark stain on the jacket where the inside of his left forearm bulged. Not too noticeable if he kept his arms close to his body.

He stole a glance at the bulletproof booth mounted on the catwalk

above the front entrance. The armed guard inside seemed to be looking straight at him. The cameras, too, would be recording his presence:
a tall man in his thirties, corduroy cap, bulky leather jacket, standing
at the vault counter, a duffel bag at his side. He wasn't sure how good a
dye job he had done on his hair, rushed as he had been, in a cafe bathroom—not as good, he was sure, as last week when he had come in to
rent the box. But the corduroy cap covered most of it.

The clerk came back. "Thank you, Mr. Aguirre. May I have your
key? Follow me, please."

When the clerk left him alone in the cubicle by the vault, Diego
emptied the contents of the safe deposit box into the duffel, stuffing
the money and passport at the bottom, leaving the gun and spare clips
closer to the top, beneath his underwear.

The album containing his stamp collection fell open in his hands.
He should have left it with Doña Asunta. What was he thinking? He
had consolidated his collection into a single album, the one that Aunt
Finia had given him to start him off, with all those U.S. Lady Liberty
stamps from her correspondence with the Altube branch of their family. The Altubes had also come to Argentina from the Basque country,
then taken off to California to prospect for gold in the 1850s, ending
up as ranchers in Nevada. As a child, Diego had treasured the postcards from his cousins in Nevada and set his heart on one day visiting
them. Maybe now he would get his chance.

He wondered if Inés would like Nevada. The name sounded cold,
but the postcards he had saved in the album showed only snow-capped
peaks in the distance. Nevada looked sun-drenched and beautiful:
Emerald Bay in Lake Tahoe; Shoshone Indians at Lamoille Creek; a
town called Winnemucca; rodeos and saddle-making—nothing at all
like the Nevada he had seen in Hollywood movies, the casinos gush-
ing fountains of neon, gangsters and whores. He suspected that very
little in the United States would fit its Hollywood image. He glanced
at the Altubes' postcard from their Spanish Ranch, in a place called
Elko. It bore his very first stamp, from 1949: the Statue of Liberty

and an American flag with a nasty-looking snake wrapped around the flagpole. *Fight Communism*, read the words across the top. He sighed. His mother would have said: *Plus ça change...*

Stop daydreaming, he grunted. You need to get to Lucas, find a safe place to stay, see Aunt Finia. Colonel Indart would have every bloodhound out by now.

The album went into the large side pocket of the duffel. He zipped the bag, replaced and locked the box, and stepped out of the vault, thanking the clerk as he signed out.

Miraculously, the pay phone in the corner pizzeria not only worked but had no waiting line behind the person using it, an elderly woman with a little girl and myriad of shopping bags. He got behind them and stared at the photograph above the phone: Carlos Gardel, smiling, hat tilted dashingly to one side. The famous tango singer would have been at the height of his popularity in 1935, the date above a smaller photo of him boarding the airplane that would crash and kill him in Colombia.

His arm felt like lead, and the woman ahead of him kept dictating her memoirs. Recipes. Home remedies for the flu. Stories about when she was young and there were few houses wherever it was she was talking about, and they didn't need curtains, and look at it now, how they're ruining the place, cutting down all the trees...

Please, lady, please.

"Gardel."

It was the little girl. She must be what—four? She was looking at him and pointing to the poster.

"Gardel," he agreed. "Do you like Gardel?"

She shook her head. "I like jazz," she said, pulling up her little skirt all the better to slide her behind down the tiled wall to the floor. This caught the woman's attention. "I have to go. Bye," she said into the phone and hung up, giving him a dirty look.

Do I look like a pervert? Diego wondered as he dialed.

"Hospital Italiano, buenos días."

"Dr. Lucas Levenson, please."

"One moment, sir."

An older man and two teenage girls stationed themselves behind him.

"Hello, this is Dr. Levenson," said a deep voice. Diego could hear other voices in the background.

"Hello, doctor. This is Francisco Aguirre. You said to call."

There was a long pause, and then Lucas spoke loudly. "Ah, yes, Mr. Aguirre. I hope you can hear me. It's very noisy here. I'm afraid that your grandmother remains in a coma."

"I'm sorry to hear that."

"Yes, we were hoping for a different outcome. I'm so sorry. She's been moved from intensive care to a private room. I regret saying this, but I think it would be best if you came to see her now."

"I understand, doctor."

"I'll leave word at the desk, Mr. Aguirre. Ask for Mrs. Ramírez's room and they will page me. Make sure you tell them it's Clara Irene Ramírez. We have other patients with the same last name."

"Thank you, doctor. I'll be there."

Twenty minutes later he arrived at the Italian Hospital in Almagro, a quiet residential neighborhood in the heart of the city. As he stepped into the ancient building, he saw at the reception desk in the center hall a policeman and a nurse standing by an elderly lady in a wheelchair. He quickly veered off into a side gallery marked "The History of the Italian Hospital in Pictures."

Through the glass partitions facing the reception area he kept an eye on the desk while perusing the old photographs and memorabilia on the walls. A caption under a snapshot of a physician on horseback explained that Dr. Medici had been hired to visit the riverfront ghettoes of Italian immigrants, a mix of seamen, Garibaldi legionnaires, and political fugitives from various Italian regions opposed to Piedmont. Indeed, Diego thought, his great grandfather Luigi Fioravanti would have been among them, if family lore could be believed, after leaving Tuscany to join Garibaldi in the New World.

Two more policemen approached the reception desk from a side corridor. Diego edged back to the door of the exhibit room, closer to the hospital entrance. He lingered there, pretending to study a painting of the Cavaliere Marcello Cerrutti, Chargé d'Affaires of the King of Sardinia, who first advocated building a public hospital for the Italian community in Argentina.

At the desk, the nurse began pushing the wheelchair toward the rear of the building. The three policemen followed. Diego felt the throbbing in his left forearm grow more intense, but he waited a while longer before approaching the receptionist.

"I'm here to see my grandmother, Mrs. Clara Irene Ramírez," he said.

"Visiting hours are almost over, sir."

"I know. Would you please page Dr. Lucas Levenson? He wants to see me. I'll be in my grandmother's room."

The receptionist gave him the room number and he made for the stairs, figuring the police and the nurse with the wheelchair would have taken the elevator. On the third floor he identified himself again at the nurses' station and was directed to a room two doors down. Too close to the nurses.

A pale, elderly woman lay on the bed, eyes shut, wearing a deeply peaceful expression. Out of the sheets pulled up to her chin, wires led to a bedside monitor.

He sat on a couch under the window that looked out on a grassy inner courtyard bordered by hedges and planted with shrubs and trees. Cats. There were cats down there. Four that he could see: one black, switching its tail by a patient on a wheelchair, an orange one sitting on its haunches near a tree, two more enjoying the sun on the cement path. He had recently asked Lucas what the hell cats were doing in a hospital. Wasn't that kind of—unsanitary? Lucas had shrugged. "To shrink the State is to enlarge the Nation," he said sardonically. "This is a public hospital. There's almost no money for soap or bandages. You think we're worried about the cats? They get rid of the rodents."

Lucas. Now Diego wished he hadn't involved his friend in his troubles. Lucas was married, with a lovely wife and two young children. The original plan had been very different and low-risk: a few lab tests followed by a medical certification that Captain Diego Fioravanti was no longer fit for service. Lucas could have made that happen without much exposure. But that plan had been crushed by events. Now Lucas was risking his life.

A figure in scrubs, his hairy arms and v-neck contrasting with the perfectly bald crown of his head, appeared in the doorway and called out, "Mr. Aguirre? I'm Dr. Levenson."

He came in and shut the door. And suddenly the reassuring figure of Lucas, a stethoscope wrapped round his thick neck, his brambly eyebrows over the heavy-lidded eyes breaking into an unconscious grin at the sight of his friend, eased Diego's turmoil.

"Well, well," Lucas said, hugging him and then putting him at arm's length to study his newly acquired black hair. "Most becoming. Nothing like a new hair job to make a man feel better about himself, eh?"

Diego smiled, his eyes on his friend's tonsure. He said, "Maybe I should have my head circumcised like yours."

Lucas chuckled, then his voice dropped. "So, you're out."

Diego nodded. He took off his jacket and rolled up the left sleeve of his shirt. Lucas's eyes started as he reached for the arm. "What happened?"

"The less you know, the better."

Lucas unwrapped the sock and let out a low whistle. "Nasty. Can't stay away from hospitals, can you? Blown up, shot at..." He shook his head. "I'll take care of this."

"Thanks. And thanks for reminding me about Mrs. Ramirez's full name," Diego's chin pointed towards the bed. "Wouldn't do for her grandson not to know it."

Lucas moved to the head of the bed. He glanced at the monitor and sat on the bed, tenderly placing a hand on Mrs. Ramírez's forehead. "I wish you had met Clara when she was well. Lovely lady. She's a widow, and her only daughter died childless last year. Clara would have been thrilled to have a grandson—not you, of course."

"Think she can hear us?"

Lucas shrugged. "You can try. She was always a good listener. She would have loved to help."

"She *is* helping."

"Yes, she's helping, isn't she." Lucas reached under the sheets, brought out her hand, and held it in his. "So you're leaving tomorrow?"

Diego pulled up a chair to the opposite side of the bed and spoke across Mrs. Ramírez's body. "I need more time. And don't look at me like that."

"Your time is up. You said so yourself."

"I know. But there's somebody I need to get in touch with first."

Lucas stroked Mrs. Ramírez's hand. "Hear that, Clara? Tell him it's a bad idea."

Diego said, "I think Clara would understand. She had a daughter, you said."

"Had, yes. Her daughter's dead."

"Clara would understand, believe me."

"Is it your girlfriend Inés? The one you've never introduced me to? Is that why you're staying?"

Diego shut his eyes. He felt light-headed. He hadn't slept in so long. And he couldn't count on doing much of it until he found and talked to the families of Beatriz Suárez and Violeta Argerich. "No. Inés is actually one reason I need to leave as soon as I can. I don't want her mixed up in my problems. But you're going to get your wish and talk to her."

He brought out a slip of paper from his pocket and handed it to Lucas. "Her friend Valeria's number. Inés has a class at the law school tonight, but she'll be at Valeria's tomorrow night, after their French lesson. I'll tell you what to say."

Lucas frowned. "I don't know what you are up to, and you're right: I don't want to know. But you're taking a huge chance."

"I know that."

"Never could talk sense into you." Lucas said, standing up. "Let me get a few things to fix you up. You're good for one night here: the grieving grandson saying goodbye to his grandma. But first thing tomorrow you'll have to leave."

The medication Lucas gave him was making him drowsy, but he was too keyed-up to sleep. He finished the sandwich Lucas had brought and stared at the courtyard below, where a cat by the privet hedge was flicking out a paw toward some prey Diego couldn't see.

There had been a flurry of activity in the hallway half an hour ago; loud voices, sounds of a gurney being rushed along, people running beside it. Now all was quiet again.

He sat on the chair by the bed and studied Mrs. Ramírez's lined face, her gray hair, the eyelids mercifully covering the unseeing eyes that he imagined kindly, understanding. He wondered what color her eyes were.

"Mrs. Ramírez," he said. "Clara—may I call you Clara? I'm Diego, Lucas's friend. He and I have known each other all our lives. Our families were neighbors and we went to school together. His father ran the Red Cross warehouse on our block. Did he ever tell you that? When we were kids we played in the ambulances, helped sort donations and put together relief packages for disasters: floods, earthquakes, wars. The Soviet invasion of Hungary—nineteen fifty-six. That was a big one. Mountains of clothing, toys, canned goods. And the polio epidemic of the fifties. You must remember that. There were rows of iron lungs in the warehouse, and all the sidewalks were washed with disinfectant—creosol, I think it was called. Our parents made us wear a lump of camphor around the neck. Did you do that with your daughter?"

He passed his hand across his forehead and felt it clammy. "Sorry. Must be fatigue. I'm not thinking clearly."

He stood up and went to flop down on the couch by the window. As soon as he put his back flat against the cushions, a bog of thick, soothing drowsiness began to suck him under. He fought it.

"Lucas became a doctor, Clara," he said from the couch. "But you know that. I joined the army. And I'm in trouble. Maybe my Aunt Finia is right: it involves women. I'm going to tell you about two women named Beatriz Suárez and Violeta Argerich, and why I'm in trouble. Deep trouble, Clara. Not even Lucas knows how deep. You are the only person I can tell."

17

"Hope I haven't kept you long," Colonel Indart said, shaking hands. His voice was soft, controlled, but it was the hard jaw, the unsmiling eyes, that drew Solo's attention.

"No, Colonel," Hardoy said, "but if you don't mind, we'd like to get on with our visit."

"By all means. I will escort you myself, though I'm only titularly attached here; Major Alvarado is in charge. I expect he has informed you that no cameras or recorders are allowed."

Solo was aware that Fonseca was shooting a glance in his direction, as Hardoy said, "That was not part of the understanding we had with your government."

The colonel shrugged. "It's for security reasons. If you prefer to take it up with higher authorities and come back once the matter is settled..."

Hardoy took a sharp breath; Solo could sense his anger and the effort it took to hold it in check. "We understand, Colonel," the chairman said evenly. "Shall we proceed?"

The colonel nodded. "Let's start with the women's quarters."

They marched out of the office just as the sergeant arrived with the coffee tray.

Military personnel had temporarily replaced the civilian warden and his staff, Solo could hear Colonel Indart explaining to Hardoy as the two men led the way towards the rear of the grounds. Fonseca and the major followed some steps behind, with Solo trailing after. The sight of these lowering buildings set him thinking once again of the Mahlers, wondering if Débora Mahler had ever been inside these gates. The thought hurt, and he tried to evict it from his mind. Whatever it was that awaited him here, in this prison at the bottom of the world, he had a sinking feeling that he had been gravitating to it irresistibly, caught in a march of events towards something momentous and inescapable.

At the far end of the courtyard a soldier opened a small gate, beyond which stood a smaller pavilion built in the same style as the larger buildings. "You may want to inspect the cells before talking to the inmates," Colonel Indart suggested.

The cells looked neater to Solo than his kids' room. Each featured freshly made bunk beds, some with current magazines lying on top. There were cutouts of popular singers pinned to the walls, along with travel posters of Mount Aconcagua, the Perito Moreno Glacier, and Iguazú Falls. Everything was clean and tidy, including the bathrooms, where Fonseca inspected the stalls for toilet paper, flushed the bowls, and ran the hot water faucet in the basin.

"Hot water you say?" he inquired, drying a wet finger on his handkerchief.

The colonel consulted his watch. "Only at certain times, I'm afraid. And the water needs to run for a while before it turns hot. These buildings date back to nineteen twenty-seven."

They passed into a large room containing two television sets and rows of sewing machines with stools. "This is where the women work," Colonel Indart said. "Major Alvarado has probably told you that they make items for their personal use and to sell outside the jail, for pocket money."

The colonel waited while Fonseca studied the machines and wrote in his notebook. Then, he said, "The women know you are here. Those that wish to talk to you are assembled outside."

They followed him out through a side door. Not far off, Solo saw a dozen or so women standing in a group flanked by two soldiers. Colonel Indart stopped in front of the group.

"These gentlemen are from the OAS human rights commission. Those of you who wish to speak with them are free to do so." He stepped to the side about ten paces, followed by the major and the sergeant, and signaled the two soldiers to do the same.

Hardoy, Fonseca, and Solo stepped forward until they were face to face with the women. In the silence that hung over them, the chairman removed his hat and spoke.

"Ladies, my name is Bruno Hardoy. I am the chairman of the commission. These gentlemen are Dr. Fonseca and Mr. Solórzano. We've come to talk to you, but I want you to understand that you are under no obligation to speak with us. If you do wish to speak, anything you tell us will be held in confidence."

Solo's eyes traveled over the women. They were all ages, some adolescent, others middle-aged, a few with a grandmotherly look about them. All were modestly dressed in rumpled street clothes that matched their unkempt hair and discolored complexion. Etiolated was the word that came to his mind, like flowers pressed in a book. Some women met his eyes; others dropped their gaze or looked away. They huddled together like cornered animals.

"Let me ask those of you who want to talk"—Hardoy glanced at Colonel Indart, who gave no sign of intending to move farther away— "that you come over to the far end of this courtyard, where we may speak privately."

He turned around and walked off, with Fonseca and Solo at his side. Solo looked back and saw a moment's hesitation among the prisoners. Then, to a woman, they drifted silently after the three men. At the end of the yard the visitors waited for the women to range themselves around in a half circle.

Solo did not have to look for a sign from Hardoy. Unprompted, he produced the tape recorder, switched it on, and held it close against his body, face out, in the crook of his folded left arm. Almost at once he felt Fonseca's hand on him.

"They said..." Fonseca began. But Hardoy's hand was already on Fonseca's, pulling it away from Solo's arm. The chairman looked at Solo and nodded.

It was as if the women had been given a signal. Suddenly, their suppressed emotion erupted into tears. Some women cupped their hands over their faces; some buried their heads in the bosom or shoulder nearest them and were racked by violent sobs. A few remained stock-still, expressionless, as if unmoved. Solo's eyes were glued to one woman, the oldest in the group, who wept silently, letting the tears brim over and stream down her cheeks. Something about the soft sag under her chin, her gentle eyes, reminded him of his mother. He sucked in a long breath.

"Ladies..." Hardoy pleaded gently. "Please, you must calm yourselves. We haven't much time."

It was no good. The women's pent-up feeling released itself in uncontrollable weeping.

"Ladies, please..."

Slowly the outpour ran its course. A girl stepped up to Hardoy. Blinking back tears she took hold of his hand. "Please, sir. Please take pity on us. We know we will pay for talking to you but we don't care. We beg you, please help us."

"We just want to die," another choking voice said. "That's all we ask. To be allowed to die."

"How can we endure this any longer?" a third cried. "We are completely destroyed, out of our minds. What more do they want from us?"

Many women began to weep again.

"How old are you?" Hardoy asked a girl to his right.

The question cut short the fresh gale of tears. Stifling sobs the girl said, "Sixteen, sir."

"And you?"

"Seventeen."

"Any more young prisoners among you?"

"There were," answered an elderly woman with Asian features, Japanese, Solo thought, "but they took them away when they heard you were coming. Like the last time, when the Red Cross came. Two days ago they took away more than half the prisoners. Then they gave us these clothes to wear and brought in the televisions and the sewing machines."

"Please, sir," the sixteen-year-old managed, "don't let them torture us anymore. Please..."

She was looking at Solo, as if her plea could not fail to move the man nearest her own age. The questions he had wanted to ask Hardoy—he wouldn't need to ask them now. The women in Plaza de Mayo, the Mahlers, the people lined up outside the hotel, the old woman berating the photographer—suddenly he had no more doubts, no questions or equivocations, only a dead certainty. He saw his knuckles whiten against the black casing of the tape recorder.

"Torture? Here?" Fonseca asked.

"Not here," several voices said at once. "They take us to other places, military installations, or to the Club, downtown."

"The Club?"

"The Athletic Club, that's what they call it."

"Where is this Club?"

"It's a house on Garay and Paseo Colón streets. We've all been there. But they haven't taken us there in over a week."

Producing a pen and a small notebook out of his pocket, Hardoy opened it to a blank page and handed it to one of the women. "Pass this around while we talk. See if each of you can draw on a different page the layout of this Athletic Club and every detail of it you can remember."

"When they finish with us," said another voice, "they bring us back to recover in that building over there." Fingers pointed to a pavilion.

"They have doctors—"

"—to make sure we don't die."

Solo saw Colonel Indart strolling towards the group and he lowered the tape recorder slightly. The man now stood close by, within hearing range, hands in pockets, ostensibly chaffering with the soldiers who had also drawn nearer. Some of the women noticed him too. Solo moved closer to Hardoy, putting more bodies between Indart and the tape recorder.

"What are the charges against you?" Hardoy asked a prisoner.

"Charges? None of us know. They said my name was in somebody's address book. We are not allowed lawyers, so what difference does it make?"

One of the prisoners pressed through to the front of the group and planted herself before Hardoy.

"My name is Silvina Schiaffino. I was kidnapped from my home in the city, in Liniers. They hooded me and took me to a place out in the country, where I could hear crickets." The woman's voice was steady, but flat, as if she had been robbed of inflection. "They put me in a room where I slept on my own daughter's bed, which they had taken from our house. That night they tied me to a metal bedspring—the *grill*, they called it. They were very excited and talked about God, saying that we the prisoners were enemies of God. They gave me electric shocks all over. The pain was excruciating, especially on my breasts because I had been nursing my baby. I went into convulsions. They told me it was all part of the training I needed in order to confess. Then they raped me. When I asked to go to the bathroom, they took me naked through a hallway full of soldiers who laughed at me. They would put me on the grill three, four times a day. I can't tell you how long it all lasted. I asked them to send me to jail, to give me anything to sign. My ears hurt so much that I kept blacking out. My convulsions came back and that made them even angrier. Time just went on and on and..."

Solo saw the woman's eyes open wide beneath her swollen eyelids, and for a moment she looked dazed.

"I lost all notion of time. It was always the same, always the howl-
ing. They would bring in a tape recording of the voice of my daughter
asking me to save her—they told me she was there too, in that place.
She was only nine, they said, but she was"—the woman bit off the
words as if struggling to bring them out—"'a nice little piece just asking for it.' By then I was only half conscious all the time."

She was small, with short dark brown hair, one of the few women
Solo had seen displaying no emotion while the others cried. She spoke
with the same detachment as Mrs. Mahler had yesterday.

"They injected me with something called Pentothal and other
drugs. I don't remember much. The doctor was there all the time while
they tortured me. They would walk me down the hallway, where I was
raped many times by soldiers or policemen—I don't know which. I
was bleeding a lot by then and was just letting myself die. I didn't care
about anything. I didn't even cry anymore."

She faced away from the group and moved off a few steps. Another woman put an arm over her shoulder and began talking to her gently. In a whisper, Fonseca asked other prisoners to spell the woman's
last name and wrote it down.

A second prisoner moved up to the tape recorder. She was tall,
handsome, perhaps thirty, Solo judged, with large amber eyes in a taut
face. Her dark hair was tied back with a rubber band. "My name is
Sara Goldberg. They kidnapped me in broad daylight in the street,
when I was waiting for my husband outside the Constitución train station. I yelled out my name, hoping a passer-by would hear and tell my
family. I was taken to the underground cellblock at the Superintendencia de Seguridad Federal, an annex of police headquarters, where you
are greeted by an enormous swastika painted on an entire wall."

A swastika, at police headquarters, Solo repeated to himself.

"That night the guard came into my cell. He put his boot on my
face and said he would send me to the grill if I didn't keep still. Then
he raped me. Next morning, when they gave us tea, he gave me a lump

of sugar 'for the services rendered,' he said. That same morning another man came into my cell shouting orders, 'Get up! Strip!' He pushed me against the wall and I was raped again. In the evening, the guard forced me to play cards with him and later raped me again."

Unlike the prisoner who had spoken first, this woman did not appear overwhelmed, undone. Solo could see that she was outraged. Color rose in her cheeks as the words tumbled out of her. But like the first prisoner, she seemed past caring whether Colonel Indart heard. *We just want to be allowed to die.* Those words still reverberated for him, still stunned him.

"They said I had been arrested 'for speaking in Jew' when I gave my last name. They tortured Jewish prisoners to get information on the Jewish community—they had lists of names and addresses of Jewish organizations and drawings of the layout of synagogues and Jewish clubs."

"How were you tortured?" Hardoy asked.

"Electric shocks in my genitals, my mouth, my armpits. And a choking bag over my head, or water to simulate drowning." The guards entertained themselves by making us dance or forcing us to place a finger on the floor and pivot round faster and faster—'oil drilling.' they called that—until we dropped and they beat us to the point where we couldn't cry out anymore. They simulated firing squads or threatened to have us 'transferred,' which meant killed. When we lay on the floor we were kicked, spat and urinated on. I saw high school students there who had campaigned for a student bus fare, and a priest who worked in the slums. Women were afraid to ask to go to the bathroom because there were always guards there waiting to—"

The sudden flash of light almost made Solo drop the recorder. All heads turned to the photographer taking pictures of the group, a heavily built man wearing a necktie and vest, shirt cuffs rolled up his forearms. He was circling them with measured deliberateness, snapping shots every few feet.

"What is the meaning of this?" Hardoy exploded, looking about for Colonel Indart. But the colonel and the major had disappeared. In their place stood the sergeant, smiling at the group. Hardoy stormed over to him.

"Why is this man taking pictures of us? We were told that no photographs would be allowed."

"Oh, but these are official, sir, to mark your visit to Villa Devoto. The colonel has instructed me to tell you that you will receive copies."

"Where is your colonel?"

"He was called away on urgent business. My commandant has gone to see him off."

Hardoy returned to the group. The women were visibly agitated.

Hardoy said, "We will deal with this later. Right now it's more important that we hear you out. Try to ignore the photographer. Mrs. Goldberg, please go on. As I recall, a bomb was planted in the cafeteria of the Superintendencia, killing some two dozen policemen."

The woman wrapped her arms around herself and began again, her words punctuated by the popping flash. Solo kept his eyes on the photographer, rotating his body to keep the recorder out of sight. "Yes, there were massive executions of prisoners in revenge for the bombing. But I had been moved a few days earlier to the Athletic Club. It was run by Indart, this same Indart." She waved her hand at the space he had occupied. "He was a major then, before they promoted him for his services there. He worked closely with the navy and Admiral Rinaldi."

Admiral Rinaldi. Solo felt the words thud into him.

All eyes were on Mrs. Goldberg. No one, Solo knew, was aware of the effect the mention of the admiral had on him. He thought of the Mahlers and felt his ears burning. And Malena—did she know about the admiral? He carefully lifted his hand from the recorder and rubbed his eyes. They smarted. A sharp stinging pain, as though Mrs. Goldberg had slapped him. *Beware the fool with initiative.*

"There were three torture rooms, each with a metal bedspring, hooks from which to hang the prisoners, and a barrel of water. The walls were decorated with swastikas. At my first torture session they told me to forget my name and said from now on you are a number. Each session lasted as long as the torturer wanted. The only limitation was death, which for us prisoners meant liberation. Some died under torture. Others found ways of speeding their own death."

She paused and Hardoy said, "Were you held anywhere else?"

She nodded. "Campo de Mayo, the large army base thirty kilometers from Buenos Aires. There, after each torture session, they kept us chained and hooded, seated on the floor fourteen hours a day in warehouses. We were forbidden to utter a single word or to move, even turn our heads. It was impossible to sleep on the floor, in the puddles of urine, because of the shrieks of the tortured."

"What did you eat?" Fonseca asked.

"Sometimes they gave us food once or twice a day, but sometimes days went by without any. It was never much—something like the small plate of beans they give us here, only worse, often nothing more than water mixed with flour or raw animal entrails. But it was a chance to take off the hood. They bathed us by hosing down the whole group, like cattle. We were so full of lice that a few times they sprayed us with insecticide. The worst days were the days of transfers."

"You mean..." Hardoy said.

"You never knew when it would be your turn," she went on. "We waited, day after day, never knowing if we would be called."

"What happened to those transferred?" Hardoy asked.

"Everybody knew. The guards made no secret of it. They said it was a Christian form of death, approved by the Church, because the victims didn't suffer. They were given an injection to make them drowsy, then trucked to the airport, loaded on airplanes that flew out over the Atlantic, and thrown out still alive."

Still alive. The words stayed in the air, lingering in Solo's ears in the silence they created. A shiver rose from deep within him, and he turned to look for Colonel Indart before remembering that the colonel was no longer there. Only the photographer remained, hovering around them, firing his camera within earshot.

"Mrs. Goldberg," Hardoy said. "Were you ever allowed to see a lawyer or brought before a judge?"

"Still alive," she repeated. "I remember one prisoner whose number was dropped from the list and was never called again for anything. They forgot him. Months went by, and one day when they were doing transfers he broke down and started shouting: 'Me! Me!' He had remained there, hooded, for six months, waiting for death. So they transferred him, because they no longer had any interest in him."

She stopped. "What did you ask me?"

"If you were ever brought before a judge or allowed to see a lawyer."

She shook her head. "The only visitor we had was the local bishop. He told us we had no right to complain because we were not cooperating with the authorities. We should tell all we knew, he said, and he offered to hear our confessions. The only lawyers I saw were other prisoners."

The tape recorder clicked. Every one waited in silence while Solo turned the cassette over. The photographer had finally left and the two soldiers had moved away to chat with the guard at the gate. They were alone in the yard now.

"I was in Campo de Mayo too, sir, before they took me to the Naval Mechanics School," a thin blonde woman said. "Graciela Escobar is my name. At the Navy School prisoners are kept in chains and there is a system of closed-circuit television to monitor every movement. Swastikas and *Viva Hitler* are painted on the walls. They torture people kidnapped all over the country, including pregnant women, in a room covered with egg cartons to muffle the shrieks."

Solo saw the corners of Hardoy's mouth quiver, before the chairman said, "Do the names Alice Domon and Leonie Renée Duquet mean anything to you?"

"The French nuns who helped the Mothers of Plaza de Mayo, yes. I was there when they were brought in, tortured into writing letters to their Mother Superior and the Pope, then photographed against posters of guerrilla organizations and transferred. The naval officers joked for days about the *flying nuns*."

Hardoy shut his eyes, then opened them. "Go on, please. Tell us about the pregnant prisoners."

Graciela Escobar barely opened her lips when speaking, which Solo realized was an effort to conceal the missing front teeth that marred her otherwise attractive face. He edged the recorder closer to her.

"In Campo de Mayo they have a hospital, with doctors and a ward full of pregnant women chained to their beds, hooded and hooked up to IV's to hasten labor. The Naval Mechanics School is not like that. When a baby is due, a doctor and other prisoners help with the delivery. I am a nurse, so I helped. If a woman needs a cesarean section, she is taken to the Naval Hospital and brought back at once afterwards. They tell her that the baby will be turned over to her family and ask her to write a letter to her relatives. Then, she is usually transferred and the baby is given away to an infertile couple in the military or the police, or sold. There are waiting lists for the babies. Admiral Rinaldi leads visitors on tours of the place. You can hear him boasting that he runs the best maternity in town."

"Sir!" the sergeant called from a distance, "the men are outside, waiting for you."

"We are coming," Hardoy shouted back.

The girl who had first spoken burst out crying and grasped his arm with both hands, like a child embracing a parent's leg. "Don't go, sir," she pleaded. "Please don't go. As soon as you leave they will..."

"Hush," another woman enfolded the girl in her arms. "The men need them too. You know that."

Solo saw Hardoy raise a fist to his mouth and cough repeatedly. He waited for the sergeant's olive uniform to vanish from sight before speaking again. When he did, his voice was rough with emotion but oddly gentle.

"We have to go now, ladies. I am sorry, but we must."

He stared fixedly at the women as if trying to imprint the image in his mind. "Nothing I say will undo what has been done to you. For that, nothing can make amends. And I won't ask you to believe that our visit will bring immediate relief from your suffering."

The two soldiers, Solo saw, had left off their bantering and were walking back towards the group.

"But two things I will tell you. One is that you are not forgotten. No matter how desperate you are, be certain that you are not forgotten. We will be doing everything in our power for you. I give you my word."

The soldiers reached the group and stopped behind it.

"The other thing..." Hardoy hesitated, lowering his eyes for an instant before raising them again, "is to apologize. To apologize to you on behalf of mankind."

The women looked at one another. No one spoke.

Then, still silent, singly or in pairs, the prisoners broke away from the group and trudged after the guards.

Solo stood with Hardoy and Fonseca, frozen, never taking his eyes off the retreating women until the building swallowed the last of them.

"Gentlemen."

The voice made all three of them turn around. A woman had come up to where they were standing.

"You mustn't believe a word those women are saying," she said. "They're playing victim for your benefit. I have never been treated here with anything but respect and consideration."

She was tall, pretty, her dark hair possessed of some luster, and better dressed than the group that had just left. She wore no make-up, but a faint trace of perfume reached Solo's nostrils.

"Are you an inmate here?" Hardoy asked, eyeing her narrowly.

"What else? I have to go and join the others now. But in the interest of fairness I wanted to tell you that those women are lying. Life in Villa Devoto is actually quite pleasant."

Before they could say anything else she was off, scurrying across the yard and into the building.

As he and Hardoy and Fonseca walked away, a fire bolt of impotent anger arced inside Solo at the thought of what awaited those women. Out of the feverish jumble in his head, one imperative stood out with desperate urgency: he had to find Malena.

18

The tears live in an onion that should water this sorrow. Inés sat back in her chair at the little desk in her bedroom and tapped the pencil against her Shakespeare textbook. This translation was the hardest yet on the list. She had finished *As flies to wanton boys and Tidings to wash the eyes of kings*, though she found both of her versions wanting. There was no music in her renderings; they were correct but soulless. She tried to retrieve herself from her wandering and focus on the assignment, but could not dismiss from her mind her visit to the Palace of Justice.

Fito was a criminal court judge. He was one of her father's oldest friends and a good man—she had no doubt about that, having known him her entire life. Judges were under orders to turn away the families of subversives, he said. What else could that mean except that people could be detained and held in secret for as long as the government felt like it? Still, as chilling as the notion was, that it *could* happen did not mean that it *was* happening. Yet what was there to prevent it? The Congress had been shut down, the Supreme Court replaced with yes-men. Maybe Diego was right. Maybe the government *could* do whatever it pleased.

And where was Diego? The whole day had gone by and still there was no word from him. She had no reason to suppose that he was away on anything other than one of his unpredictable assignments. Now more than ever she resented his secretiveness. She had no phone number or address, no way to get in touch with him.

She went to the study. Gladys Iturralde's phone number was by the telephone, where Inés had left it this morning. She sat down and dialed.

"Good evening, is this the Iturralde family?" she inquired of the pleasant young girl who answered the telephone.

"Yes, Luciana speaking. With whom would you like to speak?"

Civility and correct grammar. What a delightful child. The voice could not be more than eight or ten years old. "I'd like to speak with Gladys, please."

"Hold on. MAAAA!!!"

The painful screech still rang in Inés's ear when Luciana's mother stopped remonstrating with her daughter and picked up the receiver. "This is Gladys Iturralde. May I help you?"

"I hope so. I was given your name and number by a reporter who wrote an article some years ago about a shipwreck on the River Plate, the *Ciudad de Asunción*. The article carries a photograph of—"

"I know," Gladys Iturralde interrupted quietly, "Haydée and Leandro. Are you a reporter too?"

"No. I was hoping to locate Mrs. Madariaga on behalf of a friend of mine, the son of another passenger. But the reporter told me that Mrs. Madariaga is dead. Are you family?"

"No, I worked for her husband, Leandro. He had a business in Posadas, where they lived, exporting hardwoods from the northeast. I took care of the paperwork for shipments out of the port of Buenos Aires."

"Mrs. Iturralde," Inés said, at a loss for questions now, "did Mrs. Madariaga ever mention to you the other passenger in the picture— Mr. Solórzano?"

The answer startled Inés. "Oh, yes. I remember that."

The Iturraldes ran a small green grocery in a sleepy cobblestoned street in Belgrano and lived in the apartment in the rear. While her husband minded the store, Gladys Iturralde, a late thirtyish, large-busted woman in a print dress, her nut-brown hair crimped into a bun atop her head, sat with Inés drinking coffee, the newspaper article on the kitchen table between them. Luciana, the precocious telephone operator, had turned out to be just six years old and sat at one end of the table with her drawing pad and colored pencils, the tip of her tongue peeking out of a corner of her mouth in deep concentration.

"They were coming back from visiting relatives in Uruguay," Gladys said. "Leandro knew the captain of the *Ciudad de Asunción*. I'm sure that's why they were dining at his table that night."

And Mr. Solórzano probably knew him too, Inés thought, since he traveled so often to Montevideo.

"Haydée was seven months pregnant," Gladys said. "Did you know that?"

"No." Inés glanced again at the clipping. Only the upper half of the diners could be seen above a tabletop crowded with dishes and bottles. Haydée Madariaga wore a bright smile as she clinked glasses with her husband.

Gladys drank the last of her coffee and set down the cup. "Leandro drowned but Haydée survived. She went back to Posadas right away to be with her family and give birth. But she never recovered, and died shortly after her daughter was born. Carlota is sixteen now. She still lives in Posadas with Haydée's family."

"You were going to tell me about Mr. Solórzano..." Inés said.

Gladys nodded. "Haydée was in the hospital practically all the time after she went back to Posadas. Among other things, she suffered from pulmonary hypertension, which was aggravated by exposure in the cold water. One day—I had just moved to a new apartment and didn't have a telephone yet—she sent me a telegram. That's why I remember it so well, because she didn't write a letter but sent a telegram. She wanted me to go to the American Consulate and find out the address of Solórzano's family in the United States—they had left Argentina, you see. I thought it had to be very important to her, so I went to the consulate right away, got the address, and wired it back to her. Soon after that, she died."

They were both silent. A canary, in a cage hanging above an array of potted plants, suddenly broke into song. Inés ran her eyes over the laundry-laden clothesline above the washtub at one end of the kitchen, the pharmacy calendar pinned to the wall by the water heater, the dishes drying on a rack above the sink. A pot simmered on the stove, giving off a savory smell of stew. The scene had that familiar feeling of domesticity and comfort she had known since childhood: a mother's kitchen, a place of safety and warmth, worlds away from drownings and death. She said, "Do you know why she wanted to get in touch with the Solórzanos?"

Gladys shook her head thoughtfully. "No. But her family might know."

Luciana looked up from her drawing. "Mommy, what's pulmonary hibernation?"

The telephone rang as soon as Inés came through the front door. She heard her mother pick up in the kitchen.

"Inés! It's for you."

She was already heading for the study. "I'll take it in the study. Is it Diego?"

"No. it's your friend Alberto, long distance."

Alberto? She picked up the extension in the study and heard her mother hang up.

"What a wonderful surprise," she said. "It's so good to hear your voice. Is everything all right?"

Alberto hesitated. "I'm not sure. Have you seen Solo yet?"

"Yes," she said, suddenly disquieted. She sat down on the armchair by the telephone. "We had dinner here on Saturday, then visited his father's memorial yesterday. Is something the matter?"

"I had a message on my answering machine from my aunt Laura Mahler..." Alberto said.

"Your relatives, I know. Solo said he was delivering something to them from you."

"That's right. My aunt's message said to call her back, but nobody answers when I try. And I can't get through to Solo's hotel. It's always busy. The operator says they must be swamped with calls but she could patch me through if it's an emergency."

"Is it? Is there something I can do?"

Alberto seemed to consider this, then said, "No, I don't think so. I just didn't like the way my aunt sounded. She and my uncle..." He paused, then said, "Do you know if Solo got in touch with them?"

"He said he was going to on Sunday— Would you like me to go see them? If you give me their address..."

"No, no. I'll keep trying them. I'm sure they've just been out when I called." He hesitated again. "There's something else I need to talk to Solo about. If you speak to him, would you have him call me?"

"Sure," she said. This was not like Alberto, to be so reticent in saying what was on his mind. "He's coming by my school tomorrow evening. Is that soon enough? I can also go to his hotel and leave him a note."

"Tomorrow is fine. Look, I don't mean to be mysterious. God knows you and I were friends long before you introduced me to Solo. But it's ticklish. It has to do with his children."

She sat up. "What's happened?"

"Take it easy. It's nothing serious and I don't want to alarm him. It's just that his housekeeper told me that a car had been following her and the children when they walked to the playground."

Inés felt her heart quicken. No, wait, she told herself. Alberto was not in Argentina. He was calling from Washington. There had to be a reasonable explanation.

"I thought she might be wrong, but I kept watch in my car anyway.

She was right. I spotted the car and wrote down the plate number so the police could run it. Then I saw the driver." He paused. "It was Phyllis, his ex-wife."

Phyllis. Inés exhaled. She said, "What did you do?"

"I talked to her. She had parked to watch Lisa and John. I went up to her car and got in beside her. I mean, we've known each other for years. And we liked each other, I always thought. But she was so unnerved, almost afraid of me, like a child caught in mischief by an adult. She asked me not to tell Solo."

Alberto fell silent, then he suddenly said, "I don't know why I'm telling you this—"

"No, no," she cut him off. "I want to hear it."

"Well, I felt awful. I mean, these were her own kids she was watching."

Inés found herself moved. She had never met Phyllis, had no reason to feel any fondness for the woman Solo had married, but the image of her skulking around to sneak a look at her own children was pitiable.

Alberto went on. "Phyllis said to me, 'What harm am I doing? If you knew what it's like—not being able to see them, talk to them, be with them.' So I said, 'But you walked out; I don't understand.' And you know what she said?"

Inés waited.

"She said, 'I know. How could I leave my home and my children? If I were a man, people wouldn't ask that question; they wouldn't think twice about it because it happens all the time. But I'm a woman, so they think I don't love Lisa and John. They are wrong.'"

There was another silence on the line. Then Inés heard him sigh and ask, "What do you think?"

She wavered. Her loyalties lay with Solo, but she was not a mother. She could not pretend to know how a mother felt. "I—kind of agree with her," she finally said, and quickly added, "But you have to tell Solo. He has a right to know."

"I know. I told Monique, his lawyer, and she wanted to phone him right away. But I said I would do it." Alberto sighed heavily again. "Thank you for listening. Let's keep this conversation to ourselves."

"Yes," she agreed.

"You know the last thing Phyllis said to me?" Alberto added as an afterthought, "She said, 'They're my children. I'm not giving them up.'"

19

Stay paranoid, Diego told himself as he stood once more before a shop window, eyes combing the street in the window's reflection. Again, nobody he could see.

He knew that the pay phone in the garage next door worked because a young girl was using it. She came out and he went in.

"Hello?"

"Doña Asunta, it's me, your neighbor."

A pause, then, "Yes, dear. You're not hurt, are you? I heard shots..."

"I'm fine. But I can't talk long. Just wanted to see how you were. Is everything all right?"

"Yes, I think so. It was frightening. They stayed for hours and took away all your things. I couldn't believe it. Your father's collection of tango records, your mother's personal things—all gone."

Diego flinched. He had expected it, if they came for him, but the thought of them even laying hands on the few meager mementos he had of his parents... "Don't worry about that. There wasn't much to take. Did they talk to you?"

"They talked to all the neighbors. And two of them came to see me. They had guns. They asked me if I knew where you might have gone. I said I had no idea. And they wanted to know what I said to you before you went in."

"I'm sorry, Doña Asunta. What did you tell them?"

"I said, 'I told him that he needed to be home tomorrow during the day because the gas people are coming and they need access.'"

He couldn't help smiling.

"When they left I went to take a look. You can't imagine. They smashed the door and turned your apartment to trash. It's awful. But don't worry. I managed to get the door shut. I'll call your landlord and then I'll go in with a pail and a mop and—"

"No, please, Doña Asunta, you have to promise me that you won't do that. It's very important. They could come back. Don't call my landlord either. I don't want you mixed up in this in any way."

She said nothing for a moment. "All right, dear, I understand. And don't worry about the packages you gave me. They are in my daughter's house for safekeeping."

"Thank you," he said. "Thank you for everything. If I had you here I would give you another kiss."

He wondered if she was blushing. "Take care of yourself," she said.

He was again tempted to call Inés, and again rejected the idea. She would be worrying, but he had to stay away from her. Lucas would call her tonight at Valeria's.

He put on the shades and walked out into the bright sunlight. They had ransacked his apartment and taken everything. Well, almost everything. His father's violin and flute, some family papers and photographs—that was all he had thought to salvage, pack up, and entrust to Doña Asunta in case they came. Now, the clothes he was wearing, the gun in his pocket, and the duffel bag he had temporarily stashed in a locker at the nearby Once train station comprised his worldly belongings. Not much to show for the high hopes of his European ancestors coming to the New World, not to mention the ensuing generations of local Fioravantis and Arambillets of which he was the last of the line. His forebears might as well have stayed in Tuscany and the Basque Country.

Aunt Finia's office was four blocks away in the Barolo building. He made doubly sure nobody was tagging along. He stood for a while in the doorway of a music store on Callao Avenue, near the corner facing the shuttered building of the National Congress, examining the hectic intersection, taking in the El Molino cafe with its beautiful needle tower and motionless windmill vanes frozen in time. People jostled one another on the sidewalks, boarded buses and taxis, came in and out of stores. Nothing attracted his notice.

He set off, bordering Congress Square to Avenida de Mayo. Once the pride and joy of Buenos Aires, this boulevard still retained a faded glory in its wide sidewalks lined with sycamores, though the mansions and monumental buildings that used to house newspapers, theaters, and hotels were now uniformly gray with decay.

Ahead, flamboyant and mystical as the temple in India that had inspired it, rose the bulbous stone tower of the Barolo Palace. South America's tallest dessert was how critics had described it in the 1920s, before it was outstripped in height by the Salvo Palace, its twin in Montevideo, two hundred kilometers across the estuary of the River Plate. Every time he saw the Barolo Palace, Diego had to wonder what Dante Alighieri would have thought of this concrete-and-marble shrine to his Divine Comedy. Aunt Finia often recounted how Mario Palanti, a young Italian architect, had persuaded a local textile tycoon named Luis Barolo that Dante's remains needed to be protected from the ravages of European wars by bringing them from Ravenna to this building. It never happened. Dante's remains remained in Ravenna and the Barolo Palace functioned prosaically as offices, its façade and interior decoration glorifying the Divine Comedy: one vertical meter for each canto; seven sections in each of the twenty-two floors—the number of stanzas in the cantos. Inferno at the bottom, Purgatory in the middle, Paradise in the upper stories and lighthouse tower. It was topped by a spire, the entrance to heaven, with an ornament depicting the Southern Cross, which aligned with the Palace's coordinates in early June at precisely 7:45 in the evening. So, Diego remembered thinking as a child, the entrance to hell was in Italy, but the entrance to heaven was right here, with Aunt Finia closest to the celestial regions on the top floor.

Before entering the building, he glanced into the ground-floor passageway, a commercial arcade modeled after turn-of-the-century galleries in Milan. The plaster and stucco, the bronze, granite, and tile, the inscriptions in Latin over the arches—everything looked sadder, dingier than the last time he was here.

"Miss Finia Arambillet, at Euskal Herria," he told the young man behind the counter labeled *Conserjería*.

"Your name, sir?"

"Francisco Aguirre."

The clerk dialed a number. "Miss Arambillet, there's a Mr. Francisco Aguirre here to see you. Yes."

The concierge looked startled as he put down the receiver. New man, Diego thought, not used to Aunt Finia hanging up cold.

"Top floor. Do you know your way?"

Do I, Diego thought as he made for the elevators. In his childhood he had visited Aunt Finia countless times with his mother. While the sisters talked, he had often explored the building, discovering the two secret elevators Barolo had asked the architect to build for him, the fire pits of hell—glass circles built into the floor and guarded by evil gargoyles and snakes—and the nine vaults representing the concentric circles of the Inferno where sinners suffered indescribable pain.

The elevator climbed past the fourteenth floor. He remembered how his mother would smile and remark, "Feeling better already" as they left Purgatory and ascended into Paradise.

Stepping out of the elevator, he walked to the door marked "Euskal Herria, Basque Aid Society." There was now a bell to ring. He rang, waited for the buzzer, and pushed the door open.

As always, the silver-haired woman he saw talking on the telephone stirred in him memories of his mother: the quick green eyes, watchful and challenging, that squinted with amusement under fulsome eyelashes; the throaty voice; the way she pinched her lower lip with her teeth. But in character Aunt Finia was nothing like her younger sister Ximena. According to his self-effacing mother, Finia was the smart one, a free spirit and a beauty. She had traveled widely, and after one stay in northern Euskadi—never to be called the French Basque region in her presence—she had come back a different woman, having found her ethnic roots, and her calling. The Basque nationalist cause became the focal point of her life. She never married—not for lack of suitors, his mother said, but for lack of time.

Aunt Finia gave him a long look, assessing his dyed hair and sunglasses as she waved him to one of the old leather armchairs. He sat and took off the shades.

There were far fewer books on the wall-to-wall bookshelves, he noticed. Books could be dangerous objects nowadays, if they were the wrong kind. Above the shelves were the posters he had grown up with: Biarritz, Bayonne, the Côte Basque, the little boy in a beret and short trousers, and Picasso's *Guernica*. People knew Picasso's *Guernica*, of course, but they didn't know that the town was to the Basque people what Jerusalem was to the Jews, Mecca to the Muslims. When Franco bombed Guernica, he had struck at the heart of the Basque. He had also shot, jailed, and exiled thousands of them and banned their language. But Franco was dead these four years. Now the Basque were free to speak Euskara in public and baptize their children with non-Hispanic names. There was even talk in Spain of autonomy for three Basque provinces, Alava, Guipuzcoa, and Biscay. He smiled at the new posters above Aunt Finia's head: *Euskara: oldest language in Europe*, and *Euskadi is not Spain*. His aunt was busier than ever.

"Hello, Mr. Aguirre," she said when she put down the phone.

"Hello, Miss Arambillet."

"Come with me," she said, getting up and kissing him on the cheek before shouting, "Back in a little while, boys." There were muffled grunts from her minions in the adjoining room.

He knew where they were going. As perpetual leader of the tenants' committee to restore the Barolo Palace—nobody else wanted the job—Aunt Finia had long ago acquired a key to the lighthouse tower. Over time the tower had become her private annex, especially useful now that Basque separatism and violence were on the rise in Europe and all Basque expatriate organizations were under suspicion.

Aunt Finia opened a door in the long hallway and they climbed the narrow stairway to the uppermost region of Paradise, emerging in the confined space of the tower. The giant beacon that had signaled all the way to Uruguay the outcome of the 1923 Dempsey-Firpo heavyweight title fight in New York sat idle on its mounting, its monstrous eye blank. Newer buildings now blocked much of the wraparound view.

"How are things here, Aunt?"

She folded her arms and released a sigh. "We're being watched. I'm not sure we can trust the phones—or the walls, for that matter. Spain wants some of our associates extradited and is pressuring the police to monitor us. But we've got three million Basques in this country—they can't watch us all. All the same, a few of our, shall we say, more enthusiastic supporters have been picked up and questioned."

"Strictly *pour la gallerie*? Round up the usual suspects and all that—or are you worried?"

"Not sure, *mon cher*. We've had some ugly incidents. You saw the buzzer..."

"I did."

"Well," she shrugged it all away, "we'll survive. We've been surviving for five thousand years. Now, what about my only nephew? You were very mysterious on the phone. Trouble?"

He nodded.

"How serious?"

"I need to get out of the country."

She raised one eyebrow. His mother had been able to do that. He had tried it many times in front of a mirror, to no avail.

"What happened? No"—she shut her eyes and raised a hand—"I

don't want to know. Don't tell me."

"I wasn't going to."

She nodded. "And where are you headed?"

"Are you still in touch with our North American relatives?"

"What—you need more stamps?"

He smiled. "Do they still have their cattle ranch in Nevada? I can ride horses and get by in English."

"I'll write them. What about your immediate needs? Money? A place to stay?"

"Advice is what I need, Aunt. Expert advice on what route to follow." He looked out a window at the cityscape and the River Plate beyond. "Pinochet in Chile, Stroessner in Paraguay, military governments all around. Where do I start?"

"Have you considered Uruguay?" she asked.

"First thing. Same language, same accent. But it's too close and too small."

"Brazil is pretty big..." she said.

"Yes," he said. "Brazil may be my best bet. Lots of room to get lost in, lots of immigrants and tourists year round. My Portuguese is passable and I could try sneaking in through the triple border area with Paraguay, up north. It's a smuggler's paradise there. Then, keep going north." He turned to look at her. "But you're the expert. What do you think?"

She joined him by the window. "We do have some experience with your problem. Does Mr. Aguirre have papers?"

He nodded.

"You know," she said, pulling her ear lobe as she thought—another gesture that reminded him of his mother, "Mario Palanti, the architect of this building, was a fascist."

"I know. You've told me the story. He went back to Italy to serve Mussolini."

"Yes. But he was a visionary. He wanted this building and its twin in Montevideo to be the Pillars of Hercules of the River Plate, welcoming ships into the estuary with their beacons."

He said nothing. Where was she going with this?

"Nothing that grand would have worked farther into the estuary, where the delta narrows to only a few kilometers between Argentina and Uruguay."

He was staring at her, understanding dawning. The Tigre Delta, just north of Buenos Aires, comprises thousands of square kilometers of islands, streams, rivers and canals. He had canoed and fished there as a child, among flocks of birds and orange groves.

"Remember my little cottage in the delta? You used to love going there when you were a boy. Nicasio, the caretaker, still lives next door and runs the fruit boat. It's no speed boat, but nobody pays any attention to it."

Of course.

"Six hours to Nueva Palmira, on the coast of Uruguay. He'll know where to drop you off so as not to attract attention. You can take buses to Artigas or any other little town on the Brazilian border. Any trouble, a small bribe will get you through."

He was still staring at her.

"Why didn't I think of that?" he finally said.

There was a mischievous glint in Aunt Finia's eyes. "You're only half-Basque."

Not far from the Barolo Palace on Avenida de Mayo was a post office with a row of phone booths and a collection of telephone directories. Diego bought a handful of tokens and contemplated the long row of volumes.

No use looking up Suárez. It was such a common name; there would be hundreds of listings. Better to try the surnames of family members he had seen in Father Bauer's file on Beatriz Suárez. Safer, too, than trying to contact the immediate family. Well, maybe not safer. He was reaching out in the dark. There was no way to tell who would pick up the telephone at the other end. Argerich should be easier, a shorter list. There couldn't be that many of them in this city. But what if he could find no relatives of the two women in these books? What if the families lived in Córdoba or Jujuy or Patagonia? He could not afford the time to keep looking.

He grimaced and pulled out the first volume.

After an hour poring over minuscule print and dialing dead ends, he stepped out of the booth rubbing his eyes. His last call had finally yielded a relative of Beatriz Suárez, and in a short and cryptic conversation he had arranged to meet the woman tomorrow. He should feel some measure of relief, he thought, but his anxiety had only heightened. He stood in the doorway of the post office and scanned the street.

Half a block away, a man in a hat had stepped out of a car and stood half-turned, studying the magazines in a newsstand while his driver waited in the car. Something about him...

Diego went back inside.

"I'm at the post office near you, on Avenida de Mayo," he said when Aunt Finia answered the phone. "A dog is following me."

"Oh? Does he look as if he may bite?"

"No idea. Dark gray Ford Falcon, a driver and one other man. I may have picked them up when I came to see you."

"Could be."

"What I mean is, they may be interested in you, not me."

"I doubt that. We have an understanding with most dog owners around here. They know we bite back. My guess is he likes you."

She hung up.

Thanks, he thought.

How to shake them. The ground floor arcade of the Barolo Palace ran through to Hipólito Yrigoyen, the street behind the building. He could try losing them there. No. He needed to keep them away from Aunt Finia. Besides, if he had picked up the tail at the Barolo, they probably knew enough to watch both entrances. Assuming for now that there were only these two men in the car, he had to try to get away before reinforcements arrived. The only escape route he could think of was the nearby La Piedad alley.

Before leaving the phone booth he transferred the gun from the inside to the outside pocket of his leather jacket. Lucas had stitched up the wound but the painkillers were wearing off and his left arm hurt like hell and felt useless.

He left the post office, walked to the corner, and turned north, away from the Barolo. Another turn and he was headed down Mitre Street to the Pasaje La Piedad, a U-shaped derelict alleyway. He walked slowly, never turning his head. He knew they were there.

The alley was deserted, in shadows, as he had expected. He strolled down the first arm of the U, made the turn—and then ran to the next corner, peering out cautiously into the second arm. Empty. They hadn't split up to come in through both entrances and cut him off. That could mean that the driver was staying in the car to guard both exits while his partner followed their prey on foot.

He turned the corner, slipped into a doorway, and flattened himself against the boarded-up entrance. His gun was in his hand. Soon he heard the footsteps on his trail, coming closer. One man, from the sound of it, checking each locked door as he passed.

When the man wearing the hat rounded the corner, he stood there for a moment scanning the alley, then each doorway, until inevitably his eyes found and locked onto Diego and his raised gun.

Sergeant Maidana.

Diego's heart hammered. Every nerve in his body went taut.

"I just want to talk, Captain," Maidana said, eyeing the gun.

"Then talk." Diego did not take his eyes off the sergeant. "But don't come any closer."

"Look, everybody understands how you feel. It's been hard on us all. The colonel says it's all right, you can come back. And Father Bauer—"

Diego felt the other man's breath behind him the same instant a hand gripped his gun wrist, deflecting his aim away from Maidana as his arms were pinned in a vise. He struggled to yank his right arm free, pivoting instinctively on his left leg to twist his assailant around and place him between Maidana and himself—but an explosive kick from the sergeant drove the gun from his hand. Maidana's boot lashed out again, grazing Diego's plexus and slamming into his left forearm. A bolt of pain shot through him and his knees buckled. Clutching his arm with his right hand, he doubled over in agony.

"Nice work, Sergeant." It was Corporal Elizalde's voice. "He never saw me coming."

Diego tried to look up but his vision was blurry. Through a blaze of pain, he felt, more than saw, Maidana's teeth bare in a snarl as the sergeant leaned down and hissed, "You may experience some discomfort, captain. This is how we deal with traitors."

The gleam of the blade triggered something in Diego's body, which moved of its own accord. His knees sprang suddenly straight, catapulting his head into Maidana's jaw. There was a crunching sound of smashed teeth and Diego saw blood spurt from the sergeant's mouth.

"Sergeant...!" he heard Elizalde's voice as the corporal released him and stepped to Maidana's side.

Diego had no strength left. He dropped to one knee, waiting for the blow, the cut, or the shot that would finish him off.

It didn't come. Instead, he heard two soft thumps followed by a cry of pain and a loud gasp, and the sound of two bodies collapsing near him.

He looked up. Maidana and Elizalde lay unconscious, side by side, sprawled on the cobblestone like broken dolls. Aunt Finia stood over them, flanked by two of the biggest men Diego had ever seen. She was looking straight at him.

"Hardheaded," she said to her escorts, putting the blackjack back into her purse. "He's a Basque all right."

20

"Dr. Hardoy," Solo said when the chairman answered the phone, "I know that you're leaving soon for the polo field to meet my friend Malena—"

"Have you heard from her?" Hardoy interrupted. "Is our meeting still on?"

"I've heard nothing, sir, and I need to talk to her myself. It's very important. I want to come with you."

Solo waited while Hardoy considered this. "Your friend seems to want to keep you out of this business; you realize that, don't you? That's probably why she didn't tell you what was in her letter."

"Yes, I think so too. But I can't locate her and I'm worried. Admiral Rinaldi is her boss..."

Solo didn't say any more. He didn't think he needed to.

There was silence from Hardoy. At length, he said, "I wanted to involve nobody else in this matter until I knew more. But she's your friend. Meet me downstairs in ten minutes."

Solo put down the receiver but did not remove his hand. He looked at his watch again. Saturnina and the kids should be home from school by now, but ten minutes might not be time enough to place the call and wait for the operator to ring him back. His conversation two hours earlier with Alberto, who after many tries had gotten through the hotel's busy lines, had added fresh anxiety to Solo's deepening gloom. It was only by a stern effort of will, Solo knew, that his friend had not broken down during their short conversation. Having finally spoken to the Mahlers, Alberto had learned why nobody answered the phone until late last night: his aunt and uncle were out making funeral arrangements for their daughter. Devastated as he was by the news of Débora Mahler's death, Alberto had yet summoned the fortitude to tell him about Phyllis. The kids had never noticed his exchange with their mother, Alberto said. Still, Solo wanted desperately to talk to them and Saturnina and reassure himself that everything was all right.

The phone shrilled and Solo's hand jerked back as if from an electric shock.

"Hello."

"Solo?"

He didn't recognize the voice. "Yes. Who's this?"

"Néstor Reidlonger. Malena's friend."

Solo felt a touch of relief. Reidlonger would know where Malena had been. "Yes, Néstor, how did you locate me?"

"Malena told me you might call. And the paper says the OAS group is at the Metropole. I hope your phone is safe."

Something inside Solo froze. The phone. He was so used to being the invisible interpreter, of little interest to anyone, that he had given the phone no thought.

Before he could reply, Reidlonger went on. "Do you know where Malena is? Have you been in touch with her?"

Solo's heart sank. "Not since Washington," he said. "Her father told me she's staying with a friend."

"I know. I called his house too and spoke to the maid." His dispirited tone made it all too clear that the disappointment was mutual, that he had hoped for news of Malena from Solo.

Solo said, "That's why I called you, but you weren't home."

"Yes. When Malena didn't show up, I moved out of my apartment."

"You moved out of your apartment..." Solo echoed the phrase, disconcerted.

"She was supposed to take a taxi from the airport to my place," Reidlonger went on. "She did fly in. I checked with the airline. But she never came to my apartment."

"Wait, what are you saying? You think something's happened to her? Couldn't she be staying with another friend?"

"Listen, when she called from Washington to say she was coming, she told me she needed to talk to you, to ask you a favor."

"Yes, she came to see me," Solo said, guardedly now, trying to decide how much to tell Reidlonger. Should he let him know that he was about to leave for the polo grounds to meet Malena? Reidlonger too was her friend. But Malena had been very explicit: Hardoy, you and me—nobody else must know. If she wanted Reidlonger to know about the meeting, she could have told him herself. Solo wet his lips. Quicksand everywhere. He would let Malena worry about Reidlonger, who was not being very forthcoming himself. "She said she wanted to get together here, in Buenos Aires. She gave me her father's phone number and yours."

"Did she mention to you something called Operation Condor?" Reidlonger said.

"Condor?" Solo repeated. The name sparked no recollection in him other than the German Condor Legion that had bombed Guernica in the Spanish Civil War. "No. What is that?"

"We need to meet," Reidlonger remained infuriatingly terse. "but I have to figure out where. I'll call you if I hear from Malena."

"Néstor, you say you moved out, but when I called your apartment a man answered."

"*Puta madre...*" The softly uttered obscenity rang in Solo's ear. Reidlonger's voice was in grim earnest. "What did you say to him? Tell me exactly."

"I asked for you and said I was a friend of Malena's."

"Did you give him your name?"

"Yes."

"Your full name?

"Yes."

"Your phone number? The name of your hotel?"

Solo thought back. "No," he said.

"How long did you talk?"

"Seconds. I was on my way out. It was just a few words. Look, what is going on?"

Reidlonger's voice seemed suddenly faint with fatigue. He said, "We have to meet, Solo. Wait for my call."

The line clicked off.

The Metropole elevator was painfully slow to arrive. Solo boarded it and leaned against the back wall, staring at his shoes. A group of hotel guests trooped in on the fourth floor, whispering, clearly disgruntled. Service was appalling. And how could the guests enjoy their stay with the sight of all those people in line...

He waited in the lobby by the bank of elevators until Hardoy came down. In the chairman's hand Solo recognized the sheet of paper with the diagram from Malena's letter. They got into a cab and, true to their security routine, remained silent until they were let off at the entrance to the polo stadium on Libertador Avenue, across from the city race-track.

"The match should be almost over," Hardoy said, checking his watch, then consulting Malena's drawing as they strode through the unguarded gate into a pungent smell of turf and horses and a distant hubbub from the playing field.

The sounds grew louder as they walked along the rear of the grandstand: galloping hoofbeats, mallet strikes, shouting and cheering culminating in a loud collective sigh. As they emerged into the open space at the end of the grandstand, they could see the playing field. Solo counted eight galloping riders and two mounted umpires. A scoreboard showed a tie at ten in the eighth chukker. He had no idea what a chukker was or how many of them there were in a polo match.

They sidled up to a cluster of early-departing fans who were stealing a last look at the game before beating the rush to the exits. Ponies and helmeted riders thundered past. A minute later, a goal at the opposite end of the field set off a stadium-wide burst of cheering and applause. After a few more seconds of commotion on the field, the action stopped and the stands began emptying.

He kept behind Hardoy as the crowd poured down and churned around them on its way out. The chairman pressed through in the opposite direction, toward the stables.

Rounding a long shed with ponies stalled side by side, Hardoy pushed open a door in the rear of the building and they entered what Solo guessed was a stockroom that doubled as an office. There was a metal desk and a bookshelf displaying photographs of horses, polo teams, and players holding trophies aloft, and in one corner a kitchenette with an ancient, small upright stove. The room smelled of horses, leather, and hay. By a wall hung with saddles and riding gear stood a tall, thin Asian man wearing a dark suit and a black patch over one eye. His long, spare frame was crowned with wiry gray hair.

He came over to Hardoy and Solo and extended his hand. "I'm Dr. Alejandro Yoshida, a lawyer and friend of Miss Uriburu's." He did not smile.

"But where is Malena?" Solo asked after he and Hardoy had introduced themselves.

"Yes, where is she?" Yoshida replied, looking at them as if he had expected them to produce her. "She said we would all be meeting here"—he looked at his watch—"ten minutes ago."

"When did she tell you that?" Solo insisted.

"Last week. She called me from Washington to say a friend of hers would be arranging this meeting."

"And you haven't talked to her since?"

"No." Yoshida trained his single eye on Solo. "You don't know where she is either, do you?"

Hardoy and Solo exchanged a look, and the chairman said, "Why don't we get started while we wait for her?"

Yoshida hesitated, then nodded. From a stack of plastic chairs by the desk, he lifted out five and ranged them around the center of the room.

"Sorry for all our precautions," he said when they were seated. "Malena's uncle breeds polo ponies and keeps this small office here. She thought it would be a good place to meet and I agreed. I'm sure you gentlemen realize there are considerable, shall we say, risks associated with coming to see you at the Metropole."

Hardoy merely nodded.

"I'm not thinking solely of myself," Yoshida went on, "though self-preservation is a plea of no small merit in a country where more than a hundred lawyers have disappeared." There was no humor in the thin pencilings of his smile. "People are placing themselves at great risk by coming to see you. Sooner or later you will leave. And they will stay."

Hardoy grimaced. "Dr. Yoshida, we are wasting time."

Yoshida's eye blinked, but Solo could not tell if the lawyer was surprised by Hardoy's abruptness.

"We are wasting valuable time," Hardoy repeated. "It sounds as if you've been involved with human rights for some time. If so, you know we can't answer for anyone's safety any more than you can. People come forward at their own peril. No one should be under any illusions about that."

Yoshida nodded, as though this was the answer he expected but did not want to hear. He was truly thin, Solo noted, as the man got up and opened a door in the rear of the room. In came a youth in jeans and sweater. He had a slight build, sun-browned skin, and strong Indian features that reminded Solo of Saturnina's.

"I want you gentlemen to know," Yoshida said, gesturing for the newcomer to sit down, "that this young man's family tried to talk him out of coming to see you."

The youth shifted uneasily in his chair, and when he spoke, Solo heard a Chilean accent. "They are worried, I know," he said, "but I have to do this. Malena—Miss Uriburu—said she would arrange it. She has been so kind to my family. She found a job for my father, helped us with money. I thought she would be here..." He looked at Yoshida.

"We are waiting for her," Yoshida said. "In the meantime, let these gentlemen hear your story."

The young man said, "I'm not sure where to start. My name is Basilio Cifuentes. My family and I are from the north of Chile. We moved to Santiago six years ago, when my father lost his job as a horse trainer. My brother-in-law Bernardo was a union delegate at his factory until everything changed with Pinochet's coup. They started arresting all union people. Soldiers came to Bernardo's home and broke down the door. I was there, so they took me too. They threw hoods over our heads and took us to the stadium."

"That's the stadium in Santiago," Yoshida said.

"I know," Hardoy said.

"People were being brought in all the time in army and police buses and trucks," Basilio said. "We had to lie face down on the cement floor, hands behind our heads while they beat us and kicked us for hours. Some passed out. Others were taken to the interrogation rooms in the basement. It was very cold. Most of us never had a chance to get into warm clothes."

"Did they give you any food?" Hardoy asked.

"I got a small cup of cold coffee the five days I was there. No one dared ask for anything, sir."

"Who was in charge at the stadium while you were there?"

"A colonel. I don't know his name. From time to time he would order the soldiers to fire their guns into the walls of the stadium. We lay on top of one another, scared to death, while they did that. That first day, one man complained and the colonel ordered him beaten and taken to the basement. The man became terrified and tried to get free of the guards, so the colonel started beating him until he killed him. Then he took out his pistol and shot the dead man in the head. We all saw it. There were thousands of us. Everybody started shouting. But the colonel ordered the troops to fire into the air and the protest was drowned out."

Yoshida put a hand on the boy's shoulder. "The interrogators. Malena wants you to tell them about the interrogators."

"The interrogators, yes. Some were foreigners."

Hardoy's face darkened. He looked at Yoshida, then back at the boy.

"Most were Brazilian. All foreign prisoners were turned over to them. The soldiers called them the 'experts' because they were giving a course on interrogation at the Ministry of Defense. Prisoners were called by name over the loudspeakers and told to go to the basement. After a few minutes their screams could be heard all over the stadium." Basilio swallowed and took a moment to catch his breath. "I was allowed to go to the bathroom once. It was next to an open room full of dead bodies. Some had their stomachs ripped open. It was hard to tell they were human—they were so shapeless. The walls and floors of the bathroom were splattered with blood and flesh. There were..."

He stopped, his mouth open, his eyes wide and unblinking. With a chill deep in his body, Solo recognized that look. He had seen it at the Villa Devoto jail on the face of the first woman who spoke up. He could barely look at the boy.

Yoshida produced a flask from his coat pocket and looked around for a glass. Glad to move and actually do something, Solo got up, went to the kitchenette and opened cabinets until he found one.

"Thank you," Yoshida said, pouring out a small measure of amber liquid for Basilio. "Drink this."

"I don't..."

"Drink it. It will do you good."

Reluctantly, the boy gulped down the drink. His face colored and he started coughing. He pushed away the glass.

"Take your time," Yoshida said.

"On the fourth day," Basilio breathed deeply and exhaled, "after a very long session of torture, even some soldiers seemed to be affected by all the screaming. The colonel took the microphone and started talking about peace, about how he and his men were working to protect the people of Chile, and he asked everyone to keep calm. When he finished, something strange happened." The boy looked at the floor, shrugged. "We all clapped. I don't know why. It was very quiet applause. Then, they called Bernardo's name over the loudspeakers. I saw him being taken to the basement. I recognized the clothes he was wearing."

An invisible claw had buried itself in the nape of Solo's neck, digging into nerve endings, darting pain up and down his spine. His eyes strayed now and again to the front door, waiting for it to open and admit Malena. But each passing minute fed his growing certainty that she would not come.

"How did you get out?" Hardoy asked.

"On the fifth day they let me go. I don't know why. I was sure I was going to die there. The last two days, when they were shooting off guns, I gave my name and address to two other prisoners, so that if they got out they could tell my family that I died there. But when my turn came to be questioned they let me go, and I..." He fingered the empty glass. "They said I could go and—I didn't even ask about Bernardo. I left as fast as I could."

"Of course you did," Yoshida said. "You did the right thing. I've told you that. If you hadn't left you might be dead."

Basilio was silent, then said, "We left Chile and came here. While he was looking for work training horses, my father met Malena and she found him a job with her uncle. I found one with Mrs. Prats."

"Prats?" Hardoy asked. "Is that Sofía Prats, the wife of General Carlos Prats?"

From the newspaper he had picked up at the Santiago airport, Solo had learned that Prats was a Chilean general who had broken with

Pinochet and exiled himself in Buenos Aires. A CIA-trained assassin named Michael Townley had recently been extradited to the U.S. at the request of the Carter administration. Among other crimes, he had confessed to murdering Prats in Buenos Aires five years ago, and Letelier in D.C. two years later.

"Yes, General Prats's wife," Yoshida put in, his tone growing grave, almost mournful. "The Prats led a quiet life here. He worked as a tire salesman and she managed a gift shop—until they were both blown up in their car not far from here. Same modus operandi as the Letelier assassination in Washington."

"Mrs. Prats was worried," Basilio said. "Sometimes she would ask me to walk her home. They were receiving threatening phone calls and were being followed, she said. The Chilean consulate would not update their passports, so they couldn't leave Argentina."

Hardoy looked glumly at Yoshida. "Townley has confessed to the Prats and other murders for the Pinochet regime. Are you saying there is more to it?"

Yoshida took several folders out of a briefcase, which had remained out of sight under his chair, and placed them on his lap. "These are detailed accounts and affidavits by exiles from neighboring countries living in Argentina. They are terrified. More of them keep disappearing. We, the few lawyers still handling these cases, believe that they're being turned over to agents from their countries of origin or simply killed. There's some sort of secret arrangement between governments to murder their political opponents anywhere in the world. It's called Operation Condor. Have you heard of it?"

Solo heard Reidlonger's voice asking the same question.

Hardoy looked at Malena's empty chair. "Operation Condor. It's what Miss Uriburu's note said we would be talking about," he said somberly.

21

Three wrenching hours later, when Solo walked out of the hotel, the sky had cleared and a glossy wedge of new moon was rising over Buenos Aires. People were everywhere, drawn outdoors by the mild weather. A couple of stiff drinks had untwisted his stomach, but he still felt raw and anxious. He had called home to satisfy himself that all was well there. The kids were already asleep—he had just missed them—but Saturnina said they were fine, and she had not seen Phyllis following them again. If Saturnina was worried about her deportation hearing, she did not mention it. Neither did he.

He had less than an hour before meeting Inés at her school. Walking there would help work off the tension in his body. He needed to think, to sort things out. Before leaving the polo grounds Yoshida and Hardoy had agreed that it was best not to file a missing person report or take any other formal action involving the Argentine authorities until every means had been tried to locate Malena. The word "disappeared" had been left consciously unuttered in that conversation. Yoshida said he would put the word out to every informant he knew and report back.

Solo could not wait that long. There had to be some way he could search out what happened to her. He had called her father again and learned from the maid that he was attending a funeral in Brazil and that Malena had not called the house.

He prayed Inés could help. She might provide a lead to other friends of Malena's, or places she frequented in the city—anything he could follow up on or pass along to Yoshida to investigate. But first he had to decide what to tell Inés. Part of him wanted to spill everything to her—to hell with his professional oath of silence. No. If Malena had disappeared, he knew piercingly that he must not involve Inés. He had already blundered once by betraying Alberto's confidences to the admiral. Débora Mahler could have paid for his stupidity with her life.

And then there was Inés's boyfriend. He was in the military. What if he dragged her into something? What if he too was a psychopath in uniform, a torturer, a baby thief, a pusher of drugged prisoners out of flying airplanes? As indignant as Inés appeared to be about her government, would she even believe what Solo—an outsider with barely days back in the country—had learned that the military, and by implication her boyfriend, were doing? He could hardly believe it himself. She would think he was jealous. Which he was.

He walked by a group of jaunty porteños entering a handsome art nouveau building, from whose upper floors the sounds of a tango drifted down to the street. *Club Español* read the bronze plaque by the door. Buenos Aires was pulsing with nightlife. At this hour D.C. would have emptied out, the federal tide having ebbed back to the suburban cocktail hour and the television account of its own workday. Here, television had yet to turn life into a spectator sport. The streets were noisy with people, and he let the bustle sweep over him, douse him in its reassuring reality. It was like stepping out of a theater after watching a gut-wrencher. On the street, the drama dissipated, traffic was an instant lenitive, the sidewalk terra firma. You stepped onto it and real life resumed.

But what he had witnessed *was* real life. All of it. The Mahlers, the people lined up outside the Metropole, the prisoners in Villa Devoto. It was all happening.

Only, it wasn't happening here, on these busy streets. It wasn't

happening to these plain ordinary people going about their plain ordinary lives. That family window-shopping, the man smoking a pipe
and walking his dog, the dressed-up couple going out to dinner—it
wasn't happening to them. Or to that young woman and her mother
picking out a wedding gown in the bridal shop. Or to the browsers in
the bookstore, the diners in the restaurants. They had no idea what was
going on behind steel doors, in prisons and military installations, in
the Athletic Club.

He turned away from the broad expanse of 9 de Julio Avenue, with
its huge centerpiece obelisk, into Lavalle Street and the theater district.
Here, neon ruled the night. Behind the etched curlicues of tearoom
windows, elegant matrons chatted over pastries. Elderly couples em-
boldened by the fair weather took the air, arm in arm, sidestepping the
outdoor tables set up by the more enterprising cafes. Bursts of joviality
beckoned from bars where the smart set mingled, their tanned faces
set off by brightly colored sweaters studiously slung over shoulders.

Nobody had a clue. A place like the Athletic Club might be around
the corner, or on this very block, in some innocent-looking building.
Colonel Indart and Admiral Rinaldi might be there right now—listening to their victims' shrieks. Or they might be on the town tonight,
mingling with these crowds, dining with them in the same restaurant,
watching a movie in the same theater, then going back to Villa Devoto,
the Naval School, the Athletic Club.

Nobody knew.

Or did they?

The thought nearly brought him up short halfway through an intersection. A chorus of honking escorted him across the avenue.

Did they know? Did they even suspect? That was too terrible to
contemplate. And yet, could you live here and not suspect? People were
disappearing right and left, all over the country. Not a handful. Thousands. They were being held in secret camps, tortured and murdered
by the government—all with the complicity of the police, the courts,
the Church. And they weren't low-lifes nobody would miss. They were

lawyers, students, factory workers, priests. They had families, bosses, employees, neighbors, friends. Didn't people wonder? Or were they shutting their eyes? Could it be that people didn't want to know? *If they were arrested, they must have done something*, Mr. Maldonado said.

He walked past the neon into quiet barrios tucked away among busy thoroughfares, along tree-lined cobblestone streets, through shadowy parks tenanted by amorous couples. He envied them. He wished he didn't know.

He was beginning to think he had lost his bearings when, rounding a corner, he saw across the wide stretch of Libertador and Figueroa Alcorta avenues the light-flooded structure of the law school. It was a neoclassical enormity dwarfing any he could remember. From its Olympian podium, Ionic columns fluted up to their carved capitals, brilliant in the glare of powerful floodlights trained on them from either side.

He walked up the steps, breathing hard. Beyond the gigantic doors lay a huge inner hall with more enormous columns. A student directed him to the rear of the building, where another marble hall showcased large statues and busts of legal scholars. More marble stairs took him to the second floor. He checked door numbers against the note in his hand and finally opened a door.

He was in the rear of a large classroom. Seated on lustrous wooden benches, an audience of students watched one of their number face three professors across a mammoth desk mounted on a platform. Everyone was smartly turned out, the young men in coats and ties, the women in stylish dresses and high heels. Solo located Inés and circled the rear benches to where she sat. He eased in beside her.

"You didn't have to come," she whispered. "I could have dropped by your hotel tomorrow."

"We'll be out of town tomorrow, flying to Mendoza," he whispered back. "And I needed the fresh air."

She nodded and handed him the envelope with Mr. Maldonado's

check. "It's addressed to his bank in Miami. Just put a stamp on it and drop it in a mailbox when you get back. My father apologizes for not delivering it himself, but tonight is his poker night."

He took the envelope absently, and heard her tell him about her efforts to locate a survivor of the *Ciudad de Asunción*. He made an effort to focus, but his mind kept returning to that stadium of screams in Chile, to Villa Devoto and its women prisoners and the photographer's flash popping over and over around them.

"What's happening here? What are you doing?" he asked abruptly, and only after he said it did he realize he had interrupted her.

Students were allowed to watch the exams, she explained. Her turn was coming up tomorrow. Her translation program unfortunately included this course on copyright law.

"And you detest all lawyers," he said, looking at the three examining professors. "You and Shakespeare."

She smiled. "I had to translate that passage for a class. Kill all the translators is what Shakespeare would say if he saw my translation." She nudged him. "Let's go. I've seen enough."

They walked out, shut the door behind them, and stood in the empty corridor. Suddenly, impelled by a mutual urge they had to acknowledge, they embraced.

"Solo..." There was an old sadness in her voice, a buried longing he knew only too well. "What happened to us?"

He shook his head. "I don't know."

She sighed. "And now you're here, and I'm..." She stopped and stepped back from him.

"Diego...?"

She nodded. "I need to work this out. We were going to meet Sunday night to talk, but he didn't show. Or call. That's not like him. I haven't heard from him since Saturday." Her face was clouded with worry. "I told Valeria I'm not going to our French class tonight. I borrowed my father's car and I'm going to look for him."

"Look for him?" Solo suppressed a quick intake of breath. "Doesn't he answer the phone?"

She shook her head. "It's all very secret. Because of his work, he says. I don't even have his phone number or address. He calls me. For the time being, he says, until things cool off."

Solo gave her an incredulous look. No address, no phone number. That was all the confirmation he needed that the man was mixed up in something sinister. "So how do you propose to find him?"

"He teaches tango downtown, at a cafe called the Ideal. He should be there tonight."

"I'm coming with you."

"Solo..."

He raised a hand. "Don't worry, I won't stay. I just want to stretch my time with you."

He was ready for more objections from her. He knew he was bullying her, but he didn't care.

She surprised him. She smiled a little and said, "Thank you."

After they seated themselves at the Ideal and Inés went off to the ladies' room, Solo surveyed the place. The hall had few customers, with some seedy-looking characters here and there. On the dance floor three couples gyrated to an old tango, their sinuous dance riveting the eyes and flashing cameras of a dozen Japanese tourists in a cluster of tables.

Why hadn't he told her yet? Why hadn't he described what he had witnessed, or spoken about Malena? He had so wanted to see her, to talk to her. Then, the exam, their embrace, her preoccupation with Diego—and he had said nothing. If something happened to her because he let her go about her normal life, suspecting nothing because he had told her nothing, he would never forgive himself.

But why should anything happen to her? Wasn't it safer not to know? Most people here seemed to have no idea what was going on, or chose not to interpret the signs—and were safer for it, weren't they?

Don't get involved. But her boyfriend had to know, and he hadn't told her. Why? Solo had to find out. He had to be sure that by telling her what he knew he wouldn't somehow be causing a fatal calamity, as he had probably done with the admiral. She thought her boyfriend might be missing, and Solo knew what that meant here. The last thing he wanted was to agitate her further to the point where she might try to find Diego by contacting the military.

He should leave this place, this grimly festive dance hall. Inés had probably gone to the bathroom to give him a hint to leave. Meeting Diego now would be awkward for her, and Solo's presence would just aggravate her discomfort. Yet while the Ideal looked harmless enough, it was probably not a good place for a woman to be alone; before leaving, he told himself, he would just make sure Diego was on the premises, or would soon appear. He got up and made for the bar.

"Diego, the tango instructor," he asked the bartender. "Is he here tonight?"

"Fermín!" the bartender called out. An old waiter serving a table looked up. The bartender's thumb pointed sideways to Solo. "Looking for Diego."

The old man nodded and briefly raised his index finger asking for a minute while he snapped out change from a leather billfold shiny with age. Solo saw Inés sitting down at their table and went back to her.

"I asked about Diego," he said as the old waiter shuffled over and recognized Inés.

"Hello, miss,"

"Hello, Fermín." She smiled.

Fermín shook his head. "He's missed two nights in a row. The boss is not happy."

"No messages? Nothing?"

"Nothing."

"Something's happened to him," she said when driving Solo back to the Metropole. "It's not like him to vanish like this. And lately he's been behaving oddly."

"What do you mean?"

"Jittery. It's hard to explain."

Solo said, "Look, there's something I—"

A car flashing a blue dashboard light was overtaking them and signaling them to pull over.

Inés glanced fearfully at Solo and eased the car to the curb. The other vehicle, a dark blue Ford Falcon, double-parked alongside them, boxing them in. A voice came from it.

"Turn on your inside light and step out with your hands up.

They looked at each other, then did as they were told. Three men dressed in dark civilian clothes and carrying mini submachine guns got out of the other vehicle. The block was deserted. A mercury streetlight cast a pallid orange glow over the low-slung buildings.

One man strode up to them, waved his gun, and pushed first Inés and then Solo against the wall. Stay calm, Solo told himself, don't give them any excuse. From the edge of his eye he looked at Inés but her face was shadowed by the wall.

"IDs!" the same man commanded. He wore a loose-fitting hat. Under its brim Solo could see a white strip of cloth that looked like a bandage.

Inés produced her ID and Solo handed the man his American passport. At the sight of it, the man stared at him. He opened it to Solo's photograph on the first page and a white rectangle fluttered out. The man picked it up.

"Don't move," he said after looking at the papers. He went back to his car and leaned in to talk to someone.

Solo glanced at Inés. He could not tell if the pallor of her cheeks was a reflection of the street lamp. "Don't open your mouth," he said to her in English. "Let me do the talking."

The two men guarding them looked at each other and one of them took a step forward. But the man with the hat was coming back.

"Get in our car," he said to Solo.

Solo hesitated and motioned toward Inés. "What about her?"

"Get in the car," the man repeated in a low growl.

Solo obeyed, opening the rear door and sliding into the back seat. The man facing him had a pockmarked face and intense black eyes. He too wore a hat, a black beret with a bandage visible under it. He leaned forward and looked fixedly at Solo.

"Shut the door," he said. His cheeks looked puffy and the words came out with some difficulty, all but slurred. But there was no mistaking the menacing tone, the violence smoldering in those eyes. Solo pulled the car door shut.

"Why were you asking about Diego Fioravanti?" the man said.

The Ideal. The bartender or the waiters must have had orders to call if anybody asked for Diego. Or else a spotter had been there and had overheard him ask the bartender. Maybe these thugs were Diego's friends. Be very careful now. He shrugged. "He's the tango instructor, isn't he? What's this about?"

The man's face was a mask. "You were just looking for a tango lesson," he said.

"That's right. I'm here for only a few days and somebody recommended this Diego as a good instructor. Why? What's wrong? Who are you?"

The man nodded in the direction of Inés, still standing against the wall. "Who is she?"

If they had questioned the old waiter and he had pegged Inés as Diego's girlfriend, lying would be useless. But they seemed to think that he, Solo, and not Inés, was interested in Diego.

"She's an old friend of mine," Solo said, keeping composure in his voice. "Her name is Inés Maldonado. You have her ID."

The man's burning eyes studied Solo's face. "So, you don't know Fioravanti."

"Never met him in my life. I don't even know what he looks like.

That's why I was asking the bartender at the cafe. Now, if you don't mind, we'd like to..." he turned to reach for the door handle.

The man's right arm shot out and his fingers clamped onto Solo's shoulder.

"Where did you get this?" The man's left hand held up the white rectangle that had dropped from Solo's passport. In the orange half-light of the car's interior Solo recognized Admiral Rinaldi's business card.

"Where do you think I got it? The admiral gave it to me last week in his office."

He felt the uncertainty in the man's eyes and pressed on. "His private numbers are on the back. It's late, but why don't you call and ask him?"

The man was silent for a minute. Then, the grip on Solo's shoulder eased and the arm withdrew.

"So you don't know Diego Fioravanti," the man repeated with a sneer, his hand mockingly dusting off the lapel of Solo's jacket.

Solo started to say something but thought better of it.

"Well," the man said, inserting the admiral's card in the passport, then tapping the cover with one finger. "This card says I have to give you the benefit of the doubt. This once. Remember that if we meet again."

He handed the passport back with a disdainful smile and Solo took it.

"And if you happen to run into Fioravanti before I find him, give him this message from Sergeant Maidana: 'He's all mine.' Tell him Colonel Indart said so."

Mustering all his calm, Solo slid the passport into a pocket and drew back. His fears were realized. Colonel Indart.

The man reached past Solo to pull the door handle. The door swung open and Solo got out.

He and Inés stood on the sidewalk as the Ford Falcon drove off.

"Who were they? What did they want?" Inés asked in a quivering voice when they climbed back into her car. Nervously, she turned the key in the ignition and the idling engine responded with a loud screech.

"Let's get out of here," Solo said. "You and I have to talk."

22

"You're picking up Dr. Hardoy at the OAS office on your way to the airport," Doris said, putting down on the utility table the fresh pile of case files she had carried in. She took part of the pile and sat down at the other end of the table. "Dr. Fonseca is almost ready to go."

Solo finished alphabetically sorting and labeling the stack of complaints in front of him and reached for another handful from the new pile.

"I'm ready too," he said. Mendoza would be a change of scene from this hotel with its endless line of victims' families outside, and from the unnerving fear that still flooded him after last night.

As he and Inés sat in the parked car across from the Metropole, he had told her everything, given her an account of Alberto and the Mahlers, the admiral, Malena and Hardoy, Colonel Indart and the visit to Villa Devoto, and the meeting with Yoshida and his Chilean client at the polo grounds. Then he had related his conversation with Sergeant Maidana.

Inés listened without interrupting, her face registering disbelief, then horror. When he was done, she remained silent for a long time.

"It explains so many things," she finally said. "I should have figured it out."

"How could you? He never told you."

"No, I don't mean Diego. I'm talking about what they're doing in this country. Diego isn't one of them. I know."

He bit back a sharp reply. "How do you know?"

"I know him. That's why it worries me that he hasn't gotten in touch with me."

"Look," he said, still inwardly shuddering to think what would have happened if the brute in the car had known she was Diego's girl-friend, "you can't go around looking for him. He may not want to be found. You'll just be endangering yourself and him as well."

She didn't reply.

"Inés," he went on earnestly, "why don't you come to the U.S.? Just for a while, until things calm down. Alberto and I could help you find a job in D.C. If you stay here, you may be placing both yourself and him at risk. You see that, don't you?"

Again she did not answer, and he had known they were both too shaken and drained to argue about it anymore.

The phone rang. Solo punched the blinking plastic square and picked up. "Hello."

"Is this Mr. Kevin Zollerzaynow?" a distant female voice said in English with a Southern accent. There was a faint hum on the line.

"Yes, who is this?"

"U.S. operator, sir. I have an emergency call for you. Hold on."

Solo's heart began to thud. The kids.

Doris looked questioningly at him and mouthed, "Don't be long—you're leaving in a few minutes."

"Go ahead, sir," the operator said.

"Solo, are you there?" Alberto's frenzied voice came over the wire.

"Yes, Alberto. What's wrong?"

"The Mahlers. Their house is surrounded by soldiers. There are two army trucks outside and a helicopter overhead."

"What?" Solo drew back in his chair. The admiral. Who else could be doing this but the admiral?

"Their phone still works," Alberto went on, "but they couldn't get through to the Metropole, so they called me—"

"Doris!" Solo yelled.

"—and I had to break the connection with them to call you." Alberto was saying.

"Tell me again their number and address," Solo said into the mouthpiece, and scribbled the information on the cover of a Buenos Aires telephone directory. He turned to Doris, now standing over him. "What's the number of the OAS office here?"

She rattled it off by heart and he wrote it down, then spoke into the phone. "Alberto, I have two lines here. I am going to disconnect so I can call the Mahlers and Hardoy."

"Do it."

Solo clicked off and stabbed out the number for the Mahlers. On the first ring, a male voice answered, straining to make itself heard above a dull background roar punctuated by loud pounding and rattling.

"Mr. Mahler, Héctor, is that you?" Solo shouted. "This is Solo, Alberto's friend at the Metropole."

"It's him, it's him, Alberto got him," Solo heard Héctor Mahler say to his wife, then, "Solo, the soldiers are outside. They are banging guns on our walls and window gratings. The whole house is shaking. Do you hear that?"

Héctor Mahler had to be pointing the receiver in the direction of their front door—Solo heard shouts and the pounding grew louder. He could picture Alberto's aunt and uncle cowering in a corner of their little house, plaster falling in chunks around them, the photograph of Alberto, David and Débora on the otherwise bare walls jerking loose from its makeshift frame. He heard glass breaking, so loud it drowned out the pounding.

"Héctor, are you all right? Can you still hear me?"

"Yes, yes. The wall mirror shattered..."

"Listen," Solo frantically cut in. "Don't hang up, Héctor. Stay on the line. I am going to put you on hold while I get help on the other line. Just hold on."

Without waiting for a reply, Solo pressed in quick succession the red button, putting Héctor Mahler on hold, and the plastic square of the second line, then punched in the number of the OAS office.

"Organization of American States, good morning."

"This is an emergency," Solo blurted out. "I'm calling from the Metropole. I need to speak at once with Dr. Hardoy. He's in your office. It's a matter of life and death. Hurry, please!"

"Just a moment, please."

Come on, come on. He watched the Mahler's line blinking away. If only this was one of those newer phones that allowed for conference calls. He desperately wanted to put the OAS operator on hold and switch back to the house, but he couldn't risk Hardoy coming on while he was talking to Héctor.

"Please hurry, operator, it's an emergency!" he kept repeating every time he heard any sound at all.

Finally he heard, "Hardoy speaking."

Solo rushed to explain who the Mahlers were and that they were being attacked, and then heard the chairman say to somebody at his end, "Get me the admiral. Use this other phone right here." And to Solo, "Stay on the line, Mr. Solórzano. What is the Mahlers' address?"

Solo read it off the cover of the telephone directory and heard the man's voice saying to Hardoy, "The admiral is in Rome, sir—an audience with the Pope."

Solo endured a moment of silence, followed by, "This is Bruno Hardoy, the chairman of the OAS human rights commission. Who am I speaking to? Let let me speak immediately with the person in charge. It's an emergency!"

Fonseca came into the room and found Doris and Solo motionless and silent. Doris went up to him and said something in an undertone. Fonseca nodded, glanced at his watch. "I'll wait downstairs in the car," he said before leaving.

Solo sat tensed on the phone through another long pause before the chairman identified himself again. "Yes, Mr. Dumas. I am calling because troops are attacking at this very moment the house of a couple who talked to a staff member of our commission, and I want you to know that unless this outrage ceases at once, we'll pack our bags and leave your country this afternoon, after calling a press conference to explain the reason for our departure."

Solo heard Hardoy read out the names and address of the Mahlers. "Yes, I too hope there is some mistake, Mr. Dumas. I will hold the wire, you may be sure."

Minutes more passed in silence. "Hello? Hello?" Solo said into the mouthpiece.

Hardoy's voice answered. "Yes, Mr. Solórzano. We are waiting."

"Sir," Solo said, "I'm going to put you on hold. I have to know what's happening at the house. Okay?"

"Go ahead."

Solo switched buttons. "Héctor? Are you there?"

"Yes, we are still here," Héctor Mahler answered. The background noise had stopped and his words could now be heard clearly. "Something is happening. They've stopped banging the walls. They seem to be going away. The helicopter is gone and we can hear the trucks leaving. Thank God."

His voice cracked. Solo could hear his wife Laura sobbing softly at his side.

"Thank God," Solo echoed, slumping back in his chair. "Look, Héctor, I have the OAS office on the other line. I'm going to tell them that the soldiers are leaving. When I hang up, you can call Alberto. Okay?"

There was a muted answer. Solo pressed the buttons again. "Dr. Hardoy?"

"I'm here," the chairman said.

"Yes, sir, they are leaving."

23

"IDs!"

The two policemen had materialized in the doorway, surprising everyone in the small, quiet cafe.

Diego's stomach clenched. He had shied away from taking a table by the windows and had not seen the cruiser coming. Through the glass door he now saw the hood of the two-tone blue patrol car at the curb. His eyes fell for just an instant to the duffel bag under the table, with the gun inside.

"All IDs, please!" one of the officers repeated loudly.

Without taking his eyes off the uniforms, Diego gently pushed the bag with his foot against the wall.

The policemen collected IDs from three other tables before coming to him. One of them held out a hand.

"*Señor...*"

Diego reached into his jacket and brought out his wallet. He handed over a laminated card.

"Francisco Aguirre," the policeman said, comparing the picture next to the thumbprint with the face in front of him.

"Address?"

Diego gave an address in the western suburbs of Buenos Aires.

One policeman stationed himself by the door while the other took all the IDs out to the patrol car for the driver to radio in.

No way out. He could retrieve the gun, but there were two of them, and one more out in the car. And his left arm, since Lucas resutured it, was dead weight.

Through the windows he caught sight of Lucas's shiny pate walking past the cafe, gazing casually into the interior. He was right on time. Moments later, Lucas was standing by the newsstand across the street, ostensibly reading a newspaper.

The patrons waited, careful not to look at each other or toward the patrol car. The police presence had killed all conversation. Two tables paid up, collected their belongings, and made ready to go as soon as their IDs reappeared. Diego caught the waiter's eye and wrote in the air. He felt his fierce headache returning. From butting Maidana, no doubt. Even the jaw of that bastard was made of granite.

At last the policeman returned with the cards and started handing them back. "Thank you for your cooperation. Please pardon the inconvenience. It's for your own safety." He handed the identity card back to Diego with only a glance.

The relief was palpable as the patrol car pulled out. Diego paid the waiter. Minutes later, Lucas strolled in and sat at his table.

"I'm impressed," he said. "You fooled the world's finest."

Diego scowled. "Let's make it quick and get out of here."

"Agreed. I have to get back to the hospital. Where are you off to?"

"I located one of the persons I was looking for, and I'm meeting her," Diego said. Then, with an eagerness he couldn't suppress, he asked, "Did you call Valeria's last night?"

"Yes, but Inés wasn't there. She missed the class, Valeria said."

"Did she say why?"

"She didn't know. Inés left a message on her machine saying she wasn't coming. So I gave Valeria your message."

"Tell me exactly what you said."

Lucas recited: "I called from a public telephone, said I had a message from you for Inés, that you've left the country and will be getting in touch soon through Valeria. And under no circumstances is Inés to try to contact you."

Diego nodded, frowned. Where had Inés been last night?

"What a romantic message," Lucas remarked. "I thought of adding a kiss for the poor girl from her loving boyfriend, but didn't know if you would approve of such sentimentality."

Diego smiled as Lucas dug into a pocket and brought out a small envelope and two keys on a paper clip with an address tag. "There are a few more pain killers in the envelope. And this time try to give my stitch work a chance, will you?" He leaned forward and lowered his voice further. "It's my cousin's apartment. And it has the typewriter you said you needed. The super doesn't know me, so if anybody asks, you are me. Use the service elevator and you'll be less likely to run into neighbors. Don't answer the intercom. Or the phone, unless you hear my voice on the machine. And no calls from that phone. Got it?"

"How long?"

"Two nights."

"That's plenty." Diego tucked away the envelope and keys in an inside pocket. He hesitated. He was reading in Lucas's eyes his own thought: the possibility that this might be the last time they met, that they might never see each other again.

They stood up and embraced. Diego said, "Mrs. Rámirez..."

As he turned to go, Lucas said, "I was hoping you wouldn't ask."

Diego watched Lucas depart, then sat down again and stared for a long while into his empty coffee cup. At last, he retrieved the duffel bag and left the cafe.

He walked four blocks to Plaza de Mayo. Two tall grenadiers in red, white, and blue regimentals with yellow trim, their high caps adding to their stature, stood at rigid attention by the entrance to the Pink House. In the center of the square, under the monitory eye of the police, a group of women in white headscarves marched around the obelisk of the May Pyramid carrying framed photographs of their family members. Passers-by glanced at them, then at the police, and steered clear.

"The crazy women of Plaza de Mayo," Diego murmured as he headed into the subway entrance. The label coined by the government and popularized through the media had stuck, turning these women into objects of derision and pity, poor souls understandably unhinged by the disappearance of their family members, terrorists who had fled abroad or gone underground.

He let the first two trains go by, making sure that the platform cleared completely, then boarded the third train. At the Pueyrredón station he got off, hurried up the steps, and a block later slipped into a shopping arcade that had a side street exit. As he stepped out of the exit he flagged a passing cab.

"Recoleta," he told the driver.

A short ride later the taxi let him off by one of the enormous Australian black fig trees outside the high walls of the cemetery. He walked to the gate. A group of camera-laden tourists, Spanish to judge by their accent, thronged the colonnaded entrance surmounted by the inscription *Requiescat In Pace*.

"Along with Paris' Père Lachaise and the Genoa cemetery," their tour guide was saying as he came near, "Recoleta is considered one of the three most artistic cemeteries in the world. Truly an open-air museum of architectural styles, stained glass, and sculpture."

He walked past the group into the cemetery. The wide avenue of cypresses he followed was bordered by massive vaults of marble, bronze, and granite ornamented with angels, caryatids, and statues of every description. Stray cats sunned themselves on the polished surfaces engraved with patrician names.

He sat down on a bench in the central rotunda and looked over at the memorial to Admiral Brown, the Irish founder of the Argentine Navy, which was where he had asked her to meet him. Nobody there yet. The Spanish tourists were coming up the avenue, listening to stories about Argentine presidents, generals, writers, financiers.

There was only one tomb they were interested in, he thought as the group reached the rotunda. And their guide was sure to provide the barest outline of the most sanitized version of the story. The country, after all, was once again under military rule. But if the tourists read their foreign tour books, they could fill in the blanks that the official guide judiciously omitted. He watched the path and listened.

"We will now proceed to the tomb of Eva Perón, Evita, as she is better known. It will be the sixth alleyway on the right. You will know it by the fresh cut flowers that are always present. She died at age thirty-three and her embalmed body, a powerful rallying symbol for the followers of her husband, General Juan Perón, was stolen after he was toppled and General Aramburu became President."

Would she now tell them that it was Colonel Koenig, the head of Army Intelligence, who stole the body and became obsessed with it, keeping it at times in his office and showing it to visitors?

"For two years," the guide went on, "Evita's body was moved around in a flower shop truck to various hiding places. In one of these, the home of an army major, the major accidentally shot dead his pregnant wife because he thought Evita's followers were attacking their home to take back her body."

There was a collective gasp from the tourists. Diego heaved a sigh. Welcome to Argentina.

"Permission was then secured from the Vatican," the guide went on, "and Evita's body was secretly taken to Italy and buried under a false name in a cemetery in Milan. It remained there for fourteen years, until it was returned to her husband, then in exile in Spain."

Diego silently completed the account, reminding himself how in that same period, Peronist guerrillas had kidnapped former President Aramburu and, before killing him, unsuccessfully demanded that the military return Evita's body. Three years later that still hadn't happened, so they stole Aramburu's body and held it until Evita's was returned. Diego shook his head. I'll give you back your dead body if you give me back mine. What was wrong with this country? How could you even explain such things to tourists?

"Five years ago," the guide concluded, "Evita's body was brought back to its final resting place here—where she lies under two very thick plates of steel." She waited for the snickers she expected. "Follow me, please."

The group moved on.

And now Diego thought he spotted her coming up the path, carrying a paper shopping bag, a woman anywhere from forty to sixty—it was hard to tell, thanks to her large sunglasses and tired gait. The small sculpture of the *Hercules*, Admiral Brown's frigate, helped her recognize the meeting place. She went up to it, looked around, and settled herself next to the bronze urn cast from the ship's cannon.

He waited. Nobody approached her. No one seemed to be paying any attention to her. He got up and walked over.

"*Señora...*" He sat down next to her.

He sensed her eyes staring questioningly behind the dark glasses. "Yes...?" she said.

He was grateful that she hadn't taken off her shades, hadn't shown him the red-rimmed eyes he knew they concealed. She looked like so many of the other mothers: middle-aged, a lifetime spent in the family kitchen. He recognized inside the shopping bag at her feet the white headscarf of the Mothers of Plaza de Mayo, the rolled-up newspaper used to fend off police dogs, the framed photograph she must have been carrying not an hour ago when he saw her in Plaza de Mayo without knowing who she was. In the black-and-white photograph he could glimpse inside the paper bag, her children wore brilliant smiles.

"I'm the person who called you," he said.

He had thought and thought about how to do this, had lain awake trying to come up with the right words. It was no use. His right hand reached for her hands, clasped on her lap. They were warm, fragile.

He said, "It's about your family."

24

At the Aeroparque, the small airfield by the River Plate in the heart of Buenos Aires, dense fog delayed the takeoff of the Mendoza flight for nearly two hours. Solo tried to calm himself as they sat on the runway in the hot airplane. The sounds of the violence at the Mahlers' house reverberated in his head. It had been a close call. And there was nothing to prevent the soldiers from descending on them again. He wiped his forehead with a cocktail napkin and saw on it the Argentine Airlines logo he had seen on the airplane's tail: an AA in a circle, topped by a stylized flying condor.

The image thrust Malena to the center of his thoughts. To speculate that she had stayed away from the meeting at the polo grounds out of fear or caution was a self-comforting fantasy. Even in hiding, she would have found a way to get in touch. She had disappeared. The very word caused a tightness in his chest. She had disappeared after arranging a secret meeting with Hardoy to talk about Operation Condor. Her connection to a multi-government crime syndicate devoted to murdering dissidents worldwide was beyond his imagining. But it was all he had to go on. If she had been arrested or abducted... he couldn't bear to imagine that. But still, if she had, there had to be some way to find out. He absolutely must see her father, tell him what he knew. Malena's father was a politician, a man whose prestige transcended the tumults of changing governments; he would have the connections to locate her. And there was Reidlonger. Solo had to learn what Néstor Reidlonger knew.

Above all, he had to make sure Inés was safe. And there was only one way: she must leave the country. He had to persuade her to pack a suitcase and catch the first flight to the U.S. Would she listen now that she knew the truth?

When they were finally airborne, Hardoy left his seat next to Fonseca and came down the aisle, lowering himself onto the empty seat next to Solo's.

"The fog put us behind schedule," he said, removing his glasses and wiping the corner of one eye with the back of his hand. "We'll have to split up if we are going to cover everything. I'm afraid I had to agree to observe the military trial of a man charged with subversion, which they're holding for our benefit, so I'll stay in Mendoza proper while you and Fonseca drive out to the prison. Think you can handle it?"

"Yes," Solo said flatly, surprising himself. Ever since their visit to Villa Devoto he had dreaded going to another prison, interviewing more victims, submerging himself again in the horror he knew he would encounter. He had wondered how people like Hardoy could manage to do it for a lifetime. Now he was beginning to understand. A grim determination had taken up residence in him, blunting his sensibilities, steeling him.

Hardoy seemed to read his thoughts. "Remember: the key is to remain unemotional. You're not there to commiserate; there's no time for it. You've seen what we do. Strain out the superfluous, get the facts: dates, names of people and places, numbers, descriptions as detailed as possible. Pin everything down, and do it fast. There won't be much time with each prisoner and no second chance."

Solo nodded.

"And you won't have the tape recorder," Hardoy added. "They found out about it and have strictly forbidden it." Hardoy looked at him a moment longer, then said, "Good luck." He got up and walked back to his seat.

"Of course, major, in our line of work one doesn't know whether to go on a diet or a hunger strike," Fonseca joked as he, Solo, and their military escort strolled out of the hotel's dining room.

They had just completed a fixed-menu lunch arranged for them by the authorities of the local army garrison. The strained conversation at table, requiring occasional linguistic help from Solo, had flagged noticeably despite Fonseca's efforts to enliven it with miscellaneous legal anecdotes, an account of his latest book titled *The Juridical Nature of the Administrative Act*, and a discussion of his preference for old-fashioned first names, many of which were similar in Portuguese and Spanish. Young people today wanted nothing but popular foreign names for their children. One hardly ever met a Herculano, a Macedonio, a Nepomuceno. When was the last time the major had come across a Nemesio, a Fructuoso, even an Hilario? And female names were even worse. Try finding a Robustiana, Encarnación or Saturnina. Children today all had to be named Samantha, Vanessa, Karina.

Solo had started when he heard the name Saturnina, but Fonseca went on. What was the major's first name? Clodomiro? Ah, a name *comme il faut*, of high lineage, from the royal line of Frankish kings.

A car from the army garrison drove them to the prison camp, where the warden and other officials met them. They inspected the kitchen and received assurances about the quality of the food. Same food the staff ate, they were told. Fonseca was very interested in the *puchero criollo* stew that the warden said was served once a week, and Solo had to translate every ingredient for Fonseca to write down. The dormitories they walked through were large barracks with bunk beds stacked four high. Solo kept his face stolid, waiting for the prisoners.

The inmates were mustered in the muddy yard, one large throng with smaller clusters milling about its fringes. As soon as he and Fonseca appeared, Solo heard a murmur run through the crowd before it fell into a silence broken only by the sloshing of feet on soggy ground. The two visitors detached themselves from the group of prison officials and walked toward the prisoners.

"Good afternoon," Fonseca called out when they had drawn near the front ranks, "I am Dr. Justiniano Fonseca, vice-chairman of the OAS Commission on Human Rights, and this is my assistant Mr. Solórzano. We are here in an official capacity, with permission from your government, to hear those of you who wish to register complaints against the authorities."

Solo studied the crowd. No one stirred.

"Don't be afraid to speak up," Fonseca insisted. "We are here with the knowledge and consent of your government. Anything you say will be kept confidential."

The prisoners remained silent. Fonseca looked back at the warden, who shrugged.

"Spies... there are spies here..." muffled voices rose over the crowd. "One by one..."

"Very well," Fonseca said. "We will form two lines. Please line up to speak either to Mr. Solórzano or to me."

Some inmates moved away, signifying their unwillingness to be interviewed. The bulk of the men, however, formed themselves into two lines from which a single prisoner at a time could walk forward some twenty paces to confer with either Solo or Fonseca.

Mourning the loss of the tape recorder, Solo readied his pen and notebook. The man limping toward him was elderly, hollow-eyed, with straggling eyebrows and ruffled tufts of downy hair swirling in the wind about his head.

"I'm Kevin Solórzano. And you are...?"

The man looked at him fixedly. "Kevin?"

"Yes."

"You are—American?"

The intensity of the man's look surprised Solo. "Yes..."

The man wavered, and for a moment Solo thought he would turn on his heels and walk away.

"Does it matter?" Solo asked. "Would you rather speak to Dr. Fonseca?"

The man looked at him a moment longer, as if making up his mind. "I have to trust somebody," he finally said.

There were informers among the prisoners, he began after giving his name. Following the Red Cross inspection, the only visit the authorities had allowed, the prison officials had inflicted terrible reprisals. He was a doctor. He had been abducted after attending a mass at St. Patrick's in Buenos Aires, to mark the disappearance of a friend a year earlier. He later learned from another prisoner that the Pallotine priests of St. Patrick's, who held the mass and did social work among the poor, had all been shot to death.

The day after the mass, as he returned home, he inserted the key in the door of his apartment only to have it yanked open from the inside. He turned to get away and was shot in both legs. The intruders hooded and handcuffed him; he yelled to the neighbors to tell his family that he was being kidnapped. Save your breath, his abductors told him, your wife and daughters have already been sucked in. That was what they called their abductions, the doctor said with a querulous edge in his voice: sucking people in.

He had been taken to the Naval Mechanics School. He would never forget it. It was July 1978, just after the World Cup soccer final played in the River Plate stadium, not far from the School. To drown out his screams, his torturers turned the television volume way up. The former U.S. Secretary of State, a special guest of the government, was giving a press conference chastising his successors in the American government for not understanding that human rights were a necessary casualty of fighting terrorism.

An image of Henry in the embassy library in Washington flashed before Solo's eyes, the admiral saying to him, Yes, you've been a true friend.

Later, the doctor said, he was taken to the Athletic Club. Solo allowed himself a nod and braced himself as the man went on. The walls in the torture rooms were caked with human gore. The stench was overpowering. As soon as new prisoners arrived, they were led to the torture rooms with guards raining blows on them. Torture was always observed by a doctor and usually stopped just short of death. At that point the prisoner was taken to the infirmary and put on an IV until he recovered enough to withstand more torture.

Once, they had wrung his testicles, by hand or with a machine, he wasn't sure. "I have never felt any pain like that. Before passing out, my prayer was that they would tear them off and free me of the pain. A few days later I had a chance to peek through the hood and saw what they had done to me. When I was a medical student," the doctor said with quavering objectivity, "one of my textbooks had a picture of a man whose testicles had grown so deformed that he carried them in a wheelbarrow. Mine looked like that, except they were a deep shade of blue-black."

Solo fought down his revulsion. He kept writing, trying to focus every brain cell on the moving nib of the pen, the trail of black ink on white paper.

Special tortures were reserved for Jews. One of the men who ran the Club, until he was promoted to Chief of Police of Buenos Aires, assigned Nazi literature for his staff to read and played recordings of Hitler's speeches. One torturer had everyone call him "the great Führer." He extorted money from the families of Jewish prisoners. Another torturer knew karate and practiced by kicking and punching three or four Jewish prisoners at a time. The guards painted swastikas on them, forced them to crawl and lick their boots, to imitate animals, and to salute by raising an arm and shouting "I love Hitler!" One torture was reserved mostly for Jews: the 'rectumscope,' a tube through which the torturers inserted a rat into the vagina or the anus, then waited for it to gnaw its way out.

Solo listened with a set jaw. The key is to remain unemotional,

Hardoy had said, and in the last hours Solo had mentally rehearsed how he would handle himself. Now his mind was a flooded engine that refused to start. Snap out of it, damn it. Hardoy is counting on you.

"What else can you tell me about this Athletic Club?" he said when the doctor paused in his story.

"The police ran it, but it also held prisoners brought in by the military. It was underground, very hot and humid in summer and freezing cold in winter, with no ventilation. Prisoners were kept in tiny cells called 'tubes,' blindfolded, their ankles shackled, forbidden to speak or move. At various times of day or night guards would burst in. Anyone caught moving was beaten unconscious.

"Why were you brought to this prison?" Solo asked.

"You," the doctor said. An inspection team was coming, he had overheard the guards say, and the Athletic Club had to be dismantled. "This past Saturday, all prisoners were moved out. I was brought here. Others were going to a place in the Tigre delta, near the city. There were also two men and two women who had been brought in two nights before and placed in the first cell, next to mine. I heard one of them scratching the wall at night. The guards came to get those four before dawn, with a priest, which I thought was a bad sign."

The doctor glanced around. "There are so many of us. I'm taking up too much of your time. Let me quickly tell you about the prisoners they moved out yesterday, when they learned you were coming."

Solo listened and wrote, filling page after page, automatically, unthinkingly, no longer shuddering. Horror fatigue was setting in.

After the doctor, more prisoners filed past. Solo recorded electric shocks, hangings, drug injections, mock and real firing squads, attacks with dogs, children tortured in front of their parents and parents in front of their children. Each man chronicled his own experience. At the Superintendence of Federal Security, Solo learned, they put electrodes on your teeth, and your whole head felt as if it was shattering. Or they made you swallow the electrodes, and when they turned on the power it felt like shards of glass moving up and down your insides.

You couldn't scream or move. You couldn't even cry. Afterwards you lay in a fetal position for days on end, with the thirst worse than the torture, but you couldn't drink anything.

A man who had been imprisoned at the Naval Mechanics School told Solo that one of the doctors there was nicknamed Mengele. He tortured pregnant women by inserting a spoon into the vagina until it touched the fetus, and then applying electric shocks. Before being allowed to sleep, all prisoners at the School were made to recite aloud the Lord's Prayer and a Hail Mary, thanking the Naval Mechanics School for being allowed to live one more day. Last Christmas Admiral Rinaldi himself had attended a mass offered at the School by the local bishop, who gave each prisoner a religious medal and a hug on behalf of the Pope. To wish them a merry Christmas Rinaldi had to shout over the jangling of chains and the shrieks from the torture rooms.

"Do you have a child, sir?" asked the last prisoner. He put a hand into a pocket and without waiting for an answer slipped something into Solo's palm.

Solo looked at the object. It was a tiny automobile fashioned out of breadcrumbs.

"Give it to your child, sir. The man who was making it for his little boy was 'transferred' just before you came."

As they started the drive back to Mendoza, Fonseca took a small pillow from his briefcase and arranged it behind his head. He looked at Solo and said, "Shocked?"

"No," Solo said. Words were his stock in trade, one of his devouring interests in life. He lived by words. And if there was a word to describe how he now felt, it was not shocked. Shock had long ago worn off. Fury was what he had felt, a cold fury mounting in him as they went through the galling courtesies of saying goodbye to the warden and his staff. He had just finished taking down evidence of the most gruesome torments inflicted on helpless captives by sadists whose hands he was now expected to shake, whose day he was supposed to disturb no further, so that they could get on with their diabolical work. What kind of monstrous farce was this? In surly silence, his balled fists had ignored the proffered hands. Fonseca had taken his rage for shock.

"No, I'm not shocked," he repeated. "I'm outraged."

Fonseca patted him on one knee. "It's only natural—all those stories. You mustn't take them at face value. Remember that prisons everywhere are full of bad people. To be sure, there is always some abuse, some rough interrogation techniques, but the inmates make up stories or exaggerate for our benefit. To hear them tell it, they're all innocent and they've all been mistreated. One gets used to it."

He turned towards the window on his side. In seconds he was asleep.

Solo stared for long minutes at the back of Fonseca's head. He finally turned his gaze away and watched the sun sink behind distant promontories as the car sped over empty roads bordered by multi-colored hills and dry river beds. Night was falling over the Andes. A soft pink twilight colored valleys and mountain steeps as far away as Mount Aconcagua. Lesser peaks strung out over the landscape glowed with the same rosy hue.

Gradually the shadows engulfed the earth, extinguishing its browns and greens and grays. Higher and higher the darkness edged, stealing over shoulders and brows, splaying out across cliffs and ledges until they gained the white solitudes of Mount Aconcagua, closed in on its gleaming cusp and snuffed out the last glimmer, plunging the land into darkness and alpenglow.

A starlit darkness. A darkness pricked by infinite heavenly lights. So many stars. And so bright. He had forgotten this brightness, this closeness to the stars. There, so near that it seemed he could reach out and touch it, was Orion's belt—the Three Marys, as they were called here. And over there, a glittering Southern Cross of stunning brilliancy.

So beautiful. He wished Lisa and John were here to see this with him.

No. He didn't.

25

Diego stopped under a street lamp and looked at his watch. Too early to meet Inés's former boyfriend, Mr. Solórzano, with whom he had an appointment at ten sharp—still fifty minutes away.

It was becoming a reflex to avoid the busier avenues, where there was a stronger likelihood of police presence. This bystreet, as Homero Manzi said in one of his tangos, was bathed in silence, a yellow moon tiptoeing on the roofs.

Halfway down the next block, he came across a small group of men and women in party clothes congregating by an entrance festooned with colored lights. Above it, *Ugarte Palace* was spotlighted in large silver letters. He went up to the billboards. A dance blockbuster: Two live orchestras: the incredible Johnny Gasparino, and Tangomanía. A brand new convertible to be raffled off. Ladies free. At the latticed window that doubled as box office, he paid for admission and went in.

A new, red '79 Chevrolet convertible was on display in the entrance hall, all shiny chrome and leather, smelling of new rubber. Patrons gawked at it, wondering aloud how the enormous car had been brought in here. Diego followed a group of arrivals past a whiff of restroom ammonia into a large ballroom. He went up to the bar at one end and bought a beer.

Dancing couples were twirling to Johnny Gasparino, a tanned little man in a blindingly white suit, his silver shirt unbuttoned to the waist. He was singing a cumbia in a pleasant bass, rubbing a small barrel-like percussion instrument that produced loud grunting sounds. When he wasn't singing, Johnny accompanied the band by shaking a pair of maracas and executing violent pelvic thrusts as though in the grip of a nervous disorder—his trademark, judging from the laughter, catcalls, and applause.

Diego sipped his beer while figuring out the boy-meets-girl house rules. Every dance hall had its own. Here, most of the unescorted women sat at tables arranged on three sides of the dance floor, the fourth being taken up by the stage. Single men stood hovering on the outside perimeter of the tables, trying to catch the eye of the lady of their choice. The prettier females sat close to the dance floor, paying, or pretending to pay, no attention to the looks directed at them, while the plainer women placed themselves near the boundary patrolled by the males. After two people made eye contact, the man nodded his head, a signal the lady could accept by smiling or by standing up and waiting for the gentleman to escort her to the dance floor. When signals got crossed, a man would approach a table only to be ignored, or a woman might remain briefly standing in vain expectation. Each would then affect indifference and walk off in the direction of the bathrooms or the bar, as if this and nothing else had been their intention all along.

"Hey..." Someone elbowed him softly.

He turned. A skinny youth at his side was raising his eyebrows and tilting his head discreetly toward one of the tables. He spoke almost without moving his lips.

"See the way she's looking at you? Hadn't noticed, eh? I thought so. You're a wolf. A regular blue wolf." The kid shook his head. "You don't even look and you hook them anyway. Best looking woman in the house, too. And you should see her dance."

Diego glanced over to a table occupied by four women. One, a very pretty chestnut-haired girl in a tight blue party dress, did seem to be regarding him insistently. She smiled when she saw him return her look.

"See? What did I tell you? I've been making eyes at her all night, but she won't even look my way. She's all yours, man. So, what are you waiting for? Aren't you going to ask her to dance?"

All he needed. A busybody. He looked at the skinny guy and shrugged. "Maybe later."

His benefactor gave him an incredulous look, then walked away muttering something about God giving bread to the toothless.

Johnny Gasparino left the stage and Tangomanía came on: piano, cello, three violins, and two bandoneons.

With the first elegant strains of an old tango, Diego felt himself transported to that familiar past he had never known. Dirt streets under velvet skies. Tiled patios. Wisteria, geraniums, jasmine. Organ grinders. Love and betrayal. A knife duel in the moonlight. He felt a wave of desolation. His world too was ending.

Tangomanía launched into another Manzi tango, achingly nostalgic. The girl in the blue dress was still looking at him. Why not, he thought. His last tango in Buenos Aires. He looked at her. She smiled back. He got up and made for her table, but she was already on her way, meeting him at the edge of the dance floor.

They embraced without a word, and a deep swell of the bandoneons pulled them into the spell of the tango, shutting out the outside world, submerging them in its magical fatality, its drunken desperation, its rain of ashes and fatigue.

When the music stopped and their bodies separated, he heard clapping from the circle that had formed around the dance floor.

Imbécil, he silently cursed himself. What a way to draw attention to yourself. What if somebody recognized you?

She was beaming. "You dance like the gods. What's your name?"

He forced a smile. "San Francisco. And yours?"

"Raquel."

"Well, Raquel, thank you." He took her by the elbow, and disappointment swept across her face as she realized they were not staying on the dance floor.

He read the confusion in her eyes. They hadn't talked at all, so it could be nothing she said. Was he just shy? As he escorted her back to her table she tried to reassure him.

"I don't usually do this..." she said, "but would you like my phone number?"

He felt guilty. She was so young. "Plenty of time for that," he said. "Right now I need to excuse myself." He nodded in the direction of the bathrooms.

She seemed relieved.

He headed for the bathrooms and the exit. On his way out of the ballroom he turned and saw her questioning eyes following him out the door.

26

Daylight was long spent when the plane from Mendoza touched down at the Aeroparque airfield and the waiting chauffeur drove them back to the Metropole. As they entered the building, Solo's fingers loosened their hold on the notebook he had clutched to his chest all the way from Mendoza.

Fonseca was running late for dinner with the Brazilian ambassador and went straight to his room to change. Hardoy and Solo checked in at the offices of the commission on the third floor where, except for Doris and another secretary still typing away, everyone had gone out to eat. There was no word yet from the second group, which had traveled north to visit a prison in Resistencia. But Professor Summerhay had returned from his interview with the Archbishop of Buenos Aires and was now in the conference room next door, going over his notes. There was also an unmarked envelope addressed to Dr. Hardoy. The messenger who delivered it had left at once without identifying the sender.

Hardoy tore it open. Solo watched the lines in his forehead deepen as he read.

"Mr. Solórzano," he said when he finished reading, "I'm afraid I'll need you a moment longer."

He preceded Solo into the conference room. Professor Summerhay's gloomy, tired eyes looked up from his notes. Hardoy laid out the contents of the envelope on the table in front of Solo. It was a single sheet of paper.

"This came today while we were gone, Professor. I want you to hear it."

Solo picked up the legal-size paper. It was a photocopy of a typed letter, its borders covered with stamps, seals and signatures. He began: "Received in this Office of the President of Argentina at 11:30 a.m. on March 6. Excellency: We, the undersigned staff of this Judicial Morgue of Córdoba, have the honor to respectfully address Your Excellency with regard to certain unsanitary conditions..."

"Yes, yes," Hardoy cut in. "Skip all that. Get to the part about the hospital."

Solo ran his eyes down the letter... "And although no autopsies are done on bodies delivered by security forces... Here: we were ordered to remove the bodies from the hospital. When we opened the doors of the ward where they had been kept without cold storage, some for as long as a month, there was a huge cloud of flies. The floor was ankle-deep in worms and larvae, which we removed using pails and shovels. Some had boots and gloves but others had to work in their street clothes, with hats and surgical masks provided by the hospital. Then, with an escort of two police cars from the local precinct, we took the bodies on trucks to the San Vicente Cemetery, where a mass grave approximately forty meters long, ten wide and eight to nine deep had been dug next to an outside wall. There, with the police shining search lights because it was getting dark, and neighbors watching from the upper stories of adjacent buildings, we laid the bodies..."

Hardoy put a hand on Solo's arm. "Thank you. You needn't go on. Go get some rest."

Solo handed back the letter, nodded to the professor, and left the room.

He dragged himself to the elevator. It seemed impossible that a single day could last this long. If he could just hold out, he would, someday, go home, escape back into his own world.

He stepped off the elevator and plodded through miles of empty corridors to his room. Not until he shut the door and turned on the light did he see the man sitting in the armchair.

"You're late," the man said irritably, standing up. He was tall, with hair beginning to go gray and pale green eyes framed by bushy eyebrows. "Our appointment was for ten sharp."

Solo conquered his amazement. "Our appointment?"

"Ten o'clock," the man repeated.

Solo's surprise now took second place to his anger. "Look, I don't know who you are or what you want, but you have ten seconds to explain yourself before I call hotel security. How did you get in here?"

The man's forehead furrowed. "Didn't you get the notes I left?" he asked, with slightly less peevishness.

Notes. There *had* been a note under the door, one note, last Sunday, when he returned from viewing his father's memorial with Inés. Seeing it lying there had reminded him of Venus Adonis and he had tried to put it out of his mind. His face must have said as much, because the man walked past him to the door, pulled back the mat, and picked up a piece of paper. He frowned.

"But didn't you get my earlier note?" he asked.

"Yes," Solo admitted, "but if you don't tell me who—"

"Look," the man said, sighing and pocketing the note. "I'm sorry for sneaking in like this. I picked the lock. When I tell you why I'm here you'll see that I had no choice. I couldn't phone or wait in the lobby or the hallway. I have to speak with you."

"Who are you?"

"My name is Fioravanti, Diego Fioravanti—formerly a captain in the Argentine Army."

27

Solórzano looked and sounded nothing like the gringo Diego had pictured. He was slim and straight, with dark good looks, wavy black hair, and probing gray eyes. There was no trace of a foreign accent. And despite the palpable tension between them, he hadn't balked at Diego's request to come to this cafe. It was as if he welcomed the idea, as if he too had been hoping to meet face to face. Before they exited the hotel separately, Diego gave him directions and handed him Grandfather Arambillet's ring. "Show this to the barman," he said. "He'll know."

Now they sat stirring espressos in the rear of the musty cafe in Once, well away from other customers. Diego kept his voice low. "It's safer here than around your hotel. The bartender is a friend of a friend. He's having the front watched, and there is a back door."

A deep fragrance of coffee rose from the row of shiny espresso machines on the bar counter, permeating the air. In the front of the cafe, old men chain-smoked and played *truco* with decks of Spanish cards, while younger men chain-smoked and played billiards. A couple at a table covered with tiny plates of hors d'oeuvres read the newspaper and sipped vermouth with squirts of soda from a siphon bottle. Students surrounded by mounds of heavy textbooks argued economics.

Solórzano sipped the rich brew and, matching Diego's hushed

tone, said, "Instead of trying to get the OAS commission to help you, why don't you just go to the American embassy and ask for political asylum?"

Diego shook his head. "Argentina will never issue a safe conduct to the airport. I won't spend years trapped in an embassy. I'm leaving on my own. But I need the commission to sponsor my case in Washington."

"That's where you're headed?"

Diego hesitated. He had no choice but to trust this man. "Initially. It's where they decide political asylum, and where the commission is based."

Solórzano looked at him warily. "And why me? Why don't you contact the chairman or one of the members?"

Diego rubbed his eyes with the palms of his hands. Behind Solórzano's head he could see his own face in the wall mirror. His sleeplessness was written on his skin.

"I don't know whether they're under surveillance, and I can't take the chance. When Inés told me about you, I thought it was less likely that the interpreter was being watched."

There was far more to it than that, Diego admitted to himself, but Solórzano didn't need to know it. Curious as he was about Inés's former boyfriend, the idea of approaching him had been hard for Diego to accept. It was not just a matter of pride. He had endlessly debated whether he could trust the man he had replaced in her affections. It would be simple for Solórzano to turn in a deserter, especially this one deserter that Colonel Indart would love to get his hands on. He could do it with one anonymous phone call.

"When are you leaving?" Solórzano asked.

"Tonight." Diego produced a business envelope and placed it on the table. "This is for your chairman—a signed affidavit that recounts what I'm about to tell you."

Solórzano glanced at the envelope. "Then why do I need to hear it?"

"Because there is a part that's not in there. The part that has to do with her."

The word *her* hung in the air. There was a commotion by the billiard tables: three girls sashaying past the long windows of the cafe were being peppered with wolf whistles and catcalls. Solórzano looked again at the envelope but did not pick it up. He folded his arms across his chest and said, "I'm listening."

Eyes focused on the scarred tabletop where generations of petty vandals had carved their initials, their political slogans and sex ads. Diego began talking. The army had been his life. He had enlisted young, when his parents died, after working in printing shops and graphic studios. The army had taken care of him, made him part of something he could be proud of. He would gladly have laid down his life for the army. Yet here he was, hiding, sneaking into hotel rooms, meeting in out-of-the-way cafes for fear of being recognized, for fear that the army might find him. Diego raised his eyes to Solórzano; for some reason that he could not explain to himself, he wanted more from this man than his help. He wanted him to understand.

After the coup he had avoided field operations because of his skills as a printer. He was assigned to an intelligence unit responsible for forging documents for the task forces. They turned out passports and birth certificates, press cards, driver's licenses and police badges, university diplomas, credentials of every kind, as well as fake letters for the media from repentant guerrillas or from mothers of soldiers killed in combat. His first job was to print handbills urging workers to strike, all strikes being illegal. The leaflets, along with weapons, were placed on the dead bodies of labor union officials killed in a fake clash staged by the military, so that the media could take pictures of subversives killed resisting arrest. The unit also drew up new deeds and titles for houses and cars seized from prisoners, which were recorded in the names of the squad members or sold for cash through a civilian brokerage. Prisoners were forced to sign checks emptying their bank accounts; their belongings were trucked into the unit and parceled out among the members of the squad and ranking officers. "Cleaning" a house often took days, until every last item of value was removed.

A student from the corner table passed within hearing range on his way to the bathroom. Diego paused. He saw Solórzano was following his words carefully, his eyes straying to the student as he went by.

The squads operated using stolen vehicles they commandeered off the streets. They stopped cars, identified themselves as leftist guerrillas, and took the vehicle and its occupants' valuables. When the squad needed a truck, they waited until they could get their hands on one loaded with merchandise, preferably household appliances. The vehicles had their plates and serial numbers changed by the mechanics in the unit's machine shop, who fitted them with signs identifying them as army property. All vehicles were replaced after one or two months, at which point they were dismantled, cannibalized, and finally abandoned.

"Hey, Flea! One of your girlfriends!" the bartender boomed out to a very short man standing by a table of dice players. The bartender was nodding towards an antique phone on a corner of the bar counter, over which a faded "No credit today" sign pointed to a lidless coffee can for coins. Flea walked up to the bar and picked up the receiver. Diego assessed him, then went on talking.

His unit also dealt with human rights organizations, Diego went on, his voice growing hoarser. Some captive activists were escorted to meetings with journalists, to declare they had never been kidnapped. But most were simply made to write letters denying they had been abducted and explaining that they had gone into hiding to protect themselves from some subversive group. The letters were then mailed from abroad and the prisoners "transferred."

Diego looked up inquiringly, ready to explain the word "transferred." Solórzano nodded grimly. "What happens to the prisoners they remove when we come to inspect?" he asked.

"They are taken to secret locations or made to wear uniforms and passed off as correctional or military personnel. In some cases, your people are interviewing collaborators brought in to impersonate prisoners."

Solórzano nodded again, as if this was no surprise. Diego wondered how much of what he was relating was known to the OAS inspectors.

"Within the military," he continued, "if you have second thoughts you keep them to yourself. You follow orders and keep your mouth shut. Discipline, obedience to your superiors, and loyalty to the service are the rules you live by. Protesting is futile and dangerous, anyway. A major I knew reported a group of senior officers for stealing and selling cars and kidnapping businessmen for ransom. He was arrested and disappeared."

"And you? Couldn't you get out?"

"I tried. I was almost ready to file for a medical discharge last week, when I was called into Colonel Indart's office."

Solórzano's lips seemed to twitch, as though he meant to speak but checked himself.

"The colonel told us that three subversives, two men and a woman, were being allowed to leave the country. I would drive one of the cars to the airport. Our chaplain was coming along, too. He often does. Everybody considers him part of the team."

Diego saw a waiter by the front entrance of the cafe come towards them, swinging his impossible tray load of bottles, cups, and plates over the heads of customers.

"Everything okay here," he said to Diego. It was not a question. Diego nodded. He watched his fingers toy with the coffee spoon as the waiter went about his way.

"The guards knocked out the prisoners. We drove to a deserted area where the doctor from our unit was waiting. He injected a red liquid into the heart of each prisoner. It was poison."

He saw Solórzano blanch. Loud laughter and guffaws erupted from one of the *truco* tables as Diego paused again to let Flea walk by on his way back from the phone.

"What happened after that?" Solórzano's strained voice broke the silence.

"My behavior had drawn suspicion. Our chaplain gave me a talk, said if I performed to their satisfaction they could send me to Paris with Operation Condor—"

Solórzano's eyes went keenly alert. "Condor? What do you know about that?"

"Very little. It's an arrangement among governments to hunt down one another's exiles. They've killed them here, in Mexico, Italy, France, other countries. Everything I know about it is in there." He looked down to the envelope on the table.

Solórzano said nothing.

"Three days later," Diego resumed, "I was included in another party sent out with four prisoners, two men and two women. The older woman was pregnant."

"Was that last Saturday?"

"Saturday, yes." While you were having dinner with Inés, Diego thought but didn't say. "Sunday before dawn we picked up the prisoners at the Athletic Club. That's a—"

"I know," Solórzano broke in. "Go on."

"It was a navy operation but we were helping empty out the Club and the Navy Mechanics School because you people were coming."

"What did they do with the prisoners?"

"Most of them went to El Silencio, an island in the Tigre delta made available by the Archbishop of Buenos Aires. But our four were not going there. The chaplain blessed them and we set out in a truck and a car, taking dirt roads until we came to a desolate place. The prisoners dug a pit and were lined up in front. That was when I realized I knew the younger woman. I had trouble recognizing her because her face was—"

Diego paused and took a deep breath. The two different images of Violeta Argerich were always there now, undimmed: one lighthearted, a smile blossoming from the corners of her mouth at some silliness he had uttered on the dance floor of the Ideal; the other savaged, mauled by torments he could only guess at.

"—her face was in bad shape. I recognized her because she and her husband had come in for a tango lesson at the Ideal, a cafe where I teach. Her name was Violeta Argerich. He was an older man, a police inspector, I think."

"Was he with her at the Athletic Club? One of the four?"

"No, just the woman. I—" Diego's voice stalled and he looked away before speaking again. "I fired over their heads. But nobody survived."

For a long moment, Solórzano kept quiet. Then, "Go on."

"There's not much more. From then on I knew I was racing the clock. I got a furlough and wasn't going to go back, but they came for me. I got away and have been hiding ever since."

Solórzano looked at him sharply. "Why didn't you stop seeing Inés long ago? You must have realized how dangerous it was for her to be connected to you."

The rebuke cracked the façade of civility between them. Diego felt his face burning. What business is it of yours, he wanted to toss back. But Solórzano was right. He had leveled the unanswerable charge Diego had flung at himself time and again.

"You're right," he said. "When I found out what the army was doing, I should have given her up. But I couldn't. I kept telling myself that things would get better, that it would somehow work out. And as long as I thought that, I couldn't bring myself to let her go. So I tried to keep her out of it. I never told her anything about my work, never introduced her to my friends, never took her anywhere I might be recognized. I said it was for my sake, because of the sensitive nature of my work, until things calmed down."

"And after your escape?"

"After that, I knew I had to stay away from her. She would have wanted to see me. I had to make her think I was gone, so she wouldn't look for me. I had someone call her friend Valeria to say I left the country."

Solórzano stared at him. "When was that?"

"Tuesday night. Inés was supposed to be at Valeria's after their French lesson, but she wasn't."

Solórzano sighed and cast his eyes to the floor. Then, without enthusiasm, as if he had come to a decision against his better judgment, he picked up the envelope from the tabletop and put it in his coat pocket.

"All right," was all he said.

Diego said, "Thank you."

Solórzano looked at him and said, "I'm not doing it for you."

"I know," Diego said.

Solórzano opened the palm of his left hand. "Your ring."

"Do me another favor," Diego said. "Keep it for me. It belonged to my late grandfather but it's too dangerous to carry around with me anymore. Maybe one day, when this is over, I'll wear it again."

Solórzano slipped the ring into his pocket. "What makes you think they couldn't come after you in the U.S.?"

Diego shrugged. "They blew up Letelier in Washington, but that was under the friendly previous administration. Mr. Carter is not friendly. And I'm a small fish, not worth their trouble."

He drew back his chair. "I couldn't locate the family of Violeta Argerich. The names I phoned were dead ends. But the poisoned woman yelled out her name: Beatriz Suárez. I got into Father Bauer's files in our unit and... "

"Father Bauer?" Solórzano drew back, startled. "The go-between..."

"Yes, that's right. He often acts as middleman with the families of prisoners."

"Why was Beatriz Suárez killed?" Solórzano asked.

"The file said her husband was a leftist and a Jew," Diego said. "He and his sister had been killed as well. Beatriz Suárez was arrested with him and gave birth to twins at the Intelligence Brigade. She—"

"Twins?" Solórzano interrupted again. "At the Intelligence Brigade?"

"Yes, twin boys."

"What happened to them? Did the file say?"

"A member of the task force kept them. Babies are often given away to infertile couples or sold. I told Beatriz Suárez's mother-in-law what happened."

"How did you locate her?" Now Solórzano's voice was husky with emotion.

"The file. Her daughter-in-law's full married name was—"

"I know," Solórzano said bitterly. "Beatriz Suárez de Mahler."

28

When the phone rang, Inés stuffed the passport receipt in a desk drawer and cradled the receiver between her ear and shoulder.

"It's me," Solo's voice said. "Did I wake you?"

"No. I was thinking about you. Where are you?"

"At a pay phone near the hotel. I'm all packed. We'll be out all day and then we leave for the airport."

"Any word on Malena?" she asked.

"Nothing. Yoshida is still trying. I'm going to talk to her father and another friend of hers today."

"May I come with you?"

He hesitated. "I wish you could, but I'm going to talk to her father after he and two other politicians meet with the commission. And her friend wants me to come alone. I'll let you know if I find out anything."

They both fell silent.

"How about you?" he said. "Anything from him?"

"Not since he came to see you. If only I could be certain that he got out. You are quite sure you didn't let anything drop about how we ran into his—colleagues..."

"I'm sure. I almost mentioned it, but I thought if he knew they were anywhere near you, he might change his mind and stay. He's gone. Now it's your turn to go."

She had already heard every one of Solo's arguments to persuade her to leave at once. She had made no objection. With Diego gone, her insecurity and urgency had begun to abate, but she had no desire to stay. All the same, an immediate departure was out of the question, she had told Solo. Even if she didn't have her parents, her studies, and her job to disengage from, there was the matter of her expired passport.

"I applied to renew my passport," she said.

She could hear the relief in his voice when he asked, "How long will it take?"

"A couple of weeks, I think. And that's with plenty of Black Label to lubricate its passage inside the police department."

She heard him inhale tightly.

"Yesterday," she said, "I came by your hotel but you were out. I left you a small parcel. Did you get it?"

"No. I've kept the room key with me, so I haven't stopped at the desk."

"It's an envelope. A tango cassette, and little gifts for the kids."

"Thank you. I'll get it right away."

"So, you'll be out all day," she said, unable to swallow her sadness. "I guess we won't be seeing each other, then."

"I guess not."

"Alberto would say it's our karma." She sighed. "We never really had a chance to talk, did we? I mean, I wish we had gone to a bar and had a bottle of wine and talked about New York. Do you ever think about it?"

"Yes. Do you?"

"Very often."

They were both silent. Then, she said, "I guess we can't rewind the tape..."

"No, we can't—can we..."

29

"I expect our meeting with Dr. Uriburu and his colleagues to run less than an hour," Hardoy told Solo before they joined Professor Summerhay in the car. "You said you prefer to speak to him alone afterwards."

"Yes, sir," Solo said. "I'm hoping he will talk more freely in private, with a friend of his daughter's."

"Very well. My conscience will protest, but I won't mention her."

Sunshine drenched the grandstand erected for dignitaries in Plaza de Mayo, from which the general who had been appointed as mayor would welcome the athletes taking part in the Buenos Aires Marathon. Thousands of spectators packed balconies, windows, and roofs along the route of the runners. Sky blue-and-white flags, pennants, and bunting flew from every lamppost. Factory workers and teacher-led schoolchildren brought into town by government buses strove to get within sight of the race, swelling the ranks of roped-off onlookers already four deep.

"Sorry, but I can't get any closer," the driver finally told them after trying for some time to discover a passage and finding police sawhorses barring the way at every turn.

"All right," Hardoy said. "Drop us off here. We'll walk the rest of the way and meet you back here in an hour."

The law office of Dr. Victorino Uriburu-Basavilbaso was in an older high-rise facing Plaza de Mayo, at the very corner where the runners, having completed a full lap around the square, would make an elbow turn and head towards Libertador Avenue and the Palermo district. As they threaded their way through the crowds, Solo heard a band on the square launch into a Souza march.

Dr. Uriburu, dressed in an impeccably tailored gray flannel suit, with silver hair and vest pocket chain to match, met them in his office's reception area. Solo saw at once Malena's high forehead, her slightly arched nose and, behind the tortoise shell-rimmed glasses, her quick hazel eyes.

"Good morning, gentlemen. Sorry my staff is off today—the marathon, you know. My colleagues have already arrived."

"Please excuse delay, our automobile could not penetrate crowd," Professor Summerhay communicated tolerably in Spanish as he and Dr. Hardoy introduced themselves and their interpreter, Mr. Kevin Solórzano.

Uriburu gave no sign of recognition when they were introduced. He doesn't know I'm Malena's friend, Solo realized. In their only conversation, over the phone, he had identified himself simply as Solo. Now did not seem the time to clear that up.

Shelves lined with law books led to their host's spacious office, where Solo noted the antique furniture and the walls hung with framed diplomas, certificates and photographs: Uriburu at the Vatican, kissing the Pope's ring; Malena with her sister at the seashore; Malena on horseback in full polo gear, knee-high boots, breeches and helmet, a mallet in her hand. The weathered face of the man in a beret holding the bridle of her horse surprised him with a kind of recollection: the resemblance to the Chilean youth at the polo field was unmistakable. This man had to be his father. Malena has been so good to my family, the young man said. This was the job she had found for the exiled horse trainer.

Two elderly gentlemen got up from armchairs and came forward, buttoning their jackets. Uriburu introduced them as the leaders of two other major political parties.

"We hope," said one of them, a portly man with epicanthic eye folds that made him look Asian, "that it is not too much of an imposition to meet here rather than at the Metropole."

"Not at all," Hardoy said as they sat down. "We regret that we won't be joined by other political leaders whom it has proved impossible to locate, but the site makes little difference to us. We are here to listen. Political parties are banned, so no doubt you had your reasons for desiring a change of venue."

"Quite so," said the third politician, a small, nervous man with a shark-fin nose. "The importance of contacts between human rights organizations and the country's legitimate political leaders cannot be overstated. Even so, we felt that the Hotel Metropole is now identified in the public mind with complaints about human rights, a controversial topic. It seemed to us more, shall we say, politic, to meet on more neutral ground, if that is the word I want, so as to forestall any misinterpretations, innocent or otherwise."

"...innocent or otherwise," Solo finished whispering into the side of Professor Summerhay's head that had tilted towards him. Even as he interpreted for the professor, Solo's eyes wandered through one of the large windows to the grandstand in the square below. The lilting palms cast elongated shadows across a starting line of yellow checkers painted on the asphalt, next to which stood a podium with a young woman wearing a "Miss Argentina" sash. Microphone in hand, the mayor was addressing the crowd.

Diego Fioravanti's words replayed in Solo's mind. *It was poison.* The doctor had injected poison into their hearts. How many times since entering this chamber of horrors had Solo believed he had heard it all, that nothing more loathsome could come up? Yet every revelation had turned out to be the anteroom to a fresh abomination. The Mahlers' daughter-in-law poisoned, David and Débora killed. And

Solo would probably never know whether he himself had caused their deaths, whether the admiral had ordered them killed because a self-commissioned do-gooder had seen fit to meddle. For one careless moment he had let his good intentions outrun his discretion, and three people were dead. Beware the fool with initiative.

We are a kind, decent, compassionate people, the politicians were telling Hardoy and Summerhay. To be sure, the reorganization process instituted by the armed forces had in some cases been carried to excess; the commission itself had probably ascertained as much, though far was it from them to pry into the commission's findings, which they knew must remain classified until the OAS made them public. But this country, which had been mired in violence, endless strikes, and runaway inflation, now enjoyed peace and prosperity. Just look around you.

"We have," Hardoy said tersely.

"On no account, of course," Malena's father said, "do we condone any violation of human rights. Our records speak for themselves. We have consistently condemned any and all abuse. But human rights considerations must be balanced against the needs of national security and defeating terrorism, to which we are all committed."

Outside, the field of runners scuttled into place. Solo studied Uriburu, his patrician bearing, the earnest demeanor and calm assurance with which he delivered the familiar lines that Solo himself had mechanically translated time and again—and that now seemed a grotesquerie.

"We beg not to be misunderstood," the pudgy man said. "There may be wrongs to right, yes. What war is utterly without injustices? But it does not help matters to be continuously bombarded with demands for investigations, especially from certain quarters—not your distinguished commission, certainly, but certain quarters traditionally intent on embarrassing the government. Last week, at the annual camaraderie luncheon of the armed forces, the Archbishop put it quite well when he said it's time to let bygones..."

Miss Argentina raised her hand, and—bang—the sound of her starting gun brought the pudgy politician up short.

As cheering drowned out the echoes of the shot, the six men watched the scrambling mass of bodies barreling round the square, arms and legs churning.

"It's good to see cheering crowds in Plaza de Mayo again," the small politician mused, "instead of the crazy women."

"I know," his chubby colleague agreed. "They are so sad, those women. They keep coming to see me, as if I could do something for them."

Professor Summerhay listened to Solo's rendering of these words and looked at the politicians, then turned to Solo. "Please tell these gentlemen this for me: As they pointed out, we are not at liberty to discuss our findings. But we can assure them that those women are perfectly sane."

Solo complied, and the politicians traded glances.

Of course, to call the women "crazy" was just a manner of speaking, they hastened to clarify. But to get back to the issue at hand—and here they grew even more serious, their eyes earnestly meeting their visitors' gaze—there was no hope of restoring democracy without the cooperation of the military. Facts had to be faced. Hence the need for political leaders to say or do nothing that might antagonize the military. Concerted action was the need of the hour.

Precisely, Malena's father concurred. Set aside differences and focus on job creation, strengthening the family, and providing economic opportunity for all: a united front, a coalition from which a single electoral ticket could ultimately be picked according to, say, how well each party had done in the last general election.

That approach, I'm afraid, would be highly misleading, his short fellow leader begged to disagree. After that election, voter disenchantment with government incumbents had given his own party a commanding lead in the congressional races held just before the coup.

His colleagues were talking ancient history, the third politician put in. Everyone knew that major splinter groups had broken off both their parties and thrown their support behind his, making him the clear front-runner.

While the men bickered, Solo remembered the painting he had seen at the Prado Museum in Madrid: Goya's haunting portrayal of men cudgeling each other as they sink into a quagmire. He glanced at Hardoy and saw him looking at Malena's father, a doleful expression on the chairman's face.

Surprisingly, when they left the building the sun had been replaced by thickly overcast skies. Dark tatters of clouds swirled ominously overhead. Under the wind-agitated palm fronds of Plaza de Mayo, the crowds were melting away before the impending storm. Hucksters bundled up their wares and drove a brisk last-minute trade among the scattering spectators. The government buses revved up their engines, collected their contingents, and joined the honking jam of traffic trying to leave the area.

"We won't get far in the car," Hardoy said to their chauffeur. "Please meet us at the hotel. We'll walk." Turning to Solo, Hardoy said, "The professor and I have to sort the documents we have in the safe at the OAS office, close by. You said you needed to run some personal errands. Let's meet right here in two hours for our last visit."

Solo watched Hardoy give him a final glance as the two men rounded the corner. Without hesitation, he immediately headed back to Uriburu's office.

"Ah, Mr. Solórzano," Malena's father said as he opened the door. "Did you forget something?"

"Sir, I'm Malena's friend. Remember I phoned you a few days ago?"

Uriburu's eyes opened wider. "Oh, yes. I thought your voice sounded familiar. Come in, please. Have you heard from Malena? I'm rather worried."

"So am I. Can we talk?"

"Of course."

They sat on the couch in the reception area.

Solo took a breath and plunged in. "Have you reported Malena's disappearance to anyone?"

"Disappearance?" Uriburu's eyebrows gathered. "You're using the term loosely, I trust. She said she would be staying with friends. She's done that before, you know. The last time she came, for her sister's wedding, she stayed away for days before coming home."

"Sir, Malena called you from the airport. But she never arrived at her friend's house. I talked to him."

Solo saw the color begin to ebb from Uriburu's cheeks.

"That's not all," Solo went on. "She asked for a meeting with Dr. Hardoy here in Buenos Aires and didn't show up. She wanted to talk about something called Operation Condor. Does that name mean anything to you?"

Uriburu shook his head. He took off the eyeglasses, revealing a deep vertical ridge between his eyebrows. His voice, when he spoke, was smaller. "What has happened to her?"

"I don't know. Have you made any inquiries?"

"I'm just back from Brazil. I called her boss, Admiral Rinaldi, but he's in Rome. His office checked and told me that Malena hasn't reported for work. I wasn't sure what to do next."

"Do you know any of her friends here in Buenos Aires?"

Doubt swept over Uriburu's face. He hesitated. "How well do you know Malena? I mean, are you one of her—friends?"

Solo looked at him. "Yes. I consider your daughter a very good friend. I've known her for years. She may have saved my life."

Uriburu nodded, his face cleared somewhat, and his uncertainty seemed to fall away. "Then, you know. My wife died when Malena was very young. I did my best bringing her up, but she was always a handful. That whole business with the FLH..."

He seemed tired and much older now. Solo sensed that he was expected to be sympathetic. He had no idea what the FLH was, but did not want to stem the flow of confidences. He assented with his head.

"When this military government came, it was all I could do to get her posted abroad. Fortunately, Admiral Rinaldi and Ambassador Capdevila, in Washington, are friends of mine. I love Malena. But I'm a public figure. I have a reputation to uphold. For a man in my position—I mean, in the present atmosphere of the country... You understand, don't you?"

This time Solo knew that he could not help but look utterly mystified.

Malena's father seemed flustered, as if trying to make up his mind about something. He slipped his glasses back on, drew a hard breath, and looked at his hands. "I guess you don't know. Perhaps this has nothing to do with her absence, but I think I ought to tell you." He looked up at Solo. "Malena is gay."

Solo was stunned. Malena? The Malena he knew? It seemed preposterous. But this was her own father saying it. He stared at him, and saw in his eyes the years of worry and helplessness over his daughter, and now the predicament in which he was trapped. All at once, with a gale force of clarity, Solo wondered how much more he didn't know about Malena.

As if divining his thoughts, Uriburu said, "Gay people are barred from our foreign service. She's had to keep it a secret."

Yes, Solo wanted to say, but he had known her before she joined the foreign service. The kind of intimacy that had taken root between them, Solo now realized, had never reached into the private depths of Malena's heart.

30

He hadn't been wrong. Malena's father had exhibited an aloofness, a guardedness, when Solo first telephoned. Now it was clear. *I'm a public figure. I have a reputation to uphold.* Uriburu was wary of his daughter's *friends.*

Solo skirted the obelisk, then walked through the Toscanini passageway under the Colón opera house to emerge within two blocks of his destination: the Grand Synagogue of Buenos Aires on Libertad street.

It was a striking building. Twelve copper medallions representing the tribes of Israel ornamented the iron railing. Concentric arches on a Romanesque or perhaps Byzantine façade framed a Star of David. Solo squinted above the star, where there seemed to be large black blotches.

"Tar bombs," a voice behind him said. "They are tired of cleaning them off, so they're just leaving the spatter. Follow me."

Néstor Reidlonger handed Solo a yarmulke and put one on himself.

"I'm actually an atheist," Reidlonger whispered as they entered the building. Inside, an old man sitting at a small table in the vestibule looked at them briefly before going back to his book.

"My uncle," Reidlonger said. He produced from a pocket a small memo pad, tore off a page and handed it Solo. "My number. It's for you alone. Give it out to nobody, understand?"

The large three-nave temple was deserted. A brooding opalescence of cobalt, cranberry, and gold seeped from the stained-glass windows, tracing lacy patterns over walls designed to look like rock. They sat on one of the dark oak benches in the rear. Néstor Reidlonger looked to Solo to be in his early forties. Blond, short and wiry, with a slightly lazy eye that lost focus when he talked.

"No word?" Reidlonger asked.

Solo shook his head. "Her father's heard nothing."

Reidlonger shut his eyes. "They've sucked her in, I just know it."

Solo shivered. "How can you be certain?"

"She was worried. They summoned her back because of something she discovered, something called Operation Condor."

"What did she tell you about it?" Solo said, aware that he was not volunteering his own information. He had learned that lesson.

"Nothing. That's why I asked you. The recall must have been a ploy. They were waiting for her at the airport. They must have made her call her father's to say she would be staying with a friend and would be home soon." Reidlonger opened his eyes and looked at him. "Solo, we have to do something. Your OAS commission..."

Solo heard the anguish in Reidlonger's voice and thought of the Mahlers' refusal to seek help from the commission, lest the government kill more of their family. Which it had done anyway.

He said, "I'll speak to Hardoy, the chairman of the commission. But there's so much I don't know. Tell me about the FLH."

Reidlonger paused. "Her father told you... "

"Yes."

"And he told you about Malena."

Solo nodded.

Reidlonger took a deep breath. "Malena and I were among the founders of the FLH, the *Frente de Liberación Homosexual.* We brought together gay men, lesbians, transvestites, young and old, blue-collar and professionals. Nobody had ever done anything like that in this country. *Fags With Perón* read the sign we raised in Plaza de Mayo when Perón came back from exile. We weren't much of a liberation front," Reidlonger half-smiled. "We didn't kidnap. We didn't plant bombs. We didn't take over television stations to issue proclamations. We just wanted to change an authoritarian way of life, a hypocritical mentality."

His eyes fixed on Solo's. "You don't know what it's like—to have to constantly suppress your feelings, not be yourself. We wanted a society where we would not be lepers, where we could live openly, raise children, grow old together, and weep over each other's graves. We didn't want tolerance; we wanted respect. We wanted our human rights."

Solo maintained Reidlonger's gaze and nodded. "What happened to the FLH?"

"We were so naive. To the right, we were biological degenerates. They wanted to lynch us. To the left, we were a capitalist blight. In marches and demonstrations, everybody moved away from us. So we became pamphleteers, putting up street posters in the dead of night."

Néstor Reidlonger hugged himself against the damp. "Then came the coup with its 'Western and Christian' and its 'national security.' We were harassed, beaten in public by the police, kidnapped, murdered. Most of the FLH fled abroad. Gays are barred from the foreign service, but Malena's father got her a post in Washington."

Solo stared at the large pipe organ above the apse with its tabernacle containing the Torah. So much he didn't know.

"I thought she wouldn't last as a diplomat," Reidlonger went on. "Not our beautiful Malena who loves to outrage propriety, who takes life by the lapels and shakes it. But I was wrong. When you don't fear for your life, she told me, having a double identity can be fun, like role-playing."

Yes, Solo thought. He could see how that would appeal to Malena.

"And you? Why did you stay?"

Reidlonger's shoulders rose and fell in a drawn-out shrug. "When I was a kid I wanted to be president of my country. Then, in school, I learned that our constitution bars non-Catholics from the presidency. Now I hear the antisemitic chants at union rallies and soccer stadiums. I see the graffiti on walls, the Nazi literature in bookstores and newsstands, the tar bombs—and I ask myself the same question: why did I stay?"

Reidlonger cast his eyes to the granite floor. "My grandfather came here in 1889 fleeing the Russian pogroms. My father was born in Moisesville, a Jewish farming community six hundred kilometers north of Buenos Aires. My mother's family left Poland before Hitler invaded; they settled up north, in the city of Corrientes. Her father dressed as a shtetl Jew to his dying day, and my mother marveled that there was no ghetto in Corrientes, that people stepped off the narrow sidewalks to let them pass, instead of the other way around."

Reidlonger met Solo's eyes. "They're all buried here. I go to the cemetery and worry that their headstones may be overturned or have swastikas painted on them. But they're here."

"And so are you..."

"And so am I."

No, Solo wanted to say, that's dangerous sentimentality. How can you think that way, knowing what you know? Get the hell out while you can. "Néstor, when was the last time you saw Malena?"

"When she came to her sister's wedding some months ago. I was afraid she might be taking a chance, but the FLH no longer mattered; it had been destroyed and forgotten, and everything went smoothly. Malena was so happy. I've never seen her so radiant. At the wedding, her father was going to dance the traditional waltz with her sister, and Malena wanted to dance a tango with him. But they needed practice, had to learn to dance together. Inés, a friend of Malena's, mentioned a place with a good instructor: the Ideal. At first her father wouldn't hear of it—he didn't want to be seen in a tango parlor. Don't worry, Malena told him. Dark shades and made-up names. Nobody will know who we are, I promise. She talked him into it. I don't know—maybe he liked the idea of a little adventure, or maybe he didn't want to spoil her fun. They had the best time, Malena said."

"What name did she use?"

Solo's quavering voice made Reidlonger look up and stare at him, surprised. "The alias she always used with the FLH: Violeta Argerich."

Solo heard a strangled sound in his own throat, and a rolling tide of misery and hopelessness swept over him.

Garay and Paseo Colón streets lay a dozen blocks south of Plaza de Mayo, in an area of run-down rooming houses, decaying buildings, and shabby shops moldering away on the edge of the old business district. An hour after parting from Reidlonger, Solo stopped with Hardoy and Professor Summerhay in front of the door of the Athletic Club.

Hardoy rang the doorbell. Almost at once a uniformed policeman opened the door and inquired their business. Hardoy replied. The policeman told them to wait in the street, then shut the door.

Professor Summerhay turned to Solo and said in English, "There's still time to change your mind. Are you sure you wouldn't rather wait for us here?"

Solo shook his head. Dazed and distraught as he was when he rejoined Hardoy and the professor and narrated his conversation with Reidlonger, he yet forced himself to cling to the hope that there might be a mistake, that Diego Fioravanti's memory had played him false, that he had misread the file, misidentified the shooting victim. That it was not Malena.

"I want to come in," he said.

The door opened and a police corporal stood before them. Hardoy repeated the explanation he had given to the first policeman.

"You're certainly welcome to look around," the corporal said, "but I can guarantee there's nothing here that can possibly interest you."

They followed him inside. *As soon as new prisoners arrived they were led to the torture rooms with guards raining blows on them.* The words of the doctor in Mendoza rang in Solo's head. This was where they had brought Malena.

The place was being readied for demolition, the corporal explained while guiding them past mounds of broken bricks and tile. It was an old structure, neglected for years. He himself had been posted here last week as custodian. About the previous occupants he knew nothing.

Solo's eyes wandered over rooms that were empty or contained dust-encrusted desks, chairs, and other variously debauched pieces of furniture. The tour ended in a large tiled hall with glass doors, empty but for a number of long wooden benches, a rusty coffeemaker propped up on an overturned crate, and a freestanding, pockmarked blackboard. Layers of desiccated wallpaper curled from the plaster.

The corporal made a sweeping gesture. "This is all there is. If you gentlemen tell me what it is that you are looking for—you can see for yourselves that there's nothing here."

Hardoy looked at the hat in his hands and wiped a speck off with the sleeve of his coat. "Actually, we didn't expect to find anything. If you will show us the basement, we will take a look and be on our way."

"The basement?"

"Yes, the basement. You know—the cellar. The door leading to the steps, past the water tank."

The corporal gave him a long look. "Yes, of course, the basement. It's just that there is nothing there. It's being used to store supplies, so it's cluttered and dusty. But if you gentlemen don't mind getting dirty... Just watch your step going down."

With no handrail to hold on to, they gingerly followed the corporal down a stairway lighted by a bare bulb. Six, seven, eight, Solo counted steps in his head. At the bottom, to the rear of the dripping water tank, lay a shadowy area littered with wrecking tools and piles of materials. Chunks of mortar crunched underfoot. The air was dank and stale.

"See?" the corporal said as they looked about, eyes adjusting to the dark. "There's nothing here."

From his coat pocket Hardoy produced a small flashlight and handed it to Solo, who led the way into a narrow hallway separating two rows of cells. The corporal didn't follow them.

There were also two men and two women who had been brought in two nights before, and placed in the first cell, next to mine. I heard one of them scratching the wall at night. The guards came to get those four before dawn, with a priest, which I thought was a bad sign.

The first door on the right was open. Solo went in, followed by Hardoy and the professor, and played the beam over the walls of the enclosure. A few inches from the cement floor, on the wall dividing the cell from its neighbor, the ray of light shone on a freshly scratched inscription.

DIOS ME AMPARE

God help me, Solo's trembling lips translated involuntarily as his eyes found the name scrawled below.

MALENA

31

It was raining hard when the three men left the Athletic Club. The street was empty of traffic and people.

"I'm so sorry," Hardoy repeated as they huddled under a narrow balcony. Solo could barely register the words from the chairman and the professor.

The street remained deserted, and Hardoy cursed himself for letting their driver go. They were about to give up and start back to the Metropole on foot when a cab happened by, a tiny Renault with a cord stretched across the front passenger seat to prevent anyone's sitting there. Once the chairman and the professor managed to wedge themselves into the rear seat, the driver shook his head at Solo and raised two fingers to indicate only two passengers.

"I'll wait for the next cab," Solo said to overcome the objections of his companions, feeling almost glad to be alone.

He crossed the street in search of better shelter and found it under the mini-portico of a dilapidated two-story house. One leaf of its double door was open, the other closed. He climbed the doorsill concaved by countless footsteps, a slab of marble yellow and brown with age, and leaned back against the closed half of the door, staring by turns at the rain, the curbside freshet, the Athletic Club.

"Are you..."

More words followed through the open half of the door, but he couldn't make them out. He leaned over and peered inside. A figure in a tunic was lying on the tile floor under the mailboxes, looking at him. An old woman, he thought, until the figure started to get up and spoke again.

"You waiting to get your car?" The words were slurred, but it was a man, an old man. What looked like a tunic was a threadbare gray overcoat several sizes too big. As he hobbled forward, the man's swollen hands adjusted a peaked captain's cap on his head.

"My car?" The man must be a watchman looking after street-parked cars for tips. "No, I don't have a car."

"Oh," the old man came out to the doorsill and stood beside Solo on tottery legs. "How about a cigarette? Do you have a cigarette?"

Solo smelled the alcohol and saw the bulge of the bottle in the overcoat pocket.

"Sorry. I quit."

The old man looked at him as if to say, Are you good for anything? But he scratched the white stubble on his chin and said, with animation, "Sure, lots of people quit now. Smoking's bad for you. I never smoked when I was young. Had to be in good shape then. A boxer, that's what I was."

He raised his fists and threw a couple of feeble punches into the air. "Professional. Can't smoke when you're a professional. Screws up the lungs."

They stood in silence, watching the storm break in earnest with bursts of brilliant lightning and booming cannonades echoing across the city.

"How're you getting home?" the old man asked. "You are not from around here, are you?"

"No, I'm not."

"Yeah. I know everybody around here. Been here a long time, working this area. Lots of tourists like you, especially today with the marathon. When it rains I take a nap, see? Don't like to get wet because of my rheumatism. Then I'm out on the street again. All day, all night, out on the street. That man is a tourist, I said when I woke up and saw you standing there across the street."

"What made you think that?"

A toothless grin brightened the bloodshot eyes. "See? You're a tourist. You don't know. You never want to stand in front of that building. Not that one. And you never want to go in. No, sir. Go in and you'll come back out, all right—late at night, when there's nobody around and the truck comes and they load you on it and off you go."

He started to laugh but hiccupped instead. "You're from Uruguay, aren't you? I can tell. Lots of tourists from Uruguay here. I went to Uruguay once. Had three fights there. Lost them all." This time he managed a low gurgle of a laugh. "But I sure had fun there. Beautiful women in your country. Almost married one. You sure you don't have a cigarette?"

"Here," Solo fished a bill from his pocket. "Buy yourself a pack."

The old man took the bill without looking at it and stuffed it in a recess of his coat. "Yes, sir. Someday I'm going back to Uruguay. Visit all my friends. You from Uruguay, you say?"

"No, *norteamericano*," Solo said, stepping off the doorway.

The old man looked at him, stock-still. Solo hurried away and had gone half a block when he heard, "Hey! Mister!"

He stopped and waited for the limping figure to catch up. The old man was soaked. He seemed quite sober now.

"Mister, I'm sorry. I didn't know. You won't tell them what I said, will you? I mean, about the building. Please, sir. I could get in trouble."

Solo walked on in the rain. He walked short stretches at first, ducking into doorways, seeking shelter under lintels and balconies, stopping here and there to watch the rain pelt the roofs, the wind lash the trees. After a while he gave himself up to the blinding rain and walked without pause, slowly, deliberately, letting the water fill his shoes and climb up his socks, stepping methodically into every puddle, as he used to do when he was little and his mother would scold him for it.

Malena was dead. She had been sucked in on arrival, the day before he himself flew in and met with the admiral in his office. She was already at the Athletic Club when Rinaldi asked him if he had seen her yet. On Saturday night, she had been in that cell, her body crippled by three days of torture, scratching the wall with her handcuffs, waiting to be murdered—while he dined with Inés and her parents. At dawn, when they shot her and buried her in an unmarked grave, he had been sleeping in his hotel bed. God only knew what they had done to her to get Reidlonger's address. Diego Fioravanti's words kept coming back: *I had trouble recognizing her.* But she had not told them about the meeting at the polo field.

He wandered into a musty cafe and sat by a window, staring out at the fury of the storm, the electric sky, listening to the cracking thunder and drinking coffee and grappa in the empty barroom. When he took off his wet jacket and hung it over the back of the adjoining chair, his eye fell on the left inside pocket. There, where he had tucked it in hurriedly before leaving the Metropole, was the small manila envelope Inés had left with her gifts at the hotel. A forgotten handkerchief in the outside pocket had absorbed most of the water and kept the inner pocket dry. The envelope was from a Familia Madariaga of Posadas, in the northern province of Misiones, and was addressed to him care of Inés. She had clipped a note to it: "Mrs. Madariaga died shortly after writing your mother. Her family sent me this."

He ripped the envelope open. Inside were a sealed letter addressed to his mother by someone named Haydée Madariaga at the same address in Posadas, and a plastic passport holder.

The letter was in an old-fashioned air mail envelope yellowing with age, its borders striped a fading blue and white. Below the cancelled Argentine postage was a still-legible Return to Sender stamp from the U.S. postal service dated some four months after his father's drowning. It noted that Sra. Evelyn Solórzano was no longer at that

Brooklyn address—the rented apartment where Solo and his parents had lived before moving to Argentina, and to which he and his mother had never returned.

He hesitated. His mother was dead, yet it still seemed an obscure offense to open a letter addressed to her. Sighing, he tore open the envelope and extracted two handwritten onion-skin sheets.

Buenos Aires, November 7, 1963

Dear Mrs. Solórzano:

I hope this letter reaches you at the address the American Consulate gave me for you.

My husband Leandro and I were passengers on the ill-fated Ciudad de Asunción. He, like your husband, died in the shipwreck. I survived but have been in and out of hospital ever since, and when I recently tried to contact you I learned that you and your son had left Argentina and returned to the United States. I have in my possession your husband's passport that was in the pocket of his coat. I don't dare entrust it to the mail. I could have it delivered to the American Consulate, but will wait until I hear back from you.

Leandro and I met Mr. Solórzano at the shipboard dinner shortly after we set sail from Montevideo. It was my great fortune in this tragedy that we were thrown together again at four in the morning, when we were all roused from sleep and ordered to assemble on deck wearing our life jackets. In the dense fog the ship had veered off the navigation channel and struck the submerged remains of a freighter, knocking out all power and lights.

It was a calm, cold night. I was seven months pregnant and shivering, and your husband took off his fur-lined coat and made me wear it. As we waited for the lifeboats to be lowered, fire broke out and began to spread rapidly.

In the thick smoke and panic that followed, lifeboats overturned and people jumped into the water. Your husband kept a group of us together, upwind from the fire, until the very last minute when the flames finally forced everyone overboard.

I cannot swim. Your husband pulled me to a floating piece of wreckage and went looking for Leandro, from whom we had become separated in the dark. He did not find him. Back and forth he swam, bringing other people to the plank I was holding on to, urging us to keep moving in the frigid water. The last time he went off he did not return.

Hours after dawn the first rescue boats arrived, too late for many whose numb bodies had drifted off with the current. I now know that I survived thanks to your husband's coat and because he kept us on board until the very last. A few more minutes in the cold water might have been fatal.

I will never get over Leandro's death. But every time I look at Carlota, our beautiful baby named for your husband, I give thanks for him. Inconsolable as I know you and your son must be, I hope you will draw a measure of comfort from knowing that Mr. Solórzano risked and lost his life to save perfect strangers. The noblest of souls, he will remain in our hearts and our prayers as long as we live. With all my affection,

Haydée Madariaga

The tears Solo had long held back would no longer be denied. He let them roll down his cheeks.

It had taken him sixteen years and the words of a dead woman to learn the truth of his father's last night, which his mother had never known. This letter would have given her some of the solace she had never found after his death.

So much to cry for. Not only his father. The Mahlers, and countless others along the road of misery and horror he had walked since setting foot again in Argentina.

And now Malena, kidnapped and killed like the rest. And he had done nothing to prevent it. He didn't even know why they had killed her.

But he would find out.

He unclasped the plastic passport holder, which bore the name and logo of a Buenos Aires travel agency. The passport inside was discolored and warped, its stiff pages largely illegible, but the photograph was the same picture Solo remembered on his father's State Department ID.

There were three more items in the plastic jacket. Two were laminated identification cards, which had proved impervious to water damage. Over the name and head shot of his father, one card read *Policía Federal Argentina*, the other *Policía Nacional de Uruguay*. The third item looked like a photocopy of a larger volume reduced to a pocket-size booklet. It was swollen and misshapen, and paper flaked off its brittle pages when Solo began to turn them. But the smudged title on the cover, repeated in the header on each page, was plain enough: Kubark Counterintelligence Interrogation Manual.

Solo's hands dropped the booklet on the table.

A bolt of incandescent light ripped the air, and in its dazzling brightness a flash of insight and certainty came with stark clarity into his mind. The answers he had long sought were in Washington. And he would find them.

PART III

32

Carrying a cassette player and a large interoffice envelope under one arm, Solo walked down Seventeenth Street past the American Red Cross building to the OAS headquarters, a handsome white marble villa roofed in red tile, on the corner of Constitution Avenue. A panoramic vista of the Washington Monument and the Ellipse opened up on his left as he crossed the flag-lined driveway and began climbing the marble staircase. The first limousines were arriving. Police cars flashing rooftop beacons flanked the entrance and exit of the curving driveway, with more cruisers visible along Constitution Avenue. A police van unloaded sawhorses to fence off a group of demonstrators.

On the building façade, the familiar carvings of George Washington bidding farewell to his generals after the American Revolutionary War, and José de San Martín and Simón Bolívar meeting in Guayaquil during the South American wars of independence, allegorized the Americas. Solo reached the bronze grillwork of the three arched entrances at the top of the stairs and looked at the protesters across the street. They were unfurling banners emblazoned "Stop Argentine Nazis," and "Shut Down U.S. School of Assassins." The women among them, he saw, wore white head scarves and carried framed photographs.

He pushed through the massive revolving doors and entered the building. In the lofty entrance hall his friend Schunk, the security guard, looked up and smiled at him as he checked IDs at the reception desk. Next to Schunk stood Alvarez, the protocol officer, a stocky, good-natured man with rimless eyeglasses and a white carnation in the lapel of his suit.

"Good morning, sir, how's the foot today?" Alvarez greeted the Brazilian ambassador who limped to the desk ahead of Solo, one hand on a walking cane, the other on the arm of his chauffeur.

"Better, thank you, Mr. Alvarez. Good morning, Mr. Schunk." The ambassador looked around. "It certainly looks busy here today, doesn't it?"

Camera crews were uncoiling wires and maneuvering gear around small groups of diplomats. Beyond the entrance hall, in the adjacent glass-roofed patio from which tropical vegetation rose three stories high, Solo could see reporters clustering around the pink marble fountain, sitting on benches under jipijapa palms, or pacing, glancing curiously at the figures of pre-Columbian gods depicted on the floor tiles.

"Oh, yes, very busy indeed, sir!" Alvarez said, and Solo saw Schunk's eyes roll discreetly at him. "I keep telling the media it's a closed-door session, but they've been relentless since they got hold of the report."

"Yes," the ambassador said with a frown as he started for the Council chamber, "I expect we will hear a great deal about that today."

Alvarez smiled and turned to the next party in line. "Ah, good morning Mr. Solorzano. Ready for the big day?"

Earphones in place, Solo moistened his lips and bent the neck of the mic upward. The big day. The OAS Council would be addressing the report on Argentina. And Inés was coming to Washington. Solo looked at his watch. She would be leaving for Ezeiza airport in half an hour. And landing at National tonight. Diego would be there to meet her.

Today of all days, Tracy was late. Solo would have to go first. He turned in his chair and pushed the door of the booth shut, his eyes snagging on "The Garden of the Bureaucrats." Schunk's painting took up most of the back wall of the booth. Tracy still didn't know what to make of it. You mean Schunk painted it? she asked. Schunk, the security guard? Whenever they partnered in this booth, she would stare at the painting's depictions of rock formations growing out of walls in the skyborne garden, the lizards crawling over the back porch, the little men in black suits carrying briefcases and scurrying about.

Where the hell was she, anyway? Tracy was never late. And he had asked her as a personal favor to get here early, so he could go find Hardoy before the meeting opened.

Too late. Hardoy was walking into the Council chamber now, Professor Summerhay at his side. The chairman looked wayworn after his all-night flight from Uruguay. Solo put the tape recorder on the counter and slid the envelope containing the Mendoza papers under it. His meeting with Hardoy would have to wait. There was no way he could talk to him now, unless the man stepped out to go to the bathroom. If so, after a quick switch with Tracy, Solo could head him off outside. If Tracy showed up.

Three heavy raps in his ears. The chairman's mic had come alive.

"Ladies and gentlemen..."

Solo turned on his mic. Two more taps on the microphone from the chairman's fingers extinguished most conversation in the chamber.

"May I have a little quiet, please. This meeting of the Council will now come to order. Thank you. Will the Secretary please read the order of business?"

"Yes, Mr. Chairman. The single item is the report on Argentina submitted by the OAS Commission on Human Rights."

"Thank you. We will hear comments from the delegations and from Dr. Hardoy before opening the floor for debate..."

The door of the booth opened and Tracy came in, winded, face flushed. She picked up the pen and legal pad on her side of the counter.

"SO SORRY," read the block letters she slipped under his nose.

"HUGE TRAFFIC JAM. LET ME TAKE OVER."

He nodded, still speaking into the mic.

"The Chair recognizes Argentina."

"Thank you, Mr. Chairman. Naturally, my delegation has much to say about this report, which, whether or not the commission realizes it, plays into the hands of the enemies of freedom and undermines our war on subversion. But first, a matter of the utmost gravity. The report was leaked to the press before this Council could discuss it and my government could present its rebuttal. This is simply unconscionable. My country is now presumed guilty. Demonstrations and protests are being organized against it, one right here, in front of this building. The damage has been done, but the Council must investigate the origin of this leak and hold the commission accountable for it. My delegation so moves."

Investigate all you want, Solo thought. He glared through the glass. You'll find nothing. Alberto had been given the report to translate and Solo had simply dropped a copy in a mailbox, addressed to a reporter he knew.

"*Traduttore, traditore,*" Alberto had quipped with a sad smile.

Translator, traitor. Solo shrugged off the maxim. He did not feel like a traitor, and doubted Alberto did.

Tracy was ready, her mic open. Solo waited for the speaker to pause, gave her the nod, then shut off his mic, pulling back from the counter. Quietly, he let himself out of the booth.

Crossing the tropical patio, he could hear the demonstrators chorusing the bullhorn outside.

"What do we want?"

"Human rights!"

"When do we want them?"

"Now!"

He ducked into a phone booth by the pressroom. As he dialed his home answering machine, he thought back to his children's wild delight when he came home, how they had jumped around him and hugged him and squealed, later snuggling up to him that evening for their story. Saturnina had even grinned. This morning she was taking the kids to the park, but the recorder would give him the messages, tell him if Hardoy had responded to him. He punched in the remote code and heard the tape rewind after the beep.

"Solo, it's Phyllis. I know you don't want to talk to me, but..."

He punched nine to skip to the next message. "Solo, it's Doris. Professor Summerhay called from the airport. Dr. Hardoy's flight came in late and they're going straight to the meeting. Dr. Hardoy says he and the professor will meet you in the snack bar after the morning session. And let me know if you finished checking my transcript of the Villa Devoto tape and filling in the blanks. Bye..."

A long beep and a pause. Diego's voice came on. "It's me. I called Valeria and she was all worked up, but she says it's okay, just her imagination. She's leaving to pick up Inés. I've done a dry run to National Airport, put air in your tires and gas in the tank. Now I'm working on getting your windows open. Has Hardoy arrived yet? I'll be out—Doris asked me to come see her. Call you later."

Solo fished in his pocket for another dime and dialed again. He left a message for Doris saying he was nearly done with the transcript and then, to avoid the reporters, walked back around the patio. Diego was staying at a cheap hotel on Tenth Street, shuttling to and from a phone company call center on Thirteenth to place the international calls to Valeria. Everything was apparently on schedule. Solo wished he could be at the airport to greet Inés too, but there was no telling when this meeting would be over.

He let himself back in through the interpreters' side entrance. In the French booth, Sabine read a magazine while Marcel, the great gesticulator, worked, accompanying every word of his rendering with sweeping hand gestures. Solo entered the English booth and sat down next to Tracy. He picked up the headset. Argentina was speaking.

"... riddled with inaccuracies and unsubstantiated allegations. My delegation accordingly asks to be included in any working group set up to draft new rules for the commission. Thank you, Mr. Chairman."

"I thank Argentina for its remarks and turn the floor over to Uruguay."

"Thank you, Mr. Chairman. We in Uruguay have also been harshly criticized for defending ourselves against subversion. Like other neighboring countries, we understand and sympathize with the antiterrorist efforts of the government and people of Argentina and believe that we are all ill-served by this one-sided report. Thank you, Mr. Chairman."

"The Chair recognizes Jamaica."

"Mr. Chairman, unlike some delegations, mine believes that we are all indebted to the commission for this report, even if it gives us no pleasure to read it. It describes aberrations that we cannot and should not deny, because they run counter to the vision of a domestic and international community we hope we all share. The commission did not imagine the abductions, rapes, torture and killings, the murder of a country's own citizens within its own borders and abroad. When Mr. Letelier and his assistant and her husband were blown up only blocks from here in Dupont Circle, American intelligence agencies told us that they were probably murdered by opponents of Mr. Pinochet trying to discredit his government. Now we know better. Now we know about something called Operation Condor. It's all here, in black and white, in this report from our own commission..."

No, it was not all there. Only the smallest suggestion was there. Since returning to Washington, Solo had been unable to dig up any more information on Condor. Nobody he asked knew, or would admit to knowing, anything about it. A day spent at the Library of Congress raking through human rights reports and newspaper accounts of the three-year-old Justice Department investigation into the Letelier murders had offered some shadowy illumination and led back to an older story—a story involving his own father.

He had hated to do it, but he had no choice—to trace his father's lineage in the American government. Close inspection of Charles Solorzano's State Department ID in the box of family papers Solo kept in his bedroom closet had revealed the acronym he had overlooked: AID/OPS. Under the cover of the Agency for International Development, his father had worked for something called the Office of Public Safety, which, Solo learned from his research, was a front for the CIA within the State Department. OPS did for police in the Third World what the School of the Americas did for the military in Latin America. It recruited thousand of foreign students for its International Police Academy in Georgetown and its bomb-making school in Texas; its agents abroad funded, equipped, and trained foreign security forces. In Vietnam, OPS had dropped live prisoners from helicopters into the Pacific Ocean and taught torture techniques using a manual called Kubark, a cryptonym for the CIA. Its secret facilities in Panama and Buenos Aires designed special interrogation devices for distribution to military and police forces throughout Latin America. The accounts of torture from survivors described the interrogators with American accents, the red, white and blue USAID shield emblazoned on the small generators that produced the shocks. All this and more had come to light in 1974, ten years after his father's death, when adverse publicity from leaks had forced Congress to look into the activities of OPS and eventually shut it down. The government and human rights reports Solo had turned up provided a full enough picture of what OPS had done before and after his father's death.

By 1974, the many attempts of the Nixon administration to thwart the election of Salvador Allende in Chile—including the murder of General René Schneider, head of the Chilean army—had backfired. Allende had become president, only to be overthrown and killed in the Pinochet coup. Michael Townley, a CIA-trained killer working for Pinochet, had then been sent to Buenos Aires to blow up the exiled General Prats. More murders of dissidents and exiles followed in Europe and the Americas. In the waning days of the Ford administration, with Henry still running the show and Bush heading the CIA, Townley had struck yet again, this time leading a team of Cuban exiles to murder

Letelier in D.C. Last year, the Carter administration had finally extradited Townley and put him on trial, but he would walk, the papers reported. In exchange for his testimony, he had been granted immunity and would be set free with a new identity. He would not be extradited to answer for his other crimes abroad.

The Letelier case, the only part of the story that seemed to interest the American media because the crime had taken place in D.C., had brought to light assassinations spanning three continents, including seventy-three people blown up in a Cuban jetliner over Barbados shortly after the Letelier bombing. All these killings, the press intimated, were now suspected of being part of something larger called Operation Condor. But that was not the whole, not even the heart of the story, Solo now knew. Untold numbers of exiles throughout Latin America were being hunted down by the governments of countries where they had taken refuge. Malena had known it too. And it had killed her.

In his restless nights following the relief of his return, her image disrupted his slumber and stalked his dreams. He saw her most often as he had known her in New York, recently arrived, exultant in her new life. He hadn't then known the reasons for that *joie de vivre*—her sense of liberation, the repression she had left behind. Now it seemed as if he had never really known Malena. Or he had known her just well enough to be captivated by her, just long enough for her to kiss his heart.

"I will now turn the floor over to Dr. Hardoy, who has something to add."

"Thank you, Mr. Chairman. I'll be very brief. Three items. This week, security forces raided the offices of human rights organizations in Argentina and seized large numbers of confidential documents, including habeas corpus applications, lists of missing persons, and lists of torture centers and torturers. Also, there are reports that the government intends to declare an amnesty for all personnel involved in fighting subversion. Records pertaining to thousands of cases are to be destroyed. Lastly, the Argentine ambassador has objected to the media's gaining access to our report before today. As required by our rules, the report was distributed to all delegations a week ahead of this meeting, so that they could review it beforehand. We obviously cannot answer for any unauthorized disclosure that may have taken place after that distribution. Thank you, Mr. Chairman."

"The Chair recognizes Argentina."

"Thank you, Mr. Chairman. The searches and seizure of documents at so-called human rights organizations were carried out under a court order. Surely the commission does not claim that any entity allegedly engaged in human rights work is thereby above the law and not required to obey court orders. If such entities have nothing to hide they should have nothing to fear from our courts, which alone have jurisdiction in these matters. Argentina, I must remind Dr. Hardoy, is a sovereign republic. Now, as to the amnesty, our military have no apology to make for preserving Western Christian civilization in my country. Even so, we want to turn the page on this tragic chapter in our history. That is why an amnesty should be declared and the records destroyed, as an act of reconciliation, an act of love."

Tracy was holding her forehead with one hand, her eyes widening as she rendered these words. The glance she flicked Solo said: Did you hear that? Solo gave her a grim frown.

"Because our war on terrorism has made it necessary to suspend certain rights, the commission absurdly claims that free license is given in my country to every act of depravity. Of course there may be a few bad apples among our security forces. But if personnel in uniform have committed abuses, you may be certain that corrective action has been swiftly taken. Ladies and gentlemen, legend has it that grass never grew again where Attila's horse trod. The question we must all ask ourselves is: why is the commission bent on likening my government to Attila's horse? Thank you, Mr. Chairman."

"Thank you, sir. I see that Haiti wishes to make a short comment. Yes, Mr. Ambassador?"

"It is only about Attila's horse, Mr. Chairman. The question I am asking myself is what did they feed this horse of Attila's..."

"Order, order! Please, ladies and gentlemen. Thank you. I'm sure we all appreciate that even the most serious debate need not be devoid of humor, but I must ask the chamber to quiet down so that we may..."

Tracy was signaling. Time. Solo opened his mic and took over.

"The Chair recognizes Dr. Hardoy."

"Thank you, Mr. Chairman. The rights no government may ever suspend are few indeed: life, personal safety, due process, the right not to be tortured. These are the essential rights of all human beings. To every writ of habeas corpus, the Argentine government replies that the missing person is not in custody or is being held under so-called "national security laws" at the discretion of the Executive. No investigation is ever ordered by the courts that the ambassador says have jurisdiction. No judge has ever inspected any of the hundreds of detention facilities identified in thousands of complaints. Those locations are as well known to the Argentine judiciary as they became to the commission after a mere few days in the country. Hundreds of depositions from torture victims, people all ages, from every walk of life, concur down to the minutest detail in their descriptions of the torture rooms, the torturers, and the tortures. Those victims, and those of us who visited the so-called Athletic Club in Buenos Aires, can tell you how many steps there are in the staircase to the basement and describe the inscriptions on the walls. The names of the torturers and murderers have been reported time and again to the authorities. No one has been charged with these crimes."

Solo's eyes alighted on Professor Summerhay, sitting next to Hardoy. He too looked worn out, shoulders hunched, brow knotted. Doris said he was the new Vice Chairman, succeeding Fonseca whose term of appointment to the commission had run out.

"The Argentine ambassador talks about saving Western Christian civilization. More than two hundred clergymen in Argentina have been arrested or murdered after being savagely tortured. Over a hundred journalists are missing and their own newspapers refuse to print paid advertisements from family members looking for them. Jews, less than one percent of the country's population, account for more than ten percent of the disappeared, with the worst tortures reserved for them. This is the largest mass killing of Jews since World War II. And for these and other atrocities, the government finds warrant in what it calls its war on subversion. Kidnapping, brutally torturing and murdering defenseless civilians, stealing their children, looting their property—can these be termed acts of war? What then of the Geneva Conventions signed and ratified by every country in this chamber?"

Hardoy paused and drank from the water glass in front of him. A dense silence had descended over the Council chamber.

"A final word. The ambassador has reminded me that his country is a sovereign republic. It was, indeed, as a sovereign state that Argentina undertook to be bound by treaties protecting human rights. And as for being a republic, surely the ambassador needs reminding of the meaning of the word. A republic is a state in which supreme power rests in the people and is exercised by representatives elected by and answerable to the people. Thank you, Mr. Chairman."

"Thank you, Dr. Hardoy. I see by the clock that we are well into lunch time. The Chair proposes adjourning. Any objections? This meeting will reconvene at three o'clock."

Solo removed the earphones, leaned back in his chair and looked at Tracy. She pushed back her chair, looking shaken.

"I'm off," she said. "Sure you won't come with us?"

"I'm sure. Thanks."

She shouldered her handbag and got up. "I'm getting worried about you. I mean, this whole business—aren't you taking it too hard? Why don't you come with us? Get some fresh air, clear your head."

"Thanks, but I have to catch Hardoy. I'll get a sandwich later."

Tracy nodded and squeezed his shoulder on her way out. Solo's eyes remained on the group surrounding Hardoy and Summerhay in the emptying Council chamber. No use trying to get to the pay phones now. They would be mobbed by reporters calling in. The open door of the booth let in the voices of the interpreters assembling for lunch and, more faintly in the background, the chants of the demonstrators in the street.

Two of the delegates ringing Hardoy and the professor departed. A third picked up his attaché case. Solo took the interoffice envelope with his Mendoza notes and placed it on his lap.

Mendoza and his whole stay in Argentina now seemed part of another life, a life he stopped living the instant he returned to his home, his children, his regular job, even his name. He was Solorzano again, without the accent.

Still, he had known he had to be here, had to witness this session today. He could have said no, made up some excuse: another job, an out-of-town trip. He hadn't. He knew they would call him. He was the obvious choice, familiar with the players, the issues, the jargon. He had worked with the admiral in Washington and the commission in Argentina. That was his job, to run with the hare and hunt with the hounds, as the admiral put it. He could sit between lawyer and client, president and prime minister, because he was neutral, an observer, an onlooker. A professional sworn to silence. A professional doing his job.

His hand reached for the small tape recorder on the counter and clicked it on.

"... *my ears hurt so much that I kept blacking out. My convulsions came back and that made them even angrier...*"

He stopped the tape. At the Villa Devoto jail, Hardoy had apologized to the women. And odd as that apology must have sounded in the mouth of a stranger, Solo knew that it was the first kind word those prisoners had heard from the outside world, the first acknowledgment that the thread joining them to humanity still held.

What fresh horrors those women must have endured after he and

Hardoy and the professor left, just as Malena's friend, the lawyer Yoshida, had predicted. Even now, at this very minute, as these elegantly dressed ambassadors in this grand chamber recessed for lunch, those women were still there, suffering God knew what outrages from their tormentors.

And those tormentors were his father's disciples. Maybe some of them still remembered his father, the American expert who taught them the grisly techniques they applied to their victims, to the women at Villa Devoto. To Malena.

He inhaled deeply and expelled a chestful of air. Since his return from Argentina, his image of his father had grown shapeless, ungraspable, a scramble of countless fragmented memories that refused to coalesce into a coherent whole. His first fishing trip with his father to a lake in the Berkshires. The magic tricks with cards and rings and knots that his father had taught him and he was now passing along to Lisa and John. That morning in Rio at the house his parents had rented in Barra da Tijuca, when his father unexpectedly returned home from one of his many trips and presented Solo with a new bicycle for his tenth birthday. That day had been one of the happiest of Solo's life. He had never seen anything more beautiful than Silver, the name he had immediately given his new bicycle: a silver body with bright blue trim, three speeds, a generator for the headlamp and a shiny tire pump clipped to the down tube of the frame. After a quarter century, he still remembered Silver vividly.

Again he wondered if his mother had known about his father's real occupation. It stood to reason that the presence of a wife and child, a regular family, would have served his father's cover as a legitimate AID official, but it seemed equally clear that his covert role would also expose them to some degree of danger. Was deliberately placing herself and Solo in jeopardy the price she had accepted for keeping the family together? His parents were both dead; he could not think why it should matter now. Yet somehow it seemed important.

He would never hear his father's side of the story, would never know why Charles Solorzano had done what he had done. In fact, Solo realized, there was little chance that he would ever come to understand who Charles Solorzano was. Could the loving parent Solo had known, the hero who gave up his life to save strangers, have been at the same time a trainer of torturers and assassins, the man whose students inflicted unspeakable agonies on Malena and numberless others before murdering them?

He could, and he was. Much as his son wished otherwise, it was a fact beyond doubt, a legacy he could not escape. His head told him it was absurd to feel transgenerational guilt, that he was utterly innocent of his father's sins. But the feeling was stronger than reason; the burden of blame lay on his heart. And perhaps it was that simple. Perhaps there was nothing to unriddle, no puzzle to solve, no code to crack—nothing but a painful truth for which a son had to make amends.

The circle around Hardoy and the professor was breaking up. Solo ejected the cassette and slipped it into his coat pocket. He tucked the interoffice envelope under one arm and left the booth. Taking the service stairs, he got to the basement just as Hardoy and Summerhay were making their way along the empty corridor towards the snack bar.

"Dr. Hardoy, Professor!" They turned and their faces lit up.

"Ah, our young friend. So glad to see you again," they said almost in unison. They held out their hands and Solo wrung them.

"Sorry my flight was late," Hardoy said. "I got your message, and I see that Doris gave you mine."

The staff lunch hour was nearly over and the snack bar empty. They sat at a table by the newspaper machines and ordered coffee.

"I can stay only a few minutes," the professor apologized.

"How are you?" Solo asked Hardoy. "I heard something about the Uruguayan government taking away your citizenship or your civil rights—something like that."

"Yes. They've done it to some prominent politicians and there is talk of doing it to me. But they don't dare while I'm on the OAS commission. It's my insurance policy for one more year, you see. But I've sent my family abroad."

Solo nodded. "Diego Fioravanti is anxious to talk to you."

"Has his girlfriend arrived?"

Solo still had to blink away the reference to Inés in relation to Diego. "She is flying in today. He borrowed my car to meet her at the airport."

"Good. We are working on his asylum application," Professor Summerhay said. "I've been debriefing him, so to speak. The information he's provided is helping us establish the modus operandi of his unit and identify a number of victims, including a newspaper publisher, and people he saw executed."

"Anything more on Condor?" Solo asked.

Hardoy hesitated, looked at the professor, then planted an elbow on the table, drawing himself closer to Solo. "There is a cable, Professor Summerhay was telling me this morning..."

The professor nodded and said, "A cable sent last year to Secretary of State Cyrus Vance by the U.S. Ambassador in Paraguay."

"Paraguay," Solo echoed. "A Condor member..."

The professor nodded again. "It explains how Condor is coordinated through a U.S. communications facility in the Panama Canal Zone. The chief of staff of the Paraguayan military described it to the American ambassador, who knew nothing about it and became worried that the U.S. role could surface in the course of the Letelier investigation."

Solo felt no surprise. The telltale signs had been there all along, if he had just paid attention.

"This cable," he said, "do you have it?"

"No." Hardoy scowled. "The family of a Condor victim is asking for it in a lawsuit here in Washington."

Professor Summerhay shook his head. "And we shouldn't hold our breath. It pains me to say it, but judges in this country are trained to throw out a case, no questions asked, as soon as the government utters the words 'national security' or 'state secret.'" Still shaking his head, he got up. "I have to run. Nice to see you again, Mr. Solorzano."

When the professor had gone, Hardoy swung his briefcase onto the tabletop. "I'm afraid I haven't much time, either. I'm due on Capitol Hill in a few minutes. Did you bring it with you?"

Solo handed over the interoffice envelope. The chairman opened it and examined the contents.

"I see what you mean," he said, frowning. "I'm sorry. I tried to keep Fonseca with me to keep an eye on him. But in Mendoza we had to split up. I should have gone with you to the prison and left him to watch the show trial. It's a good thing you kept your notes. I'll take care of this."

"But why? Why did he do it? When I read the report I couldn't believe it. He made it sound as if we visited a nice rest home in the countryside."

"I know."

"He saw what I saw," Solo went on, "heard the same kinds of things I heard, I'm sure of it. He told me as much in the car. And even if he didn't, how could he leave out my part? I typed up these same notes and gave them to him in Buenos Aires."

The coffee arrived and they waited for the server to withdraw.

"Your notes, yes." Hardoy stirred his cup. "You have to understand that the commission is not in session all the time. The organization won't budget the money. Before returning to their own countries, our members handed in reports on the visits they personally took part in. Professor Summerhay lives here and put it all together. What the report says about the prison in Mendoza is what Fonseca turned in."

"But why did he suppress my notes?" Solo persisted, even though he already knew the answer.

Hardoy sighed. "Why does he travel on a diplomatic passport issued by the military government of Brazil? Why does he represent his country at international meetings? We are all supposed to be independent lawyers, unconnected with any government."

Solo bit his lip. He remembered Fonseca's hand on his arm when he was about to tape the testimony of the women in Villa Devoto. And Fonseca's opening remarks to the inmates in Mendoza—how they seemed hardly reassuring, hardly likely to encourage confidences. And later in the car, how Fonseca had shrugged off what they had both heard, before settling into a complacent nap.

"There's nothing you could have done," Hardoy said. "This was his parting shot. His term on the commission was up and he couldn't be reelected. Argentina was his last job with us and he knew he could safely ignore your notes. He was a member of the commission; you weren't. Technically, he could have found a million things wrong with your information and chosen to disregard it. The whole matter would be academic once the report came out—not even a question of your word against his."

So Fonseca was going to get away with it. Had he planned it all along, knowing that there would be no tape recording of what they heard? Was that why he had told the prisoners to form two lines, so that Solo wouldn't witness what he heard and he could just throw out Solo's notes? All those hopeless men risking their lives to tell their stories, for nothing. Except for his notes—and how much good would they do now?—it was as if they had seen and heard nothing in Mendoza, as if they had never been there. *I have to trust somebody,* the doctor in the prison said. He had trusted Solo. And Solo had trusted Fonseca.

"Look," Hardoy said. "Fonseca is not the only one. In our Chilean cases, it was all we could do to keep Pinochet's man, our Chilean member, from reading our files, sitting in on our meetings, and reporting everything back to his government. We finally forced him to disqualify himself from our dealings with his country."

"You mean Fonseca could have...?" Solo began, alarm in his voice.

"No. If you're thinking of Fioravanti, Fonseca's heard about him, but only Professor Summerhay and I have access to his file. I don't know how Doris feels about Fonseca, so I didn't tell her why, but I asked her to keep the Condor file separate. You see"—Hardoy tilted his head toward the front of the building—"half the flags out there belong to countries that are doing what Argentina is doing. It's called state terrorism."

Yes, Solo thought, there was a name for it. There was a name for what his father taught.

"In the six South American countries involved in Condor," Hardoy went on, "there are already fifty thousand dead, tens of thousands missing, half a million people in jail. Four million have fled abroad. The situation in Central America is equally grim." Hardoy removed his eyeglasses, pinched a paper napkin from the dispenser and began to clean the lenses. Dark rings of fatigue smudged the skin under his eyes. "Those same governments appoint members to our commission. Their ambassadors on the Council oversee our work, make and change our rules."

Solo was silent. Then: "So you expect them to do nothing?"

"The Council will play ostrich," Hardoy said wearily. "It will issue a toothless resolution, a penultimatum to be followed by many more."

"Then, what's the point of the report?"

"The report was never meant for the Council."

"But I thought..."

"The report was addressed to the Council in name only. It was really intended for them." Hardoy pointed to the row of newspaper vending machines lining the wall. Solo turned to scan the front pages: *IRAN HOSTAGE CRISIS ENTERS SECOND WEEK. NO RELEASE SEEN.*

"Don't look for any headlines," Hardoy said, opening his briefcase and placing the interoffice envelope in it, then lowering the lid. "It's all about the hostages now. But, as I'm sure you are aware, most papers have been carrying our story. The report was meant for them, my friend. The Argentine ambassador knew it, we knew it, and I think that whoever leaked the report knew it as well."

Solo searched the chairman's eyes and thought he saw in them a glint of approval.

33

Diego came out of the Madison Plaza Hotel on Tenth and "H" streets
and eyed Solo's Volkswagen parked across the street. It looked as if it
was begging to be broken into or stolen. Few vehicles were parked on
this block—or any block around here, he had noticed. Reconnoitering
map-in-hand east to Chinatown and Union Station, and west to Six-
teenth Street, he had seen the same urban wasteland, a moonscape of
garbage and graffiti, porno theaters, boarded-up buildings, and largely
desolate streets. It surprised him to find this squalor so close to the
White House and the Capitol.

The hotel clerk had shrugged when, in his uncertain English, Diego asked about the neighborhood. "You should have seen it in sixty
eight, after Martin Luther King was killed. But it's pretty safe as long
as you're careful," he had eagerly added in case the Madison Plaza was
about to lose a guest.

He needn't have worried. Diego had no intention of moving out
of this fleabag. With his money running low, the weekly rate payable
in advance was as much as he could afford until Inés arrived and he
talked things out with her, explained all that he had kept back for so
long, and persuaded her to go with him to Nevada. It would be a new
departure for them both, the clean start they never had. His phone call
two days ago to his cousins in Elko had floundered at first between

English and Spanish before settling on French, which an older uncle summoned to the phone spoke fluently, with an accent that reminded Diego of Aunt Finia's. Her letter to Elko, posted from Miami courtesy of some traveler, had been received the week before, the uncle told Diego, and the family was excited and eager to welcome him. Now it was a matter of convincing Inés. She might still feel hurt by his evasions and the hard truths of what he had done in the army, but she would not be invulnerable to reason. He had to make her see that the deeper they lost themselves in this vast country, the safer they would feel, and the sooner they would leave their past behind. Maybe he could enlist Solo's help in pleading his cause. He had been wrong to be wary of Solo. The man had proven himself a friend.

He decided to leave the car where it was. He wouldn't be gone long and the clerk could see it through the lobby window, at least when he wasn't sneaking a reefer in the staircase.

He walked west. The OAS commission's office was on F Street, three blocks north of the main OAS building in this northwest quadrant of Washington that housed the monuments, government buildings, and most of the white population, according to Solo. The white ghetto within the black ghetto, Solo called it.

Diego liked what little of Washington he had seen so far: diagonal avenues crisscrossed by circles and squares; a low skyline with wide open spaces of landscaped parks and monuments; handsome old row houses and stately mansions. But it puzzled him that there was scant street life outside the downtown bureaucratic beehive, and virtually none at night. In his after-hours roaming these past few days, as he walked the streets in the empty evenings of waiting for Inés's arrival, he had seen only clusters of restaurants and bars on a handful of blocks in Georgetown and Dupont Circle.

When he reached Pennsylvania Avenue, the photographer with the life-sized cardboard cutout of a foolishly grinning Carter smiled at him and offered to take his picture with the President. Two young women had chained themselves to the White House fence under signs that read "End East Timor Genocide" and "Stop Arming Indonesia." Instinctively, he looked around, then relaxed again. There were no police with guard dogs here, nobody to drag you away to a secret prison, to torture you, to make you disappear. He was gradually beginning to break himself of the habit of looking over his shoulder, checking reflections in shop windows, watching what he said on the phone. Maybe that wasn't good. He needed to stay alert, keep sniffing the wind. At least until Inés arrived.

Once again he glanced at his watch. Valeria would be back from the airport shortly and he could call her again, make sure Inés was airborne. How he ached for her. Even though he had been constantly on the move, the two weeks since his escape from Argentina had dragged on, as if his life had been placed on hold until he could see her again. The journey was now a blur: the nighttime boat to Uruguay, the bone-jarring rides that had begun with a trip north to the small town of Artigas on the border with Brazil. As Aunt Finia had predicted, Aguirre's ID card had gotten him through the border, and he had gone on to the Atlantic and Porto Alegre, a sizeable city served by airlines. Not trusting his Aguirre passport to pass muster with U.S. immigration, he had walked into a travel agency in Porto Alegre and booked a series of connecting flights to Mexico—a country that required no visa for Argentines. His itinerary had purposely kept him clear of Sao Paulo and Rio, as well as other large cities beyond Brazil, on the assumption that airport officials in smaller towns might be less likely to spot a fake foreign passport. The tactic had paid off: Francisco Aguirre, the Argentine tourist with the duffel bag, had merited no more than cursory glances at the check-in counters of the pit stops he made. As he attempted to move from Mexico into the U.S., he had a choice of two crossing points recommended by Aunt Finia's advisers: Tijuana-San Diego and Juárez-El Paso. San Diego was considered safer. But with either choice, if he made it across, the absence of an entry stamp in his passport would preclude a subsequent flight to the East Coast. That had made him choose El Paso. On the map, it was seven hundred miles closer to Washington, D.C.

The crossing fee had made a big dent in his cash, but the elderly coyote who smuggled him over the border was worth every cent. He knew every vein and capillary that would thread him into the U.S., and he knew every Gardel tango by heart; he was overjoyed when Diego joined in on "Mano a Mano" or struck up an old Mexican favorite, a Jorge Negrete or Pedro Infante standard Diego remembered from childhood radio. They had parted sworn brothers on a dusty road outside El Paso.

The rest of the trek had been grueling but uncomplicated. Hitchhiking where he could, more often boarding trains and buses, he had finally arrived, dazed, at the Greyhound bus terminal on New York Avenue in Washington, D.C. Two blocks away he had stumbled on the Madison Plaza and called Solo.

The door Diego pushed open bore the OAS logo, a fan of clustered flags, above the commission's name. He smiled at the receptionist, who returned his smile and picked up her telephone.

"Doris, Mr. Fioravanti is here."

A minute later, Doris appeared and greeted him brightly. "Hello, Diego. Thank you for coming."

She led him through the inner hallway to her office in the filing room where they usually met with Professor Summerhay. Color photographs of Rio, including a large panoramic of Guanabara Bay's Sugarloaf taken from the Corcovado Christ, relieved the gray dullness of wall-to-wall cabinets. On Doris' desk were two empty cups of espresso and a large gift-wrapped box of bonbons. The chair Diego sat down on felt warm. Doris unlocked a desk drawer, drew out a folder, and placed it in front of her.

"I know we've been over the details with Professor Summerhay many times," she said. "This is just a formality, but we need it for our records."

"I understand," Diego said, guessing what was coming.

She opened the folder, pulled out a large photograph, and handed it to him, saying, "We asked Solo for a picture."

It was an enlargement of a snapshot taken on a rooftop terrace, discolored along the outside borders where it met the outline of the frame in which it had hung. Around a sun-washed picnic table, five people sat smiling at the camera: Solo, two women, and two children. Diego didn't know one of the women or any of the children. The other woman he knew as Violeta Argerich.

Doris pointed to her. "Is there any doubt in your mind that this is the woman you saw: Magdalena Uriburu—Violeta Argerich?"

Diego wondered where and when the photograph had been taken. The boy and the girl must be Solo's children, the unknown woman his ex-wife. But the other woman with the gamine haircut was unquestionably Violeta Argerich. Even in a photograph he could feel the magnetism of those luminous eyes, the smile that had caught his attention at the Ideal. Now he knew that her dance partner was no inspector but her father, a well-known politician he vaguely recalled from newspapers and television, that they were both part of the Argentine haut monde, that she had been a diplomat in this very city. None of it had been enough to save her.

"There's no doubt in my mind," he said dully.

There was a knock on the open door of the office and a voice behind him spoke in Portuguese. "Now I promise I'm really going, Doris. I've said all my goodbyes."

Doris stood up, startled. Diego turned and saw a man standing in the doorway.

Doris said in Spanish, "Diego, this is Dr. Justiniano Fonseca, a member of the commission until recently. He was in Argentina with us. Have you two met?"

Despite the raven hair with the faintest glimmer of silver along the temples, the man looked older than his hair—on the near side of sixty, Diego guessed. Maybe it was the old-fashioned three-piece suit, the cuff links and tie pin, which looked like real gold. A shiny white silk handkerchief folded into shark teeth peered out of his breast pocket.

"No, I don't believe we have," Diego said, getting to his feet and extending his hand. "Diego Fioravanti."

"Ah, yes, Fioravanti, the first flower," Fonseca exclaimed, switching to Spanish as he shook hands. "A most illustrious Tuscan name, as I'm sure you know. No, our paths did not cross in Argentina, but I understand that you have been very helpful to the commission. I am glad to finally make your acquaintance."

"Dr. Fonseca surprised me by dropping in just before you came," Doris said. "We didn't know he was in town."

"For a very short World Bank symposium to which I must get back, I'm afraid," Fonseca said. "I'm sorry to have missed Dr. Hardoy and Professor Summerhay. Do give them my regards."

They shook hands again. Fonseca glanced at the photograph on the desk. "And please say hello to Mr. Solórzano for me," he added on his way out.

Doris waited until the sound of his footsteps had died out in the hallway, then looked at the bonbons on her desk. "Do you want this box of chocolates? I've never liked that man."

34

When Hardoy left the snack bar, Solo marched back up the flight of steps to the first floor and started across the tropical patio toward the pay phones.

"Oh, Mr. Solorzano!"

Alvarez's voice. Solo looked round and saw him guarding the door of the Council chamber. McAdams, the paunchy and ageing American ambassador to the OAS, was stepping out to face a camera and two reporters.

"No, no, thank you, Mr. Alvarez," McAdams said with a sidelong smile at Solo. "These are American reporters. I won't need Mr. Solorzano."

"Kate Oxman, TV Twelve, sir," Solo heard as he started away. "Mr. Ambassador, some of the worst offenders in this and other human rights reports are graduates of the School of the Americas that critics call the SOA, the School of Assassins. Will Congress now shut down the school...?"

Solo heard the ambassador clear his throat, but he was too far away to make out his low-voiced reply.

There was nobody at the phone on this side of the patio. He picked up the receiver and his hand stopped in midair.

Phyllis was standing a few feet away, looking at him.

"I was going to the interpreters' booths to look for you..." she said. "Please, Solo, we have to talk."

He grimaced, put down the phone, and started to move past her. "I don't have time for this."

"No, please, wait!" She put a hand on his arm. "You have to give me five minutes. Five minutes."

Something in the way she looked made him waver. He had never seen her so pale and thin, so urgent. Her makeup couldn't quite hide the puffiness around her eyes.

"Make it quick." He moved to the bench by the phones and sat down. She sat beside him.

"Solo," she said, "I love our children. I'll never get over leaving them. You have to believe that."

"Look, we've already—"

"No, let me finish. I know what Saturnina meant to your mother and what she means to Lisa and John. And to you. I would never do anything to hurt her."

"Did your lawyer put you up to this? You would never do anything to hurt her." He was unable to keep the derision out of his voice. "Is that why you—?"

"My lawyer doesn't know I'm here. He's an old friend of my father's. That was why I went to see him, just to talk, to find out where I stood."

She clasped her hands. Solo's eyes rested briefly on the pale mark on her finger where her wedding band had been.

"I loved your mother, Solo. I wrote her a letter before she died, to tell her how it hurt me to be estranged from the family. She wrote me back, and she mentioned Saturnina, how she was worried about her, how she had discussed her situation with you and you had promised to employ her and take care of her."

A letter. Now he knew the evidence that had baffled him and Monique.

"Your mother's letter was in a binder of papers I gave my lawyer.

He told me to leave everything to him. Solo, I never dreamed he would do what he did with Saturnina. You have to believe me."

He looked at her, wondering again, with a flash of unfocused foreboding, why she had come here and cornered him. "Even if I believe you, what's the use? Now I've got a deportation hearing on my hands—besides the custody battle."

"I know. I've thought so much about this. I know that you don't understand why I left. I left because I felt trapped. I wasn't sure then, but now I know it was the right decision. Are you going to make me pay for the rest of my life by depriving me of my children?"

"Oh, come on! How self-serving is that? You were the one who left. It was your choice."

She shook her head. "I had no choice. I fell in love. For the first time in my life."

Solo felt pierced. He met her eyes and they both looked away.

"Staying with you would have meant living a double life. I didn't want that. Not for me, not for you, not for Lisa and John."

"Then why not level with me? Why just pick up and leave, as though it was all my fault?"

"I'm not trying to blame you. I think you wanted to believe you loved me. But you never got over Inés. We were both fooling ourselves."

He said nothing. He didn't think she was right; he thought he had always been wholehearted with Phyllis, but now—he no longer knew for sure.

"Solo, I was desperately unhappy. Can you understand that?"

When he spoke, his voice sounded tired to his own ears. "Give me some credit. I've thought a lot about it too. When you left, it was all I thought about. And all I talked about in therapy. You think I'm using the kids to punish you. I'm not. I was bitter at first, but it's your life."

"Then, why won't you share custody?"

"Suppose I did. How could I be sure you wouldn't disappear again, this time with the kids? Can you understand that?"

"Solo, I would never..." Her eyes were misty. "You really think me capable of doing that—to the kids, to you..."

He shook his head. "I never thought you were capable of running out on the kids. Leaving me... There are plenty of better men."

"Stop it." She placed a hand on his knee. Now there were tears in her eyes. "Solo, I've never met a better man."

He looked at her uncomprehendingly.

"My lawyer told me that if the truth came out, there would be no hope of getting any form of custody. He showed me the Virginia case law: I have no rights; I am unfit to be a parent. That's why I let everybody think I was running off with another man."

Her voice died out. Then she said, "I didn't leave you for another man. I left you for a woman."

Solo stared at her, thunderstruck. He wanted to speak but there was a knot in his throat. A woman.

"I wanted to tell you. But I felt so confused. For a while I doubted my sanity, who I was, whether I even deserved my children. And I was afraid you wouldn't understand, that you would hate me for ruining your life, that you and the kids would shut me out. My lawyer told me to say nothing. He said it would be better for Lisa and John. I—I so much need to be their mother."

He wanted to say something, but thoughts churned incoherently in his head.

"It took me time to realize that my dishonesty in not telling you was eating away at me without doing you and the children any good. When I decided to tell you, you wouldn't talk to me. I wasn't sure you would even open a letter from me."

She wiped tears with her sleeve. "Solo, she and I never meant for it to happen, I swear. It just did. We fell in love. We were both so caught up with guilt about tearing the family apart. But we were also deliriously happy."

The woman—did he need to ask? Unbidden came the image of Reidlonger in the synagogue, blue light from the vitraux flecking his hair as he talked about Malena's visit to Buenos Aires for her sister's wedding. *Malena was so happy. I've never seen her so radiant.*

"Malena..." he murmured.

Phyllis nodded. "When you wouldn't talk to me, she wanted to tell you herself. But I said no, it was my responsibility and I had to do it."

He sat transfixed, buried in an avalanche.

Phyllis's faltering voice broke through. "Solo, I'm so worried about her. I've stayed home waiting for her to call but I haven't heard from her since she left for Argentina. The phone numbers she left me are useless. The embassy here knows nothing—when I call Argentina her father is never home or I can't get past the maid, and there's no answer at her friend's." Her voice grew softer, plaintive. "She said she was going to see you in Buenos Aires. Did she?"

In a smear of rapid frames, Solo was thrust back to Buenos Aires on that last day. He saw himself calling Reidlonger's new number from the telephone in the cafe, telling him what he had seen at the Athletic Club, then walking back in the pouring rain to Plaza de Mayo, to Uriburu's office—condemned to be the bearer of evil tidings, the courier of death.

He sucked in a ragged breath, then very softly, with all the gentleness he could muster, he said:

"Phyllis—Malena is dead."

Long minutes later, Phyllis was still sobbing.

Solo watched her in silence, wishing he had found in the hideous story he had just recounted a way to soften the shock, an explanation for why Malena had died. But, inevitably, the words he had forced out could be nothing but the truth. He thought he should try and touch her, maybe hold her, but that seemed too hard. For both of them.

Phyllis had left him for Malena. Could someone live with a person for years in shared intimacy, professing honesty, working to open the heart as wide as it would go, to learn the habits, motives, and mysteries of a mate—and never have a clue? He hadn't. Had Phyllis? For some reason, he was comforted in the notion that, until Malena, he had been what Phyllis wanted. Or thought she wanted. She said she had been unsure at first. He wanted to believe her. Until her inscrutable disappearance, she had always been forthright with him. And now she was telling him that she hid the truth to protect the kids and safeguard her rights as a mother. Because she was afraid he wouldn't understand.

Did he? Did he understand now that he knew?

He should feel betrayed, stabbed in the back. Why didn't he? Was it because Malena was dead, all sins washed away? Or maybe because in his inmost heart he couldn't blame anybody for falling in love with her. He too had been a little in love with Malena.

"I think I know why they murdered her," Phyllis said, and Solo's head jerked. "Because of something she learned. A secret."

She was looking at him, blinking tears from her eyes. "She told me about it. She first heard of it in Argentina, from Chilean exiles she was trying to help. Then, here in the embassy, a package meant for one of the military attachés was delivered to her and she opened it before realizing the mistake."

Solo's mind went knife-sharp. "What was in it?"

"Documents. Documents on something called Operation Condor."

"What did she do?" he demanded.

"She put everything back, resealed the package, and rerouted it to the military attaché. But first she made a copy. Her first impulse was to send it to the media anonymously, she said, but she was afraid that if it got traced back to her it would endanger her family in Argentina. She was thinking what to do—and then they summoned her back."

Solo shut his eyes.

"She was frightened, Solo. She tried to hide it but I could tell. The recall could mean somebody suspected she had intercepted the package. If only she hadn't gone..." Phyllis's voice cracked but she went on. "She finally decided to talk to the OAS people in Argentina. She hated asking you to set it up because she felt so guilty about me. But she knew she could count on you to do it—even if she didn't tell you what it was about."

"What about the copy?" Solo asked.

"I don't know. She may have put it in the safe in our—in her bedroom closet. The combination was in her Rolodex, she once told me. When I didn't hear from her I looked through the cards, thinking something in the safe might help me locate her. But I couldn't find the combination. I'm going back to look again."

"No!" he blurted out. "You're not. Give me the keys."

She drew back. "Solo, those bastards killed her. I want to..."

"Don't argue, please." A sharp edge was now in his voice. "You have no idea what you're dealing with."

Phyllis hesitated. "Then we'll go together."

"Please," he said again, trying to keep his voice calm. "You cannot go back to the apartment. You have to let me do this alone."

She looked at him a moment longer, then reached into a pocket and handed him a small silver key chain with two keys.

"Phyllis..." he said, and stopped. He was about to ask another question he knew the answer to, now that the pieces were falling into place, now that he understood the admiral's interest in him—Kevin Solorzano, a friend in whom Malena might have confided about Condor. Still, he asked. "You said the package was addressed to one of the military attachés. Which one?"

Phyllis said, "The naval attaché."

35

Inés wedged her suitcase and carry-on into the back seat of Valeria's tiny two-door Fiat 600, then slid back the front passenger seat and got in.

"Wait," she said, closing her eyes after pulling the car door shut, her fingers uncurling as she counted, "Passport, ticket, traveler's checks... Okay."

Valeria adjusted her purple, punked hair, then unstrapped her platform shoes and discarded them by the gearshift between the front seats. Her small bare feet rested on the pedals, their toenails enameled bright purple, a golden ring on the little toe of her right foot. She wore jeans with beads for a belt, and a tie-dyed shirt with no bra underneath. "How come you didn't want your parents to see you off?" she asked, starting the car.

Inés sighed. "I hate goodbyes. My mother would do nothing but cry."

And not just my mother, she thought. She had cried saying goodbye to her boss, her friends, her parents. And soon it would be Valeria's turn; she was putting on a brave face but already looked glum and weepy.

"Besides," Inés added, "it's awkward. I know they're not buying that I've got a job interview in Washington."

Valeria worked the car out of the tight parking space. "So why do they think you're going?"

"To see Solo, probably. That's why they're not asking more questions."

Valeria kicked the car into second and leaned an elbow out the window. "That's just as good, isn't it? I mean, all Diego said was to make sure you didn't mention him. To anybody. His words."

"I know. I feel so—helpless, as if my life is being decided for me. I'm dropping everything, my courses, my job, my family, and rushing off to Washington."

Valeria shot her a look. "There are two very good reasons. I haven't met the second, but if he's anything like the first—I'd be going too." She sounded sad, upset, as if she wished she were leaving too.

She was right about Diego and Solo, Inés thought. They were in Washington, and she was elated at the prospect of seeing them again— as well as relieved to escape the suffocation of Buenos Aires, now that she knew its heinous secret. These past two weeks, while waiting for her passport and making departure arrangements, she had been a prisoner of her nerves. Before he disappeared, Diego had warned that she must do nothing to attract attention or monitoring—just follow her routine until she was safely out of the country. Now, on the day of her flight, she felt calmer. She was taking action at last, even if she was still uneasy at blindly following Diego's instructions delivered secondhand through Valeria.

They covered a dozen blocks and stopped to wait behind other cars at the grade crossing on Honduras Street. Vendors worked the line of cars, holding up newspapers, fruit, bouquets and pennants of soccer teams.

Valeria stared into the traffic. "I think I gave Diego a heart attack when he called this morning," she said. "He asked me if I thought anybody was following me."

Inés shook her head. "He asked me the same thing. What did you tell him?"

"That I'm the nervous type, always seeing suspicious characters. Wrong answer. He had a fit. But I calmed him down."

Clanging bells and flashing lights muted their conversation while a long freight train rolled past, wheels clacking loudly—sowing its mystery of goodbye, as a Manzi tango put it. Something told Inés that this might well be goodbye to Argentina for her. Since the night she and Solo had sat in the car outside the Metropole and he had revealed to her what he knew, her anger and repugnance had only deepened, along with a mounting sense of betrayal, and the growing certitude that she would never again be able to trust this country. She hadn't told Valeria that, and did not intend to. It was too close to home. Valeria's sister had fled the country, and in her new expatriate home in Canada, she probably felt the same way Inés did now, and would never return.

The bar lifted and they moved off, crossing the tracks and turning left on Juan B. Justo Avenue. Inés glanced at Valeria. Her spiked purple hair was not the best choice for her pale complexion, Inés decided affectionately. It made her look like an electrocuted chicken. Something else she wasn't going to tell her.

"I have to drop off my cousin's keys." Valeria said, signaling a turn. "It's on the way. Won't take a minute."

A right turn from the broad avenue bordering the railroad tracks and they were in a residential area of older houses, some with small front gardens and iron fences, the kind of neighborhood you could still find in many barrios of Buenos Aires, Inés knew, though such homes were quickly disappearing as more high rises sprouted like giant weeds on every block.

Two more turns and they drove down the length of the block to an open garage door near the corner. Valeria swung the car in. The garage door dropped shut and lights came on.

"Valeria..." Inés began—but she was stopped short by the sight of a powerfully built man in the rear of the garage, wearing fatigues, boots, and a ski cap. He approached the passenger side of the car. His hand made a swiveling motion to Inés.

Cold needles of apprehension raced through her as she rolled down her window.

"So," he said, baring teeth in a leer and resting a forearm on the roof of the car. The dark eyes set in a pockmarked face seemed to bore into her. "One of the admiral's little friends."

She turned to look at Valeria. But her friend's face was buried in her hands.

"I'm sorry," Inés heard her say. "My sister—she's not in Canada. They have her."

36

From the pay phone by the patio, Solo watched Phyllis make her way to the front entrance of the building. She seemed but a wind's breath away from falling, knees ready to buckle. Schunk looked up from his security desk and said something to her, but she appeared not to notice. Her body leaned heavily on the revolving doors and she exited into the shock of open air.

Solo turned his gaze to the phone. He dialed the Madison Plaza and asked to be connected to Mr. Fioravanti's room. A hoarse holler answered on the first ring.

"It's me, Diego, I—"

"They've sucked her in, Solo, they've sucked her in!"

Solo was struck dumb. There was hissing static on the line and Diego's voice began to break up.

"Did you hear me, Solo? Inés! They've got Inés!"

Solo found his voice. "What happened?"

"I just called Valeria again. She couldn't stop crying. Two cars cut them off on the way to the airport. They took Inés away."

"Oh, my God..." Solo could say nothing more. He felt his heart pumping wildly.

"They let Valeria go to give me the message. I'm going back, Solo. It's me they want."

"Wait! Let me think! There must be something we can do..."

"Are you still at the OAS?" Diego asked. "Is Hardoy there?"

"No, he left for a meeting on Capitol Hill."

Diego cursed. "I'll call Doris at the commission, tell her what's happening and see if she can track him down. Can you get Summerhay or anybody else there to help? Valeria said she'll call me back. I'm waiting a few more minutes and then..."

There was a crackle followed by a long buzz and the line went dead.

Solo clicked the line over and over, but all he got was a dial tone. He ransacked his pockets for more coins and, finding none, dropped the receiver and ran out of the booth.

The hallways and the Council chamber were deserted. In the delegate lounge to the rear of the Chamber, two diplomats sat chatting in opulent armchairs. They looked up startled as he barged in and darted out again, nearly knocking over Alvarez.

"My goodness, Mr. Solorzano! Are you all right?"

"Mr. Alvarez, where is Professor Summerhay?"

"Why, I don't know... No, wait. I think I saw him leave with a group of delegates. They were going to a restaurant, I believe."

"Which restaurant?"

"Let me see. Professor Summerhay was talking to the American ambassador and his deputy, who were about to walk back to the State Department. The professor joined other delegates going out to lunch. No, I don't believe they mentioned the name of the restaurant. Are you sure you are all right? You don't look well. Why don't you sit down? Let me get you a—"

"No, please, I need your help. I have to find the professor or Dr. Hardoy. It's an emergency! You've got to help me find them."

"I'll be glad to, but—"

"Please. Call anybody you have to. Find them for me and tell them to call Doris at their office. Immediately!" Solo ran back the way he had come.

At the reception desk Schunk was nowhere in sight. Solo tore off the top sheet of the pad on the counter and scrawled a note, wedging it halfway into the top drawer, where Schunk couldn't miss it. He leaned against the desk to keep his balance, took in a harsh breath, made himself think.

The safe in Malena's bedroom. The documents. If he could get his hands on them, he might be able to make a deal, trade the documents for Inés. No, by the time he got the safe open it might be too late—and Phyllis wasn't even sure the documents were there. Even if they were, they might not be important enough to get Inés released.

The State Department. He could try to find McAdams. The ambassador knew him, had just seen him a few minutes ago. Alvarez said McAdams had just left on foot for the State Department.

He tore down the stairs to the basement, ran past the snack bar, and out the door to the outside parking lot on C Street. Still running, he crossed Eighteenth Street and caught sight of two figures on Virginia Avenue walking by the monument to Simón Bolívar on their way to Foggy Bottom.

"Mr. McAdams! Sir!"

They turned, recognized him and stopped.

"Why, Mr. Solorzano, you look deathly pale," the ambassador said with concern as Solo came up to them. "What on earth is the matter?"

"I need your help, sir," Solo panted.

"Yes, of course. Please calm yourself. Take a moment to catch your breath."

"Would you like to sit down?" The deputy, an elderly man whom Solo knew by sight, pointed to a bench by the monument.

"You must help me, please!"

"Certainly. What can we do for you?"

"A friend of mine has just been kidnapped in Buenos Aires by Argentine security forces. You know what that means, sir. You've read the report."

They stared at him.

"I tried to get in touch with Hardoy or Professor Summerhay," Solo went on, "but I can't locate them. There's not a moment to lose, sir, I beg you..."

"Yes, yes, I understand." Ambassador McAdams looked at his deputy, then sharply back at Solo. "Now, are you certain that this is no routine police matter? I mean, do you know for a fact that Argentine security personnel are involved?"

"Yes, sir. There is no doubt."

"I see. And I take it that this person is an American citizen."

The statement stabbed him. He had to say it. "No, she isn't."

"A U.S. resident, then."

"No, sir. She is Argentine and lives in Buenos Aires."

The ambassador frowned. "I can see how distressing this is for you, but you can understand that under these circumstances, that is, if the matter is purely Argentine, if it concerns an Argentine citizen and the local authorities in their own country, then it is hard to see how the American government would have any standing to interfere."

McAdams saw the dismay in Solo's face and quickly went on. "Our present relations with the Argentine government are not the warmest, as you know, so contacting our embassy in Buenos Aires might prove—counterproductive. But our previous ambassador is a friend of mine and has many contacts in Argentina. Let me see if I can get in touch with him and ask him to call and make some inquiries with the authorities. Can you give me the information on your friend?"

His hands shaking, Solo brought out his address book, copied Inés's name, address, and phone number on a blank page, tore it off, and handed it to the ambassador.

"I will get back to you as soon as I hear, Mr. Solorzano. Perhaps as early as tomorrow or the day after, assuming I can reach my friend and he's able to find out something for us. But you really are looking awfully pale. Shall we sit with you for a few minutes?"

Solo shook his head. "I'm okay. I have to go."

He turned and started back. As early as tomorrow or the day after.

As good as never.

At the OAS building he climbed the stairs to the main floor and found himself walking back to the booth. Inés was not an American citizen. Of course the American government would not get involved. But who, then? Think! If he could just find Hardoy. Or was that also a bad idea? If the kidnapping was reported, would that seal Inés's fate?

Suddenly, another thought jolted him, and for an instant he stood idiotized. *Our previous ambassador,* McAdams said. That had to be one of Henry's ambassadors, before Carter replaced him. Good God. He had just identified Inés to McAdams, who was going to pass the information along to Henry's man—probably another good friend of the admiral's.

He fought a dizzying nausea. Should he try to locate McAdams at the State Department right now and tell him to forget the whole thing?

He went into the booth and collapsed on the chair. His head swam. Diego was right: It was him they wanted. Inés was mixed up in it only because of Diego. If Diego went back and turned himself in, she would be saved.

No, she wouldn't. They wouldn't let her go. They would just kill them both. Two more lives meant nothing to them.

A wave of despair and rage swept over him. His fist struck the coarse drywall of the booth, drawing blood from his knuckles.

"Solo..."

Schunk was looking at him from the door of the booth.

Solo sucked in his breath and reached for the handkerchief in his coat pocket. "Yeah, Schunk..."

Schunk said in a hush, "I just thought you might be mad at me for letting Phyllis in."

"Phyllis...?" Solo said with a blank stare.

Schunk nodded. "She said it was urgent, that she had to talk to you."

"Phyllis, sure. That's all right. Don't worry about it."

"I found your message and called the two restaurants the delegates usually go to. They are not there. They may have taken cars and gone farther away. I can call some embassies to see if one of them left word about where they were going. Are you okay?"

Solo wasn't listening. He was staring at the handkerchief and the cassette tape in his bloodied hand, the recording of the women of Villa Devoto that he had to return to Doris. He felt as if he had been roused out of sleep.

"Do you want me to..." Schunk began and stopped.

Solo turned to the counter and began writing on the yellow pad.

"Two more favors, Schunk," he said. "Let me use your phone. Then, after I leave, call this number and ask for Diego Fioravanti. Give him your number and tell him I said to do nothing until he hears from me."

37

Do nothing. Solo's friend, the guard at the OAS, said to do nothing until Solo called.

How could he do nothing? They had Inés. Thanks to him. How could he just sit in this dump of a hotel waiting for something to happen when it was all his fault?

And what could Solo do anyway? Even if he located Hardoy and they went through official channels, it would probably be too late for Inés. It might be too late now, no matter what anybody did. Going public would be useless too. Argentina would simply deny holding her. Then, one more body would be found, the work of subversives. Or it might never turn up at all.

Diego scooped up his belongings and threw them into the duffel bag. In the hallway he stabbed the elevator button, then changed his mind and took the stairs from the fourth floor, two steps at a time. The desk clerk was lurking behind the door that led to the lobby, a joint curled under his hand. Diego nodded curtly and pushed through the door to the lobby and the street. Solo's car should be okay parked there for a while, he thought, and Solo had another key.

He followed the by-now familiar route past the dingy Art Deco Greyhound station on New York Avenue to the corner of Thirteenth Street, then turned left. For the third time today he walked into the phone company call center, this time headed for the long row of public telephones near the entrance. Phone books encased in metal sleeves hung from a rod under each phone. He swiveled up the yellow pages and quickly found what he was looking for: a travel agency advertising *Se habla español*. He brought out pen and paper and picked up the receiver.

Ten minutes later he had his reservation to Buenos Aires. He checked his watch. Not much time. He inserted another coin in the machine and dialed Solo's home.

"Solo, it's Diego. Your car is across the street from the hotel. I'm leaving for the airport, going back. I would have rather seen you, talked to you, instead of leaving a message on your machine, but there's no time. I'm so sorry. I'll never forgive myself."

He hung up.

Leaving the pay phones, he approached the counter marked *International*. Same young Puerto Rican woman, bilingual and friendly. A smile broke over her face when she saw him coming. "*Hola*. Another call to Argentina? Definitely our kind of customer."

She saw the hauntedness of his face, and the flirtatiousness she had exhibited this morning, when he believed everything was going according to plan, fell away. She took down the number he gave her and pointed him to a booth. He sat down in it and waited.

When the phone rang, he picked it up and heard the regimental headquarters operator identify herself. He drew a deep breath.

"Colonel Indart's office, please."

"Who's calling?"

"Captain Diego Fioravanti."

"One moment, please."

A long silence. He became aware that his thumb was rubbing the spot on his left finger where his ring had been.

"Hello, Diego."

Father Bauer.

"We had a feeling you would call."

Diego felt his Adam's apple glide up and down as he said, "Hello, Father."

Father Bauer said, "I suppose I need not tell you how disappointed we all are in you. Especially your comrades. Sergeant Maidana, most particularly. He is very upset with you. And not at all well disposed towards your young lady."

Maidana. Inés. The thought sickened him.

"Father," he said. "Let her go. She has nothing to do with this."

"It's not up to me, Diego. It's in your hands."

"I'm coming back, Father."

"Of course you are," Father Bauer said.

"Tomorrow. I'll be there tomorrow. I'm on my way to the airport now. Please don't let them do anything to her. Please. I'm begging you."

He imagined the smirk on the priest's face, and wondered if he was in his own office or taking the call in Colonel Indart's, with Indart at his desk, listening in.

"We have been very patient and forbearing with you, Diego. I think you know that. We had high hopes for you. Our confidence was misplaced and you let us down, but we never imagined that you would betray your country and inform against your comrades."

"Father..."

"Don't bother denying it, Diego. We know what you've been up to in Washington with the OAS."

Diego's lips were parched. How? How could they know? Thickly, he said, "Father—please. I'll do anything you say."

"I know, Diego. And I'm glad you've come to your senses. It's never too late to repent and seek forgiveness and absolution for our sins. We are Christians; we understand contrition. Sergeant Maidana has been given a free hand in this matter, but I will do my best to intercede for you. Pray that it's not too late by the time you get here."

"Tomorrow," Diego said. "Please—"

Bauer broke the connection.

Diego paid for the call and rushed out. Not a taxi in sight. He stood on the corner of New York Avenue, waiting, his hand up in the air, until a cab stopped.

"National Airport," he told the driver.

They even knew what he had been doing here in Washington. He had deluded himself into thinking he could escape, but they had always been a step ahead of him. His blunder had doomed both him and Inés. It was pointless now to wonder how or when they had found out about her. They had her. And no matter where he ran, they could simply reel him in. There had never been any true chance to get away, just as there was no chance now that they would let Inés go, plead and bargain as he might. It didn't work that way. He and she were as good as dead. At best, he was only buying a little time.

A little time to go back and die with her.

38

Inés tried to stave off panic. The hot rush of anger and disbelief she had felt at Valeria's betrayal was giving way to a fear that seemed to irrupt from within her and threatened to palsy her mind. She had to focus, think, reason herself into a calmer state before the thug with the pockmarked face came back. He must be Maidana. That was what Solo had called him, Sergeant Maidana, the head of the gang that was after Diego and had stopped her and Solo on the street the night they went to the Ideal.

Maidana had dismissed Valeria and pushed Inés down a set of stairs and into this windowless room, locking her in and leaving without a word. She was sure that the sickening odor in this cavernous chamber would soon turn her stomach. A single lit bulb in the high ceiling glared down on a battered wooden table and three chairs, a filthy sink bowl serviced by a single faucet, and a metal bed frame with bedsprings but no mattress. A grime-encrusted bucket in one corner obviously served as the bathroom. There were large dark stains on the walls paneled with some sort of soundproofing padding. Her breath pounding in her chest, she steadied herself against the table and eased down onto one of the rickety chairs.

Valeria had set her up. Valeria, her best friend, her confidante. How long had she been an informer? Long enough, in any event, to know as much about Diego as Inés herself did—probably more, since she was working for the military. Ever since Diego's escape, Valeria had been his sole intermediary with Inés, privy to all their communications, handling his telephone calls, relaying their mutual messages. But even before that, Inés had kept no secrets from her. Valeria knew everything about her best friend Inés, about her family, her job, her friends, Diego, Solo, her whole world. Valeria was even intimately acquainted with Inés the leafleteer. With numbing clarity, Inés now recalled telling Valeria about the planned protest at the law school. It must have been Valeria who supplied the information for the police raid that Inés had blamed on Diego.

The spasm of anger and disgust at her friend's duplicity died down as quickly as it arose. Despite her bitterness, a part of her wanted to excuse Valeria's treachery. Her sister was not in Canada, as Valeria and her family had given out. The military were holding her hostage, which meant they could extort absolute obedience from the family, manipulate them like marionettes. The degradation Valeria and her family must have sunk to in their efforts to preserve her sister's life— Inés could not bear to think about it.

A key was being worked in the heavy metal door.

She sat up in her chair. The man framed in the doorway was about fifty, well-groomed, with sparse, silvering hair and hawk-like eyes. He wore a gray houndstooth jacket over a plum-colored crewneck sweater and matching lilac shirt with the buttondown collar favored by Americans. His expression was dour, his eyes dark beads.

"Miss Maldonado." He greeted her gravely, coming forward and taking a chair across the table from her. She was fleetingly grateful for the woodsy smell of cologne that emanated from him and blunted the stench of the room. "I am Father Bauer. Perhaps Diego has mentioned me to you..."

A memory stirred in her mind. The chaplain. The priest Solo had heard about from the Mahlers, and later from Diego. She felt a chill dart down her neck.

Wetting her lips, she said, "Why have I been kidnapped?"

No sooner had she spoken than she wished she hadn't. There was a constriction in her throat. She had heard the fear in her voice.

The priest smiled. "Kidnapped? Detained, young lady, lawfully detained. Surely you know that agitating at a university and distributing subversive pamphlets is a very serious offense. So is associating with a dangerous defector and fugitive. You were planning to join him in Washington, weren't you?"

She felt her cheeks burning. Out of sight under the table her hands curled into fists. "What do you want from me? I know nothing."

He held up a quieting hand, the amicable smile still in place. "We all know more than we know, my dear. As a doctor friend of mine says, that is in fact the purpose of interrogation: to help people remember what they know."

She made no reply. Why was he toying with her?

He looked around and wrinkled his nose. "It doesn't smell very good in here, does it—" Drawing from his pocket a silk handkerchief the color of oxblood, he passed it gently back and forth under his nose. "Let's hope you won't have to stay long in this dreadful place. It's really entirely up to you. You must be completely truthful and conceal nothing when they question you."

"Conceal?" she repeated. For a moment, the absurdity of it all almost made her forget her terror. They can do anything they want, Diego had told her. There is nothing to stop them.

"Yes," Father Bauer was saying. "You will be given a chance to redeem yourself, to help your own case as well as your country by cooperating fully with the authorities."

She looked at him. "You mean—the way Valeria does?"

The smile came back, spreading across his pale lips. "Precisely. Valeria's services have been very helpful to the government. Yours could be equally valuable. They could also help Diego."

Diego? What was he talking about? Diego was in Washington, safely out of their clutches.

Father Bauer continued placidly. "I just spoke to him. He called from Washington. He's very worried about you. In fact, he told me that he is coming back tomorrow. Perhaps I can arrange for you to see him."

She knew he saw the fright and hopelessness in her eyes.

"Think about it," he said, rising to his feet. "You needn't give me your answer now. There will be plenty of time after your initial interrogation."

39

"Mr. Solórzano, forgive me for saying so but you look awful," Malena's secretary remarked as she shook Solo's left hand in the foyer of the Argentine embassy. "And what happened to your hand?"

It was plain from Fernanda's manner that she did not know what had happened to Malena. As far as the embassy staff were concerned, Solo realized, Ambassador Capdevila's right-hand woman, Third Secretary Magdalena Uriburu-Basavilbaso, was still on official leave in Argentina.

"My hand—it's a long story," he said, climbing the stairs behind her to the second floor. "Thanks for doing this, Fernanda. I really appreciate it."

"Well, as it happens, you're in luck. Your OAS report hasn't made us the most popular embassy in town. The ambassador is not entertaining or going out much anymore. I told him what you said, that it couldn't wait."

She ushered him into the library where only weeks ago, in another lifetime, he had sat between Henry and the admiral. A shudder ran through him.

"Take a seat," Fernanda said. She hesitated by the door, looking unsure of what she was about to say. "Mr. Solórzano—I read the newspapers, then the report. I had no idea..."

Solo nodded. His head tilted towards Ambassador Capdevila's office. "Did he?"

Fernanda raised her shoulders. "I don't know. Oh, it's so awful," she said, then withdrew.

Solo sat down and tried to control his breathing. A grandfather clock, with two sailboats painted on its face above the words Thomaston, Conn., kept time in one corner of the room. In an oil painting on the wall opposite his armchair, an elderly gaucho gripped a tattered hat, his hair unkempt, his calloused hands and leathery face bearing the stamp of the outdoors, his kind eyes watching Solo intently.

Ambassador Capdevila opened the door. Solo had never seen him looking so haggard, his necktie pulled wide of center. I must look as bad or worse to him, he thought when the ambassador glanced at his injured hand.

"Mr. Solórzano, sit down, please. We meet again under most inauspicious circumstances. I'm sorry that your trip to Argentina was not, what shall I say—more pleasant. What can I do for you? Fernanda tells me your business is urgent."

"Extremely, sir. Every minute counts. A little over an hour ago in Buenos Aires a woman named Inés Maldonado was on her way to the airport when she was intercepted and kidnapped by Argentine security personnel."

Capdevila's brow creased.

Solo rushed on. "She was about to take an Argentine Airlines flight to this country approximately one hour from now. I've come to ask that she be released and put on that flight."

The ambassador folded his arms. "Inés Maldonado. The name is unfamiliar to me. Is she an Argentine citizen?"

"Yes, sir. That's why I've come to you."

"How do you know that the people who kidnapped her, as you put it, are Argentine security personnel?"

"They are. You can take my word for it."

"And I suppose I must also take your word that she has done nothing wrong, nothing illegal."

"Yes, sir." Solo worked to suppress the anger in his voice. "The people who kidnapped her know that too."

Capdevila took out a silver case, extracted a cigarette and tapped it with infuriating slowness against the case before lighting it.

"Mr. Solórzano, what if I were to tell you that this is an internal matter for the Argentine authorities to..."

Solo shook his head fiercely.

"I see. I take it that this person is very dear to you."

"Yes." Solo took a deep breath and placed on the coffee table the tape recorder he had been holding in his lap. He pressed the "ON" button:

"I had been moved a few days earlier to the Athletic Club. It was run by Indart, this same Indart. He was a major then, before they promoted him for his services there. He worked closely with the navy and Admiral Rinaldi. There were three torture rooms, each with a metal box spring, hooks from which to hang the prisoners, and a barrel of water. The walls were decorated with swastikas...."

The ambassador grimaced, raised a hand. Solo turned off the tape.

"I've read the report," Capdevila said.

"I know. But most people haven't." Solo pointed to his watch. "In half an hour I'm meeting a nationally syndicated radio host at a studio downtown. Unless Inés Maldonado is delivered to her flight safe and sound, the tape will be broadcast—with me interpreting it on the air."

Capdevila stared at him. He took a long pull on his cigarette and exhaled a steady stream of smoke. "Mr. Solórzano, if you go through with this plan, there could be some very serious consequences for you. You are a professional interpreter. The information on that tape is confidential and you took an oath not to divulge it. You may never work again. You could be prosecuted."

"I know that."

Capdevila got up. He thrust his hands into his trouser pockets and paced a full turn around his armchair before speaking again. "Unless

I'm mistaken, that tape includes the names of complainants that were omitted from the OAS report in order to guard against reprisals—"

"I have a transcript of the tape. We'll edit out the names and scramble the voices."

Capdevila seemed to be debating something. "Are you absolutely certain of what you've told me happened to this Inés Maldonado?"

"I am," Solo said. "Please, sir, let's not waste any more time."

Capdevila ground out the cigarette on a silver ashtray and looked at Solo. "Mr. Solórzano, let me be blunt. If you do this, you will earn the enmity of some very powerful people."

Solo didn't answer.

"Very well. I see that your mind is made up. Please wait here."

Solo's eyes were riveted on the hands of the grandfather clock in the corner of the room. Don't think about her. She's going to be all right. She's going to be all right.

What if Capdevila couldn't get through to Indart or Rinaldi? What if they thought Solo was bluffing and decided to call his bluff? He couldn't allow himself to think about that. Broadcasting the tape would mean certain death for Inés. He knew that. If they refused to let her go, if they dared him to air the tape, he knew he could not become her executioner. There was no radio host waiting for him.

The clock ticked away. Three more minutes and it would rap out the hour. The gentle eyes of the old gaucho never left his.

Ages later, the door opened.

"You are a very persuasive young man," Ambassador Capdevila said. "Miss Maldonado is on her way to Ezeiza Airport. I myself called the Argentine Airlines officials there. They've been asked to hold the plane for her."

A tide of relief broke over Solo and suffused him. He felt like crying. Thank God, he mumbled, and heard the tremor in his voice. An enormous weakness had descended over his limbs. It took all his strength to lift himself out of the armchair.

"One more thing before you go," Capdevila said, and seemed to hesitate. "I know that you and Malena were close friends."

Solo looked at him, startled by the past tense.

"Yes, I know what happened," Capdevila said. His face betrayed his distress. "When there was no word on her return and the Ministry said she never reported in, I called her father. We've known each other for years, from politics. He related his last conversation with you, and asked me to keep the news to myself until there is—confirmation."

Solo nodded. His word, the word of a stranger, was all that Malena's father had for the death of his daughter. Her body had not turned up. It might never turn up. Like all the families of the disappeared— like Solo himself when his father vanished—Malena's father was sentenced to hope.

"I wanted to tell you how sorry I am," the ambassador said, offering his hand. "I don't expect we'll be seeing each other again. I've tendered my resignation."

They shook hands and Capdevila escorted him to the door of the library.

"One word of advice, Mr. Solórzano. If I were you, I would stay out of Argentina. Admiral Rinaldi and General Indart are not men to cross."

"*General* Indart?"

"Yes. Didn't you know?"

40

Malena's apartment was not far from the embassy, on the third floor of an early Victorian townhouse neighboring the Phillips Gallery on Twenty-first Street. Solo glanced up at the cloud banks of boding rain and quickened his step. A clap of thunder broke with shattering rage over the city and rolled away northward to die convulsively over Maryland.

The old-fashioned red phone booth on the corner of Malena's street was vacant. Using a phone in the embassy had been out of the question, and for no reason that he could explain to himself he was not going to use the phone in Malena's apartment.

"Madison Plaza, good afternoon."

"Mr. Diego Fioravanti, room four-oh-four, please."

"Oh, I saw him go out. He's not back."

Gone out? Solo's gut didn't like that. Diego was supposed to stay put. "He hasn't checked out, has he?"

"Oh, no. I can see his car parked out front. He's just been in and out all day."

Solo made the man repeat the strange message he was leaving for Mr. Fioravanti: They let her go, she's flying in.

He dialed Schunk's number at the OAS to leave the same message for Diego, but got a busy signal. The first raindrops spattered the booth as he hurried across the street and let himself into the building. The ancient yellow-pine staircase groaned under his weight. He had been here so many times visiting Malena with Phyllis and the kids, for weekend asados and candlelight dinners on her terrace. The first time they came, John and Lisa had found the house excitingly spooky. Is it haunted? they asked. Now it was. For him.

On the third floor he put the key in the lock of the apartment door and froze when the mere pressure of his hand swung the door open. The couch and chairs lay overturned, their guts exposed where the upholstery was slit open. Books and records littered the floor. The contents of the china cabinet were strewn over the dining room table.

He stood motionless in the doorway, ears cocked for any sound inside the apartment, then stepped in and shut the door behind him.

Malena's collection of silver maté gourds was gone from its display case, as were various other small antiques he remembered. They must have been watching the house, waiting for Phyllis to leave. Maybe there was a lookout still posted outside. He went over to the bedroom window and used one finger to push aside the edge of the voile curtain. Rain riddled the panes and drove at the roof slates all along the street. Nobody he could spot.

Stepping around the debris, he went into the bedroom. The mattress and box spring sat halfway off the bed, their fabric slashed, and the two night tables lay belly-up. Paintings on the walls dangled crookedly, having been turned over and inspected, he guessed. On the bedside rug he caught sight of a framed photograph of Lisa and John and felt an inexpressible emptiness and loss. His children. By the bed that Phyllis and Malena shared. He picked up the photograph and placed it on top of a ransacked bureau.

The closet door was open. Dresses had been pushed aside on either side of a safe built into the back brick wall. Its door was shut. It looked like an ordinary hotel room safe, the kind he encountered more and more when he traveled, though he had yet to use one.

Had they taken the envelope? Then, why turn the apartment inside out? To make it look like a run-of-the-mill burglary? They had found the safe. That meant it would be empty if they knew the combination. If not, they would be back with heavy tools or whatever it took to open it. And soon. They had left the apartment door unlocked.

He crossed the hallway to the den. In the dull gray light slanting in from the small terrace beyond the sliding doors, his eye was drawn to the framed photographs of Malena's sister's wedding hanging cock-eyed on the walls: the bride and groom gazing into each other's eyes; Malena and her father dancing tango.

The drawers of her desk had been removed, gone through and stacked with the telephone and desk calendar against a wall, leaving a trail of rubber bands and paper clips. All that remained on the desktop was an article on Ottoman ceramics bearing Phyllis's editing marks that he knew so well. And the Rolodex.

He rotated the knob until the A came up on the index tabs, then flicked through the cards looking for A.V. There it was. Even before he saw on the card an entry for N.R. with a number he thought he recognized as that of Néstor Reidlonger's defunct phone in Buenos Aires, he knew that this was the card for Argerich, Violeta. There was another notation farther down: three two-digit pairs separated by hyphens. He pulled out the card and went back to the safe.

Left, right, left. That was the standard pattern he remembered from high-school lockers—the last time he had used a combination lock. He turned the knob to the numbers and pulled.

Nothing.

Again. Left, right, left. Pull.

Nothing.

Just then, through the wall of the closet, he heard heavy creaking from the staircase. He stood still to listen. More than one person, judging by the footfalls. On the first flight of steps. They could be going to the second floor. Or here. And then what? Confront them? Call the police? He might be dead before the police arrived.

He shut his eyes, trying to visualize his homeroom locker, his gym locker. Left, right left. Yes, but when changing directions, go *past* the first number to the third.

He turned the dial again. The footsteps on the staircase did not stop on the second floor but kept climbing, louder and closer.

Left, right, left. Pull. This time there was a muted click and the door swung open. Inside the safe was a single thick manila envelope. He grabbed it, shut the door, and spun the knob.

They must be at the apartment door now. He seized Lisa and John's picture and dropped it on the bedside rug on his way back to the den. Sliding the door open, he stepped out into the plant-filled terrace and pulled the door shut. As noiselessly as he could, he covered the few steps to the doorless utility shed and eased in, making himself small behind bags of potting soil—the hiding place Lisa and John had always squabbled over when they played hide-and-seek here. He was too big for it. And nothing more than a right angle concealed him from the den. If anybody stepped out it would be all over.

He willed his breathing to even out and to still his body. His nose twitched with the smell of soil mingled with burnt grease from the barbecue grill. He tried to listen past the street noises blunted by the steady drumming of rain on the metal roof of the shed, the blare of horns, sirens, the rumble of trucks. There were voices inside the apartment, but he could not make out words.

Suddenly he heard the sliding door squeal open. He held his breath. Somebody was standing there. He could feel it.

A glowing cigarette butt sailed across his field of vision, struck the terrace railing in a shower of sparks and dropped out of sight. The door slid shut again.

Ten minutes. Fifteen. The skin around his wristwatch glistened with sweat. All sounds inside the apartment had ceased, he thought, though he hadn't heard the apartment door close. He could have missed it—a motorcycle, a sputtering muffler.

Wait.

Finally, he could no longer stand it. Still crouching, he left the shed and inched his way to the door of the den to peer inside. Nobody. He slid the door aside and stepped in. A cautious reconnoitering confirmed that they were gone. Inside the closet, the safe yawned open.

He sat down at Malena's desk and looked at the fat envelope, now smudged with soil and sweat. In red ink, Malena's handwriting across its face read: *Operación Cóndor.*

He opened it, took out a thick wad of photocopies and inspected them. Surveillance reports. Shipments of equipment. Money transfers. Manuals. He picked out something titled *Coercive Interrogation Manual* and began to read.

41

Two boarding calls for his flight had come and gone.

"Organization of American States, reception desk." The voice on the phone belonged to Solo's friend, the guard.

"Chunk?"

"Schunk, yes. Who is this?"

"Diego Fioravanti. Anything from Solo?"

"No, he's not back and he hasn't called. Look..." Schunk hesitated. Diego could hear other voices close to Schunk's. "I can't talk now. Why don't I call you as soon as Solo calls me?"

"Sure. It's just that I'm not in the hotel."

"That's all right. I'll call you. Where are you?"

"At a public telephone."

"Well, give me the number."

"It's a public telephone," Diego repeated as if Schunk hadn't heard him. Then it dawned on him. "Can you do that?"

"Do what?" Schunk's voice was impatient now.

"Call me here."

"Why not?"

He must think I'm an idiot. Of course. In the movies they called public telephones all the time, drug dealers especially. The number was printed in the center of the dial. He read it off.

"I'll call you the minute I hear from him," Schunk said and hung up.

Diego disconnected and fed the phone another dime. The unit digested it with a metallic burp.

The desk clerk answered, "Madison Plaza, please hold."

Diego held. Something that passed for music came on—hundreds of strings playing the same note while the voice of a woman under heavy sedation licked his ear. The soupy music went on. And on. The pothead must have gone off for another smoke.

His phone curse again. Now he knew what happened in a country where the phone system worked. For him, it made no difference.

"Última llamada de embarque para el vuelo siete cero ocho de Braniff con destino final a la ciudad de Buenos Aires..."

Listening to the last boarding call for his flight, he gently pressed the metal tongue in the center of the handset cradle and reached into his pocket for another coin. Then he paused. No. There was nobody left to call.

The dial tone in the receiver in his hand gave way to an angry beeping. He turned and handed it to a waiting elderly woman with blue hair and a kindhearted expression that reminded him of Doña Asunta, then picked up his duffel bag and headed for the boarding gate.

A man coming towards him was staring at him, saying something and pointing over Diego's shoulder. Diego turned. The old lady was holding up the receiver in one hand, signaling him with the other to come back.

42

Solo checked his watch as he climbed out of the taxi. From the Dupont Circle drugstore where he had called Schunk, the ride to Capitol Hill had taken less than ten minutes. A Buenos Aires cabbie would have made it in under five, perhaps delivering cab and passenger in one piece. The meeting at the OAS was about to resume and Tracy would have to cover for him.

He went into the Capitol by the same side entrance he and the admiral and the ambassador had used weeks before, the day they came to meet with the lawmakers. A young woman carrying a stack of folders pointed him to the underground passageway that led to the Cannon House Office Building, where he asked again for the office of the New York congresswoman. Minutes later he found it. His hand was on the doorknob when he saw Hardoy coming down the hallway in his direction. He waited.

Their eyes met. Solo was about to speak, but the chairman made no move to acknowledge his presence, walking past him as though he hadn't noticed the figure gripping the door handle of the New York congressional office.

Solo pushed the door open and went in. Plausible deniability, he remarked to himself. Another of Tracy's favorite terms.

"I need to see the congresswoman," he told the young man behind the desk. A picture of Governor Hugh Carey and shots of Albany were interspersed among the large maps of New York State that dominated the walls

"Do you have an appointment, sir?"

"No, but she'll want to see me. Please give her this." He handed over the small envelope he had taken from one of the drawers of Malena's desk. Inside it was the note he had scribbled. It read: "It's about Operation Condor."

"I'm terribly sorry," was all Congresswoman Susan Segal said after raising her eyes from the last photocopy in the pile scattered on her desk. She said it feelingly. While he told his story, Solo had seen in her soft eyes a mixture of disgust and indignation, but more often sadness.

"How much of it did you already know?" he asked.

"Some," she said. "Three years ago, before he became mayor of New York City, my fellow representative Ed Koch sponsored legislation to cut off our military aid to Uruguay. The Uruguayan military put out a contract on him. That was around the time of the Letelier murders here in Washington. Koch asked for protection from the CIA and got none. That was my introduction to Operation Condor, though I didn't know its name then."

Solo nodded. He hadn't paid much attention to her the last time he had seen her, at the meeting with the admiral and the ambassador, and had now been scrutinizing her while she read. She was in her fifties, he guessed, small, attractive, if drably dressed in the customary business suit by which the American female executive emulates the uniform of the male.

She glanced at the empty manila envelope. "This confirms what I suspected. The military attachés in each embassy run the local chapters of Condor. Our country coordinates, finances, and provides equipment and information: untraceable guns and explosives, secure communications, and surveillance reports on political exiles."

"And training," Solo added acidly.

"And training. These assassination handbooks and torture manuals..." She flicked a hand over the pile of booklets and shook her head, her upper lip curled in disgust. "We managed to shut down US-AID's Office of Public Safety in the State Department, but they simply change their names and relocate to one of our hundreds of military bases in this country or abroad."

Solo felt the quick flush on his face. No, of course she didn't know. His father had died a full decade before the stories broke and OPS was disbanded. She was unaware of the nerve she had touched within him.

"This one..." She picked up a booklet between thumb and forefinger, wrinkling her nose as if holding a cockroach. "School of the Americas—we've been trying to put them out of business for years, with no success. Your friend, the murdered diplomat..."

She broke off, but Solo completed the thought in his head. His friend the diplomat had not realized until too late how in over her head she was. And neither had he. For all his cynicism, his self-image as a savvy Washington insider, he had been slow to recognize in the deadly web Malena had stepped into, the tendrils that led back to this city. Nor had he been perceptive enough to guess the bloody secret in his own lineage.

He exhaled loudly. "What now?"

She crossed her arms and leaned them on the desk, looking at him. "Our committee needs to hear your story. Will you testify?"

"Yes."

"Good. I don't know how your security clearance and your oath of confidentiality square with giving testimony. We may have to issue a congressional subpoena to get you off that hook. But we'll let our lawyers figure that out. It'll be a closed-door session, naturally, and yet—" she hesitated, "it's likely that your identity will, in the end, come out. What I'm trying to say is that, for starters, it may mean the end of your career."

"I understand."

She gave him a motherly look. "Do you?" She hesitated. "Your life may also be at risk."

She waited, but he said nothing.

"We could have the FBI—"

The horrified look on his face brought her up short.

"Mr. Solorzano," she said gently, "This is America. We are the good guys, remember?"

He wasn't sure if there was any irony in her tone. Yes, he remembered. We are the good guys. He had grown up with it; it was ingrained in him. His father, too, no doubt considered himself a good guy, a patriot, a man devoted to duty, serving his country.

But Solo also remembered the car watchman in Buenos Aires who, when Solo told him he was American, pleaded, *You won't tell them what I said, will you? Please, sir, I could get in trouble.* And the doctor in Mendoza, who seemed to cringe when he learned Solo's nationality, as though the mark of Cain had bloomed on his forehead.

"Mr. Solorzano," she said in the same gentle tone, "You have to trust somebody."

43

Evening. Solo stepped out of the OAS building. The heavy rain that had escorted him back from the congresswoman's office had finally stopped, but the air was heavy and warm, pregnant with more rain. The demonstrators were still across the street, still waving their signs, going round and round more slowly now, under the bored eye of the only remaining police car.

He walked along the top of the staircase to one of its flat marble abutments. It looked dry. He sat down. He was so tired.

In the livid sky framing the Washington Monument, caravans of colored lights crisscrossed an early, watery moon. Airplanes were leaving the city, flying away to tropical beaches caressed by turquoise waters, with palm trees and rum drinks and warm sand in which to bury your body and sleep. He could just let himself drift and doze off right here, on this marble, let himself sleep and dream of release and retreat.

"What do we want?"

"Human rights!"

The hoarse chanting woke him. He tilted his wrist and checked the time. Diego should be here any minute, after meeting Inés at the airport and dropping her off at Alberto's apartment, where they would all be having their reunion dinner after all.

How strange that they were being thrown together like this again: he, Inés, Alberto. And now Diego. Almost like old times, like the dinner they never had in New York the night of Venus Adonis.

No, Malena was gone. And they were all different people now, irrevocably changed, scarred. The old times would never return.

But Inés was safe. And there might be a chance of finding the missing Mahler twins—if Alberto and his family could trace their whereabouts before it was too late, before they grew up with the man who had kidnapped, tortured, and murdered their parents—calling him father.

A car horn. The brown Volkswagen was coming up the driveway, a tango pouring out of the windows.

> *Your song*
> *Has the chill of the last encounter*
> *Your song*
> *Grows bitter in the brine of remembrance*
> *Who is to say*
> *If your voice is a flower of sorrow...*

Solo recognized the song. "Malena." Diego had found Inés's tape. And he had managed to open the windows.

The car stopped in front of the building and Diego killed the engine and got out. Solo hurried down the steps. It still surprised him how much younger Diego looked without the black coloring and gray streaks concealing his reddish-brown hair.

"Is she okay?"

Diego nodded, as if he didn't trust himself to speak. He took a step forward and they embraced.

"She's all right," Diego said, "just very shaken. Her kidnapping wasn't quite the way Valeria told me, but it doesn't matter now. Inés says it all happened so fast—her release, the drive to the airport, that they didn't have time to do whatever they had in mind for her."

"I don't want to think about it," Solo said.

"Neither do I. Alberto offered to come pick you up, so I could stay with her, but I thought you deserved better."

Solo smiled. "Yes, you too have experienced his driving. But you didn't have to come. I could have taken a taxi."

"I had my own reasons," Diego said. In the waning light, his eyes were half-shrouded in shadow. "I wanted to talk to you alone, to thank you for saving us."

"Look..." Solo began.

"No." Diego cut him off. "I know that you don't need to hear it, but I need to say it. Just this once. Thank you. I'll never be able to repay you."

The demonstrators across the street had stopped marching and were huddled together.

"You know," Diego said, "the night I met you in Buenos Aires in your hotel room..."

"What about it?"

"What I said about not knowing whether Hardoy was under surveillance—that was true. But there was another reason I wanted to see you. I needed to meet you, see what you looked like, know who you were."

Solo didn't reply. He had gone to the Ideal with Inés for the same reason.

"But just before coming to see you...you'll never guess what I did."

Solo shrugged. "You were on the run."

"Yes, but—I know this will sound crazy, but I went dancing."

"You went dancing," Solo echoed, no incredulity in his tone. Nothing seemed outlandish any more.

"I was killing time, waiting to go to your hotel. I walked by this dance hall and went in. I remember thinking it was nostalgia, because Inés and I met dancing. It wasn't."

Diego gazed across the street, where glimmerings of white were appearing. The demonstrators were lighting candles.

"I had never felt so sad, so utterly alone. It was my last night in Argentina. If they caught me, I knew I would be killed. Or worse."

Killed or worse. The phrase skittered along the surface of Solo's mind, raising hardly a ripple. Just weeks ago, the linguist in him would have snickered.

"Or I might get lucky and make it out of the country, only to keep running. Either way, all that mattered was that my time with her had run out."

His eyes held Solo's. "You are the only one who can understand that."

Solo nodded. Across the street, the demonstrators were sitting down in the expanse of grass bordering the sidewalk.

Diego glanced at his watch. "You said you have another set of car keys."

The statement surprised Solo. "Yes, I gave you the spare."

"Good. I need your car for one more trip. It means a little more trouble for you, but consider it the cost of getting your windows open. I don't want you to drive me where I'm going."

"Where you're going? What do you mean?"

"I don't want you trying to talk me out of it. I'm not coming with you to Alberto's."

Solo stared at him.

"I'm going away. Alone," Diego went on, then paused and looked again at the protesters sitting on the grass. In the deepening dusk, their lighted candles formed a flickering cross. "I'm a marked man. Before today, I hadn't fully understood it. I would have been selfish and foolish enough to take her with me, if she would come. Now I know I can't."

Only weeks ago, this would have been what Solo most wanted to hear, all he had wished for. Now he said, "Shouldn't that be her decision?"

"No. She wouldn't want me to go. Or she might want to come with me. And I don't want to change my mind. That's why I haven't told her."

He turned, opened the door of the Volkswagen and climbed in. "Remember my Nevada relatives that I told you about? I have twenty minutes to catch my train. I'll leave the car in the station garage, the keys under the floor mat." He smiled a little. "Seems I'm always leaving you things under floor mats."

The door slammed shut, the engine cranked, and the haunting sound of "Malena" once more filled the air. Solo watched the beetle drive past the police cruiser at the brightly lit corner of Constitution Avenue and turn east towards Union Station.

Suddenly, with a deafening detonation, the brown car sprouted wings of flame and lifted off the ground.

Wheels turning, it crashed down and skidded over the curb, dragging along the pavement the splintering debris of the car floor. The crumpled mass of the vehicle rammed an empty park attendant booth and thudded to a halt against the guardrail behind it. Broken glass and charred metal showered the smoking wreck. It burst again into flames.

Stunned, ears ringing, Solo ran toward it.

The driver behind the Volkswagen had slammed on the brakes and stopped her vehicle a dozen yards before what Solo saw was a smoking saucer-shaped crater in the pavement. The blast had shattered the windshield and side windows of her car. Solo ran past her as she opened the door and stepped out on rubbery legs into the stench of burning chemicals and flesh.

"Get back! Get back!" A policeman had bounded from the cruiser and now blocked Solo's way while his partner, a small fire extinguisher in hand, cautiously approached the fireball lighting the night.

Solo stood back petrified, his heart kicking wildly, his body rigid with horror.

He felt a gust of hot wind on his face and saw small bits of paper dancing in the air. One fluttered down to his sleeve. He looked at it. It was a postage stamp.

44

"Good afternoon," Judge Manley greeted the courtroom as he entered and climbed the bench. "We have before this court," he read, "an application from Ms. Phyllis Kirk, formerly married to Mr. Kevin Solorzano, for joint custody of their children Lisa and John, ages six and four respectively. The applicant and respondent and their attorneys are here. Counsel for the applicant is Mr. Myles Granville. Mr. Granville, are you ready to proceed?

"Yes, Your Honor."

The judge looked at Monique. "And respondent's counsel, Ms. Monique Nguyen, are you ready to proceed?"

"Yes, Judge."

"Very well. Ms. Nguyen, I understand that you wish to present a witness on the preliminary issue of respondent's childcare provider, one Saturnina Arce, an issue raised by the applicant and referred to the appropriate immigration authorities."

"That's right, Judge."

"Who is your witness, Ms. Nguyen?"

"Respondent calls Mr. Bruno Hardoy, Your Honor."

"Any objections, Mr. Granville?"

"No, Your Honor."

Hardoy rose from his seat in the gallery. He made his way to the witness stand and was sworn in.

"For the record, sir," Monique began, "please tell the court your name, address, and occupation."

"My name is Bruno Hardoy," he said in good English with a slight British accent. Solo realized it was the first time he heard the chairman speak English. "I live at Llambí thirteen-fifteen in Pocitos, a suburb of Montevideo, Uruguay. I am a lawyer by profession and the chairman of the Commission on Human Rights of the Organization of American States."

"Mr. Hardoy, are you familiar with the case of Saturnina Arce, my client's live-in housekeeper, and her immigration status in this country? Please tell us in your own words what you know."

Hardoy nodded. "At the request of Mr. Kevin Solórzano, the respondent, I looked into the case of Saturnina Arce. She is a Bolivian national from the Cochabamba region. Her husband, one of the leaders of the nineteen seventy-four peasant uprisings against the military government of General Hugo Bánzer, was killed along with their two teenage sons in the brutal government repression of peasants known as the Massacre of the Cochabamba Valley. Mrs. Arce fled the country and eventually found her way to the United States. Our commission believes that past persecution is proven, and that she has been legally entitled to apply for political asylum. It is our view that, for humanitarian reasons, she should not be forced to uproot herself again. We have consequently endorsed her petition to remain legally in this country."

"Your Honor," Monique said, "I have here copies of the relevant documents, which I should like to enter as evidence. On the strength of the endorsement from Mr. Hardoy's commission, the U.S. State Department has added its favorable recommendation to the application filed with the Immigration and Naturalization Service."

She approached the bench and handed the papers to the judge.

"Mr. Granville?" Judge Manley said after examining the papers.

Granville looked at Phyllis, sitting next to him. "No objection, Your Honor."

"Very well. Mr. Hardoy, the court sincerely appreciates your presence here today and the testimony you've given. You may step down. Are we ready to proceed with the rest of the case, Ms. Nguyen, or do you have other preliminary matters?"

"I do, Judge," Monique said. She glanced at Solo, sitting beside her.

"Go ahead, Ms. Nguyen."

"Your Honor, the dominant principle in child custody cases is the best interest of the children. Mr. Solorzano insisted on retaining sole custody because he harbored doubts about the wisdom of sharing custody with his former wife. Those doubts have now been dispelled. Maximizing contact with both parents, my client now realizes, would be in the best interest of the children. Mr. Solorzano is prepared to accept joint custody with equal access and visitation rights."

Phyllis looked dumbfounded. When her eyes found Solo's, they were brimming with tears.

Solo smiled. Again he saw Reidlonger in the synagogue, and his words rushed back: *We did not want tolerance; we wanted respect. We wanted our human rights.*

How long since he had smiled like this, with genuine feeling? Not once in the two weeks since Diego's death. He glanced round to the seating area behind him, where Inés sat between Alberto and Hardoy, a smile at long last brightening her grief-stricken eyes. In the rear of the courtroom were two of the FBI agents assigned to investigate the car bombing and protect the Solorzanos. There were more of them in Alexandria, watching his home.

So far there had been no mention of Operation Condor in the media, and perhaps he would never know whether the bomb, with its remote-control detonator, was meant for Diego or for him—or both. But he did know that Diego had saved his life. Diego had paid him back.

Friday morning he shaved, with Tita licking her paws and watching from the terry cover of the toilet lid and Lisa and John sitting on the long counter top of the vanity, overflowing with energy and questions. What was his favorite song? His favorite color? Could he fog up the mirror so they could draw pictures? The kids used the shaving cream to make themselves up into clowns until a dispute broke out over nozzle-pressing rights, causing tears to well up in John's eyes. Tita, who found crying distasteful, leapt off the toilet and left. The crisis passed, but Lisa sulked and John kept a stiff lower lip long after. Solo sighed. He knew the two of them were excited and anxious in anticipation of spending their first weekend with Phyllis in her new apartment in Bethesda.

That afternoon, waiting for Phyllis, he built the first fire of the season, cuddled with the kids on the sofa facing the fireplace, and read to them from their favorite book, a children's illustrated volume of legends of the indigenous peoples of the Americas. Malena had given it to them.

Lisa and John listened, rapt, to the stories of Viracocha, the old god who made the world with its mountains and volcanoes, its woods, rivers, and streams; and the great spirit Makunaima who populated the earth and the skies and the waters with animals and birds and fish and then set the wind to bring the different seasons at the proper time; and the first human beings, a race of giants who rebelled against their creator and were turned into stone statues that you can still see on Easter Island.

When the bell rang, Lisa and John vaulted from the couch, grabbed their backpacks, and hurled themselves at the front door.

"Sunday, six p.m...." Phyllis managed to call out to him after the kisses and hugs while her children tugged and dragged her to her car. Her doleful eyes gave way to a beam of pleasure.

Again he waited, now in the abrupt silence broken only by the crackling fire and Saturnina's rhythmic raking of her vegetable garden behind the house.

An hour later, Alberto dropped off Inés and sped away, waving a hand from the window of his erratic car.

"Brandy, quick!" Inés said, collapsing on the couch and wiping her forehead with the back of her hand in mock relief. "Thank God for seat belts."

"You do look a little pale," he said.

He poured cognac into two snifters and they sat watching the fire. "You miss them already, don't you," she said.

He nodded.

She smiled. "I will stay and hold your hand." Her fingers squeezed his, and he knew for the first time with unalloyed certainty that they were taking their first steps together to reclaim each other. It would be a long road.

He would have been content to simply sit here, watching the dancing flames, but there was one more thing he needed to do. He had considered not doing it, sparing her the pain, but he was done keeping secrets from her. He brought out from his shirt pocket the ring he had forgotten to return to Diego, and placed it on the children's storybook. Diego's ring on Malena's book.

He saw the emotions rise to Inés's face, saw her eyes flash at the sight of the sunburst and laurel wreaths engraved on the face of the ring, then gradually soften and blink away a tear.

After a moment she said, "It's all he left behind, I know, all I will have of his—but I can't bear to look at it. Not now."

A warm, pale ray of afternoon light caught in the sill of the picture window and bled into the room. Solo's eyes traveled through the pane to the kneeling figure of Saturnina at the far end of her garden, spade and trowel at her side, She too was a survivor of the same murderous madness. He now knew that the lines the icy winds of the Andes had traced on her face were not as deeply scored as the scars in her heart, which bore the imprint of the massacre in the Valley of Cochabamba. He watched her lovingly lower her first plantings into the soil, then dress them in earth with an almost ritual tenderness. There was in her gentle motions a quiet conviction, a silent certitude, the felt presence of a stubborn faith in the future. Life, her movements said, will rise again, tenacious, resilient, perennial. And he understood that for him and Inés, too, life would bloom again, that they were engaged in the ancient battle for it, that they could and would win back their future.

He reached for the ring and returned it to his pocket, then gently covered her hand with his. Whatever lay in their future, the past would always be present—that bitter brine of memory, as "Malena" the tango put it.

I will keep the ring, Diego, he said to himself. Maybe someday she will ask me for it. Someday, when this is over. Someday, when Argentina heals. God knows Argentina needs to.

And God is Argentine.